"The old ones here, they traveled off world."

We plodded along in the heat and on either side were more ruined buildings. I asked Micah about them and he said, "A few of them, we think, were temples or exhibit halls. There were old things in some of them . . . bones and stones from long, long ago. One temple had some paintings of flying machines, made from metal. And in that one temple . . . ships that traveled off the world, into space."

I wiped my face one more time. "I've heard those tales as well."

The tone of his voice changed. "They are not tales. The old ones here, they traveled off world."

I said, "Well . . . some of our science men, they know that they sent instruments and such off world . . . but to think people traveled there . . . they believe it's just tales, or imaginings . . ."

Micah stopped and gently took the bottle of water from me, took a sip, and said, "My grandfather . . . he told me once . . . that when he was a boy, an elder, who was part of the College, let him touch a stone from one of these buildings, a stone that came from the moon."

"The moon?" I couldn't help myself, I chuckled. Tour guides . . . how ignorant do they think tourists can be?

—From "A Souvenir to Remember"
by Brendan DuBois

D0683448

Also Available from DAW Books:

Mystery Date, **edited by Denise Little**
First dates—the worst possible times in your life or the opening steps on the path to a wonderful new future? What happens when someone you have never met before turns out not to be who or what he or she claims to be? It's just a date, what could go wrong? Here are seventeen encounters, from authors such as Kristine Katherine Rusch, Nancy Springer, Laura Resnick, and Jody Lynn Nye that answer these questions. From a childhood board game called "Blind Date" that seems to come shockingly true . . . to a mythological answer to Internet predators . . . to a woman cursed to see the truth about her dates when she imbibes a little wine . . . to an enchanting translator bent on avenging victims of war crimes . . . to a young man hearing a very special voice from an unplugged stereo system . . . these are just some of the tales that may lead to happily ever after—or no ever after at all. . . .

Fellowship Fantastic, **edited by Martin H. Greenberg and Kerrie Hughes**
The true strength of a story lies in its characters and in both the ties that bind them together and the events that drive them apart. Perhaps the most famous example of this in fantasy is *The Fellowship of The Ring.* But such fellowships are key to many fantasy and science fiction stories. Now thirteen top tale-spinners—Nina Kiriki Hoffmann, Alan Dean Foster, Russell Davis, Alexander Potter, among others—offer their own unique looks at fellowships from: a girl who finds her best friend through a portal to another world . . . to four special families linked by blood and magical talent . . . to two youths ripped away from all they know and faced with a terrifying fate that they can only survive together . . . to a man who must pay the price for leaving his childhood comrade to face death alone. . . .

The Future We Wish We Had, **edited by Martin H. Greenberg and Rebecca Lickiss**
In the opening decade of the twenty-first century, many things that were predicted in the science fiction stories of the twentieth century have become an accepted part of everyday life, and many other possibilities have not yet been realized but hopefully will be one day. For everyone who thought that by now they'd be motoring along the skyways in a personal jet car, or who assumed we'd have established bases on the Moon and Mars, or that we would have conquered disease, slowed the aging process to a crawl, or eliminated war, social injustice, and economic inequity, here are sixteen stories of futures that might someday be ours or our children's, from Esther Friesner, Sarah Hoyt, Kevin J. Anderson, Irene Radford, Dave Freer, and Dean Wesley Smith, among others.

FUTURE AMERICAS

EDITED BY
Martin H. Greenberg
and John Helfers

DAW BOOKS, INC.
DONALD A. WOLLHEIM, FOUNDER
375 Hudson Street, New York, NY 10014

ELIZABETH R. WOLLHEIM
SHEILA E. GILBERT
PUBLISHERS
http://www.dawbooks.com

Copyright © 2008 by Tekno Books and John Helfers.

All Rights Reserved

DAW Book Collectors No. 1444.

DAW Books is distributed by Penguin Group (USA).

All characters in this book are fictitious.
Any resemblance to persons living or dead is coincidental.

If you purchase this book without a cover you should be aware that this book may have been stolen property and reported as "unsold and destroyed" to the publisher. In such case neither the author nor the publisher has received any payment for this "stripped book."

The scanning, uploading and distribution of this book via the Internet or any other means without the permission of the publisher is illegal, and punishable by law. Please purchase only authorized electronic editions, and do not participate in or encourage the electronic piracy of copyrighted materials. Your support of the author's rights is appreciated.

First Printing, June 2008
1 2 3 4 5 6 7 8 9

DAW TRADEMARK REGISTERED
U.S. PAT. AND TM OFF. AND FOREIGN COUNTRIES
—MARCA REGISTRADA
HECHO EN U.S.A.

PRINTED IN THE U.S.A.

ACKNOWLEDGMENTS

"Introduction," copyright © 2008 by John Helfers

"A Souvenir to Remember," copyright © 2008 by Brendan DuBois

"Suffer the Children," copyright © 2008 by Barbara Nickless

"Better Guns," copyright © 2008 by Jean Rabe

"The Baby Store," copyright © 2008 by Ed Gorman

"Jesus Runs," copyright © 2008 by George Zebrowski

"The Rotator," copyright © 2008 by Pamela Sargent

"Acirema the Rellik," copyright © 2008 by Robert T. Jeschonek

"Family Photos," copyright © 2008 by S. Andrew Swann

"Our Flag Was Still There," copyright © 2008 by Steven Mohan, Jr.

"The Last Actor," copyright © 2008 by Mike Resnick and Linda Donohue

"The Great Chain of Being," copyright © 2008 by Brian Stableford

"Attached to the Land," copyright © 2008 by Donald J. Bingle

"The Thief Catcher," copyright © 2008 by Theodore Judson

"Unlimited," copyright © 2008 by Jane Lindskold

"Switching off the Lights," copyright © 2008 by Peter Crowther

"The Power of Human Reason," copyright © 2008 by Kristine Kathryn Rusch

CONTENTS

Introduction

by John Helfers

ALTHOUGH I DO not believe in predetermined destiny, I do believe in serendipitous coincidence. Take this introduction, for example. A few days before beginning the final assembly of the anthology you're holding, my wife and I were watching the classic SF film *Logan's Run*. While it now seems rather quaint watching Michael York and Jenny Agutter move through the sterilized, antiseptic blandness that typified much of the era's science fiction films (notable exceptions being *The Omega Man* and *Soylent Green*), and only in the 1970s would Hollywood believe that people would still be wearing miniskirts two hundred and fifty years later, at the time I'm sure it was seen as a daring exploration of the themes of potential overpopulation and population control, concerns that were very much at the forefront of society's mind.

By now, anyone who has seen the movie will have drawn the obvious parallel to the theme of this book; that when Logan and Jessica escape the city, they are in a future version of America that had destroyed itself long ago, with only ivy-covered ruins standing where the Capitol and Lincoln Memorial once towered in Washington DC. While post-apocalyptic and dystopian stories of a future America and the rest of

1

the world have been popular for decades, it takes a special vision to look at our nation as it currently is, and even try to imagine what life might be like one hundred, fifty, or even twenty years in the future. Authors have done so in the past, from Aldous Huxley's dystopian satire *Brave New World*, which was heavily influenced by a visit he made to America in the 1920s, to more recent books like William Gibson's *Neuromancer*, forecasting the ubiquitous World Wide Web and the rise of multi-national corporations and their influence on government, as well as the effects of each on a near-future society.

As we come to the end of this first decade of the twenty-first century, there is little doubt in my mind that America is at a crossroads, or more of a six-or eight-way intersection. With social, religious, economic, governmental, and world cultural pressures bearing down on our nation from all directions, who can possibly guess what the future might hold (although I doubt it will be all handsome, jumpsuited men and beautiful, miniskirted women living in hedonistic, idle pleasure in domed cities)? Predicting the future is hard; just ask the people who have tried, whether it was the end of the planet as we know it, or the adoption of a new method of transportation, or, more famously, predicting that something wouldn't catch on, and then being completely wrong.

What can be theorized is that sweeping changes are coming on the horizon, but whether they will be for good or ill remains to be seen. But the concept is simple; what might an America of the future look like? In many ways, it is practically impossible to theorize or extrapolate what the future might hold, yet writers try every year. However, I'd imagine it would be much like if we were to somehow bring a man or woman from a century ago forward in time to today. Who knows what their reaction would be to the mechanized, technologized world they would find themselves in? Just as they would be lost in a sea of strange and wondrous sights, trying to imagine the future from what we know today, we would most likely be just as lost walking down a city street a century in the future. Some things would be familiar, like cars and houses, and some would be utterly foreign, like the personal computer, or a cell phone, or whatever someone is eventually going to invent to replace both of those.

Regardless of how accurate anyone's predictions can be, it is still very enjoyable to ask others for their views of the future. Sixteen of today's finest authors responded to my invitation to write stories supplying their version of an America of tomorrow, and their takes on it may surprise you, as they surprised me. There are stories that cover almost every aspect of the issues that will shape—and possible fracture—our nation, from the two very different political ideas explored in the stories by George Zebrowski and Pamela Sargent, to the disturbing concept of future art posed in stories by S. Andrew Swann and Mike Resnick and Linda Donahue. The society of the future is laid bare in stunning pieces by Barbara Nickless, Ed Gorman, Steven Mohan, Jr., and Don Bingle. And, of course, where America goes, conflict often follows in its wake, as shown by the fiction of Jean Rabe and Theodore Judson. Finally, I do not think a collection like this would be complete with a tale of America reformed after a catastrophe, and Brendan DuBois kindly obliged with his story of an America that is at once familiar, yet so very different than the one we know today.

I hope you enjoy these tales of an America that may be, but isn't—at least, not yet.

A SOUVENIR TO REMEMBER

by Brendan DuBois

Brendan DuBois is an award-winning author of short stories and novels. His short fiction has appeared in various publications, including *Playboy*, *Ellery Queen's Mystery Magazine* and *Alfred Hitchcock's Mystery Magazine*, as well as numerous anthologies, including *The Best Mystery Stories of the Century*. He has twice received a Shamus Award for his short fiction and has been nominated for three Edgar Allan Poe Awards. DuBois' long fiction includes six previous books in the Lewis Cole mystery series, as well as several other suspense thrillers. DuBois lives in New Hampshire with his wife Mona.

I THOUGHT OF Father's words as I stood there alone on our hotel room's balcony, looking out over the small town, the warm morning air thick and still about me.

"Be careful for what you wish for, Armand," he had said a week ago. "You just might get it."

True enough. When Father had earlier told me of his trade mission to the south, I had begged, pleaded, and begged once again to let me go with him. I had never traveled with Father but always knew he went to wonderful places and met interesting people, and I didn't want to pass up this chance. I hadn't bothered trying to bring Mother into the fight; she was a traditionalist, one who focused on my sisters and the household, and she let Father take care of me and his position in Court. But after one evening dinner, as the servings and plates were taken away, when the servants were preparing cafe au lait and dessert for Mother and Father, she had said, "For once, Roland, listen to the boy. Let him go. It will be a good experience for him, to see what his father does with his time. And besides, he's coming of age. He might meet others of influence, ones who can help him later on when he goes away to school."

That was an insult for Father, one that I had seen instantly—for Mother had always chided him for not making enough of the right friends and allies in Court—but Father, still giddily in love with Mother after all these years, had just smiled and said, "Very good, dear. Of course."

Which is how I found myself, two weeks later, on the good airship *Pitseolak*, gliding our way south, past the borders of the empire, to the unorganized territories and squabbling city states that were our empire's poor southern neighbors. The trip took less than a day, and Father spent most of that day in our stateroom, going through his papers, preparing for his days of meetings with the trade delegation representing a collection of southern coastal city-states, all vying to sell their sugar cane for our industries. I spent the time looking out the windows at the slowly passing landscape beneath me, excited at first, and then deathly bored. Just klick after klick of mountains, hills, and forested areas, punctuated here and there by crumbling ruins of some old city. And even when we landed at the small town—called Tomac—it was at night, so there wasn't much to see, even on the short drive from the air station. So most of the trip had been one long bore.

And now, bored again. Father had warned me that his days would be taken up with meetings and trips to the sugar cane fields, and, alas, I could not come along, which meant I spent my time alone in the hotel, small and clean and secure, but not much else. There were books to read and a radio to listen to, but I had a hard time with the language. It was something like *franglish,* but not quite, so I had listened to the music instead. There was a rawness to it that I had liked, but how long can you spend the day alone in a room, listening to the wireless? The hotel had restaurants and a manmade pond for swimming, but it took all of a day before I had seen it all.

I attended one formal event—when the leader of Tomac and the surrounding territory, called Prez Thomas III, sponsored a reception in honor of Father and the rest of the delegation—and I dressed in the only formal suit I had brought in my luggage. Polished boots, black trousers, scarlet tunic with ruffled sleeves, and for the entire night, being the youngest one there, I was ignored, as Father worked the room, plump and short in his own formal wear. Once, a couple of local women, drinks before them on white tablecloth, looked at me and then whispered and giggled behind their manicured hands. It was at that point that I wished I hadn't come along. I was out of place, I didn't belong.

Now I breathed in the muggy morning air. Tomorrow we would return north to home, and for all the time here . . . I had seen this hotel room and the reception hall. So what? A wasted trip, for Father had been busy and had forbid me from leaving the hotel.

"I don't want you to get into trouble, Armand," he had said. "So be a good boy and stay here while I'm out working."

I grasped the stonework of the balcony. Leaving tomorrow without seeing more of Tomac and its lands than what I could see from this room. I should go out, poke around, see the ruins that were supposedly the most dramatic in this part of the world. . . .

And I hesitated.

Father had said be a good boy.

Don't get into trouble.

And stay here.

I felt a smile coming across my face, as the part of me that belonged to Mother rose to the surface. I was being a good boy, and would always be a good boy, for while Father was kind and gentle in the household, on most days, I know from rumors and such from my friends at school that he did have a temper, was strong, and that there were several men at work in the tar pits out west due to his displeasure at finding corruption in the Trade Ministry.

And yet . . .

I left the balcony, tossed on a short cape, and went out and locked the door behind me, and went downstairs to the lobby. It was quiet as I walked across the stone floor to the front desk, past the dark, rough-looking furniture, and the bellmen, standing at attention, white-gloved hands held before them. There was an older woman there, flipping through some papers, and she looked up at me with a smile as I approached. Even in the heat, she had on a long skirt and some sort of dark blouse, her dark hair rolled up in a bun at the back of her head.

"May I help you, young sire?" she asked.

"Yes," I said. "I'd like to arrange for a tour to the ruins."

Her smile seemed to flicker a bit. "Are you sure?"

"Yes, I'm sure."

She nodded. "All right, then. If you go toward the front, by the doors, you'll see some tour guides by a table. They are all bonded, licensed, and insured. All operate through the cooperation of the hotel. Use one of them. They are all safe."

"Are there any ones you recommend?"

She shook her head. "No, they are all legitimate . . . but if I may add, you should go with the one you feel comfortable with. Examine the brochures, talk to the tour operators . . . and oh, one more thing."

From underneath the counter, she took out a white sash with a gold eagle centered in the middle. She passed it over to me and said, "Here. Wear this."

I slipped the sash over my left shoulder, looked at her. "Why?"

A slight shrug. "The ruins are safe during the day . . . but we want to ensure without a doubt that our guests will be safe no matter the time or place. While wearing the sash, it means you're under the protection of the Prez. No one will dare hurt you, or harass you, or cause you any trouble."

I touched the sash. The cloth was rough, like it was hand-woven. "And suppose someone ignores the sash?"

A tight, worldly smile. "Then he or she will be sentenced to the cane fields. For life."

I followed the directions and passed through the doors, which were made of glass, a fair expense for this part of the world. Uniformed guards with peaked hats and short swords kept an eye on the guests and visitors coming through. Off to the left was a long table, and behind the table was a collection of men and women. There were expensive signs before them, professionally printed in the local dialect and *franglish,* and they all looked at me expectantly as I came forward.

And yet . . .

They seemed too slick, too polished, like something Father or somebody else in the Trade Ministry would choose. I looked at the far end of the table, where a young man sat, almost about my age, dark-skinned with close-cropped black hair. He was dressed plainly and before him was a hand-printed sign, on white cardboard, *Honest Tours, Honest Ways.* He caught my eye and then I just decided to walk over to him.

And I thought of Father.

Be a good boy. Well, I was being a good boy. I was polite to the desk clerk and I was going to be polite to this young man before me, and I was going to pay him some money, which, judging by his haircut and clothes, he could use.

And trouble . . . yes, I was going to stay out of trouble. And with the sash about me, that was going to be guaranteed.

One more thing. What had that been?

Oh, yes, stay here, he had said. But he hadn't defined here, had he? Here could mean the hotel room. Or the hotel. Or the town and its ruins.

So I had listened to Father. Of that I had no doubt.

I went forward to the young man.

"I would like to arrange a tour."

The young man just nodded. I thought he might have been excited at getting a paying customer, so early in the morning, but he just bent over a tablet of paper and started laboriously writing with a pencil.

"Your name, sire?" He spoke *franglish* well, with just a bit of a southern accent.

"Armand de la Cloutier," I said.

"Your room number?"

"Suite twelve."

"And your home address, sire?"

"Mansion de la Cloutier, Torontah, Empire of the Nunavut."

"Very good, sire," he said, writing some more.

As he wrote, a well-dressed older man leaned over in our direction. "Sire," he said in a low voice. "That's not what you want. Come with us, we'll show you things you've never imagined, things you'll remember the rest of your life."

The young man said in a quiet but firm voice, "You're poaching, Alex. You know what the rules are for poaching."

The other man laughed. "Not poaching. Just offering an interesting alternative, something he won't get back home. Like the counting houses. Hear that, sire? Off the cane fields, the young ladies that work there, it's quite hot and humid. The way they dress, leaves

very little to the imagination, and for just a bit more
payment—"

The young man tore off a slip of paper and passed
it over to me. "One brass sovereign, if you please,
sire. And then we'll be on our way."

I opened the leather pouch at my side, pulled out
a sovereign and passed it over. He pocketed it and
stood up, now smiling, the hand drawn sign now under
his arm. "My name is Micah. Shall we go?"

"Yeah," I said. "Let's go."

Outside, the tropical air was thick and heavy, and
the sky was overcast, threatening rain. Before us was
a curved driveway, with taxis arriving and leaving,
guests and others milling about, and young beggars
and urchins, out there among the crowd, holding out
their palms, pleading, begging. Occasionally, one of
the guests would toss a coin to the ground, and they
would fight for the treasure, scrambling and yelling.
But though they saw me and the way I was dressed,
none approached. The sash was like an invisible
shield, not letting anyone near me, and I'm embarrassed to say, it made me feel more important than
I should.

Micah led me down to a line of luxury vehicles, and
I recognized the names painted on the side with those
of the tour guides inside the hotel. I wiped at my
brow, looking forward to being inside a cool vehicle,
but Micah kept on walking, until we reached the end
of the line of vehicles, where there was—

A pedicab, with a parasol on the top, and with a
sign hanging by cords from the rear. *Honest Tours,
Honest Ways.* He looked to me and then smiled. "I
see you look disappointed, sire. If you would like a
refund and go with someone else, please do. That's
your right."

If I had been Mother or one of my sisters, I'm sure
that's exactly would have happened. But I liked his

look, liked his smile, and liked his attitude. I was going with what the woman at the front desk had recommended.

"No, Micah, this would be fine."

He kept his smile. "That's good. Where would you like to go?"

"The ruins," I said. "I hear they're quite dramatic."

"That they are," Micah said. "But if what Alex said has any interest for you—"

"No," I interrupted. "The ruins. That's what I want to see."

"Very good, sire," he said. "If I may suggest . . . your cape will be too warm. May I take it?"

I unhooked the cape and passed it over to him, and he placed it within a small leather container at the rear of the pedicab. He then led me over and said, "Please climb in."

He helped me in the rear of the pedicab, to a clean and padded seat. Before me was a low shelf, with plastic bags of nuts and fruits, and bottles of water. He got forward, undid a hand brake, and started pedaling. There was a mirror so I could see his face, and he said, "Is this your first time to Tomac?"

"Yes, it is," I said.

"And are you here on business or pleasure, sire?"

I laughed. "My father is here on business, and I'm supposed to be here on pleasure, but so far, all I've gotten is boredom."

He paused at the road, and then went out, joining the traffic. The road was well-paved and wide, and though I didn't see any signs, it seemed there was a series of lanes for different modes. People walking or pushing wagons were on the far right, and then were bicycles and pedicabs, then horses, and then powered vehicles. Micah pedaled at a fair pace, and I had to smile at what I saw next. From the roof of the parasol a small fan was suspended and with a complex set of gears and chains, the fan spun as Micah pedaled, send-

ing air across my face. It was very hot, and I undid
the top few buttons of my tunic, enjoying the movement of the breeze.

"It won't take long," Micah said, "and we'll stay
out in the ruins as long as you'd like."

"Thank you," I said, as I turned here and there, to
see our progress. The land was flat and was jammed
at each side of the road with thick growth, though on
occasion, a dirt road would lead off deep into the
jungle, ending up God knows where. It was hot, but
I found I was enjoying the ride, and though I felt just
a bit of guilt over being pedaled there by Micah, I
thought I had paid him well, and it would work out
for the best.

The sun was strong and the clouds moved away,
and I saw two airships, up there in the distance, and
felt a bit of pride. Only my home empire had airships
this large and powerful, and it felt good, to see them
up there, like they were somehow watching over me.
After a while the road rose up a bit and the jungle
fell away, allowing us a fair view off to the east. Micah paused and I looked out, where I saw a few
plumes of smoke rising up.

"The cane fields," he pointed out. "The old fields
get burned. Part of the growing cycle."

"I see," I said.

He grunted something and then said, "Look. Up
ahead. That's where we're going."

Before us, the road swooped down and to the west,
and there was a flash of white out there in the distance, of old buildings, poking up through the jungle
and growth. I felt my pulse quicken some. It had been
one thing to read about the ruins and to see the news-
reels; it was another to know that in a few minutes, I
would be right there, in the middle.

And if I knew then what I know now, I think I
would have paid Micah, one more time, to turn
around and take me back to the hotel.

*   *   *

With the downward slope of the road, we made good time, the breeze washing over us, and then there was a fork in the road, and Micah aimed the pedicab to the left, to a stretch of road that was much narrower. I held onto the side of the pedicab as we came to a large sign that I couldn't understand—the language being written in Tomacese, or whatever—and then we came to a large dirt area, seemingly carved from the jungle. There were powered vehicles here, from large buses to smaller vehicles, some with the engines idling. Micah pedaled to the far side of the lot, where there were a few other pedicabs. There was a small group of young boys and girls, dressed in ragged clothes, barefoot, and the tallest of them came forward, holding a large staff. Micah got out of the pedicab, said something quickly in the local patois, and the boy with the staff laughed, and the other kids scattered.

I got out, stretched my legs, and said, "What was that all about?"

Micah shrugged. "That was Lucas. He keeps an eye on my cab while I'm touring."

From the front of the pedicab, he pulled out a yellow scarf, which he draped about his neck. "Take one of the waters," he said. "You'll need it."

I did just that, as we went down a well-packed dirt path, past a group of men with short swords and yellow scarves that looked like they were gatekeepers of a sort. There were other tourists there as well, some with bulky cameras, and I kept pace with Micah as we walked deeper into the jungle.

"What do you know of this place?" Micah asked.

"The ruins? That they're very, very old. That it's believed they were the capitol district of the city-states that were here, a very long time ago."

Micah grunted again. "I suppose."

"What do you mean?"

"I guess that's what they teach you up north, right?"

"That's right," he said. "And what's wrong with that?"

There were other paths off on other sides of the jungle, but Micah obviously knew where to take me, as he ignored my question. He said, "Up ahead, there's an observation tower. We'll climb up there and you'll see where we're going."

Which is what we did. There was a gaggle of young people at the base of a wooden tower, but they scattered at Micah's words and—I'm sure—by the sash I was wearing. We climbed up the steep stairs to a platform about six meters to a side. I was out of breath and took a sip of the warm water I carried as we emerged. The viewing platform was crowded again, with tourists and some of the dark-skinned beggar children, but Micah led me to one side and said, "Look."

Before us was a jungle-covered plain, with more lumps of white stone emerging from the growth, but this close, I could make out the shapes better. There was a large building before us, with a dome that was collapsing upon itself, with vines and saplings and trees poking through the old stone. On either side of the dome were two wings of other buildings, more obscured than the dome. Off in the distance there were other buildings, plus one that was fairly clear. It was shaped like a box with pillars of some sort, and before this building was a long, open pond.

Micah said, "We'll be going to the large building first, and then, depending on the time, the temple at the end." He smiled. "That place is my favorite."

I could make out the language of the tourists, and heard that some were from home. They were wearing white sashes similar to mine. An older man and woman, and they both laughed as the man scattered coins on the floor. The children fought over the coins and the man laughed again. "Barbarians," he said. "Little brown monkeys. Look at them."

I was suddenly ashamed to be there, with Micah,

but if it bothered him, he didn't show it. He leaned a bit over the railing and said, "This place . . . these people . . . what do you know about them?"

I wiped at my face again. "A very rich, very powerful, very corrupt empire. An empire that polluted the air, the water, even the very cultures of the world. An empire that tried to rule the world . . . until the other peoples fought against them, and brought them down, just as the earth was rebelling against it as well, with droughts, storms, and floods."

"And what was it called?"

"It had a number of names. Merka being the most common."

Micah turned to me. "Not bad for a tourist. Come along, Armand, let me show you the ruins of my people."

After a half hour of slogging along the path, we came out before the large domed building, at what seemed to be its front entrance. Other tourists were there as well, and more of the ragged children, either begging or trying to sell iced drinks or carvings of the various buildings that were still hidden among the jungle. There were wide stone steps leading up to the main dome, and we went up, and Micah talked to me. "This is the most lavish and decorated building here among this collection of ruins, and most believe that this is where the assembly or parliament met."

I noted the collapsing stone, the empty windows, the birds flying in and out of the ruins. "Is it safe?"

"No, not really," he said, "but we'll go to places that are fairly safe. There are many, many small rooms in here, which we think were where the representatives met, or lived."

At one of the doorways Micah spoke to another man who wore the same yellow scarf, and he reached below a stone counter and came up with a lantern. He lit the lantern and spoke quickly in patois, and Micah laughed and looked to me.

"Ready?"

"Yes," I said, feeling my heart thump right along.

"Then let's go back in time, Armand."

And I followed him into the darkness.

The air was dank, thick with odors and old things. We went up another set of crumbling stone steps, the lantern leading the way, until we came out onto a wide stone floor, which was beneath the dome. I felt my head go back, looking up overhead, at the dome, and with the awe of seeing what the ancients were able to do, there was a tinge of fear, feeling that the tons of stone above me could collapse at any second. Micah stood next to me, looking up as well, the lantern in his hand.

"Don't worry," he said

"Worry about what?"

He laughed. "Every tourist thinks the same. That the dome will collapse on them and kill them. Don't worry. It's been up for centuries, and it'll be up for centuries more. The ancients—" and then there was a note of pride in his voice, "—my ancestors, they built this place well. They built it to last."

And then he looked to me. "One wishes, sometimes, that other things they built lasted as long. Come, let's take a look around."

We walked further across the stone floor, and despite its age, I had to admire the handiwork that went into it. There were other tourists in here as well, accompanied by other guides, all wearing the same yellow scarf as Micah. Up above on the walls were heavy wooden frames, empty although it looked like they once held paintings. There were statues there as well, most of them shattered and broken and on their sides. I looked and saw that all had their faces disfigured, like they had been the focus of some rage, so many years ago.

"Who were these people?" I asked.

Micah said, "Oh, the great ones. We don't know

their names, or who they are, or what they did. But this building, being so big and ornate, they must have been very important."

I followed Micah as we went down a long hallway, filled with more broken statues, more empty picture frames, and then I saw something odd. There was one statue, standing by itself, but it wasn't broken, or torn down. It stood there and I felt chilled. It wasn't fully human, that was or sure. There were offerings of some sort at the base of the statue, fruit and nuts and flowers from the jungle.

"What is this?" I asked, standing still, looking at the form. It was tall and had a folded, leathery skin, with some sort of square shape at its rear. There was a human head on top of the shoulders, but its arms . . . held another head, it seemed. A blank, bulbuous head, held in its arms, like some sort of trophy.

"No one knows," Micah said. "Most people think he was a shaman, or a priest, or some mighty hunter . . . and that he carries the head of some monster in his arms, a monster he had killed."

I looked again at the brave face of the man. "So that's why his statue was left alone."

"Maybe so. My father's father told me that even back then, people left the statue alone."

We continued down the wide hallway, our footsteps and others echoing on the stone. Torches had been placed along the walls, lighting up the way. Birds still flew overhead, and I unbuttoned two more buttons on my tunic. It was still very hot and muggy, and I wiped again at the sweat dripping down my forehead. Up ahead, the hallway seemed to widen some, and there was a crowd of tourists, and some beggars as well that must have snuck in past the keepers at the entranceway, but no one molested us as we went through an open arch. We were now in a great room, with balconies overhead, some of the stonework having fallen down. There were rows of benches of some sort before us, torn up, shattered, lying in heaps. At the other side of the room was a large rostrum or higher place, and other tour guides moved their small collection of visitors among the ruined benches and tables.

Micah took a breath. "This is where we think the people's assembly met. At least, that's what the old stories and legends tell us."

I looked around at the size of the room. "There must have been hundreds of them, to fit in such a space."

"Yes, you're right," he said.

"It must have been a large empire, back then," I said.

Micah replied, a bit of pride in his voice. "Greatest in the world."

"Are . . . are there other places like this among the ruins?"

"Yes, on the other side of this complex. A smaller room, but set up the same, with a raised platform. Some feel that's where the judges held court, or another assembly, perhaps representing other groups of people."

"How fascinating," I said, and I meant it. Micah rubbed at his chin and said, "May I ask you a question, sire?"

"Of course."

"Your empire . . . isn't there an assembly, similar to this?"

"Not really," I said. "We have . . . a council of sorts. Of elders from our tribes, clans and the cities. They advise the emperor, but, of course, it's up to him to decide whether he accepts their advice. More often than not, he does. Our elders . . . they're wise. They know the lands, they know our peoples . . . and you folks, what do you have?"

Micah seemed to grimace. "We have Prez Thomas III. And the Prez is selected by a group called the College."

"College? Like a university?"

"No," he said, shaking his head. "This College is

made up of guild masters, traders, and the like. And every eight years, they meet and select the Prez."

"I see," I said. "And how long has Thomas III been Prez?"

"My entire life," Micah said. "Look, would you like to see the other assembly room? It's on the other side."

"Is it like this one?"

"No, much smaller."

By now I was getting tired of being indoors, among the gloomy stones, the sounds of water dripping, the fluttering of the birds overhead. I wanted to be outside, as hot as it was.

"No, let's move on."

"Fine," he said.

After retracing our steps, we returned the lantern to the gatekeepers and resumed our walk down the wide stone steps. There were pools of water before us, and wide packed dirt roads, and more buildings, lining each side of a wide and long field that was kept close-cropped. We walked down more series of crumbling stone steps until we reached the ground, and by now I had my tunic almost unbuttoned all the way.

"It's so hot!" I said, wiping at my face with a kerchief. "How could any empire be governed from such a hot place?"

Micah smiled. "And this isn't the hot season, not quite yet. Well, there are stories and legends, that this whole area had once been cooler, with more land, which I think is true. Some of the fishing craft, out in the bays and channels, their nets often drag up old pieces of metal and stonework from the ancients. There are a few stories that this place even had frozen water during the cooler months, if you can believe that."

I wiped again at my face. "That would be a change now, a change I would like."

He turned to me. "Is it true, up north, that the water sometimes falls from the sky, frozen?"

"Quite true. Even where I live, the water falls like that. We call it snow. In fact, some of our clans, they have more than thirty names for different kinds of snow."

Micah shook his head. "Frozen water . . . I see it in cooled drinks, on occasion, but to think of it on the ground and in the air . . . not natural."

We plodded along in the heat and on either side were more ruined buildings. I asked Micah about them and he said, "A few of them, we think, were temples or exhibit halls. There were old things in some of them . . . bones and stones from long, long ago. One temple had some paintings of flying machines, made from metal. And in that one temple . . . ships that traveled off the world, into space."

I wiped my face one more time. "I've heard those tales as well."

The tone of his voice changed. "They are not tales. The old ones here, they traveled off world."

I said, "Well . . . some of our science men, they know that they sent instruments and such off world . . . but to think people traveled there . . . they believe it's just tales, or imaginings . . ."

Micah stopped and gently took the bottle of water from me, took a sip, and said, "My grandfather . . . he told me once . . . that when he was a boy, an elder, who was part of the College, let him touch a stone from one of these buildings, a stone that came from the moon."

"The moon?" I couldn't help myself, I chuckled. Tour guides . . . how ignorant do they think tourists can be? I took the bottle and after wiping the opening clean with my hand, took a warm swallow of the water and then recapped it. "If you say so . . . but these buildings, is there anything of interest to see?"

Micah resumed walking. "Perhaps, but after we visit the temple at the end of this walk, then we'll see how much time is left. Some of these buildings are nothing but empty rooms, with nothing much of interest."

We walked and walked in the heat, sometimes followed by young bands of boys and girls, trying to beg or sell us hand-carved souvenirs, but with a few shouts from Micah, and their eyeing of my sash, they left us alone.

As we passed another open pool of water, the passing breeze brought cooking smells to me, and my stomach grumbled. In the heat, I had forgotten how hungry I was getting. By the shores of the pond stalls had been set up, with all types of food being served. Most of the people at the stalls seemed to be locals, and I looked to Micah and he said, "Are you hungry, sire?"

"Yes, I am . . . but it seems that these stalls are only for . . . the ones who live here."

Micah smiled. "True, sire . . . and at the far, far end of these ruins, are restaurants for visitors, but if you wish to have a local meal, well, I recommend these places. The food is fresh and satisfying."

We walked closer to the stalls, my stomach grumbling even louder, and Micah said, "If you allow, I will go there and get something for you. Will that be acceptable?"

"Quite," I said, finding a large boulder underneath a palm tree that was shaded. I sat down and stretched my legs, and Micah stood there, not moving.

"Yes?"

His face was set. "My apologies, sire. Perhaps I did not make myself clear. This food is for sale. If you wish some, I must politely ask you for some money."

"Oh." I felt even more warm and foolish. I reached into my side pouch and asked, "Will a brass sovereign be acceptable?"

He nodded, took it from my hand, and then he walked away. Then something came to me and I called out, "Micah!"

He turned. "Sire?"

"Is . . . is there enough there to buy something for you as well?"

A faint nod. I called out again. "Then do so."
And then he moved into the crowd.

I sat there in the heat, legs stretched out, took another swallow from the water bottle, gauged the time
by the placement of the sun. As much as I would have
liked to see the other ruins, time was getting on. Father kept a fairly regular schedule with his meetings,
and I wanted to make sure I was back to our room
in plenty of time . . . so it would probably be the
temple at the end of this mowed area, and then back
to the pedicab and the hotel.

A young boy approached, about the age of my
youngest sister. He was wearing a tunic that looked
like it had been a sack for holding grain or vegetables,
with a length of cord as a belt. His feet were bare,
caked with dirt, and his brown arms were covered with
scratches. One of his eyes were cloudy, like it had
been injured at an earlier age. In his hands, he held
out a wood carving.

"Sir, sir, sir," he said. I barely understood his words.
"Please, please, please."

He held out the carving, and I took it in my hands.
The workmanship was remarkable, showing a man's
head, like a tiny bust, in dark wood. I looked again
at the little boy, snot running down his nose, and I
took in the ruins. Centuries ago, his ancestors had
built and populated this place, and even had ruled
most of the world, if the old stories and fragments of
books were to be believed. And now? He and his kind
were poor, diseased and corrupt, scrabbling for life
among the ruins of such glory. Even in the heat, I
felt chilled.

"Please, please, please," he said again.

I began to look at it even closer when there was a
shout and Micah approached, carrying a small bag.
The boy snatched the carving from my hand and ran
away, and when Micah reached me, I saw his face
was flushed.

I stood up. "It's all right, no need to be angry . . . the boy wasn't bothering me."

I could sense Micah trying to control some anger, and he bowed for a moment. "Forgive me, sire. I wasn't angry with the boy. I was angry with you."

I was shocked. "Me? Whatever for?"

Micah said, "If one of the gatekeepers saw what was going on . . . the boy bothering you as you sat there, with the white sash, then the boy would have been in the cane fields by this evening hour."

"He wasn't bothering me!"

Micah said, "It doesn't matter. All here know the law, especially what it means, for one to wear the white sash. You should have known better, sire . . . and not put his life in jeopardy."

I said nothing else for a few moments.

Our meal was cold drinks of some sort of fruit mixture, and bits of meat and vegetables, cooked on a long skewer of wood. The food was tasty and spicy, like nothing else I had ever eaten, and I asked Micah what the meat was, and he demurred. "Hard to explain, sire. Just enjoy the taste, and leave it at that."

When we were finished, we resumed our walking, and we came up to a small rise of land, and at the top of the rise was a collection of square stones, tumbled in one place. Micah pointed to them and said, "My grandfather told me that his grandfather told him that years ago, a mighty stone column stood here, rising up to the sky. No one knew who it was built for . . . just a great man, many, many centuries ago. . . ."

I eyed the pile of stones as we walked past. "What happened to it, then?"

Micah said, "One of Prez Thomas III's predecessors, many years ago, tore it down for the stone to build his own monuments." He pointed off to the right. "There was a place over there, before I was born, where another monument was found . . . buried under stone and dirt and weeds. Flat stone that had letters carved in it . . . names, it seemed like. That stone, too, was removed for other purposes."

Now we were skirting around a pond that was rectangular in shape, moving toward a building that Micah called the temple, at the other end of the pond. I said to him, "Micah . . . then who owns this place? And why hasn't more stone been removed?"

"Prez Thomas III . . . his great-great-great grandfather, Prez George II, ruled during a time when trade was increasing . . . with your empire and other lands, and he sensed that tourists would enjoy coming here, and spending money, and learning about the city of Tomac . . . and so he issued a decree. This area of ruins was to be protected, as best as we can afford."

"I see," I said.

We came closer to the temple, and crossed a boulevard of packed dirt and broken stone, and then approached another set of stone steps. We walked up the steps, most of them cracked and shattered, and before me I saw an incredible sight. The temple was open to the outside, with pillars before us, and hidden in the shadows, beyond the pillars, was a huge statue of a seated man, staring out at us. He sat in a giant stone throne, staring out, wearing a coat and trousers and boots, his giant hands resting on each side of his throne. His face was somber, looking out with an old but knowing gaze. His eyes were firm but tender, and he had a beard, but no moustache. It was odd, I had the strangest feeling I had seen him before, and then I recalled: the young beggar from just a while ago, with the carving. The carving had been of this man's face. I looked up at him and even with the tourists, the place was quiet. It seemed to be one of the holiest places I had ever been.

"Who is he?" I whispered.

Micah sounded proud. "One of our ancestors, one of the great leaders. Father Abram. That's his name. Father Abram."

"What made him great?" I said.

"He freed slaves," Micah said simply. "All of the slaves in the empire . . . Father Abram freed them, freed them all."

I looked up and saw that ivy and other weeds had grown up on the walls, but the statue was clean of all growth. I pointed this out to Micah and he said, "When there are no gatekeepers around, the people who live nearby, they make sure Father Abram is clean, and is safe. It's a sacred duty to them."

Then I noticed more offerings, piled at the base of the giant statue, of fruit and stones and wooden carvings. I said, "Do they pray to him, as well?"

Micah looked at me with surprise. "Of course."

"What for?"

"To come again, sire. To come again and free the slaves."

My mouth was dry, and I took another swallow of water. "Slaves? Really?"

He looked to me and then gently turned me about, to look out by the wetlands by the approaching bay. Columns of smoke rose up from the cane fields. "Sire . . . who do you think works out there, all day and all night?"

"Workers . . . servants . . . who else?"

"Sire . . . there are slaves out there . . . who do the work . . . slaves that cut the cane that is brought north to your land, so you can make the fuel that runs your engines, and your airships. And I know that there are slaves, even in your lands, even in your household. Am I not right?"

I shook my head. "We have servants . . . they are not slaves."

Micah laughed, but there was no humor there. "What kind of servants are they? May they leave when they wish, to take position elsewhere? Do they earn any type of salary, or does their pay go to their debts . . . as indentured servants? Tell me, sire . . . tell me about your servants."

I thought about what he said, and there was a truth

there, that I had never thought about. It had seemed . . . normal, for it was in our household, and the household of other families, that we all had servants, servants whose families had incurred debts, years and years ago. Their labor, day after day, went to reducing the debt. . . . Day after day, without end, without stopping.

"Come, sire, do you know of any servant who has ever left someone's employ? Do you?"

"No," I said, my voice sounding weak and shallow here, in this temple. "No, I do not."

Micah said, "A slave is a slave, no matter what they are called. Working in the cane fields, working in your lavish mansion, up there in the northern lands. If they are not free, they are slaves. And it's as simple as that."

He turned and looked up to the statue, his voice firm and quiet. "I know what you and the others think of our ancients, of our lands, of the empire that was here. We know of the troubles we were accused of doing, the hate and wars we supposedly started . . . I don't know the truth of that. It is in the past. But what I do know is that this empire that was so hated once, produced a man like Father Abram, a man who freed the slaves. And any empire that can bring forth such a man . . . well, not enough of its true history is known."

I looked back as well. Something about that steady gaze and knowing who he was, I felt small.

Micah said, "And perhaps, someday . . . another Father Abram will return to these lands. Come, sire, it's getting late. We must leave."

Which is what we did, though I almost fell twice, walking down the stairs, looking back up at that steady gaze.

When we got back to the hotel, Micah was nearly out of breath, sweating, as he stood there in the gathering twilight next to his pedicab. I shook his hand

and before I could say anything, he said, "Sire . . . when you return to your empire, remember your trip here. Talk about us, who we are . . . and of Father Abram . . . and . . . well, I must show you something."

From his own pouch he took out a very small round coin or medallion, which he held up to me. It was old, nearly obscured, but I held it close and felt something close about my chest as I recognized what was on the medallion. On one side was the temple, and on the other side, there was a carving of Father Abram. I held the medallion tight and said, "Micah . . . I must have this."

"Sire, please, it's something I've had—"

I reached into my pouch, took out a silver sovereign, and then a gold one, and pressed them into his hand. "I need to take this with me, as a reminder, Micah. I really must."

He bowed. "As you wish, sire. It was . . . it was an honor to be your guide today, sire. Do have a safe trip home."

And then he got into his pedicab and left, and I went into the hotel, to return my sash, and to get to my room before Father arrived.

The next day, as our luggage was being prepared by the hotel's servants (slaves, I thought, slaves) Father looked to me, as I rummaged through my pouch, and said, "Armand, what's that coin?"

I took out the medallion and passed it over to him. Thinking quickly, I said, "I . . . I bought this from a local. It's a medallion, to honor a great man who once ruled the old empire here."

Father took the medallion, examined it, and then laughed. Tossed it back over to me.

"Armand . . . I'm sorry, I truly am, for leaving you alone for so long, for you've been taken. This is just an old, old coin from the days of the old empire here . . . and even at the empire's height, this coin was used everywhere. Billions of them must have been created . . . and you can find them in almost any of the ruins. You said you paid for this coin, Armand?"

"Yes," I said, my face warm with embarrassment.

Father kept on smiling. "I'm so sorry, son, but you were robbed. Even when it was being used during the old empire here, it was often ignored or thrown away. That coin is without value, no value at all."

I looked at the coin, rubbed the edge and the faded face of Father Abram. Thought of the statue, thought of the temple, thought of the pride of Micah in his ancestors and this old man. I rubbed the coin even harder.

I raised my gaze to him. "I'm sorry, Father," I said. "I think it's priceless."

SUFFER THE CHILDREN

by *Barbara Nickless*

Barb Nickless' short stories have appeared in a wide variety of magazines and anthologies, including *All Hell Breaking Loose*, *New Writings of the Fantastic*, and *Fate Fantastic*. Currently at work on her second mystery novel, she lives in Colorado with her husband and two children.

THE GAWDERS MOVED us seasonally, like we was birds. Skinny, bent-over, plucked-to-the-skin birds.

The winter afore my change, the Gawders hauled us to the north end a Miner 3B and turned the temp down five degrees so we'd know it was winter. The holographs went from lily fields to black rivers and dead grass. Needled trees stood all solid in the distance like Gawd's soldiers. The light was fainter, and everybody looked blue, as if we didn't have enough air.

None a us had ever knowed real seasons or seen real flowers or trees. In the domes there wasn't nothin like that. But we liked the holographs. If you touched the picture, words like *Colorado Ponderosa* or *lichen* lit up and a bell chimed to remind us to pay attention, like the bells at prayer time.

29

"When you gonna need a word like *pon-der-o-sa*?"
Flea would ask, and we'd laugh and laugh.

But every member a the Flea Pack would've given
anything to see a real, live Colorado Ponderosa.

When we wasn't workin, the Pack sat near the
vents. We'd take turns leaning over the grillwork,
waiting for the fans to kick on so we'd get a full blast
a air. The higher we got on the ventilator chemicals,
the more dreamy-sad we got, like the way you feel
when you just know things gotta change on account a
you can't take them the way they is any more. The
Gawders hadn't caught on to what we was doin. Or
maybe they didn't care, we had this one thing.

Sure, we didn't have nothin else.

It was Seven-Day, and the mines was closed. The
haulers and loaders and scoopers all stood still, silver
flamingoes roostin outta the rain. Rings leaned over
the vent. Flea was fixin his crutch where the rubber
foot had cracked. His muscles was all bunched, and he
had a little frown between his eyes. He was hummin
somethin he'd sung afore, some song he brought
from North.

I twirled a bit of hair round my finger and wondered
if he'd walk me home again.

Fox Girl poked my arm. "Willow."

Rubbin my arm, I looked over at Fox Girl.

"What?" I said.

Fox Girl was givin me the eye. She winked at me,
then licked her lips at Flea.

"What?" I said again. Fox Girl gets bored, likes to
cause trouble, that's what Flea says.

Fox Girl made a circle with the fingers of her left
hand, then stuck her right index finger in and out of
the hole, in and out. She nodded toward Flea.

I knowed Flea was right. I should pay no nevermind
to Fox Girl. But I'm not myself all these last seven-
days, my body all shook up like it aint quite mine no
more, and bein tall and tall and gettin taller till I don't
know who I am. I tried to close my mouth, but trouble

boiled up inside me and I frowned at Flea and let loose his secret.

"You goin streamin today, Flea?" I asked.

Flea flipped up his shades and stared at me. I could just about read his mind. *Supposed to be our secret, Willow,* he was sayin. *No one else supposed to know about that tunnel.*

Right off, I was shamed.

"Just jokin," I said.

But Fox Girl was on me quick. "You're not. You think them stupid stories are true."

Rings sat on his heels and flicked Fox Girl's arm. "Sometimes you too mean."

I shrugged, all not-caring like. "Not so stupid, them stories."

Streamin was a myth, a dream, like Flea said half the stories in the Praise Book was just made-up. All us wantin to believe and refusin at the same time on account all that hopin can hurt.

We was a sorry pack a birds, ha!

Flea should a told me it was a bad joke, left it at that. Stead, he dropped his shades, said, "Don't know if I'm going, Willow. You?"

The fans clicked on and I put my face in the spray and snorted, feeling the sting deep inside. *Breathe deeply, my child,* like the preacher said to me on baptism day.

I pulled my head back and sneezed. "I'm thinkin I might, you show me that tunnel."

Fox Girl jumped to her feet. "Stupid talk! Nobody ever got out a the Praise Dome. We gonna stay here and work till we nothing but bones, and then we'll have babies so our babies can work till they nothing but bones. And they'll all be stupid or crips or crazy, just like us. There no tunnel. They was sealed up afore we was born." She stomped her foot. "Get true."

Her voice echoed along the gray tiles of the shaft, booming around like a bird that lost its way and kept bangin into things.

I looked at Flea. "There a tunnel?"

"There's a tunnel. An old mining duct from before they built the Bios Domes."

My arms pimpled and I rubbed them.

Every six months, outsiders from the Bios Domes come to check on us, to ask us questions like how we doin and to listen to us pretend to read. Every time they come, the Praise Dome opens up a crack like there was all the sudden enough good air to lift us up and carry us away, just like them invisible updrafts the birds float on in the canyon hologram.

"Think I will, then," I said.

Fox Girl sank to the floor. "It's a sin, hopin for something not gonna happen."

"Fox, you not much a saint, anyway," Rings said. Rings is taller'n all a us, with gray eyes and hair dirty-white. He's got a death wish and eyes that go flat when the Gawders talk. "Flea says there's a tunnel, there's a tunnel. Let's do it, Flea Pack."

My heart was poundin now. But Flea looked at me and smiled.

"You the brave one, Willow. You find us all a home."

Fox Girl snorted, but it was a soft, weak sound.

Rings cocked his head. "Gawders."

Flea swung up on his crutches. "Sublevel 1," he mouthed. "Behind the secondary shaft."

We flew from the Gawders like we had wings.

I made my way toward Sublevel 1 by cuttin through Blessed Park. It was my favorite place in the Prayer Dome. It had bright grass that looked real, and if you didn't go barefoot you could pretend it was soft like everyone said real grass was. Up above, a patch a dome was lit like it was blue sky outside stead of the rain. It was nice to have somethin between the gray and us. All that color shook me up, made me feel a touch deep inside, better than the air vents.

I couldn't enjoy it none today, though.

Honor thy Gawder. And Gawders don't believe in streamin.

We wasn't like the mainstream kids. We was the lucky ones. Snatched from the very jaws a death, praise be, and given homes and jobs. Never mind some a us was crips or crazies, and we wouldn't a been if we was mainstream. We'd a had gen-screens if we was mainstream, and we'd a been fixed afore we was born.

Course, we wasn't sposed to be born.

I slipped through the crowd, walkin slow and casual. Walkin with downcast eyes, proper like. But there must a been somethin on my face, somethin fierce or scared. Suddenly there was a Gawder walkin next to me.

"Praise be," he said.

I walked slower. "Praise be."

The Gawder was tall and old, with long gray hair and stone eyes. His hands looked tough and stringy like the roots in the holograms. My heart hammered like to leap out a my chest.

"What is work, girl?" the Gawder asked me.

"The way to purity," I answered.

"And where do idle thoughts lead?"

"To the deepest place of all, the very mineshaft of the devil."

Quick as a snake he reached out and grabbed my wrist, squeezing it hard, jerking me to a stop. "You look idle, girl."

"I'm not, Elder." Tears stung in my eyes from the pain in my wrist, and my breath was comin too fast.

He pushed closer to me and his hand jumped from my wrist to my shoulder. "You be needin a pinch from Gawd's hand?"

"Oh, no, Elder."

"Do you know about pride?"

I nodded, feelin his hand quiver on my shoulder,

his fingers curlin neath my coveralls to press against
my flesh. His face got red, and his mouth hung open.
His breath was all hot.

"Do you think you're beautiful, girl?"

"No, Elder."

"The devil works through beauty."

His fingers dug into my skin, stoppin afore he gave
me the pinch that would send the burnin down my
back. His other hand traced the letters a my name on
my coveralls, just over my breast. *Miriam 237*.

"Where is your flock, Miriam?"

"Doin their wash."

"What dorm you in?"

"Block C, Row 12, Column 41."

"Go to your room, girl, and wait for me. Maybe I'll
come and see you. Gawd's work."

"Yes, Elder." I let the crowd sweep me away from
the Gawder, but I felt his eyes flamin into me, like
the eyes a the devil himself.

It's a sin to think a the Gawders that way.

But streamin was a sin. Bad things happen to sinners, even I know that.

When I saw Flea ahind the secondary shaft, I said,
"We can't go."

He was the only one there. He pulled me ahind the
pipes and kissed me.

"You're brave, Willow," he said. "I loved you before, but I love you even more now."

"We can't do it. The Gawders know. They know
everything."

"They only want us to think that."

"A Gawder stopped me in the park. I'm supposed
to be waitin for him."

Flea's face got red, and he punched the wall.

"You'll hurt yourself," I said.

"It's because you're beautiful. You're almost fourteen. You're almost onto your Change. They won't
leave you alone much longer."

I turned my face against his shoulder.

"I'm afraid a being a sinner."

"Willow, you're no sinner. You're just a girl trapped in a sick place."

"The Praise Dome, you mean?"

"I mean not everyone thinks it's a sin if you're not working all the time. Like the lilies in the field. How can you love anyone or anything if all you do your whole life is haul shale through rain that'll eat you to the bone?"

"You know all this on account a you're from Outside."

"It's different up North."

"Without the rain."

"With only good rain."

I knew the story. I'd asked Flea to tell me a thousand million times about how his uncle hid him away in the hills on account of his leg. But I'd hear it a thousand million more times if I could.

"There's real trees," I said.

"And tall green grass with feather tops made of seeds. A silver moon that rises and sets. Mountains where the snow stays always, and where you can drink from the lakes right next to the deer. Waterfalls louder than the loaders. Things we don't have in the holograms."

"The wind."

"Like to blow you over."

"And you'd a stayed there if someone hadn't found out."

"Forever."

"But someone saw your uncle goin back and forth. Then the coppers arrested him and you had to live with the Gawders."

"Where I met you, Willow."

This was my favorite part. "And gave me my name."

"And fell in love with you. Someone to dream with. I'm going to take you North."

I wanted to curl up against him, make him promise. "Flea, you still got your leg. They won't want us."

"I've heard it's different now."

"I'm not smart."

"They don't care."

"You promise?"

"Sure, Willow."

I wrapped my arms around him. "What you see in someone like me?"

He reached back and took my hands, crossed his fingers between mine. "Smarts aren't everything, anymore than having straight legs. I love you because you've got a good heart, Willow. Honest and true."

"There really a tunnel not closed?"

"Yes."

"And we can get through it?"

"It took hard work to get it open, but it wasn't welded shut. It's been opened before. Maybe someone else went through that tunnel. Maybe they got away. Could be it's blocked farther along, but we won't know till we try. Trying is half the game, right?"

"How come the Gawders haven't found it?"

He shrugged and grabbed up his crutches. "Because it still looks sealed, I guess. And because you have to be small and skinny to fit through it."

"What if we get out a here, Flea? I mean, for real-like?"

"Then we'll go far away. We'll get married and raise a family."

"They'll find us."

"Not up North. I know how to hide."

"How we gonna get North?"

"I'll figure something. Do you trust me, Willow?"

"I trust you."

I touched Flea's face, and he put his fingers over mine. I wanted to tell him how much I loved him, even though it didn't need sayin. A course a nobody like me would love Flea. But Fox Girl was there, all the sudden. And Rings.

Flea loosened the screws on each corner a the screen, and the screen just sat there till he grunted and lifted the whole thing away from the opening. He leaned the screen against the wall and dropped the screws in his pocket. He snapped his fingers, and we slid, one by one, into the tunnel and through the door. Me first, then Fox Girl. Flea and Rings was last. When I heard them two pull the grill back into place, somethin clanged in my heart. I didn't know if it was death's gong or a bell a freedom.

I touched Flea's leg as he crawled past me draggin his crutches. I touched his twisted leg, down near his foot where his ankle was hot and smooth.

It was dark in the tunnel and cold. Flea had brought two glowlights, and Rings had a third, but the lights was sorry in all that black. At first, I didn't so much mind. We was on an adventure, and it's not a proper adventure, there's no scary parts.

But pretty soon I started to feel like this was purgatory, and we'd be stuck here till Judgment. And then I thought it was hell, and we'd be stuck here forever.

When my brain had become a little shriveled thing, all scared and talkin to itself, Flea signaled us to stop. We'd been real quiet, on account a the tunnel would go right under the Prayer Dome for a long way. But now Flea said we was past all that, and we could talk in whispers.

He grinned at me. "How's freedom feel, Willow?"

"Like I gotta pee," I said truthfully.

We all laughed, but Flea looked at me a real long time, and I figured if this was purgatory, then it was okay long as Flea was around.

It got harder after that.

Sometimes the tunnel was vertical, and we'd have to haul ourselves, hand over hand, up the slurry-car cable. Sometimes the tunnel was nearly filled with water pipes that had fallen from their brackets, leavin just enough room for us to squeeze through. The old rails hurt our knees when we had to crawl. Sometimes we'd go one way and find the tunnel had fallen and we'd have to back out, stirrin up the dust and tryin not to cough. Worst, sometimes we heard the rain beatin on the dirt over the tunnel from somethin like a hundred miles away. I thought of all that rain, eatin its way to us.

But Flea got us through. He had to drag his crutches, and I knowed it was harder for him than for the rest a us, but he never said nothin.

We stopped for another water break in an old processing room. We fetched up against the dead furnace and stared at each other till our grins was like to split our faces. I was startin to think it might all be real, and my heart stuck in my throat. When we started again, I kept movin by watchin Flea's skinny back and flat bottom twitch and shimmer in Rings' light like he was a rabbit in one a them springtime holograms and this was his hidey-hole.

After forever, we went through another door. After that, Flea raised his hand. We huddled ahind him.

Twenty feet afore us, light poured through the grillwork, broken up by the screen into thousands a tiny stars. We heard voices, lots a voices, like the roar a the generators, but like music, too.

"We done died," Rings said.

"It's heaven," Fox Girl whispered.

Flea reached through and undid the screws and the grill hung in place, just like at the other end. Through the grill we saw the Bios Dome was filled with people rushin here and there on sidewalks and streets or just sittin in chairs with their legs crossed and their arms wavin and lookin happy like they didn't have to be nowhere.

There was music, and it wasn't nothin like the music in the dome. It jumped and snapped and hopped sideways like it couldn't hold itself. Real trees in the distance, leaves shimmerin like as if they wanted to move to the music. A snippet a air floated by, filled with what I thought might be how leaves and grass smelled. My stomach rumbled.

Flea said we had to wait for everyone in Bios to be

lookin the other way. We waited and waited, tryin not
to cough or sneeze. My stomach was tight as my fists,
sayin to me, *This is wrong, girl,* and my mind thinkin
back, *So what?*

Finally, Flea said, "Let's go," and he lifted out the
grill.

We scrambled through the tunnel opening, and we
was out! We straightened up and smiled a little shaky
at each other and didn't hold hands on account a we
was in Bios and we began walkin.

Noise and things rushin and more noise. The people
all strong and full a good color. Not a gray-hair or
wrinkled face or any backs bent over. Big white teeth,
high shoulders, strong hands. They pushed past other
people all unafraid, and they nodded and showed their
teeth and the scent that rose off them said they hadn't
ever been scared or hungry.

There was places filled with clothes in colors like
flowers. There was jewelry all shiny like the snow on
the ponderosas. A picture of a woman and two children the way the Book said it was supposed to be,
and I looked at that picture and wanted it like I
wanted the music, and Flea said, "Come on, Willow,"
and pulled me along.

We went past the trees and touched the leaves, and
I took off my shoes and Fox Girl ran through the
bushes, her voice all high and happy.

Smells was comin from some places like to drive
me mad. Flea said you could walk into them places,
if you had credit, and order yourself anything you
wanted. And eat as much a it as you wanted. I knowed
about that. It was part a the myth.

After a long time we began to hitch and slow, feelin
too much. I saw that people was lookin at us. Maybe
it was Flea's crutches. I didn't see nobody else with
crutches. Maybe it was our clothes, which I could tell
was all wrong. Or maybe it was on account a Rings
bein all white and Fox Girl all pinched and me with
my slow eyes. We wasn't streamin very well.

It was Rings that noticed we was bein followed.

"A man's watchin us," he said. "All dressed in shiny blue."

"A copper, I'll bet," Flea said. "They're Law here. This way." He ducked down an alley quick as a sin, crutches or no crutches.

We began movin fast again, changin directions. Bios was bigger than the ocean must be. It went on and on and on like to never end, and my heart got small and quiet. Then we passed a huge room filled with light. Glass, to tell it true, but glass that held the light. Glass that tripped up the light and sent it round in a thousand million colors. Glass in the shapes a people and animals and the flower called American Beauty Rose that I'd seen in the holographs. And tiny trees in more shades a brown and green than I'd a figured there could be.

I stared.

After some time I became myself again and realized wantin somethin so bad was a sin. I forced my eyes away from the light. The Flea Pack was gone, and there was a fat man dressed all in bright blue standin at my elbow.

He looked me in the eye. "Hey, girl, you one of the Praise kids?"

I thought to run, but it wouldn't a helped much, bein without an idea how to find the tunnel. I opened my mouth and shut it.

"Thought so," he said. "Word is out that four of you bolted. Get tired of all that singing and digging?"

I blinked and shook my head, knowin soon as I said somethin he'd know what I was. I looked round for Flea.

The Law frowned. "You guys are nothing but trouble. Bad luck and trouble all rolled up in one little praise package." He had a long, brown stick, and he began feelin it up, like he had an itch. "You've got no business hanging around normal folk. You're a bunch of crips and retards and loonies. Sick in the head from all that praise stuff. World's bad enough without your kind."

Just then a woman came runnin up. "Maria!" she cried, lookin at me. "There you are. Niece, you gave me a fright. Now stay with me and be a proper tour guide, or I'm going to have a talk with your mother."

My mouth opened again. Suddenly I knowed how badly I didn't wanna go back to the Praise Dome. I made a smile. "I'm sorry."

The man glanced at the woman, his face confused. "She with you?"

"Oh, yes," the woman said. "She's my niece. She offered to take me around, but it looks like she lost me. Or I lost her. Thank you for looking after her."

The woman tucked her arm through mine and pulled me away. She leaned close and whispered. "Let's stroll about a bit until the policeman gives up, shall we?"

"Thank you, ma'am."

She patted my arm. "My pleasure."

She was from Outside. I could tell on account a her skin was dark and there was wrinkles at her eyes and she was *round* like she'd eaten real food her whole life. Her arms her hips her breasts her stomach. Rollin like the hills in the spring holograms.

We walked round, and looked here and there until my naked feet was afire, and if the fat man was followin us, he'd know for sure I wasn't no mainstream kid. I couldn't stop my mouth from fallin open. I tried to look for the Flea Pack, but the woman clung to my arm and dragged me in and out a shops and finally took me back to the store a glass and light. She bought me a little tree she called a maple. The leaves was red.

"There are still maples. Did you know?"

I nodded, though I didn't know about the maples. I held it tight and gentle.

"Now we'll go to my sister's, and you can tell me why that policeman was following you. I've just arrived here, and I'm afraid I don't know much about this place. But I'm sure terrifying children isn't the normal code of ethics. He looked about to hit you! Diane—that's my sister—will know what to do."

I thought I saw Flea twice and Rings once as we walked through Bios, but every time I stopped and turned to look closer, they vanished. Maybe they was followin us, maybe I was just wishin. Either way, I was stickin with the woman till I was sure that copper was gone.

Diane laughed and shrieked when she saw her sister, and hugged her. Then she looked at me and screamed again, but it wasn't the same kind a scream. She waved us in, then rounded on her sister.

"Anna, I thought you'd given up bringing home strays."

"She was being terrorized."

"Well, you can't keep her," Diane said, closin the door. "She's a Gawder."

"A what?"

"From over near Deep Water. The Praise Dome. My dear Anna, what have you done?"

A look a understandin showed on my rescuer's face. "She was to be aborted?"

"Apparently."

"Why didn't her mother have a gen-screen?"

"Maybe she did."

"And she couldn't afford to do anything with the information."

"It happens all the time."

Somethin dark showed in Anna's eyes. "Poor child."

"Amen," I said, like we was supposed to when people talked about bein saved.

"And the mother?" Anna asked.

"An eye for an eye," Diane answered.

I bent my head. "Amen."

We all sat down and was quiet awhile, and Diane gave us tea to drink. I sipped mine careful like. It was wicked hot.

Somewhere, somethin ticked.

"Abortion wasn't always a crime," Anna said.

"It is now." Diane slapped a plate a cookies on the table. The little cookies hopped up and down.

I grabbed a cookie and took a quick bite, then slid the rest of the cookie into my pocket.

"But they use the children in the mines!" Anna said. "Why save them for a life like that?"

"It's still a life!" Diane snapped. "They're fed and taught to read and write a little, and cost the domes nothing. Most of the children are content to stay, even when they're of legal age."

Anna snorted. "They stay because they're not qualified to make a living anywhere else. And they're probably too scared to try." She grabbed a book from the counter and slapped it open in front of me. "Can you read any of this?"

I shook my head. "Sorry, ma'am."

But Anna didn't look upset. She was studyin me like I was a praise song that needed memorizin. Then she glanced at Diane. "They can be adopted, can't they?"

"Anna! For heaven's sake! You don't even know this girl."

But Anna was again lookin at me. "You have a name?"

"Maria?" I asked.

"That was only for the policeman's benefit."

"Miriam 237."

"Miriam," Anna said softly. "My little girl's name was Lilith. She would have been twelve, now. How old are you, Miriam?"

I smiled hopefully. "Twelve."

One corner a her mouth lifted. "No, really. How old?"

"Almost fourteen."

Diane poured more tea. "It's the lack of sunlight. Everyone raised here looks young for their age."

"I'm going to adopt her, raise her as my own. She's not going back to the mines."

"Anna—!"

There was a knock on the door. It had to be Law. I snatched up the maple tree. Would they make me give it back?

But it was the Flea Pack. They nodded politely to Diane when she opened the door and then pushed on past her afore she'd said a thing. They stood round the kitchen with its daffodil-yellow curtains and ponderosa-green walls. With all that color, the pack looked like them icicles on the frozen river in the hologram. I laughed, but it sounded like a hiccup.

Diane looked scared and left the room. But Anna got to her feet and pulled out the chairs so everybody could sit.

"These friends of yours?" she asked me.

"The Flea Pack. That's Flea, and Fox Girl and Rings. Our real names are John 511 and Ruth 423 and Daniel 367."

"Numbered children," Anna said. "Sit down, all of you. I'll get you something to eat and drink."

Flea squatted by my chair and took my hand. "Rings, watch out the window for that copper."

Rings grabbed a cookie, and Fox Girl did the same, and then they went to stand at the window. Diane came back into the room. She smiled okay, but when she took the teapot to the sink, I saw her hands was shakin..

"You okay?" Flea asked me. "What're you doing here?"

I grabbed his hands. "I'm streamin, Flea. We're all streamin. These women, they want to help us."

Flea narrowed his eyes. "Not us, Willow. You."

"All of you. It's wrong, what they do." Anna looked all the sudden sad. "I mean, I can't help all of you. I don't have that kind of money. But there are others like me. Isn't that so, Diane?"

Diane rattled the tea pot.

"You gonna leave me, Willow?" Flea asked.

Tears squeezed out from beneath my lids. "I'm not leavin you, Flea."

"You could. You could, and wait for me. I'm almost eighteen. I won't be all that long."

"She not gonna wait for you," Fox Girl said.

I glared at Fox Girl. "Flea named me Willow on account my roots go deep. I don't go over."

"Coppers," Rings said.

Flea looked at Anna and Diane. "Is there a back way out?"

"Only a window," Diane said. "It's too far to jump."

"Well, praise shit," Flea said.

Fox Girl ran into the kitchen and grabbed a knife.

"Drop that!" Diane shrieked.

But Fox Girl didn't pay no nevermind. She looked all stupid-scared. Just like I felt. By the window, Rings jerked down the long, metal bar holdin the curtains. He held it up like it was a spear.

Flea didn't say nothin.

The coppers didn't knock. They busted the door down. They came in swingin clubs. They saw Fox Girl, still standin stupid with the knife. Rings threw the metal rod at them and clear missed them and they hit him in the stomach. When I jumped up, one a them smashed me in the nose.

My face exploded. Blood blasted out like vent air. The maple tree flew out a my hand.

"Willow!" Flea screamed.

Flea jumped the one that had got me and hit him hard till another copper turned and clubbed Flea in the back a his head. Flea fell to the floor, and they clubbed him again and he quit twitchin.

"Flea!" I cried.

Anna and Diane was screamin and Fox Girl was wailin. Rings was holdin his stomach, his mouth gapin open like a Great White Shark from the summer hologram.

But Flea didn't say nothin. I saw his crutches by the door, and that's what I remember. His crutches throwed down near his feet. The maple tree lay smashed into a glitter a light near the special shoes Flea wore on account a his short leg. I stood up, meanin to go toward the crutches, toward the heat a Flea's skin where his leg met his foot.

The Law lifted up his club.

"Stop!" Anna moved toward the copper. "She's going to be my little girl."

Diane hauled her back. "Look at her, Anna. She's *dull.* Stupid. It's why her mother tried to get rid of her. You don't want a child like that. You can't have a child like that."

Poof, went Anna's face, all crumpled like. She sat down hard, like her legs just quit.

I understood things real clear then. I understood we was the ones shouldn't a been the way we was. We could a been perfect, only it takes money to be perfect. I understood no one would ever want us but the Gawders, them people who look at us not like we was made a flesh and blood, but as if we was dollars and cents. Bein made a dollars and cents was how we gave back to the world when otherwise we'd be worth nothin.

"Flea," I sobbed.

Flea wasn't movin.

I let my hand fall back.

It was a long time afore Fox Girl and Rings and me was sent back to the Praise Dome, on account we had to pay for our sins.

After we got back, the Gawders moved us south. Temperature went up five degrees. We changed into our short-sleeve coveralls. The holographs sprouted leaves and grass and names like honey maple, Miriamac, weeping willow. I couldn't say the words no more on account of havin paid for my sins, but I whispered them in my head.

No one will say one word about Flea. He's in some in-between space like that second between when you see the rock break loose in the shaft and afore it reaches where you're standin at the bottom. He can't be dead, on account a when someone dies the Gawders have a big celebration to show the deceased is gone to a better place. But he's not here either.

It's like he never was.

Every Seven-Day I sit by myself, tryin to figure it out. I sit still, all still and watch the holograms like I got roots and can't move.

But the holograms don't make much sense anymore. I mean, what kind a name is weeping willow?

What call would a tree ever have to cry?

BETTER GUNS

by Jean Rabe

Jean Rabe is the author of more than twenty novels and more than forty short stories. In addition, she has edited several DAW anthologies. When she's not writing (which isn't often), she delights in the company of her two aging dogs, dangles her feet in her backyard goldfish pond, and pretends to garden. She loves museums, books, boardgames, role-playing games, wargames, and movies that "blow up real good." Visit her web site at: www.jeanrabe.com.

"**A**H TINK MY gun's better'n yours, Cousin Cletus."
Cletus snorted and wiped his nose on the sleeve of his Tennessee Titans sweatshirt. "Matter of opinion, Jimmy-Don, and your opinion'd be wrong on that count. What you've got there is a Colt, army model 1860, a .44 caliber six-shot revolver, double-action. It were used in what they called the Western theater."

Jimmy-Don held the gun in front of him so that the moonlight revealed its old tarnished glory. The teen-ager brushed a hank of wheat-blond hair out of his eyes with his free hand, some of the strands sticking to the sweat on his forehead. "Well, Ah dunno, Cousin Cletus. Ah still think it looks better'n yours.

Ain't so nicked up as that piece you got, and Ah'm pretty sure it . . ."

"Shut your pie-hole, Jimmy-Don." Cletus glared for good measure. He was sweating, too, despite it being the first day of winter and despite them being outside crouched on a frost-tinged lawn. At least Jimmy-Don had thought to wear a coat, dark like the shadows that stretched from the pines and maples that ringed the property.

Smart boy, Cletus thought. *Might even be community college material someday.*

"That there gun of yours, Cousin Cletus . . ."

". . . is a Le Mat, boy, the best foreign-designed revolver that were used in the Civil War. See?" Cletus drew the gun from beneath his belt and held it so Jimmy-Don could get a good ogle. "It's got two barrels, this top one here can fire nine .40 caliber bullets, and the bottom's loaded for a 16-gauge shotgun ball. It were made by Jean Alexander Francois Le Mat, a French doctor working for the Confederacy."

"So you really think yours is better 'cause it were a Confederacy gun?" Jimmy-Don shook his head. "The Union won, Cousin Cletus." He waved the Colt for effect and grinned, showing an even row of bright white teeth. "Ah know my history, Cousin Cletus. Ah'm gonna be graduating junior high come June." He waved the gun again.

"Careful with that, Jimmy-Don." Cletus ground his stubby teeth together. "These guns ain't ours. Your Uncle Bodean loaned 'em to us."

"From his Civil War museum down by the turnpike. Ah know." Jimmy-Don nodded. "On account of the gun laws now, Uncle Bodean had to borrow them to us, else we wouldn't have anything to shoot with. Them government men confiscated the ones Ah had stockpiled. My deer rifle, that .357 magnum, the Walther PPK like James Bond used in the movies. They even got my old Derringer, too, the one that Grandpa gave me when Ah finished the sixth grade and that

Ah'd been hiding in my sock drawer. Got all of them. Got my mom and dad's stash, too.'' The teenager wistfully wiped at the Colt's barrel, treating the revolver almost reverently now. "Ah'm surprised they didn't pull all of Uncle Bodean's guns from the museum."

"Them government men didn't consider museum pieces dangerous," Cletus said. "Probably figured putting that big Cabela's out of business down at the 'I,' closing our sporting goods shops and the gun shows were enough, raiding homes and hunting clubs, disbanding the NRA, making it more illegal to buy a gun than to buy . . . And all of that in the span of a couple of months. Don't you get me started, boy."

"Sorry, Cousin Cletus." Jimmy-Don blew at the Colt and tried to polish the handle. "Hope this packs a punch. Sure wish Ah had that .357 right now."

Cletus sucked in a lungful of the chill air and held it deep. A moment later he let out a big breath that feathered to hang suspended in front of his lips like a woman's lace hanky. He shivered, though not from the cold, and stretched out on his stomach, the breech-loading carbine that he'd slung over his shoulder lying uncomfortably across his back.

It was nerves that had caught a firm hold on him and Jimmy-Don, Cletus knew—which was why the boy was talking so much, and why he was sweating like he was sitting in the YMCA sauna. He couldn't let the boy realize how rattled he was by this venture. He needed to look brave. This had been his idea, after all, and he'd only brought Jimmy-Don along because the boy's eyesight was so good. Why, Jimmy-Don could spot a June bug in a mass of spring willow leaves and could shoot the gold circle off a Campbell's soup label at fifty paces . . . when no one else was looking, of course. Firing ranges, skeet, target-practice, hunting . . . none of those things were legal anymore. Five months past the Bill Of Rights had been rewritten to eliminate the right to bear arms.

What had this country come to?

"Someone's coming, Cousin Cletus." Jimmy-Don held a finger to his lips and mouthed: *My turn.* He stuffed the Colt in the pocket of his jeans and drew a bowie knife from a homemade sheath on his belt.

Jimmy-Don scuttled forward, reminding Cletus of a big toad, back all hunched and legs in close, mouth gaping open as if to catch a fly. Good thing he'd brought the boy along, Cletus thought, as he hadn't heard the guard approach.

The man wore black, looking like a piece of the night sky come to ground. He was lean and broad-shouldered, and Cletus knew he was armed, though he couldn't see a gun. Cletus wouldn't have seen the man at all if it hadn't been for his breath easing away from his face like a little cloud of fog. Probably how Jimmy-Don noticed him. The guard, maybe a secret service man, was patrolling the grounds, certainly only one of many with such a task. Enviably quiet, the man's course took him near Jimmy-Don and into a patch of moonlight.

He had night-vision goggles, and they allowed him to see the teenager springing at him.

Again, the image of a big toad rushed at Cletus. He clamped his teeth together so tight his jaw ached, and he held his breath and prayed.

The man brought up a gun, sleek and black and almost two centuries newer than what Cletus and Jimmy-Don toted. Probably deadlier, too, but he didn't get the chance to pull the trigger. Jimmy-Don barreled into him, knife leading and sinking into the man's neck before he could cry out a warning. Cletus had told Jimmy-Don that the guards were all no doubt wearing some type of fancy body armor, and the boy had taken the words to heart, going for exposed flesh.

Jimmy-Don gave a soft victory whoop and the guard made a gargling sound that didn't last long. Then Jimmy-Don pulled the body back and stuffed it under a big pine next to three other bodies that Cletus had put there minutes ago.

"You done good, boy."

Jimmy-Don's grin splayed wide across his face. "Let me get the next one, too, Cousin Cletus. Ah'm getting the hang of this."

It looked like the boy was having fun, and that notion chafed in Cletus' craw. This wasn't about fun or adventure. This was about taking something back, fighting for a just cause and teaching the politicians . . . what was left of them . . . a lesson. Forcing them to grow a backbone.

Cletus closed his eyes and in the back of his mind pictured the footage that had played over and over for weeks upon weeks this past summer and into the fall. The west wing of the White House imploding in the passing of a heartbeat, the Washington Monument toppling, the Smithsonian Air and Space Museum vaporized, the Lincoln Memorial the site of the dirty bomb that wiped out the city and a good chunk of Arlington and into Baltimore. Smoke and fire and screams and death, caught by news crews stationed on street corners intending to capture Fourth of July activities and recording destruction instead. News crews that died days later in hospitals.

Radiation got them.

Practically all of Congress wiped out in minutes, most of the rest of them succumbing within the month, some of them still lingering in hospice care.

The president, vice president—gone. Speaker of the House, cabinet members. Only a political skeleton was left behind, those folks who weren't in Washington that day. The ones who were in their hometowns for celebrations or overseas on some diplomatic mission or other were spared.

Like the secretary of agriculture, a former soybean farmer from south of Nashville who was pushing eighty, born in the fall of 1980 like Cletus' father. That old coot was the Commander in Chief now, and he was somewhere in the building that loomed ahead of Cletus and Jimmy-Don.

What had this country come to? Cletus wondered again.

Didn't matter.

He and Jimmy-Don, Bodean and the others, they were going to take back a little piece of it. Set this particular patch of Tennessee soil to right again.

Cletus peered across the lawn and to the palatial building, the white columns practically glowing in the moonlight. He blinked and tried to get some water going in his eyes, tried to get a better fix on the guards tucked in by the trellis. Hard to see them nestled close to the front door. He crawled under the pine where the bodies were stashed and retrieved a pair of night-vision goggles and two of the fancy guns. One he stuck into his back pocket, the gun was small enough and he turned it barrel out. The other he passed to Jimmy-Don, who grinned wider and put the bowie knife away.

Cletus fitted the goggles on. He was on the far side of fifty, and his vision was getting a tad fuzzy, though he was certain he would be able to shoot well enough when they got closer. Point, aim for a man's middle if he wasn't wearing body armor, pull the trigger, and pray you hit something vital. Shoot a couple of times, just to be certain. He had a pocket full of ammunition for the old Le Mat, two bowie knives, and an old Ketchum grenade, all from Bodean's Civil War museum.

The goggles didn't improve on the fuzziness, but they held back the dark well enough and tinted some things a ghastly green. Jimmy-Don didn't seem to want a pair. He was doing fine on his own.

"This one's mine, too, Cousin Cletus," he whispered.

A few moments later Jimmy-Don tugged another body under the tree. This one he'd shot with the new pistol. It had made a spitting sound, some sort of silencer built in.

Too bad the guards were going to have to die, Cletus thought. They were only doing their jobs, protecting the former secretary of agriculture and his lackeys. Too bad a lot of people were going to die tonight.

The government should have kept itself seated in Washington DC . . . what was left of it anyway. Or at the very least settled itself as close to Washington as the lingering radiation allowed. Shouldn't've tucked its tail and run to the country's middle. All of them surviving politicians that thought they'd be safe here, thought it would be better to hide in the heartland rather than to hold their ground on the crumbling coast . . . well, Cletus and his little militia would show them. Show them that they should have left the Bill of Rights alone. Shouldn't have had no knee-jerk reaction to all the in-country riots that followed the Fourth of July destruction. Shouldn't have made it illegal for good-hearted, God-loving American citizens to have guns.

Showed them all that they should have stayed strong and stayed put. Stayed proud and defiant and righteous.

Stayed away from Memphis.

Damn the radiation!

"Don't shoot if you don't have to, Jimmy-Don," Cletus cautioned. "Even with that quiet gun someone might hear. Use the bowie knife first and . . ."

"Ah understand, Cousin Cletus. Ah ain't stupid."

Cletus tried to rub at his eyes, his fingers clunking against the goggles. He truly wished he could see better. He hadn't been about to sashay into one of those government-operated clinics for that corrective surgery that promised 20-20. Even before the Fourth of July bombing you couldn't trust them. You never knew if those government-paid doctors were going to implant some sort of tracking device when they were lasering your cornea. Better just to buy some cheap reading glasses at the Wal-Mart Supercenter.

If only Cletus hadn't left those reading glasses next to his bed.

"Uncle Bodean's coming, right?" Jimmy-Don lowered his voice to a whisper, and Cletus had a hard time hearing him. "He and Jeb Miller and them? Ah heard them say they were gonna be along."

Cletus didn't answer. He crawled forward on his belly, elbows and knees propelling him like he'd seen the men do in footage from the Iran War, breaking the brittle grass off as he went, his breath coming in lacy puffs now. Iran, that ended a little more than twenty years past . . . the last official war the United States participated in. These skirmishes with Canada during the past several months—retaliation for the bombs that the radical Canuks had unleashed in Washington—hadn't yet escalated to a full-fledged war.

But it would escalate, Cletus knew. Like the conflicts of the past in the Middle East. The U.S. just needed another month or so to get all its troops in position, the National Guard ready, the bombs loaded on the planes and into the tanks. News reports showed the Army and Marines spread out along the border, the Navy ships along Canada's eastern coast.

"Any day now it'll start," Cletus whispered. "Double-damn Canada all to hell and gone. If it hadn't been for them idiots from Quebec who couldn't even speak English, we wouldn't be resorting to this. French sons-o-bitches. Couldn't be like old Doc Le Mat who helped the South. Hell, no! These Frenchmen bombed Washington and ruined Memphis in one fell swoop."

He heard Jimmy-Don scrabbling behind him, clumsy in his youth and excitement, huffing and dragging the tips of his boots.

"Think they got any of them motion detectors or bombs, Cousin Cletus?"

"Ain't had time to install them yet, boy. We got us

a spy inside, my next door neighbor's in the kitchen staff and she's been keeping me posted. That's why we're doing this now . . . before they have a chance to hook up all their gadgets. Only got this little window. This very, very little window to save Graceland."

They froze when a light swept this side of the lawn, then crawled forward when it passed. The light wasn't a new addition, it had been there for decades, illuminating Graceland so the tourists driving along Elvis Presley Boulevard could see it at night. Tourists weren't allowed inside anymore, not since just before this past Thanksgiving when the former secretary of agriculture got it in his head to move the nation's capitol here.

Until then, 3734 Elvis Presley Boulevard had been open to the public. For a modest admission fee one could visit the mansion, then walk across the grounds to the Elvis Auto Museum, which now housed the new presidential limo, take a gander at Elvis' custom jets . . . the presidential helicopter took up that spot now. They could walk across the street and stay at the Heartbreak Hotel, which the rebuilding House and Senate had claimed. Graceland had been a magical experience, Cletus remembered—as he'd had a season pass.

He knew by heart the steps Elvis had taken to become the greatest musical superstar in history. Recalled with clarity the clothing, mementos, and row of gold and platinum records that had been displayed inside. They'd all been removed, of course, transported to Nashville and stuffed in the already crowded Country Music Hall of Fame.

Cletus spat at that notion. Elvis might well have had country roots, but he was the king of rock and roll.

Cletus couldn't count the times he'd been through Graceland, with his second ex-wife—they'd been married in the Chapel in the Woods adjacent to the mansion—and later on his own or with Bodean. Toured the planes with his VIP ticket, walked through

every inch of the Sincerely Elvis Museum and Elvis
After Dark. He honeymooned with his third wife in
one of the theme rooms at Heartbreak Hotel, the one
that looked a bit like a 1950s diner.

Tears threatened the corners of Cletus' eyes.
"Damn the French Canadians," he cursed again.
"Hell's too good for them. Just wait'll we ram one of
those tactical nukes."

"Cousin Cletus. Got two more coming our way.
Maybe Ah could use a little help this time."

If only the U.S. had quit paying attention to the
Middle East and had instead trained a wary eye to
the north. Graceland wouldn't have needed rescuing
if this country would have been watching the real
enemy. Wouldn't have gotten so paranoid about ban-
ning guns. Wouldn't have forced Cletus and his
nephew to pick off secret service men on Graceland's
front lawn.

Wouldn't have ruined everything.

They'd killed four more by the time they reached
the tall oak that shaded the front drive and word must
have spread that something bad was going on. Lights
appeared in windows that previously were dark, and
shapes moved back and forth, bursts of static hissed
in the air, hinting that people were chattering back
and forth across the property.

"Ah been thinking, Cousin Cletus." Jimmy-Don
shimmied close and pointed at the guards at the front
door. "We've gone and killed quite a few. And now
Ah'm wondering if maybe we should quit. Maybe
we've made our point and they'll move the government somewhere else. Maybe we should stop killing,
Cousin Cletus."

Cletus groaned. "Too late for second thoughts,
boy."

"Ah just didn't think it would get this bad, you
know? At first it were fun, Cousin Cletus, like playing
some sort of high-fangled computer game. But Ah got
me lots of blood on my jeans, and . . ."

The rest of Jimmy-Don's words were drowned out
by an explosion on the Chapel in the Woods side. It
was followed by another and another, none so devas-
tating as any of the bombs dropped in Washington or
used in the riots since.

"Ketchum grenades, boy," Cletus said. "Your Uncle
Bodean and his buddies have arrived." Cletus tugged
his own grenade out, easy to see in the lights that had
flared on in front of the mansion. "They've seen us,
Jimmy-Don." He stood and hurled the grenade for all
he was worth, the plunger striking one of the front
columns and detonating. The column split like a tree
struck by lightning, and the overhang it helped support
tumbled down to the pavement, crushing two guards
who were just emerging from the mansion.

"You were right, boy, the North did have better
weapons, like these here Ketchums." Cletus pulled his
other grenade and tugged Jimmy-Don behind the oak
just as the bullets whizzed their way, poked his head
out and threw the Ketchum, hitting a guard who'd
been jogging toward them.

"Don't look," Cletus warned. The grenade shred-
ded the body armor and tore the guard to pieces.

Jimmy-Don had looked anyway, blinking furiously
now as blood rained against his face.

Lights flared at the rear of the property, and a whin-
ing, sputtering, rat-a-tat-tatting cacophony erupted.
Screams and barked orders were heard in the gaps
between bullets.

"Take that!" Cletus bellowed as he started running
toward the noise. "Serves the lot of you right for turning Elvis' jungle room into the new oval office. This
place was meant for the King, not for the president."

He glanced over his shoulder, seeing Jimmy-Don
standing stock-still with a deer-in-the-headlights look
on his blood-spattered face. "C'mon, boy, or we'll miss
the good part. Your Uncle Bodean's done brought the
heavy stuff."

Cletus paused only a moment, then shook his head

and kept running, figuring Jimmy-Don would catch up when he shook off the shock. But Jimmy-Don wouldn't be running anywhere. One of the guards had survived the Ketchum onslaught and took cover behind the remaining pillar. He sighted Jimmy-Don and put a bullet through the boy's forehead.

Behind the mansion, smoke filled the air and bullets continued hammering the secret service men that spilled out the back door. Cletus unslung his breech-loading carbine and took a shot at a man leaning out a second-floor window. Despite his fuzzy vision, he hit the man dead-center and dropped him. Then Cletus reached for the gun he'd taken from one of the dead guards and started shooting at the other second-story windows, hoping to catch anyone who risked looking out. When he was out of bullets, he dropped the weapon, retrieved the Le Mat, and headed toward Bodean.

The old man was firing one of two Gatling guns he'd hauled here from the museum. It was a multi-barrelled, .58 caliber repeating machine gun that was spewing death and a hellish noise Cletus had never heard before. The cartridges were being fed by a hand crank "at sixty-five rounds a minute," Bodean shouted. As the old man turned the crank, the barrel spun into place before the breech, collected a cartridge, and an empty shell was extracted.

Bullets whizzed back from secret service men popping up at windows and darting out the door, all of them falling to the might of the old Gatling guns.

Earl, Bodean's best friend, was shooting the other one, whooping and singing an old Civil War tune.

Should be singing an old Elvis song, Cletus thought as he took aim with the Le Mat at a figure appearing in a lower window. "Jailhouse Rock", he mused. They'd all be in the jailhouse for the rest of their lives if they didn't get out of here pretty soon. Cletus suspected someone inside had called for the local police, the sheriffs, whoever else they could summon.

The figure in the window looked a little familiar, all the glare from the lights and the weaponfire making it easy to pick out the details.

It was Hiram McKinley, the former secretary of agriculture turned president of the United States. Cletus hesitated and stared at the barrel of the Le Mat.

Hadn't intended to shoot the new president. Just scare him out of Graceland. Cletus sucked in a breath and grimaced. The air was still chill, but it was foul with the tang of blood and smoke from the Gatling guns and burning wood—the Ketchums had started the Chapel in the Woods on fire.

He pulled the trigger again and again. Fired all nine of its .40 caliber bullets, and the bottom barrel's 16-gauge shotgun ball.

"Jimmy-Don!" Cletus called. "I killed him, boy. I killed the president." But his words didn't travel much beyond his face, with the spitting Gatling guns so close. Not even Bodean and Earl heard him.

Behind the Gatlings sat a crate of Rains and Adams grenades. They were spherical hand grenades, similar to the Ketchums, but with paper fuses. Not quite as good, but the South never did have quite as good weapons as the North. Cletus pulled three out; at six pounds each, they rested heavy cradled in his arm. He edged closer, crouching low like the toad crawl Jimmy-Don had used, then with his free hand fumbled in his pocket for a cigarette. They were illegal, too, but Cletus had a stockpile of them from his grandfather, had been rationing them through the years. He set it in his lips and lit it, took a deep drag and couldn't taste it—all the blood and smoke and burning wood settling in his mouth more strongly.

He took one of the grenades and held it to the cigarette to light the fuse, drew it back over his shoulder and hurled it. The thing didn't travel that far, but it landed in a patch of winter-dead flowers and sent a shower of dirt in all directions.

He toad-crawled closer and threw the next one at the back door.

All the while the Gatlings kept firing, Bodean and Earl's buddies helping supply the ammo. Cletus knew the guns could be fired for a long while without overheating, could fire well longer than they'd need.

"Have to skedaddle right quick," Cletus said.

Well to the west of the Gatlings, Otis manned a Dictator, a contraption similar in appearance to a Gatling, but it was actually a large mortar that launched a two-hundred-pound shell. Otis launched one as Cletus watched. The shell struck the roof and exploded like fiendish fireworks, fragments shooting everywhere and digging up shingles and bricks, thudding into the ground around Cletus' churning feet.

He headed back toward where he left Jimmy-Don, seeing more of Bodean's buddies coming at the front now.

There was Alvin and Ralph-T, Travis and his little sister, all of them ducking behind a pair of Napoleons, smoothbore, muzzle-loading, twelve-pounder howitzers that were used by both sides in the Civil War. These were cast from iron, Cletus knew from seeing them in the museum. Since the time they'd appeared in the U.S. artillery in the 1850s, they'd been made of bronze. But the South ran short of that metal and resorted to casting them in iron. Alvin and his pals were about a hundred and fifty yards back from the ruined entrance, well closer than they needed to be for the range of the Napoleons.

Cletus hurried to the oak.

"Jimmy-Don? Boy?"

He dropped to his knees at the boy's side and smoothed the blood away from his face.

"I'm sorry, boy. Didn't intend for this. Just wanted to put some backbone in them. Didn't intend to kill the president."

Cletus continued to blather, as if Jimmy-Don were

listening. All around him, guns continued to fire, from both sides. Above the battle sounds sirens screamed, and lights flared from far overhead.

"Attack copters!" Otis had abandoned the Dictator and was nudging Cletus. "They've done called in attack copters, Clete. We've got to . . ."

". . . skedaddle, I know," Cletus said. He tried to pull Jimmy-Don with him, but the boy was dead weight, and Cletus was too tired. "Can't leave him, Otis."

"Got to, Clete." Otis crouched when a missile struck the lawn near what had once been the Sincerely Elvis Museum. A high-pitched whistle indicated another one was falling. "They's fighting back, Clete. Didn't think they'd fight back, did you?"

Of course, you idiot, Cletus thought. *Of course I thought they'd fight back.* "Thought we'd be out of here before they called in the air power," he answered, as Otis steered him toward the Napoleons.

In the distance, Cletus spied the Thompson family set up at the end of the drive behind the fence. They were firing three-inch ordnance rifled guns and parrott rifles, accurate to about two thousand yards and all borrowed from Bodean's museum. Too-tall Miller was with them, aiming a muzzle-loaded rifled cannon that was said to have been decisive at Vicksburg and Atlanta. Behind him was Muley with a canon that fired shells weighing up to ninety pounds.

"Serve them all right," Otis said, "for taking away our guns. Can't nobody change the Bill of Rights."

"Yeah, we showed them," Cletus said. The Le Mat slipped from his bloody fingers and landed in the frosty grass, its old tarnished glory practically gleaming in the battle light. "Things kind of got out of hand, though, Otis."

They cut past a row of pines, and slipped beneath the branches of the tree where Cletus and Jimmy-Don had stashed some of the bodies. They paused there to catch their breath and to listen to the continuing ruckus. It wasn't quite so loud as before.

"Bet Bodean and Earl are starting to pack up. Bodean's a smart old coot and knows when to hightail it. He and Earl fought in the early years of the Iran War, after all."

They ducked under more branches, and then toad-crawled to the side fence, where Jimmy-Don had sliced a way through with the bowie knife.

"They're gonna know it were us," Cletus said as they started down a side street. "Bodean'll have to leave the Gatlings there, and the Napoleons and the Dictator. They'll be traced back to the museum."

"Bo's got a place to run. Didn't he tell you? His sister's got a winter home in Freeport, and he and Earl have plane tickets. Me? They can't hook me to any of this, Clete. Probably not you, either." He paused and rubbed at the stubble on his chin. "Well, some of them guys in what's left of the government are pretty smart. Maybe they can hook you. Not me, though. I don't even have a Social Security number."

Cletus thought of Jimmy-Don. They'd trace him that way, through the poor, dead boy. He was Jimmy-Don's second cousin and was listed in the city directory.

"I'll have to go up into the mountains," Cletus said to himself. "Got me some shirttails I can hide out with."

"All worth it," Otis said. "All of it. We saved Graceland, Clete. We're true Americans."

Cletus felt his chest grow tight as he slipped into the driver's seat of his rusty Ford Explorer. It was four-wheel drive and operated on a converted engine with an animal fat and grease concoction. It would make it up the back roads in the mountains. Otis hefted himself up into the passenger's side.

"Graceland's ruined, Otis. We didn't save it. Didn't think none of this through properly," Cletus said. He thumbed the CD player; practically antique, it still worked. Elvis started to croon softly through the speakers. "Grenades, bullets, that big shell from the Dictator. Graceland's pretty much gone."

Otis shrugged. "Someone'll rebuild it after the politicians leave. And if they don't . . . well, as you said last Thursday, Graceland was built for the King, not the president. The King's long dead."

The president, too, Cletus mused.

"Next in line for the presidency is some woman from St. Louis," Otis continued. "Let them set up a new White House there. We saved Memphis from the Democrats and Republicans." Otis sagged against the seat and closed his eyes. "It's been a long night, Clete."

Cletus nodded as he drove toward the outskirts of the city, Elvis singing about being lonesome. Well behind the Explorer, the sky was still lit from the conflagration.

"A long, good night," Cletus pronounced with a touch of sadness in his voice. "But the South won this time, Otis. This time we finally had the better guns."

THE BABY STORE
by Ed Gorman

Ed Gorman was born in Minneapolis, Minnesota, and he currently lives in Iowa with his wife Carol, who is also a writer. He spent twenty years in communications, working at various times as a political speech writer, a writer-director of television commercials, a copywriter for several advertising agencies, and owner of his own small agency. He's been a full-time fiction writer for almost a quarter century, working in suspense (his favorite genre) and Westerns, with a handful of horror short stories and novels. His fiction reflects his primary influences—Richard Matheson, Robert Bloch, and Cornell Woolrich—and among his best-known books are *The Autumn Dead* (mystery), *Cage of Night* (horror) and *Wolf Moon* (Western). He recently collaborated with Dean Koontz on *City of Night*, the second novel in Koontz's modern Frankenstein series. His work has won the International Horror Guild Award, the Anthony, the Shamus and the Spur. He has also published six collections of his short fiction, and has contributed to a wide variety of publications, including *The New York Times*, *Redbook*, *Penthouse*, *Ellery Queen's Mystery Magazine*, *The Magazine of Fantasy & Science Fiction*, *Poetry Today* and *Interzone*. With Martin H. Greenberg, he has edited more than twenty anthologies.

"Y OU KNOW HOW sorry we all are, Kevin," Miles Green said, sliding his arm around Kevin McKay's shoulder and taking his right hand for a manly shake. "It's going to be rough and we know it. So whenever you need some time away, take it. No questions asked. You know?"

"I really appreciate it, Miles. And so does Jen. Everybody here has just been so helpful to us."

Miles smiled. "If you're not careful, you're going to give us lawyers a good reputation, Kevin." He checked the top of his left hand where the holo was embedded. "Time for me to head out for LA. The rocket leaves in three hours."

The Miles incident had occurred at the top of the day, just as Kevin had been about to settle himself into his desk chair for the first time in two months. The firm of Green, Hannigan & Storz had been generous indeed with one of its youngest and most aggressive lawyers. But no amount of goodwill could quite take away the guilt he felt for the death of his son. No amount of time off could erase the blame he felt.

By day's end, Kevin had been consoled by fourteen different members of the staff, from the paralegals to the executive secretaries to the firm's reigning asshole, Frank Hannigan himself.

Hannigan had said: "I know Miles told you to take all the time you need. But if you want my advice, Kevin, you'll get back in the game and start kicking some ass. And not just for the sake of your bonus this December. But for your mental health. You're a gladiator the same as I am. The battle is what keeps you sane." Hannigan frequently spoke in awkward metaphors.

As Kevin was leaving the office, he heard a brief burst of applause coming from one of the conference rooms. As he passed the open door, David Storz waved him in. "C'mon in and celebrate with us, Kevin. My son just graduated at the top of his class at his prep school."

Reluctant as he was to listen to even ten minutes

of Storz's bragging, Kevin stepped into the room and took a seat.

Storz, a balding enthusiastic man with dark eyes that never smiled, said, "This is quite a week for this firm, I'd say. Phil's son jumped from second grade to fourth after taking a special test. Irene's daughter wrote a paper on George Gershwin that's going to be published. And now my boy is at the top of his class."

The people Storz had cited were sitting around the conference table, pleased to be congratulated by one of the firm's founders.

No one seemed to understand that inviting Kevin in to hear people bragging on their children was a bit insensitive given what had happened to him and his wife. But then nothing ever seemed to deter the lawyers here from bragging on their kids.

More than winning cases, more than accruing wealth, more than performing as talking heads on the vid networks, the greatest pleasure for these men and women came from congratulating themselves on how well they'd designed their children at Generations, or what the populist press disdainfully called "The Baby Store." Of course it wasn't just this law firm. Designer children had become status symbols for the upper classes. An attractive, bright child obviously destined to become a prominent citizen was now the most important possession you could boast of.

These parents were unfazed by the media criticism insisting that the wealthy and powerful were creating a master race by genetically engineering their progeny. After all, as Miles had once said, "You design the child yourself. And it's no sure thing. Every once in a while somebody designs a dud."

Kevin was able to leave before the liquor appeared. It would be a long session. Six fathers and mothers bragging on their children took some time.

"May I help you, sir?"

Only up close did the woman show even vague evidence of her actual age. The plastic surgery, probably multiple surgeries in fact, had been masterful. In her emerald-colored, form-fitting dress, with her perfectly fraudulent red hair, she looked both erotic and efficient.

"Just looking, really."

"Some very nice ones. And feel free to read their biographies. Some of them are pretty amazing."

"I don't have much time today. I think I'll just look at the holos."

"Fine." A smile that would have seduced a eunuch. "I'll just let you look. If there's anything you need, just let me know."

He spent equal time with male and female holos. They were all so perfect they began to lose individuality after a time. As Miles had said, people did, of course, design duds. The looks didn't turn out quite right; the intelligence wasn't impressive or even, sometimes, adequate; and then there were personality flaws, sometimes profound. Most of these problems resulted from parents who wouldn't listen to the advice of the scientists and programmers. But their arrogance could be tragic.

Given what had happened, he settled on looking at the girls. These were finished products, used to guide the buyers in creating their own girls. He was particularly taken with a dark-haired girl of sixteen whose fetching face was as imposing as the amused intelligence that played in her blue-eyed gaze. Yes, good looks—and intelligence. Requisites for a leadership role later on.

He doted on the girl, imagining the kind of boasting you could do in a session like the one he'd just left. Even up against the likes of Storz and the others, this girl would undoubtedly triumph. Whoever had designed her obviously had known exactly what they were doing.

But then it was time to catch the bullet train home.

He just hoped Jen was free of her depression, at least for a few hours.

He was never sure how to characterize the sounds she made—"crying" was too little, but then "sobbing" was probably too much. He usually settled for "weeping."

She was weeping when he got home that night. He went upstairs immediately to knock softly on the door of the master bedroom. "Is there anything I can do, honey?" he asked, as he'd asked every night since the death of their five-year-old son two months ago.

"Just please leave me alone, Kevin," she said between choked tears. "Just please leave me alone." Even given the loss they'd suffered, could this tragedy alone fuel so many endless days of bitter sobbing sorrow?

Dinner alone. By now he was used to it. An hour or so in front of the vid with a few drinks. And then bringing her a tray of food. Otherwise she wouldn't eat. He'd come to think of all this reasonably enough as The Ritual.

After eating—she'd lost fifteen pounds from an already thin lovely body—Jen usually went into the bathroom and showered for bed. Afterward was when they talked.

"Somebody at the office told me about a very good doctor. Very good with depression."

"Please, Kevin. No more shrinks. I couldn't take another one."

"I wish you'd take the meds."

"The headaches they give me are worse than the depression."

Sometimes he wondered if she wasn't purposely punishing herself. Maybe her depression was her way of dealing with what she saw as her negligence in the death of Kevin Jr.

"You know the doctor said he'd never heard of anybody getting headaches from this particular med."

"That's what I mean about doctors. They say things like that all the time. *They* don't take the drugs. *We* do. We're their guinea pigs. And when we complain about something, they tell us we're just imagining it."

And so on.

The best part of the night was when she lay in his arms in the darkness, responding finally to his patience and kindness, trusting him once more as she had always trusted him in their young marriage. Sometimes they made love; sometimes the day-long siege of depression and tears left her too shattered to do much more than lie next to him.

Tonight he was afraid. He didn't know if he should tell her what he'd done. He certainly didn't want to set her off. But maybe the idea would appeal to her. Maybe she was ready now to talk about the rest of their lives. Maybe a talk like this was exactly what she needed to hear to make her forget—

He'd tell her about his impulsive visit to the Baby Store and—

But then he smiled to himself, for there, her regal blonde head on his shoulder, came the soft sweet sounds of her childlike snoring.

In the next few weeks he stopped at the Baby Store three times after work. On the second visit he asked if he could talk with one of the consultants. He kept assuring the doctor that he was only asking questions while he waited for his train. The doctor kept assuring him, in turn, that he understood that quite well.

On the third visit, his words seeming to come unbidden, Kevin explained how five-year-old Kevin Jr. had drowned in the small lake that came very near the front porch of their summer cottage and how Jen blamed herself for it. She'd been on the phone when he walked into the water. Kevin had been in the backyard dealing with some particularly aggravating gopher holes.

The doctor, a middle-aged man with kind blue eyes,

said, "It's especially traumatic when you lose a child you designed yourself. It's a double loss."

"I guess I hadn't thought of that. You're right. And we spent so much time making sure he'd be just right."

The doctor, whose name was Carmody, spoke gently. "I know why you're coming here, Kevin. And I think you've got the right idea. But what you're worried about is convincing your wife."

Kevin smiled. "You're a mind reader, too."

"Oh, no. It's just that I've been through this process with a number of people over the years. Something unfortunate happens to the child they've designed and they're not sure if they can deal with designing another one."

"That's right. That's exactly right."

"Usually the man is the one who suggests it. The woman is too lost in her grief. And he knows that she won't like the idea at all. Not at first. And her feeling is perfectly natural. You'll both feel guilty about designing another child. Kevin Jr. is dead and here you are going on with your lives—and replacing him."

"I'm already feeling guilty. But I think that's what we both need. A new child. While we're still in our early thirties. With our lives still ahead of us."

Dr. Carmody nodded. "But it won't be easy. She'll resist. She'll probably even get very angry. And she'll feel even more isolated than she does now. She'll think you don't understand her mourning at all."

"So maybe I shouldn't suggest it?"

"Not at all, Kevin. All I'm saying is that you should prepare yourself for some very heated discussions. Very heated."

"I don't know how you could even *think* about another child now," Jen said at dinner that night. "We loved him so much. It's not like buying a new pair of shoes or something."

"Honey, all I said was that it's something to think about. You're so sad all the time—"

"And you aren't?"

"I guess I don't have *time* to be sad most of the time. I'm always rushing around with work and—" He knew he'd said the wrong, insensitive thing. He eased his hand across the candlelit dinner that the caterers had prepared so nicely. He'd wanted the right mood to introduce the subject. He knew that convincing her was somewhere in the future. "Why do you think I don't sleep well? I'm thinking about Kevin Jr."

By the look in her blue eyes he could see that he'd rescued himself. And what he'd said hadn't been untrue. He couldn't sleep well these nights. And a good deal of the time during those uneasy hours, he thought of his son, his dead son.

"I don't even want to talk about it now," she said. "Or think about it." Her smile surprised him. One of the old Jen smiles, so girlishly erotic. "Tonight I want us to drink all three bottles of wine and just be silly. It's been awhile since we've been silly."

He slid his hand over hers, touching it with great reverence. His one and only love. He missed her. The old her. "Well, if you want silly, Madame, you've come to the right guy. Nobody's sillier than I am."

And they toasted his silliness. In fact, before they managed to stagger into bed and have some of that old-time sex of theirs, they'd toasted a good many things. And every one of them had been silly. Very, very silly.

Then came the day when he got home from work and found Jen's personal holo filled with images of children from the Baby Store. Jen often forgot to turn the holo to FADE when she was done with it. His first inclination was to rush up the stairs to the exercise room and congratulate her for beginning to show interest in designing another child. But then he realized it would be better to let her interest grow at its own pace.

He was disappointed that she didn't mention the

holo that night at dinner. But the fact that she'd come down to dinner at all told him that the old Jen had not been lost to him after all. The old Jen was slowly returning to the shining presence he loved so much.

She didn't mention anything about the holo—or subsequent viewings of the Baby Store holos—for the next eight evening meals. And when she brought it up, the reference was oblique: "Sometimes it's so quiet here during the day. Bad quiet, I mean, not good quiet."

It had rarely been quiet when Kevin Jr. had been alive.

Dr. Carmody said, "I think a little nudge might be appropriate here, Mr. McKay."

"What kind of nudge, Dr. Carmody?"

"Oh, nothing confrontational. Nothing like that. In fact, something pleasant. I had a patient who was having a difficult time getting her husband to visit us. They'd only recently come into some money and her husband still had some of his old attitudes about designer babies from the days when he'd been not so well off. But she surprised him. Invited him to his favorite restaurant, which just happened to be near here, and after the meal she just happened to steer him in our direction—and four days later, he came in and signed the papers and started creating not one but two children. Twins."

"Well, one of Jen's favorite restaurants is near here, too. We go there for our anniversary every year."

"When's your next anniversary?"

"Two weeks from tomorrow."

Dr. Carmody smiled his Dr. Carmody smile. "That's not very far off, is it?"

She was late getting into the city and for a frantic half hour Kevin was afraid that Jen had known that this would be more than an anniversary dinner. He couldn't contact her on her comm, either. Maybe she'd decided not to meet him. Maybe she was in the bedroom, weeping as she once had. He stood on the street corner lost in the chill April dusk and the shadow crowds racing to the trains and the freeways.

And then, golden and beaming, tossing off an explanation for her tardiness that was both reasonable and reassuring—then she was in his arms and they were walking like new lovers to the restaurant where their reserved table waited for them.

After her second glass of wine, she said, "After dinner, let's go for a walk. I don't get down here very often. And I still love to window-shop."

The center of the city gleamed in the midst of darkness, an entity constantly reinventing itself, taller, faster, more seductive in every respect, the streets patrolled by android security officers. The androids were without mercy.

The store windows Jen stopped at were alive with quickly changing holos of haute couture. He was happy to see her interested in her appearance again. She even talked about making one of her shopping trips.

He made sure that they kept moving in the direction of the Baby Store. As they turned a corner, entering the block the store was on, she said, "I think I've got a surprise coming up."

"A surprise?"

She leaned into him affectionately, tightening her grip on his arm. She laughed. "You've been steering us in a certain direction since we left the restaurant."

"I have?"

"We're going to the Baby Store, as you've always called it."

"We are?"

But of course they were.

A small staff kept the three-story building open during the nighttime hours. As Kevin had arranged, Dr. Carmody had stayed late. He greeted them in the lobby and led them back to his office.

"Happy anniversary to both of you," he said.

"Thank you, Dr. Carmody. I guess I knew somehow we'd end up here tonight. Sometimes I can sort of read my husband's mind."

"I hope you're not disappointed, Mrs. McKay."

She shrugged in that sweet young-girl way she had. "No, maybe Kevin's right. Maybe this is what I need."

"We'll certainly do our best," Carmody said.

And so they began.

Coffee cleared their minds and numerous holos of designed girls—that was the only thing Jen knew for sure; a girl this time—sharpened their imaginations. They began to form a picture of the infant Jen would carry. And what this infant would look like at various stages of her life. And what kind of intellectual acumen the child would have. In a world as competitive as this one, superior beauty without superior intelligence was nothing.

Dr. Carmody had left them alone in front of the enormous holo console. They were so infatuated with the prospect of a new child that they became infatuated with each other, friendly kisses giving way to passionate ones; a breast touched, long lovely fingers caught behind Kevin's neck, pulling him closer. "Maybe the wine hasn't worn off after all," Kevin said. And laughed.

But Jen said, "We really should be looking at the screen now."

After forty-five minutes they stopped browsing through holos and began talking seriously about the child they'd come to create. Hair color, eye color, body type, features—classic or more contemporary? What sort of interests it would have. The level of intelligence—some parents went too far. The children had serious emotional problems later on.

Kevin asked Dr. Carmody to join them.

"Did you like any of the holos you saw?"

"They were all very impressive, Doctor," Kevin said. "In fact they were all so good it got kind of confusing after awhile. But I think we've started to have a pretty good idea of what we're looking for."

"Well, we're certainly ready to proceed with the process anytime you are," Dr. Carmody said, his perfectly modulated vid-caster voice never more persuasive. "We just need to look over our standard agreement and get to work."

"I'm sure that won't be any problem," Kevin said. But as he spoke, he noticed that Jen no longer seemed happy. The tension of the past two months had tightened her face and given her eyes a somewhat frantic look.

Dr. Carmody had become aware of her sudden change, too. He glanced at Kevin, inclined his head vaguely toward Jen. He obviously expected Kevin to deal with this situation. It wasn't the doctor's place to do so.

But as Kevin started to put his hand on her arm, she stood up with enough force to make herself unsteady. Kevin tried to slide his arm around her waist to support her but she pulled away from him. She was suddenly, violently crying. "I can't do this. It's not fair to our boy. It's not fair!"

And then before either man could quite respond effectively, Jen rushed to the door, opened it, and disappeared.

Kevin started to run after her. Dr. Carmody stopped him. "Just remember. She's been through a lot, Kevin. Don't force her into this until she's really ready. Obviously she's having some difficulty with the process. There's no need to rush."

Kevin, scarcely listening, rushed out the door after his wife. She was much faster than he'd imagined. She wasn't in the hall nor, when he reached the lobby, was she there. He hurried outside.

The sidewalk was crowded with people his own age, of his own status. Drink and drugs lent them the kind of happiness you usually saw only on vid commercials.

He didn't see Jen at first. Luckily, he glimpsed her turning the far corner. He ran. People made wary room for him. Somebody running in a crowd like this instinctively made them nervous. A running man meant danger.

There was no time for apologies, no time for gently moving people aside. When he reached the corner, his clothes were disheveled and his face damp with sweat. He couldn't find her. He felt sick, scared. She was in such a damned vulnerable state. He didn't like to think of what going to the Baby Store might have triggered in her.

He quit running, falling against a streetlamp to gather himself. He got the sort of cold, disapproving glances that derelicts invited. While he was getting his breath back, he smelled the nearby river. The cold early spring smell of it. He wasn't sure why but he felt summoned by the stark aroma of it.

In a half-dazed state, he began moving toward the water, the bridge that ran north-south coming into view as soon as he neared the end of the block.

She stood alone, staring down at the black, choppy water. Though he knew it was probably best to leave her alone for awhile, his need to hold her was so over-powering that he found himself walking toward her without quite realizing it until he was close enough to touch the sleeve of her coat.

She didn't acknowledge him in any way, simply continued staring into the water. Downriver the lights from two tugboats could be seen, like the eyes of enormous water creatures moving through the night. In the further distance a foghorn sounded.

He leaned against the railing just the way she did. He remained silent. He smelled her perfume, her hair. God, he loved her.

When she spoke, her voice was faint. "I killed our son."

"Honey, we've been over this and over this. You

were on the phone and he didn't stay on the porch
like you told him. He went into the lake despite everything we'd warned him about."

She still didn't look at him. "I lied. I ran out the
door in time to save him. I could have dived in and
brought him back to shore. But I didn't. I *wanted* him
to drown, Kevin, because I was ashamed of him. All
the women I know—they were always bragging about
their sons and daughters. But Kevin Jr.—we did something wrong when we created him. He just wasn't very
smart. He would never have amounted to much. And
so I let him drown. I stood there and let him drown
while you were in the backyard."

He'd always felt that her grief was more complicated than the death of their son. And now he knew
that his guess had been correct. In addition to loss, she
was dealing with a kind of guilt he couldn't imagine.

"You just thought I was in the backyard."

For the first time she turned and looked at him, her
face in shadow. "But you *were* in the backyard."

"True. But only for awhile. I heard him scream, too.
I ran around to the side of the house. I was going to
save him. That was all I thought about. But then I
stopped myself. I started thinking—you know how in
just a few seconds you can have so many different
thoughts—I started thinking the same things you did.
I loved him, but we'd created a child who just couldn't
compete. Who'd *never* be able to compete."

She clutched his arm. "Are you lying to me,
Kevin?"

"No. I'm telling you the truth. And I'm telling you
that we're both equally guilty—and that we're not
guilty at all. We made a terrible mistake. We didn't
listen to our counselor. We designed our son badly. It
wasn't his fault and it wasn't ours. I mean, we had the
best of intentions."

"But we let him die."

"Yes, we did. And you know what? We did him a
favor. We'd already seen how mediocre his school-

work was. What kind of future would he have had? He wouldn't have had any kind of enjoyable life." He drew her close to him. "But now we have another chance, Jen. And this time we'll listen to our counselor. Dr. Carmody will help us. We'll create the kind of child we can be proud of. And when Storz and everybody at the office start bragging about *their* kids, I'll finally be able to brag about *mine*."

She fell against him. This time joy laced her sobbing. He could almost psychically share the exuberance she felt knowing that he was as much to blame for Kevin, Jr.'s death as she was. There was such a thing as the saving lie, and he was happy to relieve her of at least some of her guilt. And in fact he'd sometimes wondered if he shouldn't have killed the boy himself.

A numbing wind swept up from the river. She shuddered against him.

"We need some coffee," he said. He slid his arm around her shoulders and together they started walking back toward the center of the city.

"We never did decide if we want our daughter to be blonde or brunette," he said.

"Or a redhead," she said. "I've got an aunt with beautiful red hair."

An image of an ethereal red-haired girl came into his mind. One who inspired lust and myth in equal parts. That was the kind of daughter they'd create. He couldn't wait to see the envy on Storz's face when the daughter was fifteen or so. It would be something to exult about for weeks.

JESUS RUNS

by George Zebrowski

George Zebrowski's many novels include his classic *Macro-life* (recently reissued), and the John W. Campbell Award Best Novel *Brute Orbits*. His more than one hundred short stories have been collected in hardcovers, among them *Swift Thoughts* and *Black Pockets*, both *Publishers Weekly* starred books. He writes in search of reasons to live and to think better of his own kind.

> "This race of men . . . I am sorry
> that I ever made them."
> —God, *Genesis* 6:7-8

THE BONES GAVE up their DNA—a dozen times or more, so it was claimed—helped, many also claimed, by a generous history that could only have been God's gift to secular science. But who knew the provenance of the bones, and could identify whatever greasy stuff it was that they scraped up from the old tombs? Where were the long-lived police who had preserved the unbroken chain of evidence? Where were the affidavits along the *via dolorosa* of history's abysmal record-keeping to confirm the unimpeachability of the evidence? The Romans had long ago lost the transcript of their trial and execution order for the man from Nazareth, if they had ever made or kept such a record. In fact, no usual records of the existence of Jesus had ever existed, except for the Gospels. The only provenance for the DNA came from fragments in a tomb, with the same name attached, and this much was unquestioned: the tomb had belonged to someone human, no more, no less.

Two thousand years after he had died and failed to save humankind from itself, Jesus ran for the presidency of the land that still called itself the United States of America. By the 2080s, our much divided land could hardly be called united, but the divinely inspired purpose of the religious states was to bind the country together again through moral revival and reform, by putting forth a candidate, in the best tradition of personality worship, behind which had always stood the well-known American ability to discern character.

Americans had always voted for a man's character above all other considerations, and though it went unsaid, the DNA would surely have transmitted divine character along with the claimed historical fact. *His* qualifications to be president and to bring virtue to governance were self-evident, given his origin as a clone of Jesus; and so his character, if not his divinity, at least suggested trust, bolstered by his DNA, however he had been resurrected.

Divine contact had to be present because God the Father would not have permitted the blasphemy of a false clone; a worship-worthy divinity would not have allowed it. The clone of Jesus Christ had to be another resurrection of God's Son, a new incarnation of the original missionary from beyond, who had come to us and then returned to his vengeful Father in Heaven, whose heart he had softened toward humankind by suffering and dying for its sins. The DNA match could not be anything but a form of divine contact, a message from the past, rebuttal enough against the horrid objection that the biology of cloning confirmed only that some long dead Middle Easterner had been cloned.

Nevertheless, endless claims were made by various groups, until at last, quite rightly as it turned out, the case confronted the Supreme Court; but in the three decades before the identity of Jesus became a legal problem, eleven other resurrections of the so-called Jesus pattern had also grown to manhood, in relative obscurity, until they were discovered and united in this case.

The ways of the Bush era had long ago run their course, but the hopes of the Republican Right again filled the party like black bile swelling a devil's leathery cocoon toward a hideous explosion, as one long-memoried columnist wrote. Dark candidates began to seek the presidency of a Britainnically shrunken United States, surrounded now by an enlarged world struggling to adapt to climate change, disease, and cosmic dangers. The same mean-spirited columnist imagined the Earth as a giant convertible filled with screaming souls careening around the Sun.

Interestingly, these twelve resurrectees of Jesus each felt the call to justice against the Caesars of America. Sociobiologists speculated on an "ethics" gene that seemed to be identical in all twelve expressions of the DNA, while self-serving educators chalked it up to education's early light of upbringing. Believers, of course, claimed that divine grace and the continued concern of a merciful God had preserved the DNA into these perilous and needful times, when the attentions of the all-powerful were once again necessary to save his human creation. Cynics pointed out that at one time He had declared Himself finished with humanity, and had drowned the creatures in a watery genocide, but had been kindly enough to save one family and a very incomplete list of animals, and had then provided a sentimental rainbow, a cheap "get well" card to mark the occasion. And *then* His Son had to come by to suffer and die, to placate the abusive Father so he would not try again to clear the slate.

And now the savior's job had to be done all over again—even as it seemed, the cynics cried, that humanity was well on its way to doing Old Testament Joe's work for him by destroying itself. It was the first creature of its kind on the earth to have that capacity, so He wasn't taking any chances, in keeping with His reformed New Testament ways of mercy and compassion, and had made sure by sending a team of twelve sons.

But with a dozen clones of Jesus claiming the same DNA, professed divinity took second place to the untangling of priority. It still seemed unlikely that the clone who prevailed in the highest court would be recognized as the Son of God, or even be nominated and win an election, but first things had to be decided first, by ID-ing the clone.

To comprehend how this case was presented and resolved—and recall that it was resolved—we must keep in mind the nature of the enhanced Supreme Court that sat in those decades before our New Enlightenment. It was a court that had refused to die, and so had in practice come to be ignored in favor of more accountable local and state courts, beyond which, in practice, no cases were allowed to proceed.

The Supremes became irrelevant primarily because of the often odd and one-sided decisions handed down during the White House residency of George W. Bush. These decisions still stood, but varied in their degree of application from state to state, even as the majority members of the court became hated and ridiculed pincushions, even within their own families, for their protection of large corporate structures, their championing of faith-based programs that violated separation of church and state, for their support of arbitrary deadline juggling by judges to confuse case filings, and their strengthening of an animal husbandry-like male control of women's pregnancies—whose bodies belonged to the society at large when it came to childbearing, according to Justice Kennedy's assumptions—not to mention the ways their decisions froze the country into a rigid *de facto* form of racial segregation by denying school districts, through a host of smaller decisions, any practical way to move toward a genuine integration of Americans, leaving that to happen locally, where and how it could. It became an obvious, much repeated complaint, that Justices Roberts and Alito had lied to the Senate during their confirmation hearings in their assurances that they would not weaken and disable lawful abortion, turn back the clock on segregation, or justify price-fixing for large manufacturers as a protection against those who would undercut them according to free market ideals. Even dissenters Souter and Ginsburg were seen as pitiable figures whose integrity was compromised by a corruption of judicial ideals, and so rendered ineffectual. Some states approved of the court, others did not, often over the same issues, producing, overall, a net independence of the states.

The members of the court lived concealed, protected lives, fearing laughter and contempt more than physical violence. The time when they might have shed their immunity to being moved by any group was long past.

It was to this exhausted, confused and cowering court, charged with decades of backward marching through one-vote victories and stalemated decisions, that the candidacy of Jesus Christ for president was brought, and the court welcomed the case—any case at all would have been welcomed; but happily this was also a case of great moment, and the justices were grateful to have such significance laid before them, given their irrelevant and vestigial state.

To see why and how the case was decided, we must keep in mind who these justices were, where they had come from, and where they saw themselves as taking an America of differing resurgent states, whose liberties were controlled by lesser and greater hypocrisies of vice and self-interest, with restrictions weakening and falling away as one climbed higher on the pyramid of money-harvesting and the power it bought.

The most recently appointed justices were still John G. Roberts, Jr. (2005), the Chief Justice, and Samuel Alito, Jr. (2006), an Associate Justice. The other Associate Justices, John Paul Stevens (1975), Anthony Scalia (1986), Anthony M. Kennedy (1988), David Souter (1990), Clarence Thomas (1991), Ruth Bader Ginsburg (1993), and Stephen G. Breyer (1994), were all still sitting as of 2080, thanks to stem cell rejuvenation and replacement of all their organs, except their brains, of course, which could not be replaced without loss of memory. Only Thomas' state was ever questioned, as it had been in 2036, when his skin had become miraculously lighter, but ever since that year his ability to raise his hand during deliberations had been accepted as sufficient if not conclusive proof of brain function, as the satirists put it in their more tolerant, even affectionate monologues and riffs.

Since no justice could be retired except under extreme circumstances of legal or medical challenge, the sitting court was seen as "continuing to sit" for as long as it wished, and acceptable to all despite its constant irrelevance through the absence of cases, a stability which no state wanted to alter.

"First things first," said Chief Justice Roberts. "Let's establish *who* is here before us—before we consider . . . deeper issues."

It had been rumored for some time that religious experts intended to confirm divinity through a miraculous demonstration of some kind, and so establish God's rule against the horrors of science once and for all—and make Jesus Christ, from the storied House of David, America's permanent president, more powerful than any king, fulfilling the decades of longing for an American superhero who would bring order and justice, not from Krypton but from God Himself. His human mother, if she would so honor the country, would become the first lady, since Jesus was unlikely to marry, but she was still in hiding until the outcome of the case, and no one could explain how she would reenter human history—as the original or a clone from the tomb's pasty residues. As the host mother of a clone, hers would also be a virgin birth, if that turned out to be the method. No one knew as the case came to trial whether the same mother of Jesus had hosted all twelve births.

"Can anyone suggest," Roberts continued, "how in . . . heaven we can decide this case?" He coughed once, then said, "Pardon me." The word hell had struggled to emerge from his mouth, and I recalled the old heretical claim that both heaven and hell were in the same place, suggesting an agreement with Jesus saying that we should not search far and wide for wisdom because the "kingdom of God is within us." As a Roman Catholic, this had always puzzled me, since from that notion it's only a hop-and-skip to believing that hell is other people, made possible by their free will, a state of affairs which even the pagan gods had despaired of controlling. Humankind had made good its escape from its makers.

Thomas did not stir when Roberts asked the question. His eyes stared as if he knew all mysteries and had already made his decision about the twelve men before him, each of whom was a clone of the God-Man who had come to save humankind from itself. There was no doubt in his eyes, as if he were looking out through their dozen eyes, at the court, at himself.

"I want to understand," said Chief Justice Roberts, "how you can all come before us as the same person, and be represented by yourselves rather than legal counsel. Granted, you all look somewhat alike, but . . . do please explain, if you can." He spoke in his secular voice, which I knew only disguised his deeper convictions.

The Twelve had all taken numbers. Jesus One got up and stepped forward from the seated eleven.

"We should throw out the case for lack of credible evidence," Justice Ginsburg said. "They're merely twins of whoever is playing this game with us."

"We should not have taken the case," Justice Souter said, "but it's too late now."

I saw the opposed fires in the eyes of the Chief Justice. Lacking a case in decades, his exiled court now had the chance to mean something again, to alter politics, even reunite the country, he thought, as clearly as if the words were written on his forehead.

"Yes," Roberts said, "it's much too late. So tell us, Jesus One, how is it possible for all twelve of you, political competitors all, presumably, to be defending against a suit from The League of Women Voters and the ACLU for fraud and racketeering . . . and all together? How . . . can you all be together?" Hell was again struggling to snake from his mouth, but he said, "How in God's name can you all be together?"

"And why no lawyer?" Ginsburg demanded.

Jesus One said, "We can have no better counsel than Our Father in Heaven."

"What?" Souter asked, appalled.

"We are He," Jesus One said. "How could it be otherwise?"

"He?" Ginsburg said. It was not a question.

"I defend," Jesus One said, "only our right, divine and secular, to run for office."

"Indeed," Souter said. "You can't all be Jesus, of any kind. You are clones, exact twins, brothers without a doubt, but nothing more."

"Certainly they can run," Justice Scalia said as if it were a track meet, then smiled. "We cannot presume to circumscribe God's ways, now can we?"

I gazed at this intellectual warrior and wondered how this man who had outlived his nine children could ever smile, alive today thanks to the progress of medical therapies that he had sought to suppress.

"If we decide for one of you . . ." Ginsburg began, ignoring Scalia.

"Or for none of you," Souter added.

"What happens to the rest?" Ginsburg added.

"She means if only one of you prevails," Souter said unnecessarily.

Jesus One said, "All will find their place to serve."

"The case here," Ginsburg said, sighing, "is one of fraud, not of claims to divinity. I see no way, short of the miraculous, of deciding that any of you are the historical Jesus, or the son of God, or God, for that matter—beyond the fact that you have the same DNA, which I will, provisionally, admit."

Uneasiness quieted the justices. Long diminished in their influence and authority, a finding for this multiple resurrection of Jesus Christ, Son of God, member of the Godhead Trinity, might strike the final blow against the secular power of this Supreme Court, if not American judicial power in general, whatever its individual members believed or did not believe. As a court, their interests and fears were the same: continued survival or atrophy, and finally death. Enhanced, their bodies might persist indefinitely, but it would be a continuation of their living death, depending on how they decided this case. An excess of disagreements would hurt them all. The court's resurrection and ascent might well be decided by this case, which God in his mercy, some of them believed, had given to them to save America—if they could stick together without seeming to do so. A court with renewed authority, whatever its biases, would have a chance to grow again, to seek new ways rather than sit stagnant and powerless. Any kind of court, as long as it was listened to and its decisions implemented, was preferable. It would at least have a chance, to progress through continued debate and internal conflict, I told myself, renewing my own hopes, so long delayed.

The irony was that in fact all the justices were squirming past their differences. In years past, Justice

Thomas had lamented, usually to young clerks, that all those who had appointed him were dead, or so vastly changed that he had been forced to reexamine his loyalties. He felt sorry for himself and his previous ways, now so clear to him after more than a century and a half of life. "God, forgive me, I should have gone with the great ones of my people!" he cried. Even at the start of the twenty-first century, Thomas had spilled his guts to unknowing school age audiences, pitying and justifying himself as he hoped to forestall the incoming shell-fire of history, not about his love of pornography and Coca-Cola but doubts about his intellect and contempt for his loyalty to his masters.

"The case before us," Jesus One continued over the inner anxiety of the justices, "will be to prove the legitimacy of the candidacy of any one of us."

Kennedy cried out, "Are you planning a dynastic theocracy, in which sinners would be compelled not to sin!" It was a horrified statement of derision, not a question. As one of the five Roman Catholic justices, he valued the God-given necessity of free will, by which human beings could choose to sin or be virtuous—how else would they be capable of being praised or blamed? God-fearing men had known the worthier moral leash of divine command, and I often lamented its loss to free will. But that was another time and a god who had changed his mind and spared the rod.

"Do you," asked Ginsburg, navigating the singular, "propose to . . . demonstrate divinity?"

"All DNA is immortal," Jesus One said. "But we do claim unity with the Father. We are, also, the Father, obviously."

"Real contact?" Scalia asked as if there could be an unreal kind.

"Obviously," Jesus One said, "since We are also the Father."

"And the Holy Ghost?" Ginsburg asked with a smile.

"He's everywhere, of course."

"He?" Ginsburg asked.

"Divine spirits can be anything," Jesus One said. "Therefore *He*."

"Secular reason," Souter said, "does not recognize any of this kind of talk." He sighed as if a devil were squeezing his lungs, but did not cough.

"I speak with Divine Reason," Jesus One said.

"Seems hardly fair," Souter added, clearing his throat.

"And from the wellsprings of Divine Knowledge as well," Jesus One added, "more than you can ever encompass."

Souter shook his head in dismay.

This wild form of discussion, keep in mind, was well known as the tradition of the Supreme Court's historical informality. It was now back in force, and would run its course, even as these Twelve of Faith and Godhood passed judgment on themselves and the Court, claiming their own invulnerability to reason and evidence through a much maligned circular insistence. Another kind of court stood above the Supremes, a court of preordained decisions, proving its conclusions by knowing, enemies would say assuming, their truth from the start. Divine Reason, as always, was moving in mysterious ways. Inexorable and blind were the disapproving descriptions of the secular skeptics. Take your premise for a conclusion, with no space in between for facts or reasoning, and you can have whatever you want come out at the other end. No fairly played game can be won against you. Never visit a sausage factory. Their derision was without restraint.

Justice Thomas, holding his head up with his left hand, blinked several times, but said nothing.

"Are you going to prove your divinity," Souter asked, "or simply ask us to assume it? You can't prove a conclusion by assuming it's true."

"We can," Jesus One said, "by direct introspection of the preexisting truth within us."

"Seems to me," Scalia said, "that they don't have

to prove anything. They have a right to run, whoever they are and whatever they believe, and let the voters decide."

"Not if they are a fraud," Ginsburg said. "It is the answer to that question that lets them run or not."

"And that is the point we must decide," Justice Roberts said, "not the truth of the theology. If they believe themselves to be what they claim, they cannot be a fraud. Wrong, perhaps, but honestly so."

"Even if they are a fraud," Ginsburg quipped.

"Even, if . . . by some external view, they are fraudulent," Roberts said as if choking on the admission. "Unintentionally so," he added.

"That's absurd!" Ginsburg shouted. "Ignorance of your own delusion, or of the law, is not a defense."

Thomas yawned, sat back, and stared, and this further sign of life sent whispers through the spectators. His fellow justices looked at him in wonder. Was he in doubt about something and about to question it? But after a moment, he seemed disinclined to contribute.

Thunder sounded outdoors. I mused about George Bernard Shaw's challenge to God to strike him dead for his unbelief. Many of us were uneasy at this point, myself included. The spell of the discussion had taken hold. If the Bible can have it both ways, then I might just as well pray, nay demand, that the Lord tear open the sky and cure my doubts. Shaw, they claimed, had held up a watch and permitted God a few minutes to visit his punishment—but when the time had run out and Shaw declared himself still living, some were sure that his soul had not escaped an appointment with damnation. Many years later, in his late 90s, he died when a tree fell on him, some claimed.

"It seems to me," Scalia said softly, "that we may have a problem with these thirty-five year olds being natural-born American citizens. How were they born—surrogate human flesh or artificial wombs? How?"

Ginsburg smiled, knowing that the distinction would come into play only if the decision was taken to let the Jesus Gang run.

"Anything," she said, "that is born in our universe is natural born, of course, including all Americans. My colleague has the list of states in which they were born. He should consult it."

Scalia looked disappointed. In one dramatic stroke the case might have become moot, and I wondered whether he might now speculate that the clones were alien inseminations from another solar system, if not from heaven. As the record finally showed, each clone had been born of a different surrogate mother, virgins all, of course, because it could not have been otherwise.

Only two hours had passed according to the large digital display above the bench, in what would stretch into a month-long casemaking, even as the world struggled with much greater problems of life and death.

We waited in silence for the case to continue, but in the next minute the schedule was changed to resume on the next day.

The court was in no hurry to dispose of the case, given that it had so much at stake, both from a long continuance and possible outcomes. Whatever the result, I was sure that the justices wanted to benefit the court's future more than their individual ways to glory. I and many others found this selflessness admirable, and hoped that the example being set would remain on display for a longer time.

But Chief Justice Roberts seemed to threaten an early end when he said, "Can we be given an indication of what kinds of evidence you will be offering beyond argumentation of a metaphysical nature which seems only to demand self-evident acceptance or proof by self-reference?"

Not bad for a believer trying to sound fair-minded, I noted, even if it was all smoke. Still, it was almost as good as what might have been expected from a hostile skeptic like Hitchens—the ancient one, not the reclusive monk who now spoke to God every day and embarrassed even the faithful with wild visions and overly exact prophecies.

"Yes," Jesus One said. "We will raise the dead right here before you."

Souter said, "Resuscitation is well known . . ."

"Not the recently dead," One said, "but the long dead."

Thomas opened his eyes in delight. At last, he seemed to think, the final vindication had come! He had been waiting for it all his life, and he had been right to wait patiently into his extended life.

"It would follow, then," Roberts said as if speaking for the twelve, "that if you prove by this miracle that you are not frauds, you will therefore be eligible to run for the presidency."

"Exactly, Chief Justice," Jesus One said. "May I proceed?"

Roberts nodded, but he seemed unsure of where he had arrived or whether he had fully meant to paint himself into a corner, if it was one. It all depended on whether he had ever witnessed a miracle, or was content to rule on the evidence of a magician's trick. His thinking was as obvious as that of a clock open to show its works.

At that moment a man in a black business suit stood up in the gallery and announced:

"I, Judas Iscariot, am called here by my Master to warn of these twelve frauds who are in cahoots . . . they are conniving to distribute the cabinet and various executive positions among themselves, and seek to found a dynasty . . ."

Roberts shook his head as the guards came, as if his clockwork had jammed and he no longer knew which way to jump to gain something from the moment. Thomas seemed puzzled, but the other justices showed a head shaking solidarity with their Chief.

"I never died!" Judas cried out in a voice suddenly muffled by his forced exit into the gallery passageway.

As the chamber quieted, an empty hospital stretcher was wheeled in. The justices leaned forward, except for Thomas, to gaze at the empty, sheet-covered conveyance, and I recalled my law school days, so long ago now, before the many changes made to my body, when "conveyance" meant a transfer of title to property, the document that accomplishes the transfer, and I wondered who it was that remembered and sat here now. Were my memories my own, or was there a higher power working through me to shape my thoughts and feelings? Whoever, whatever I was today, was where these memories now lived. Who knew then, who knows now, what was coming? Here I am, conveyed from the past. Get over it, get on with it, I told myself with a deepening hope.

The stretcher.

Big wheels.

White sheets.

There was no doubt that it was empty. That much must be understood, before anything else that followed can make sense. I saw its emptiness.

Jesus One pointed to the empty conveyance and said, "Here we have the body of great President Ronald Reagan."

The chamber was silent, its people expecting the body to appear. No one dared to shout out that the stretcher was empty. That seemed to be the given, and of no consequence. Wait and see, because it was inconceivable that Jesus One, or anyone, would lie so blatantly in such a place and expect to be believed.

The eleven stood up and chanted, "He-breathes-before-us, to-prove-that-we-are-the-world's-savior-come-again-as-twelve-but-one-in-Heaven."

"We see him!" a group chanted in the gallery. "Let Jesus run, let him run, his proof has come."

Justice Thomas rose to his feet and cried, "I see him, Great Reagan come to help us again. I see him, may the Lord be praised!"

And I, too, expected the empty stretcher to be suddenly occupied, as my brain limped along to catch up with my besieged faith; but the conveyance remained insistently empty, even unwilling, a defiant betrayer of belief, an obstacle to the proof that was so dearly needed before the road to salvation would be opened.

Was I one of those who would be left behind, blind and damned? Fear shook me, but my mind said no, I would go forward to the destiny prepared for me. A tree would not fall on me.

Thomas raised his hands heavenward, and stood waiting, as rigid as a sculpture. Roberts stared at him in disbelief, a man of faith embarrassed by one of his own. Ginsburg had covered her face with her hands. Souter sat back, smiling at the charade. Scalia's eyes were wild with expectation. Kennedy was stone-faced. Stevens was weeping. Breyer sat with his eyes closed. Samuel Alito sat shifty-eyed, as if afraid to make a choice.

And suddenly I prayed to see Reagan rise and greet his summoners, the Twelve, and his nation. And for an instant I did see him, as the name and broad smile vibrated in my mind, and the tall, stout body formed around the grin . . . and I thought that they should have brought him a white horse to mount. . . .

But I was wrenched back from the part offered to me by this theater of delusion, as some distant part of me realized that this kind of acceptance was unworthy of the body and brain given to me by the science that had extended my life to this very day, to this shameful day that would have to be repudiated because it played fast and loose with divinity, with God's own plan for man.

But would the charade be rejected? Was that how things were going? Or would it be confirmed as true? Waves of faith had spilled from our human depths, and we could conjure up whatever we wanted until stopped by what could not be wished, by the unmade reality around us that was deaf to all pleading. I almost prayed to Aristotle's rational god, to Spinoza's all-encompassing universe, to Teilhard de Chardin's emergent God at the end of time, to the best in us when all else fails. . . .

The hall erupted into violence. People were thrown down from the gallery. Soldiers marched in and stood as a barrier before the great bench of the court. I cowered in my seat at the rail, waiting for the return of order, which would come when it would or not at all.

It came—and we all stared at the empty stretcher, our faith brutalized.

"He's gone!" someone shouted.

"They stole the body," another voice added.

"Kidnapped!" a boy shouted.

"He's escaped!" a woman cried. "Thank God!"

"We don't deserve him!" a man wailed.

"He's gone into hiding," said another in the returning silence that crept in around our doubts and crushed out hopes.

"He'll be back," said a pleading voice. "They won't kill him this time."

"He wasn't killed," another said. "He got old and forgot everything!"

"Oh, yeah?"

As I sought desperately within myself how to say yes to whichever would be the winning side, Justice Thomas collapsed back into his seat. His head slumped forward as if it would fall off, I sensed that he had died, but it went unnoticed. Stupidly, I realized that he hadn't noticed either. He sat there much too long to be revived.

"Pray!" a voice shouted, "for a decision from the one great court."

"Yes!" another shouted. "And pray that the magnetic field does not reverse and the Sun's wrath fry us!" Clearly a man of faith and science, holding fast to both.

"Pray!" massed voices cried, as if launching a ship of songful harmony into the heavens. But it was not that. Strange dissonances shook the building, cracking floors and ceilings, rattling chandeliers, exploding toilets and bursting water pipes, and people fled out into the street as if hell itself was erupting through the foundations of the building.

When finally the great chamber was quiet, the stretcher of resurrection still stood empty. Men in white coats came and rolled it out. The judges were the last to leave. They got up, abandoning Thomas in place, and departed as if from a tomb.

The decision of the court that would declare the Twelve frauds who should be denied a run for the presidency, or not, was long enough in coming to give the clones time to travel and proclaim that the court would find in their favor and America would be saved once and forever, while their new-found lawyers argued that the delay was unfairly handicapping their run and would only become even more of an injustice if the decision to let them run came too late.

Reagan sightings became common. In western states he was seen on a beautiful white horse, sometimes driving a twenty-mule-team wagon across a desert horizon. Silhouette shots of him and his team were offered as proof of these sightings. In southern states he was seen in the company of Elvis. The raising of Reagan had been a success, if not exactly a miracle.

Justice Thomas' seat remained unfilled. Few wanted to suggest anyone to fill it during an upcoming election. No side dared guess what the court would decide. Would it cut a Gordian Knot, unbake the pretzel, and raise itself up into a new life of wise guidance?

The justices' opinions came many weeks later but earlier than expected:

John Paul Stevens, although he sympathized with the religious contribution to ethics and laws, could not see how these clones could possibly have the authority of God beyond that of the common mankind from whom their DNA was drawn. Lacking proof of that clear authority, if there could even be such, meant that their claims had to be regarded as doubtful if not fraudulent, and so they could not run for office.

Antonin Scalia simply said that they were not who they said they were and that ended the case for him, even though he insisted that it was possible for him to be wrong.

Anthony M. Kennedy expressed his view that superstitious belief and fallacious argument and complete lack of evidence clearly denied these twelve men the legitimacy they wanted from the court.

David Souter simply voted against granting the claim.

Ruth Ginsburg stated that the American people deserved a rational decision based on common human values. Faith-based ideas were to be tolerated, but they could not be permitted to rule in a country of diverse views.

Stephen Breyer voted against the claim of the twelve with no comment.

Samuel Alito extolled the need for religiously based values, but made no decision about the identity of the twelve.

Chief Justice John G. Roberts, Jr., also praised the legitimate need for religious values and a belief in God, but dismissed the twelve as imposters, although perhaps well-meaning ones. He also claimed that Justice Thomas, before his death, had expressed a faithful belief in the true identity of the twelve, and said that he had been granted a proof of this during the attempted resurrection of Ronald Reagan, but that this revelation was unfortunately unavailable to the Court and could not be verified. However, was this not what faith was all about—that we should believe in the absence of proof? Any fool could believe *with* proof, but that would be no test at all. Roberts regretted that Reagan had not been raised, "because the nation might have drunk of his vitality again and been morally refreshed."

Ginsburg added a postscript, saying that "Chief Justice Roberts had very neatly had it both ways, avoiding the fact that because faith spoke in tautologies that were true by arbitrary definition, it could be accepted or exempted from reason. Every schoolchild knows it's wrong when a parent insists that something is so simply because the parent says so, and all parents know that it's not so simply because they say it, so they lie. Youth knows that tautologies are false. Grownups should not speak in tautologies." Her last statement had echoed the words of a great scientist, Erwin Chargaff, who had contributed greatly to discovering the structure of DNA.

To this Roberts replied that the Twelve were to be commended for their traditional "imitation of Christ," and referred Ginsburg to *De imitatione Christi* by Thomas à Kempis, circa 1418, an instructional work that sought to guide the soul in Christian perfection with Christ as the Divine Model, and pointed out that it was the most widely read spiritual work next to the Bible.

Ginsburg made no further comment.

But the fact of a great victory could not be denied, that the court had rejected the claim of these twelve resurrectionists on rational grounds. Faith further lost its sway and reason had returned to America at last, some argued in triumph.

But it was irony and hypocrisy that prevailed, I thought as I again looked forward, thinking back to my own strange days at the century's start, when my accounts were seized as my patron, the once doubted and now proven fraudulent president, finally left office and I fled to Mexico, where the World Court sought me out because I was easier to find, when the longer-lived classes began to take over the planet and the short-lived underclasses perished, when the very earth and sky threatened us and we managed to escape the wrath of a godless universe by diverting an Extinction Event asteroid, at a cost that had finally bankrupted the last of the Fossil Fuel Family fortunes, intent as they had been on burning the last lump of coal, the last therm of gas and the last drop of oil, and being paid for it. . . .

Strange days indeed, as "truth and reconciliation commissions" took hold in the human family, which finally sought to shake off the past. Strange days indeed, when people valued a public airing and admission of the truth above so much else that still needed to be done. . . .

When President Jeb Prescott was sworn in after the three-party elections of 2084, he appointed me to replace Judge Thomas, and I was confirmed by the Senate's mercy, along with Harriet Miers, newly rejuvenated with only a small loss of memory to replace the recently committed John Paul Stevens. I then spoke these grateful words:

"I, Alberto Gonzales, tried and rehabilitated by the Hague Tribunal, and newly recommitted to our Constitution and to International Law, now take office as Associate Justice of the Supreme Court."

This, of course, was where I needed to be, but not as an Associate Justice. Briefly angered, I know now that a rational Providence had only prepared a more careful way for me to my rightful place.

My time as a criminal, when I was Attorney General in the first decade of the twenty-first century, remains a great lesson to me—to go with whomever or whatever gets you there. That was my way from the time George W. Bush made me his general counsel in the mid-1990s, then appointed me Secretary of State in Texas in the late '90s, and then gave me a place on the Texas Supreme Court until 2000, before making me his White House Counsel and finally Attorney General of the United States in 2005.

It is from this last service that I most regret my actions. What was I thinking? What was *he,* my previous self, thinking? I am not the man I was decades ago, the man who needlessly, as it turned out, supported torture and termed the Geneva Conventions "quaint" and "obsolete," who denied the intent of *habeas corpus* in our very own Constitution, who agreed to warrantless domestic wiretapping of Americans, who wrote capital punishment briefs for Bush when he was governor of Texas that made it impossible for the future planetary boy king, as he was called by his critics, to pardon anyone on death row. I was the one who smiled into the television cameras in such a sickly way that millions of Americans developed an unkindly hatred of me. As a Roman Catholic I regret that most of all, that my face brought out so much hatred in my fellow Americans. Hatred is not good.

I always gave George what he wanted, and he nicknamed me Fredo, after the weak and traitorous brother executed by Michael Corleone in those frightening "Godfather" movies. What was that all about? That he would have me killed if I refused to be a "yes man?" I was glad to be one, so why the obvious threat on my life?

I remember what it was to be that man, and what it took to open his eyes and change him, as the shadows of the future took on substance and grew teeth. Justice needs teeth, but they need time to grow. Our history is a teething child, but I imagined that I could make of it what I wished, around myself and my family, as if I could repeal gravity. The junta told me, especially Karl Rove, that they could do anything, even make two and two equal five.

But the teeth of justice have deeper roots than those who pull them, and they grew back, I learned when I was released from prison, where they gave me new organs and increased my modest intelligence. Without this help I would not have understood Vice President Cheney's death, Bush's pardoning of Wolfy, Rummy, Rice, Rove, Libby, and himself, with many others, just before his disappearance. Oh, how I repent of the man I was. I am not he, and never will be again! Never, never, never!

But now the Twelve have chosen Jesus One as their candidate and another, Jesus Two, as his vice president, and despite being banned from running for office, Jesus One has proclaimed that the two of them will win on a write-in.

My time has come. Chief Justice Roberts has resigned in despair, saying that he now knows too much to function with a clear conscience. I have taken his place, and our court stands ready.

Is theocracy the worst form of government, as some have claimed? Where are values to be found? Where does the buck of moral judgment stop? Where should it stop?

My conscience whispers to me that the rule of Jesus would make all courts unnecessary—for no one would govern us better than the Son of God, if he would truly come to us, and stay. If we could truly know that it was He, we would rejoice that there is a being in whom all problems dissolve, from whom we can learn how we should live and what we should know about our universe, because he loved us enough to send us a savior out of his own cosmic body, to die at our hands in payment for our sins, past present and future, and to show us that death is nothing to fear.

But Jesus One and Two are not the Sons of God. On their tour before the court's decision went against them, they proclaimed their social agenda of so-called love and sharing; but this professed goal is not of the Kingdom of Heaven. One and Two would take everything from the strong and leave them with nothing but insults about rich men and camels unable to pass through the eyes of needles. The Twelve have insisted that they will not bargain with private wealth and privilege, give no preference to prideful individuals and families whose hearts hold back allegiance to universal love and sharing. The Twelve only lie to us when they say that theirs is a kingdom not of this world, because it will take our world from us if their ways are accepted.

If they seize the presidency, my court will strike down the election. If by some strange chance they take office and attempt their destruction of our history, my court will strike down their laws. For only ours is the kingdom that is One with God.

Twelve legal crosses await the imposters.

THE ROTATOR

by *Pamela Sargent*

Pamela Sargent (www.pamelasargent.com) has won the
Nebula Award and the Locus Award; she has been a final-
ist for the Hugo Award, the Theodore Sturgeon Memorial
Award, and the Sidewise Award for alternate history. She
is the author of several novels, including her Venus trilogy,
The Shore of Women, the historical novel *Ruler of the Sky*,
and the alternative history novel *Climb the Wind*. Her most
recent novel, *Farseed*, a sequel to *Earthseed*, is out and will
be followed by a third volume, *Seedship*. She lives in Albany,
New York.

> "To these I set no bounds in space or time;
> They shall rule forever."
> —Vergil, *The Aeneid*

ALL OF THIS HAPPENED in worlds nearby.

The tanks rolled down Pennsylvania Avenue and
stopped at the edge of Lafayette Park, near the White
House. To the east, more tanks were rolling along
New York Avenue, while other tanks had also been
spotted on 14th and 17th Streets and on Constitution Avenue.

They were closing the circle, surrounding the White House. No one knew where they had come from, but there they were, a procession of Abrams M1A1 tanks, all with the markings of the United States Army. No one had stopped them, and whatever the tourists and bureaucrats and police standing around in Washington's streets might think, none of the guards stationed on the White House grounds seemed to be at all concerned when the tanks rolled to a stop and two uniformed men in desert camouflage with stars on their shoulders climbed out, followed by a balding, white-haired, out-of-shape bespectacled man who looked a lot like the vice president.

"What the hell?" somebody milling around in the crowd of sightseers near the Ellipse muttered. "Something's up," an old wino said to his homeless companion in Lafayette Park as they shared a bottle of Night Train. Then again, the unusual and even the unthinkable had become so commonplace by now that even the networks didn't seem to be covering the movement of tanks that had seemed to appear out of nowhere. There was no sign of satellite trucks or of any TV personalities doing stand-ups in front of cameramen.

"Who are they?" a child asked his mother as the two uniformed men and the heavyset man who looked a whole lot like the vice president started to walk in the direction of the White House. She had no answer for him, and sometimes, especially these days, it was better just to mind your own business.

The vice president said, "No way around it, Mr. President." Whenever he was alone with the guy, he normally dispensed with the usual courtesies, "Mr. President" and "Sir" and the like, but this particular occasion seemed to require them. "We've got to get out of here."

"We do?" the president asked, glancing around the Oval Office. He had his usual blank, what-me-worry expression on his face, the one that people who didn't know him that well could easily mistake for a sign of strength and self-confidence rooted in his religious faith and a deep inner calm.

"Yes, we do," the vice president replied. "We've counted the votes seven ways from Sunday, and we've lost them, there isn't a chance now. The House is going to impeach both of us, and the Senate's going to convict, thanks to all those turncoat bastards who finally deserted us. It isn't even going to be close."

"Well, fuck them." The president still wore his look of serenity. "History is what's with us, and we've got the Almighty lookin' out for us. We sure as shit don't need the House and the Senate. Someday down the road, people'll know we were doing the right thing. When the history's all written, they'll—"

"That's all very well," the vice president interrupted, "but in the meantime, we're dealing with this goddamn impeachment coming up out of nowhere. They're going to throw both of us out on our asses and put that bitch from San Francisco behind your desk until the next election." And that wasn't the worst they might be facing. He'd overheard a few low-level staffers muttering something about the World Court and war crimes tribunals and the Hague the other day when they thought he had left the room. "But I'm not waiting around to witness that travesty. We're all set, thanks to a secret project I've been keeping an eye on and shepherding along, just in case it might turn out to be useful. I'm getting the hell out of here, and you're coming with me."

The president's eyes became slits; he looked confused. "That's your idea, cuttin' and runnin'?" he asked, sounding a bit petulant. "And just where are we gonna go?"

"Well, in a way, we aren't going anywhere. In a sense, we'll be staying right here." The vice president would have to explain the complexities of his escape plan very carefully. "Here's the deal," he continued in as gentle a tone as he could muster. "What if you could go someplace where everything's exactly the same as it is here, but where you aren't going to be impeached, where you'll still be the president right up until the end of your term?" And maybe even beyond that term, if certain irons the vice president had in the fire got properly smelted. "I'm talking about a place where we can both avoid impeachment altogether."

"Sounds purty good." The president frowned, making his eyes look even smaller. "But it still smells like cuttin' and runnin' to me. Anyway, how the hell do we do all that? Round up the Congress and ship 'em out for some enhanced interrogations?"

"We've got an even better way out than that, thanks to the research teams at DARPA." The vice president paused. "They got up something for us called the Rotator."

"The Rotator?"

"The Alternative Stochastic Variability Actuator and Rotating Transporter," the vice president explained, "but it's simpler to just call it the Rotator. And that's basically what it does, rotates you out of one continuum—er, place, and puts you where impeachment isn't going to happen, executive privilege is upheld, and we can do our goddamn jobs."

"You make it sound mighty simple."

"It is mighty simple. What happens in the end is mighty simple, anyway." There was no point in trying to explain the complexities of the technology and the assumptions underlying it to the president, especially since he didn't really understand them too well himself. "It's like this. We'll head out of here for the secure and undisclosed and meet there with everybody who's coming along with us. Then we get rotated, and before you know it, you're back in this office going about your business, but without impeachment pending and your poll ratings right back up where they should be. Hell, maybe we can even get them back up in the forties."

"So I'll be back here," the president said, "but in a way I actually won't be back *right here*. I'll kinda be like somewheres else that's sorta the same."

"That's it." Somehow the kid had grasped the big picture.

"And everything'll be the same as here?"

"Everything except the stuff we don't want to have happen to us."

"What about my wife?" the president asked. "I wouldn't want to get rotated unless she's gonna get rotated right along with me, and she won't be back here at the White House until the weekend."

The vice president scowled. His own wife was coming along with him; she had made damned certain of that once he had revealed his plans to her, but he hadn't counted on bringing the First Lady along on this journey through the variant probabilities. For one thing, he didn't want anybody coming with them who wasn't absolutely trustworthy and close-lipped. This had kept the number of people to be rotated at a minimum; there was no point in getting where he wanted to go only to end up with some traitor whistle-blowing before some Congressional committee or other there. For another, he had doubts about the First Lady's ability to carry out what would need to be done after they were rotated and confronting their variant counterparts. His own wife was coldblooded enough to do what she had to do, but the First Lady probably wouldn't be up to it even with a triple dose of Xanax.

"She won't have to come along with you," the vice president said very slowly, "because she'll already be there, see? I told you, everything's going to be the same except that everything'll be going our way and we won't have to put up with all this oversight and impeachment crap. Believe me, except for that, you won't notice any difference." The president probably wouldn't have noticed any difference anyway, given the useful bubble of obliviousness that usually surrounded him, but he had to know enough to avoid confusion.

The president's eyes got really tiny and squinty then, as they always did whenever he was trying to summon up anything resembling a thought. "And my ranch? That'll still be the same, too?"

"You'll have plenty of brush left to clear there, believe me." The vice president cleared his throat. "Um, we'd better get going."

"Right now?"

"Yes, now." Better to get out of here fast, before any of those nerds working on the Alternative Stochastic Variability Actuator and Rotating Transporter got tempted to spill the beans to the media. He had never been able to tell the ethical ones from the opportunists.

They were all there in the underground chamber of his secure and undisclosed location, his wife, his medical team, and those completely trustworthy souls who were to be rotated along with him and the president. The guys he needed from the Defense Advanced Research Projects Agency were there, too, along with a couple of officers who understood the research and how to operate the Rotator and other soldiers to man the tanks. He had, however, made sure that the scientists responsible for the actual research and for calculating his course were absent. He wasn't sure they had wholeheartedly approved of his plans, and they had always seemed somewhat too anxious to outline the possible drawbacks of the Rotator, what with their talk about opening doors and altering events in other continua that might be mirrored throughout a long run of variants and that maybe there were certain doors that should stay closed. All he had needed to know was that he could get to where he wanted to go, and they had assured him of that.

It was too bad, he thought, that his old buddy, the former secretary of defense, couldn't be here with him to take advantage of DARPA's Rotator. But there'd be somebody just like him in the next continuum, and maybe, if everything worked out, they'd be able to reappoint him to his old Cabinet position. After all, where they were going, there was even a chance that they were actually winning the war on terror and securing the oilfields, if what the scientists had told him about all the possible variants was correct.

"All we have to do, Mr. President," one of the Army officers was saying, "is go outside and get in the tanks, and before you know it, we'll be on our way to the White House."

"Tanks?" the president asked.

"To protect us while we're being rotated. You'll notice what you might call a kind of rippling in the atmosphere, but as long as you're inside the tank, you'll be protected from any ill effects when we're rolling through the gateway."

"The get-away?"

"The gateway." The officer had a patient look on his face. "The gateway through to another continuum that the Rotator's going to open up for us."

The president screwed up his eyes. "This isn't gonna be one of those deals where I have to put on a uniform, is it?" he asked.

"Not at all," the officer replied, still wearing his patient look.

" 'Cause prancin' around in that flight suit on that carrier deck didn't work out so well in the end." The President let out one of those laughs of his that sounded like a mixture of a snort and a whinny.

"You won't need a uniform for this trip," the vice president said, stepping forward, "but you are going to need this." He handed the president a Glock automatic. "Can't miss with this baby. Even I won't be able to miss my target." He allowed himself an avuncular chuckle.

The president hefted the automatic in one hand, then slapped it into the other in a way that made the vice president grateful that the weapon wasn't yet loaded. "And exactly what am I gonna be aimin' at?"

"Well, it's like this." The vice president paused, knowing that he would have to phrase things very carefully. "After we're rotated, we're going to run into—well, I guess you could call them our doubles."

"Our doubles?"

"Our twins." That didn't seem like the right word either. "You could even call them our clones."

"Clones?" The president grimaced in disapproval. "Can't say I approve of that. Thought I signed a bill to make that illegal."

"I wasn't talking about that kind of clone," the vice president said. "It's like this. You see, when we get to where we're going, there's going to be another president there—that's you—and another vice president— that's me—sitting in the Oval Office. *Our* Oval Office. I mean, *your* Oval Office," he added, correcting himself. "And we have to take their places. I mean we have to take *our* places in their place."

The president pursed his lips and screwed up his eyes even more, looking extremely perplexed.

"Look at it this way," the vice president said. "Think of that other guy who looks like you as an imposter. What he's doing is taking up space that's actually yours, and you can't have two people in the same place at the same time. So you're going to have to take him out."

"Didn't count on anything like that." The president stared at his weapon. "Couldn't we just send 'em back here? We'd be gone, and they could have our spots."

The vice president shook his head. "Too complicated. Might not even work. There's no way to guarantee they'd even end up here."

"Yeah, but who cares?" The president's voice rose to a whine that could have shattered glass. "At least we wouldn't have to kill them, and they'd still be alive."

That didn't sound like the guy who had refused to pardon any of those inmates on death row while he was still governor. On the other hand, it did sound like the guy who had made sure he had landed a cushy berth in the Air National Guard during wartime. "Too complicated," the vice president said. "We'd have to convince them to go, maybe force them to leave. Tie up the loose ends—shoot'm and be done with it."

"I dunno."

The vice president struggled to contain his exasperation. If the president got cold feet now, well, he wasn't about to wait around here and get impeached and removed from office, even if he did have to get rotated by himself. And if the president started blathering about the Rotator to those Fox News gasbags and all the other sycophants he had been inviting to the White House more frequently these days, they'd just assume that he had finally cracked under all the pressure.

"You're up to it," the deputy chief of staff piped up. "You've got the balls for it." His eyes roved around the room, then peered at the president through his thick glasses. "Look at it this way—that look-alike'll be taking up a space that's rightfully yours. You'll need to take his place if you're going to go after all those goddamn liberals and lefties. You're the decider, not him."

"Besides," the vice president added, glad of the help as he picked up the conversational ball that the deputy chief of staff had thrown his way, "you won't be able to go after the terrorists *here* if you're impeached. But once you're rotated, you can go after them *there*."

The president's face brightened. His eyes took on a glow. "Then I guess we better get goin'."

The vice president had been somewhat apprehensive about being rotated, even though he had been assured that his pacemaker would remain unaffected. To his relief, the rippling of the air and the sudden feeling of disorientation passed quickly, leaving him feeling only slightly nauseated afterward. It helped to be inside a tank, and he didn't bother to ask about looking through the periscopes to see what was going on outside.

"We're rolling down Pennsylvania Avenue, sir," the officer sitting in front of him at the commander's station announced. "We should be passing the Old Executive Office Building in about five minutes or so."

"Any sign of trouble?" the vice president asked.

"Folks are just watching us pass," the officer at the gunner's station replied, "like we're some kind of parade."

Good, the vice president thought. He had been wondering if they might encounter some of the groups that had been gathering outside the White House in recent days, knots of people who looked mean and angry and carried signs with obnoxious slogans like IMPEACH THE COMMANDER-IN-THIEF and REGIME CHANGE BEGINS AT HOME and MY TOYOTA GOT BOMBED BECAUSE IT'S SMALL, FOREIGN, AND FULL OF OIL and other phrases that dared to compare him and the president to Nazis and criminals. Apparently, they'd arrived in a variant where the citizenry was more docile and less likely to cause them any trouble, which would make it easier to do what they had to do now.

At last the tank rolled to a halt. Two officers climbed out ahead of him, while another was just behind him, ready to help heave him out of the vehicle if necessary. He was panting by the time he clambered over the side. The driver was already standing below him, and held out an arm to help the vice president down to the ground.

The sky was cloudless and blue, the morning air crisp and cool without a hint of global warming. By now, his wife would have taken care of her counterpart and, with the help of the trusted aides and Secret Service officers with her, secured the vice presidential residence. Other officers and aides were climbing out of tanks and sprinting across the White House gardens, knowing that they would not be challenged; after all, the vice president was with them.

He looked around and finally spotted the president; it was important that they head for the Oval Office together. He waited as the president trotted up to his side. "All set?" the vice president growled.

"Yeah." The president had taken on his steely-eyed look, the expression he occasionally wore whenever that old bag who was still hanging on in the White House press corps shot off one of her more impertinent questions at a press conference.

The vice president slipped a hand inside his pocket, feeling his weapon; too bad all those jokers who insisted on making wisecracks about all of his draft deferments would never know that he could be one hell of a brave warrior when it counted. "Then let's go," he muttered.

He and the president were the last ones to enter the White House. They made it all the way through the hallways without seeing anything more disturbing than a glimpse of the deputy chief of staff standing over his dead counterpart before the door to his office closed. It would have been a lot easier if the bodies could just fade away and disappear, the way they had done in a sci-fi TV series he used to watch, but the Rotator didn't work that way; the DARPA researchers had told him that they would have to dispose of the bodies themselves.

Two Secret Service men, two that the vice president could trust completely, were moving down the corridor ahead of him and the president. Among other things, the pair had made sure that the Veep wasn't left holding the bag when that clumsy pal of his got in the way during their hunting excursion and ended up with a face full of buckshot. A couple of Secret Service officers were outside the northwest door to the Oval Office, and maybe it was just his imagination, but they both looked just a little bit heavier than their two rapidly approaching counterparts.

"Mr. President?" one of them said, looking puzzled. "Nobody alerted us." He tapped at his earpiece. "Thought you were still inside," and then his eyes widened as he stared at his own twin.

The president cackled. "Thought I'd slip out into the Rose Garden and catch some of that nice weather we're havin'. Decided to take the long way around and come back inside this way." He struck his chest. "Stayin' in shape. Every little bit helps."

Even as the Commander-in-Chief was yacking, the four Secret Service men were reaching for their weapons, but the two who had been rotated, knowing what was coming, had drawn theirs just a second or two faster. They aimed and fired, one round each, right at the heads of their alternate selves, and two men lay dead on the floor. The vice president reflexively clutched at his chest, hoping his pacemaker would hold up under the strain; this was where things could have really gone wrong, and they weren't exactly out of the woods yet. The president had a sickly look on his face, as if he was about to toss his cookies.

They passed through the door into the Oval Office. A quick look around the large round space revealed that the same volumes of history the president had lately been browsing through were still on the bookshelves, the same paintings of Western scenes still hung on the walls, the same slightly uncomfortable sofas faced each other, and the same brightly colored rug with the presidential seal lay on the floor. He stared past the sofas and the rug with the seal and saw the two men right where he had expected them to be. The president's counterpart was behind his desk and his own doppleganger sat in one of the armchairs near a window.

The sight of his double unnerved him for a moment. He hadn't realized how bald he was getting, and how jowly his face was, but those cold glittering eyes behind his spectacles looked reassuringly familiar.

"What the fuck?" his double muttered.

The president's double stood up behind the desk. The vice president was reaching inside his pocket for his gun when, next to him, the president shouted, "Nobody else gets to be me!"

"What're you talkin' about?" the president's double said.

"I'm the president, and you're takin' up my space!" The president whipped out his gun and fired. "I'm the president!" he shouted as his double fell across the desk, nearly drowning out the staccato sound of the vice president's gun as he shot his own twin.

The balding man fell. A red stain was spreading across his chest. "Fuck you," his doppleganger said with his last dying breath.

"Fuck you," the vice president replied, aiming carefully, and shot him again.

"Holy shit," the president whispered. They sat down on the sofas, facing each other, and waited for the cleanup crew who had been rotated with them to arrive.

It was taking the president a while to recover. The two bodies, their heads covered by black hoods before they'd been stuffed into body bags, had been taken away. The laptop the vice president had requested had been brought to him, and still the president was sitting at his desk, staring up at the presidential seal on the ceiling, perhaps seeking some heavenly guidance. He looked like he could use a stiff drink, and the vice president could have used one himself, but that would have to wait until he was back at his own place. He and his wife could toast themselves with some of that single-malt he kept in one of his underground vaults.

An hour of Googling various news sites and blogs had already told him what he needed to know. In this variant, they'd held on to a majority in the Senate and had a two-seat edge in the House—slim margins, but enough so that they wouldn't have to worry about hearings or oversight, let alone any impeachment proceedings. There would be no challenges to claims of executive privilege or declarations of extraordinary powers. They had landed in a place where their people were worthy of their efforts, where they'd be free to secure the world's resources and their own interests and cement their status as the world's one and only superpower. He thought of what the DARPA scientists had told him about the possibility of events being mirrored across the continua. That might mean that if they succeeded here, then they'd be increasing the odds of America's dominating all of the other variants as well. Maybe well out to infinity.

Master of the multiverse, he thought. The title had a kind of appealing ring to it.

The president coughed. "This is weirding me out," he said from behind his desk.

"What's weirding you out?"

"Can't figure out if I'm the president or an assassin."

The vice president was about to reply when he heard the door behind him open. He turned to face himself, a gun in his hand, with the President standing right behind him. "What the fuck?" he muttered, and then a hammer struck him in the chest.

He fell forward, then rolled to one side. Somebody was shouting; he recognized the president's voice. "I'm the decider," he was shouting, "and nobody else gets to be me!"

The vice president looked up and saw a dark form bending over him. "Fuck you," he managed to say, wondering how many times this was going to happen.

"Fuck you," his double responded before everything went black.

ACIREMA THE RELLIK

by Robert T. Jeschonek

Robert T. Jeschonek has written fantasy and science fiction stories for *Postscripts*, *Abyss & Apex*, *Loyalhanna Review*, *ScienceFictionFantasyHorror.com*, and other magazines and Web sites. He has also written for *War*, *Commercial Suicide*, *Dead by Dawn Quarterly*, and other comic books. Robert's Star Trek fiction has appeared in an e-book and anthologies, including *New Frontier: No Limits*, *Voyager: Distant Shores*, and *Strange New Worlds* Volumes III, V, and VI. His story, "Our Million-Year Mission," won the grand prize in Pocket's Strange New Worlds VI contest. Robert has worked in radio, television, and public relations, and currently works as a technical writer for a defense contractor in Johnstown, Pennsylvania. His Web site, www.robertjeschonek.com, features news, original fiction and The Flog, a fictionalized blog with an emphasis on fantasy.

THE GREAT STATE of Missouri lay across the Speaker's bench at the front of the House of E-representatives, wrapped in the American flag. His eyes and mouth gaped, and his arms and legs hung over the sides, dripping blood on the carpet below.

"Oh, God," said Connecticut, her shaky hand hovering over Missouri's motionless chest. "He's not breathing."

Manitoba stood on the next tier down and wouldn't come any closer. "Is there a—what's it called? Heartbeat?"

Connecticut lowered her hand, then jerked it away. "That's in the throat, right?" Nervously, she scrubbed her palms on her smart red pantsuit. "Or is it the arm?"

That was when Nevada had finally had enough.

Without a word, he pushed his tall, lanky body through the crowd on the floor of the House and charged up the steps to the Speaker's bench. Without hesitation, he pressed two fingers against the side of Missouri's throat and felt for a pulse.

But nothing was there.

"No pulse." Nevada said it loud enough for the whole crowd to hear. "The Speaker of the House is dead."

A great gasp went up from the crowd—the computer-generated, artificial intelligence-driven avatars of ninety-eight of the one-hundred states of the United States of America. Though none of them had flesh-and-blood bodies that could be murdered in the physical sense, they were stunned by what they had seen and heard.

"But how?" Connecticut slipped off her gold-rimmed glasses, let them hang by the diamond-studded chain around her neck . . . then slid them back on a second later. "And why?"

Nevada pushed up the sleeves of his tuxedo. He took Missouri's head in his hands and turned it gently to one side, exposing a gruesome wound. "Blow to the back of the head." Accepting the wound for what it appeared to be instead of what it was—an electronic simulation of a wound—he looked around for a simulated weapon that could have caused it. "What did it and why, I don't know."

"What's that?" Connecticut pointed at bloody marks on Missouri's left arm.

Nevada put Missouri's head down on the bench and walked over to look at the arm. Wiping some of the blood away, he realized the marks followed a familiar design.

Someone had cut a number into Missouri's arm. "One hundred," said Nevada. "It's the number one hundred."

The crowd murmured and moved restlessly. Nevada could tell the e-reps were confused because they usually acted more decisively.

They were AI avatars of the United States, guided by the aggregate preferences of the human electorate in the world outside. Perfectly attuned to the people they represented, perfectly immune to corruption, they never hesitated or doubted themselves.

That was why their confusion was unusual . . . and it didn't last long. As Nevada examined the body on the Speaker's bench, three of the e-reps broke from the pack and stormed toward him with jaws and shoulders set.

Sinaloa, in the middle, flipped his red-lined bullfighter's cape over his shoulder. "This is impossible." An American state since Mexico had disbanded twenty-five years ago, Sinaloa cultivated an air of insolence and false bravado. "What we see here is the product of a server malfunction."

"Exactly." South Africa tossed his glossy blond hair beside Sinaloa. "This is a bug. The Developers will fix it."

Nevada rubbed the stubbly cleft of his chin and met South Africa's blue-eyed stare. "Like Idaho?" he said slowly.

South Africa straightened his khaki safari shirt and looked away. So did stocky Kamchatka, the recent Russian convert, who had followed him up the steps.

Sinaloa glared. "I hear that might have been someone *else's* fault. Not the Developers."

A cold, threatening smile spread across Nevada's face. He knew exactly whom Sinaloa was talking about.

He was talking about Nevada.

"Then maybe you'd best be careful." Nevada adjusted his gold pinky rings and cracked his knuckles. "Just in case he can hear what you're saying."

"If, by some wild chance, the same person is responsible for this crime, I hope he *does* hear me," said Sinaloa. "I want him to know he won't get away with what he's done."

"Tell him yourself, when you catch him." Nevada started to walk away.

"*I* won't catch him." Sinaloa caught Nevada's shoulder and held him in place. "*You're* sergeant-at-arms of the House, aren't you?"

Nevada sighed and nodded. "As of twenty-four *hours* ago. What makes you think I'm ready to catch a *killer*?"

Sinaloa let go of Nevada. "We all know you've done this job before." He tightened his bolo tie, pushing the turquoise slide higher into the neck of his black silk shirt. "Five years ago, yes?"

"So what?" said Nevada.

"So you've got experience," said Sinaloa. "Not just with being sergeant-at-arms, but with losing e-reps on the job."

Nevada felt the urge to clock him in the face. Sinaloa couldn't resist bringing up Idaho—his black mark, his greatest failure, his darkest moment.

His deepest love.

"You're better qualified than any of us. You have more motivation to solve this than anyone," said Sinaloa. "You have quite a lot to prove, don't you?"

Nevada smirked and loosened the collar of the frilly shirt under his tux jacket. "You just don't want to get your hands dirty. None of you ever do."

Even as he said it, he knew Sinaloa was right. He knew what people thought of him.

He knew he had a lot to prove.

Sinaloa laughed and walked away. "You'll do it. We can all rest easy."

"Or rest in peace, pally," muttered Nevada, running a hand over his slick black hair. "Whichever comes first."

"Missouri and I walked out together," said Antarctica, her beautiful silver eyes staring into space. "He went back in for some papers he'd forgotten, and I left him there." She tucked her long, platinum hair behind her ears, and a single tear rolled down her pale cheek. "That was the last time I saw him alive."

Across the table, Nevada watched Antarctica's reaction closely. She was the last person to have seen Missouri before the murder, and that earned her a spot on the list of suspects.

She was also a sweet kid, and Nevada didn't buy her as a killer. She was the youngest e-rep, in fact, from the newest, hundredth state; Antarctica had joined the U.S.A. only one year ago, in 2299. Strikingly beautiful and shining with inner light, the junior Congresswoman gave Nevada an impression of innocence and honesty, not wiles and lies.

For a moment, Nevada looked away from her, directing his gaze across the chamber at the bloody Speaker's bench. While Nevada interviewed witnesses in the back of the room, other e-reps were up front, clearing the crime scene.

"Did he say anything unusual?" Nevada flicked his eyes to Antarctica, then back to the cleanup crew. They'd already removed Missouri's body, but the blood was another matter. Soap and water didn't exist in the digital realm, so the e-reps couldn't scrub out the soaked-in stains.

"Nothing." Antarctica adjusted her white fur wrap. "Just small talk about today's vote."

As Nevada considered his next question, his fellow e-reps gave up trying to clean the Speaker's bench. Instead, they draped a red tablecloth over it to hide the blood. "How close were the two of you?"

"He was a mentor to me," said Antarctica. "Even

though he was Speaker of the House, he still took the time to show me the ropes."

Nevada nodded. He thought the e-reps should've left the bench uncovered. Not seeing the blood made it seem bigger and brighter in his imagination.

"And there was nothing else between you?" Nevada locked eyes with her. "Nothing of a more personal nature?"

Antarctica didn't flinch. "No. Nothing."

Nevada believed her. His intuition rarely misled him, and he followed it again. "Okay, fine," he said. "Thank you for your time."

With that, Nevada rose from his chair and called out to the e-reps milling around the chamber. "Panama," he said. "Will the great state of Panama please report to the sergeant-at-arms."

When Nevada turned back to the interview table, he realized that Antarctica was still sitting there. Her pale hands were folded neatly in front of her, and her silvery eyes were focused coolly on Nevada.

"You're dismissed, sweetheart," said Nevada. "Unless you got something else to say?"

Antarctica nodded grimly. "I want to help you," she said. "I want to help find who killed him."

Nevada sniffed and fiddled with his tuxedo cufflinks. He could think of two possible reasons for her offer. One, she really did want to do her part to bring the killer to justice.

Or two, she *was* the killer. Maybe she wanted to divert attention from her own guilt.

Either way, Nevada figured he could use her.

"Why not?" he said. "As long as you don't mind getting your hands a little dirty."

"I'll do what I have to." Antarctica rose, smoothing the glittering, ice-blue gown that she wore under her fur wrap. "Missouri was a great state."

"Aren't they all?" said Nevada.

* * *

Panama was no help. Neither was Jamaica or Wyoming or any of the other states who had been around Missouri before his death.

After hours of questioning one e-rep witness after another, Nevada was no closer to solving the murder. According to the witnesses, Missouri hadn't said or done a thing out of the ordinary, and no one in his orbit had said or done anything suspicious.

Whatever had happened to Missouri, the only part that wasn't a mystery was the fact that he was dead.

Frustrated, Nevada marched out of the House chamber through big double doors and into the halls of the digital Capitol building. "I need some fresh air." Antarctica followed him.

Except for Nevada and Antarctica, the halls were empty. The e-reps, whose sole reason for existing was to vote on legislation according to the will of the electorate, rarely ventured outside the House chamber. Neither did the e-senators.

Nevada was the exception to the rule. For him, the peace and quiet beyond the chamber were a bonus. Except for the glitz of Las Vegas, he was a state of wide-open spaces; he did his best thinking away from the endless chatter of his fellow e-reps.

"What's next?" said Antarctica.

Nevada shrugged. "Missouri's office, I guess. Root around for some kind of clue."

"Like what?" said Antarctica. "What are we looking for?"

"How should I know?" said Nevada. "I'm no detective."

Antarctica frowned. "What did Sinaloa mean when he said you have experience losing e-reps on the job?"

Nevada sighed. "Didn't anyone ever tell you about Idaho?"

"I'm new around here," said Antarctica. "There's a lot I don't know."

Nevada was relieved that there was one person left who hadn't heard the story. He almost didn't tell her, just so he wouldn't lose that one last unspoiled innocent.

Then, he decided just to get it over with. "Idaho disappeared five years ago," he said. "Without a trace. I was sergeant-at-arms at the time, and I couldn't find her."

"So they blame you for losing her?" said Antarctica.

"Some of them." Nevada listened to his lizard-skin cowboy boots echoing down the corridor. "And some think I might have *killed* her."

"What?" Antarctica gaped at him. "How could they *think* that?"

"Because we were lovers," said Nevada, and then he stopped in front of a door. "Well, here we are." The print on the frosted glass bore the name of Missouri. Nevada turned the knob and pushed the door open, following it into Missouri's office.

Antarctica walked in after him and closed the door. As Nevada rifled drawers and flipped through papers on Missouri's desk, Antarctica circled the perimeter, watching him with a newly guarded expression.

Nevada knew exactly what she was thinking. He'd seen that look a thousand times before on other faces.

She was wondering if he'd killed his lover.

"Nothing here." After ransacking the desk for a while, Nevada planted his hands on his hips and shook his head. "Nothing out of the ordinary."

"What about that?" Antarctica pointed toward the door through which they'd entered. At the base of it, a single sheet of blank paper lay flat on the floor.

"Someone must have slid it under the door while we were busy," said Nevada.

Antarctica picked up the paper. "Why would somebody slip us a piece of paper with nothing on it?"

"Depends." Nevada reached out, and she gave him the paper. As soon as his fingers touched the page, black lettering appeared on it. "Depends who it's addressed to."

Antarctica leaned in close enough that Nevada

could smell her sweet gardenia perfume, and they read the note together.

Statue of Liberty, 3PM. Come Alone.

"It's an invitation," said Nevada. "Somebody wants to tell me something."

"Or maybe this is from the killer," said Antarctica. "Maybe he wants you to 'come alone' so he can kill you."

"There's only one way to find out." Nevada crumpled the paper into his tux jacket pocket and headed for the door. "And I'd better hurry, since three o'clock is just ten minutes from now."

From the windows in the tiara of the Statue of Liberty, Nevada gazed out over the digital realm that was his home.

He could see everything spread out before him— a world of simulated American landmarks, brought together in a single electronic space. Who cared that in the real world, they were nowhere near this close together? All that mattered was that the e-reps and e-sens had plenty of picturesque American backdrops for their speeches and pronouncements.

In the middle of it all, Nevada saw the gleaming white dome of the Capitol building. Northwest of the Capitol jabbed the ivory needle of the Washington Monument; to the southwest rested the Lincoln Memorial. The Liberty Bell hung in a golden tower to the southeast, and Plymouth Rock perched on a pedestal to the northeast.

Straight across the bubble of the digital realm from the Statue of Liberty, Mount Rushmore spanned the horizon, its giant presidential heads gazing out over the city. Niagara Falls roared to the east, and the Grand Canyon sprawled to the west, glowing forever red in the never-dimming sunrise.

As Nevada gazed out at it all, he wondered what it would be like to see such landmarks in the real world. As amazing as they looked in the digital domain, how much more spectacular would they seem in True America? Would he feel different to stand in their presence, to breathe the air and walk upon the soil of the nation he served and loved?

Or would it turn out to be a letdown? For all he knew, it was better in here, in this idealized, compressed simulation. Maybe he had it better than he knew.

Even if he wasn't going to live forever, the way he'd once thought. Even if Missouri's death was a precursor to his own.

"Nevada." The whispered voice from across the room surprised him. Nevada shot his gaze into the shadows . . . and saw an intercom speaker mounted in the wall there.

"Nevada." The voice spoke again, still no more than a whisper. Nevada crossed the room and stood close to the speaker, straining to identify who was doing the talking.

And failing. "Nevada. Are you there?"

Nevada pressed the button to transmit and spoke into the grill in the wall. "I'm here. Who is this?"

"Call me Looking Glass." The voice belonged to a man, but that was all Nevada could tell. "I know where to look."

"For what?" said Nevada. "Or who?"

"For Yukon's murderer," said Looking Glass.

A sharp chill raced up Nevada's spine. "Don't you mean Missouri's? Yukon isn't dead."

"She wasn't," said Looking Glass, "when you got on Lady Liberty's elevator."

Nevada took a deep breath and released it. He burned with rage at the thought of a second murder taking place while he investigated the first . . . but he knew that he had to keep his cool. Looking Glass was on the line, and Nevada might still be able to get information out of him.

Nevada pressed the intercom button and spoke. "Did you do it? Is that what this is about? Did you bring me here so I'd be out of the way while you killed Yukon?"

"Here is your first clue," said Looking Glass. "When is one one-hundred?"

Nevada scowled. "Just tell me if you did it. Tell me if you killed them both."

"When does one plus zero equal two?" said Looking Glass. "That's your second clue."

"If you didn't do it, who did?" said Nevada. "I can't get to you from up here, can I? So just tell me."

"No more for now," said Looking Glass. "See you after three and four."

With that, the line went dead.

Nevada slammed the button with the palm of his hand. "Looking Glass! Get back here! Talk to me!"

But Looking Glass was gone.

"Damn!" Nevada pounded the intercom speaker with the side of his fist. He hadn't felt so angry for a long time . . . or so helpless.

He hadn't felt this way since that day, five years ago, when Idaho, his love, had disappeared.

Yukon sat on the toilet in the women's lavatory, fully dressed and covered in blood and toilet paper. Her long, brown hair covered her face like a shroud, as if her killer had tried to spare her the sight of her own murder.

"When did you find her?" Nevada stood in the doorway of the stall, hands on his hips.

Nervous Connecticut stood at his left. "A half hour ago." She took off her gold-rimmed glasses, then put them back on . . . then took them off again. "We c-came in together for a sidebar. She was f-fine when I left."

Nevada nodded. Since the e-reps hadn't been programmed to simulate excretory functions, bathrooms in the digital realm were used mostly for sidebar meetings and secret deals. "Let me guess. No one noticed anything unusual."

"Not exactly, señor." Sinaloa stood at Nevada's

right and clapped him on the shoulder. "Some of us noticed *you* leaving the House chamber shortly before the murder. Would you call *that* unusual?"

Nevada ignored him and stepped into the stall. Gently, he parted the hair over Yukon's face with his fingertips, revealing a gruesome palette of cuts and bruises.

Pushing the hair away from her throat, he saw the biggest visible wound—a bloody gash from ear to ear.

"And no murder weapon left behind." Nevada was thinking out loud, repeating what Connecticut had already told him. "No bloody footprints, no fingerprints, no nothing."

"Tell me." Sinaloa flipped the red-lined bullfighter's cape over his shoulder with a flourish. "How is your first investigation going? Can you tell us who murdered Missouri?"

Nevada spotted the edge of a bloody symbol sticking out from under the toilet paper wrapped around Yukon's forearm. Tearing away the paper, he saw that there were two symbols underneath—two numerals carved into Yukon's flesh.

Two nines, carved side by side. Together, they made the number "ninety-nine."

Just as the number one hundred had been cut into poor Missouri's flesh.

"Well?" said Sinaloa. "Can you tell us who murdered Missouri?"

"Same person who murdered Yukon," said Nevada. "And there'll be more to come."

"What makes you say that?" said Sinaloa.

"Because he's counting down from a hundred," said Nevada. "A hundred of us."

Nevada sat at the end of the reflecting pool, gazing across the still water at the Lincoln Memorial. Antarctica, who was sitting beside him, had kicked off her crystalline shoes and dropped her pale, slender feet into the water.

The ripples from her feet disturbed the scenes playing over the pool's surface—visions of life beyond the digital domain in True America. Men, women, and children worked and played in softly swirling moments, flickering across the sunlit water like memories.

It was here that the e-reps and e-sens came to watch the proof of their good work—the results of the legislation they passed on behalf of the American electorate. It was here that they came to see the faces of the people they served and strengthen their resolve to preserve the American dream.

"You're sure the killer won't stop?" said Antarctica.

"There are one hundred e-reps," said Nevada. "The first victim was marked one hundred, and the second was ninety-nine. Ninety-eight is next, then ninety-seven . . . all the way to one and zero."

Antarctica sighed and frowned. "I can't believe the Developers are letting this happen. Can't they just reprogram the source code to bring back the dead and stop the murders?"

"Maybe not." Nevada stroked the dark stubble on his chin. "Maybe they've lost control of the simulation."

"I hope not," said Antarctica.

"Or maybe they're *letting* it happen," said Nevada. "Hell, maybe they're *making* it happen."

Antarctica looked shocked. "The Developers wouldn't *do* that, would they?"

Nevada shrugged. "How should *we* know? The Developers keep to themselves."

"But it doesn't seem possible." Antarctica shook her head and gazed into the water. "None of this does."

"Got that right." Nevada stretched out on his side, propping an elbow on the cement. Even with everything that was going on, he felt a sense of peace in this place, a clearheaded perspective that came to him more strongly here than anywhere else.

Of all the places in the digital realm, the reflecting

pool would always be the most special to him. It was here that he'd last seen Idaho before she'd disappeared from his life.

It was here that he'd last made love to her.

"What about Looking Glass's clues?" said Antarctica. "Do they mean anything?"

"I'm sure they do," said Nevada, "but I haven't figured them out yet."

" 'When is one one-hundred?' " Antarctica narrowed her silver eyes in thought. "He must have meant the one hundred e-reps of Congress, right?"

"Probably," said Nevada.

"Or he might have meant *me*." Antarctica's eyes widened. "I'm the one-hundredth e-rep, from the one-hundredth state! What if I'm the next *victim*?"

"I don't think so," said Nevada. "The killer counted Missouri as number one hundred for some reason. Maybe reverse order of importance. Missouri was speaker of the House, number one in terms of power . . . so the killer counted him as last, as number one hundred."

"And Yukon was the minority leader." Antarctica sounded relieved. "Second most powerful. So you don't think I'm next, Nevada?" She smiled over her shoulder at him.

"No, sweetheart." Nevada smiled back at her. "I don't think you're on the killer's radar right now."

Just then, without warning, Antarctica shot forward and disappeared under the water.

Heart pounding, Nevada scrambled to the edge of the pool and stared at the spot where she'd gone under. Since the water was murky with projected scenes of True America, he couldn't see below the surface. No trace of Antarctica or whatever had pulled her in was visible.

Then, suddenly, one pale hand broke the surface of the water. Without hesitation, Nevada lashed out his own hand and locked onto it.

Determined not to lose Antarctica, Nevada pulled

up hard . . . but whatever had hold of her wouldn't let go. Nevada didn't want to hurt her, but she was running out of air, and he had to act fast. Leaning out farther, he clamped his other hand around her wrist . . . and then he pulled as hard as he could.

The underwater force resisted, and Nevada redoubled his efforts. Finally, the thing in the pool released its grip, and Nevada hauled Antarctica free with one great heave.

The two of them tumbled backward on the edge of the pool. Nevada cradled her in his arms as she coughed up water and gasped for breath.

Finally, her silver eyes flickered open and met his gaze. "Guess what?" Her voice was shaky as she said it. "I think I'm on the killer's radar after all."

Nevada stroked the platinum-blonde hair out of her eyes. "Who pulled you in?" he asked. "Did you get a look at them?"

Antarctica shook her head. "All I know is, their touch was beyond ice cold. It was so cold, I couldn't *stand* it, and that's really *saying* something."

Nevada stared at the surface of the pool, which was as smooth as if nothing had happened a moment ago. He wondered who had attacked Antarctica, and why.

He came up with three possibilities. First, maybe the killer's hit list was more random than he had thought, or followed a more complicated formula. Second, maybe the killer had tried to murder out of order because Antarctica was helping with the investigation.

Or third, a more ominous motive had fueled the attack . . . a motive that explained why the underwater assailant had finally let go of Antarctica.

"We've got to get back." Nevada tipped Antarctica so her feet touched the cement. "Back to the House."

Antarctica frowned. "Why is that?"

"I don't think you were a target," said Nevada. "I think you were a diversion."

*　　*　　*

Pieces of the great state of Zacatecas were scattered all over the House chamber—head on the flagpole, foot on the Speaker's bench, arm on the podium. Blood was spattered everywhere, and ragged shreds of flesh stuck to the furniture and walls.

Many of the e-reps were also stained and clotted with their colleague's remains—including Connecticut, as she explained to Nevada what had happened.

"Half an hour ago, the power went out," said Connecticut. "We heard Zacatecas screaming, but we didn't know why until the lights came back up five minutes later. We found him . . . like this." She looked down at her bloody hands and clothes. "Blown up . . . or chopped up. Both, maybe."

Suddenly, Sinaloa stormed toward them, scowling with rage. "Arrest this man!" He grabbed hold of Nevada's wrist and wrenched it in the air. "He killed my Mexican *hermano!*"

"That's enough," said Connecticut. "Let him go."

"Who among us was mysteriously *absent* when Zacatecas was *murdered?*" Sinaloa shook Nevada's arm for the crowd. "*This* man! *This* man only reappeared when the killing was *finished.*"

Antarctica pushed forward. "I was with him when this happened!" Her long hair was still damp from the Reflecting Pool, and she'd had to abandon her soaking-wet white fur wrap. "I tell you, Nevada didn't kill *anyone.*"

"Then what *was* he doing?" said Sinaloa.

"Saving my life!" said Antarctica. "I was attacked at the Reflecting Pool!"

"How do we know for sure?" Sinaloa locked eyes with her and sneered. "Perhaps you were his *accomplice* in this atrocity."

Fed up with the grandstanding, Nevada tore his wrist free of Sinaloa's grip. "This is exactly what they want."

" 'They' who?" said Sinaloa.

"You're right about one thing," said Nevada. "More than one person is involved in these murders."

With that, Nevada headed for the front of the chamber. The crowd of e-reps silently parted to make way for him.

Sinaloa followed. "Of course I'm right," he said, "but what makes you admit it?"

"Someone attacked Antarctica at the Reflecting Pool while the murders were underway here." Nevada walked up to the podium, where Zacateca's left arm rested. "That tells us at least two people are involved. Maybe more."

"Maybe more?" Sinaloa sounded skeptical.

Nevada gazed at the severed arm on the podium, its hand curled into a loose fist. "In five short minutes, power was cut to the House, Zacatecas was torn to pieces, and power was restored. That's a lot for one person to do alone in that amount of time."

"I don't know about that," said Sinaloa.

Nevada turned the arm over. "In that same five minutes, someone also did this." Nevada held up the arm for the crowd to see. "Cut open Zacatecas' coat and shirt sleeves and carved the number '98' into his flesh."

The watching e-reps gasped and mumbled.

"The countdown continues," said Nevada, "unless we start working together and find who did this."

Sinaloa glowered at Nevada for a long moment, shoulders rising and falling with rapid, angry breaths. Then, he spun and marched up the aisle toward the back of the chamber.

"You're right," he said over his shoulder. "It's time to get some answers."

Nevada frowned and put down Zacatecas' severed arm. "How do you plan to do that?"

"By making a call," said Sinaloa. "You're welcome to join me."

"Making a call to whom?" said Nevada.

"Who else?" said Sinaloa. "The Developers."

In the center of the vast rotunda beneath the dome of the Capitol building, Sinaloa came to a stop on a single glowing tile. Nevada and Antarctica, who had followed him from the House chamber, stood to one side and watched.

When Sinaloa placed his right hand over his heart and recited the Pledge of Allegiance, a shaft of light burst up from the glowing tile, striking the middle of the dome. Smoothly, the dome split on one side and rolled open, revealing a starry night sky overhead.

The shaft of light from the tile spiked straight up, never dimming as it shot into the heavens. This was the holy connection to the godlike Developers in the world outside, the fabled *soulpipe*.

Nevada shivered as he watched the soulpipe disappear in the unknowable distance. As often as he'd seen it in action, the sight of the climbing, blazing conduit still filled him with awe.

"I've never actually seen a soul call before." Antarctica's voice was soft and slow with wonder and surprise. "Will the Developers answer?"

Nevada shrugged. The same question was foremost in his own mind at that moment.

Since the murders, the role of House Speaker had fallen on Sinaloa, which qualified him to make the soul call. As a rule, though, the Developers didn't answer every query from the digital realm. In the past, they'd already gone years without responding to a call, so there was no way to know what would happen this time.

In the blazing light of the soulpipe, Sinaloa gazed upward and spread his arms wide. "O Masters of the Source Code, I beg you—hear my prayer!" Sinaloa's feet left the floor. Spinning slowly, he rose into the air, following the soulpipe's beam. "Representative Sinaloa . . . transmit *now*!"

Suddenly, Sinaloa exploded upward, streaking along the soulpipe in a strobing blur. There was a distant sonic boom as he vanished in the heavens, flashing out of sight among the flickering garlands of stars.

"Wow." Antarctica walked around the base of the

soulpipe, staring up into Sinaloa's rippling wake. "He's in True America now?"

"Somewhere between here and there," said Nevada. "A hub outside their firewall."

"Don't you mean fire *ball*?" said Antarctica.

"Fire *wall*," said Nevada.

Antarctica frowned. "It's just that I see one now. A fire *ball*."

Nevada squinted upward . . . and then he saw it, too. A clutch of flames far above, burning in the firmament.

Burning and falling.

Without another moment's thought, Nevada lashed an arm around Antarctica's waist and ran with her, racing her away from the soulpipe. Just as they reached the far wall of the rotunda, a thunderous impact crashed down behind them, shaking the cavernous chamber.

Nevada and Antarctica stumbled as the floor buckled. Bracing each other, they managed to stay on their feet . . . and as the tremor faded, they turned.

The soulpipe was gone. In its place, in the center of the rotunda, was a smoking crater.

"Stay back," Nevada told Antarctica, and then he ran toward the crater. In spite of his order, he heard Antarctica running close behind him.

When Nevada reached the broken rim of the crater, he saw what had caused the impact. He saw what had fallen from above like a fiery comet.

The body of Sinaloa lay in the crater's heart, curled like a fist and charred from tip to toe.

Antarctica drew up alongside Nevada and gagged. "Oh, no."

"I guess they're not taking our calls." Nevada stepped over the edge and eased into the crater. He saw that parts of Sinaloa were still smoldering, glowing cherry red in familiar patterns.

There were messages on Sinaloa's body, burned instead of carved into his flesh.

"Ninety-seven." Nevada pointed to Sinaloa's left

arm, where the numbers had been branded. Then he pointed at the letters seared into Sinaloa's right arm. "A-C-I-R-E-M-A. Acirema."

Finally, he read the smoking words on Sinaloa's charred chest. "'ANSWERS IN HOUSE NOW!'"

Leaping into action, Nevada clambered up the crater's slope. Antarctica gave him a hand clearing the rim.

And Nevada started running the instant his feet hit the floor. His heart hammered in his chest as he headed for the House chamber.

Even though he already knew.

"I don't understand." Antarctica caught up and ran beside him. "Why would they kill Sinaloa and tell us we'll get answers in the House?"

Nevada didn't answer, though he knew. He knew all too well.

He knew that he was too late.

Four figures wrapped in star-spangled robes waited outside the big double doors of the House chamber. Their faces were hidden in the depths of shadowy hoods, arms folded across their chests.

Nevada and Antarctica stopped running, staying well back from the hooded figures. Even from a distance, Nevada could see that the blue-and-white robes were stained with smears and splotches of dark red.

They were bloodstained.

Holding back Antarctica, Nevada took a step forward. "Stand aside," he said to the four figures. "The sergeant-at-arms has business with the House."

To his surprise, the figures moved to comply without hesitation. The two in the middle turned and opened the doors to the chamber—but they did not usher him inside. Instead, a fifth figure emerged, clad in red-and-white-striped robes, also hooded.

Before Nevada could get a look inside the chamber, the two figures who had opened the doors pulled them shut once more.

The fifth robed figure glided forward, face hidden

like the rest. The voice that flowed from under the hood was that of a man . . . hoarse and muffled, but clearly a man.

A familiar man.

"Hello again," he said. "I told you we would meet again after three and four, didn't I?"

"Looking Glass." Nevada had a terrible sinking feeling, but he squared his shoulders and tried not to show it. "I've been thinking about you."

"Victims three and four are dead, so here I am." Looking Glass bowed his head. "Have you deciphered the clues I gave you?"

"No," said Nevada.

Looking Glass chuckled. "Then prepare to have your mind blown."

Nevada took a step back, pushing Antarctica along with him. He briefly considered running, if only for her sake . . . but he waited. How could he run when he had yet to see inside the House?

When he had yet to confirm what he already knew in his broken heart?

"Meet the welcome wagon," said Looking Glass, gesturing at the robed figures on his right.

Silently, the figure on the far right reached up and tugged off the star-spangled hood, revealing a face. A man's face, grinning.

Nevada couldn't help gasping when he saw who it was. Heart slamming like a piston in his rib cage, he froze in place and gaped, holding on to Antarctica's arm.

Antarctica said the name for them both. "S-Sinaloa?" She scowled in confusion. "But you're dead!"

The robed man with Sinaloa's face took a bow.

Then, the next figure unmasked. This time, the face under the hood was also familiar—a man most recently seen in pieces in the House.

"Zacatecas." Nevada's head was spinning. He fought to make sense of what he was seeing, but could not.

"More where that came from," said Looking Glass,

turning to gesture at the two hooded figures on the other side of him.

The next to unmask was a woman with long, brown hair—unmistakably Yukon, also back from the dead. Beside her, the last of the four in the star-spangled hoods, was the man who had started it all, the first to go: Missouri, former Speaker of the House, peeled back his hood and smoothed his neat white hair with a toothy grin.

"What's going on here, Nevada?" Antarctica sounded dazed. "How can they all be alive?"

"The Developers, maybe?" Nevada felt dazed, too. Again, he was seized by the urge to run . . . and again, he fought it back. "Maybe they fixed the glitch and resurrected the dead e-reps?"

The four who had come back to life looked at each other with knowing smiles and giggled.

"Wrong," said Looking Glass. "Not even close."

"Some kind of practical joke, maybe?" Nevada heard what could have been a muffled scream from behind the double doors to the House chamber. "A stunt to delay a key vote on legislation?"

"It *is* kind of funny," said Looking Glass, "but no. I assure you, this isn't a joke or a stunt. Would you like me to give you a hint?"

Nevada heard a loud thump and a crash from behind the doors. "Sure," he said. "Why not?"

"Here goes." With that, Looking Glass reached up and pulled off his red-and-white-striped hood.

And Nevada felt the world of logic and reality dissolve around him.

His mouth fell open. He hand dropped away from Antarctica. His mind went blank.

What he saw in front of him—*whom* he saw—was impossible. Completely, inarguably impossible.

Looking Glass, without the hood, had a very familiar face—*frighteningly* familiar. He wasn't someone returned from the dead, or anyone Nevada had ever expected to see.

Outside of a mirror, that is.

The face staring back at Nevada was his own. Looking Glass was his identical twin.

"I bet I know what's going through your mind right now." Looking Glass smiled. " 'What a handsome S.O.B.,' am I, right?"

Nevada didn't answer. He was dimly aware of Antarctica's hand on his shoulder—and other than that, the world around him was sunk in fog.

Stepping forward, Looking Glass extended a hand. "The name is Adaven," he said. "Pleased to meet you, Nevada."

Without thinking, Nevada took Adaven's hand. It was ice-cold to the touch—*beyond* ice cold.

Then, Adaven gripped Nevada's elbow, freezing him right through the sleeves of his tux and shirt. With a whoop, he swung Nevada around to face the four seemingly resurrected e-reps.

"This is Aolanis." Adaven pointed at the reborn Sinaloa, and then he moved down the line. "This is Sacetacaz, Nokuy, and Iruossim. They're not who you think they are." Adaven leaned close and whispered in Nevada's ear. "You've never met them before."

Nevada frowned. Everything sounded crazy. He wondered if there had been a malfunction in the simulation somewhere.

"Now come on." Adaven led Nevada toward the doors. "Let's meet the rest of the gang, shall we?"

Grinning, Sacetacaz and Nokuy pushed open the double doors to the House chamber. Adaven guided Nevada inside . . . right into a nightmare.

The huge room was splashed from top to bottom and side-to-side with blood and gore. Body parts were scattered everywhere, the way the pieces of Zacatecas had been scattered. Corpses were piled like cordwood in the corners of the room.

They were the corpses of Nevada's e-rep colleagues . . . or at least they appeared to be.

Even as Nevada recognized the dead faces of e-reps in the corpse heaps, he saw e-reps with the same faces moving around the room. The moving and the motionless looked exactly the same, except some were living and some were dead—and the living versions weren't behaving the way that Nevada ever would have expected them to.

Specifically, they were killing their fellow e-reps.

As Nevada watched, Arkansas, South Korea, and Israel teamed up against Costa Rica, howling and whooping as they tore her limb from limb. Across the chamber, Florida and Japan were hacking up Chihuahua with knives, cutting out his organs while he screamed in agony.

Antarctica's identical twin slogged past not ten feet from Nevada, dragging a charred and disemboweled corpse by the feet. She paused on the way past to snarl at Nevada's Antarctica, then continued on her way.

Staring at the hellish scene, Nevada could think of only one thing to say, one question to ask: "Why?"

"Why what?" Adaven laughed and clapped him on the shoulder, sending a frigid blast through his tux coat. "Why redecorate, you mean? Why have a surprise party?"

"I don't understand," said Nevada. "Why are there duplicate e-reps?"

"Remember my riddle? 'When does one plus zero equal two?'" Adaven looked at Nevada as if he were a moron. "The answer is, when *one* casts a reflection in a *mirror,* of course. In a looking glass."

"You reflect us?" said Nevada.

Adaven made a twisting gesture with his hand. "Other way around."

Antarctica crowded in close, shivering against Nevada's arm. "So there's two of everyone?" she said.

"One from America." Adaven raised his right hand, palm up, like the tray of a balance. "One from Acirema." He raised his left hand, also palm-up, alongside the right.

" 'Acirema,' " said Nevada. "That word was burned into Sinaloa's body."

Adaven threw an arm around Nevada's shoulders, freezing him again. "You know it by another name," he said. "'True America.'"

Nevada stared at him in surprise, too stunned to speak.

"You e-reps have been living in a fantasy," said Adaven. "Thinking True America was a paradise of liberty. Thinking you were the voices of a just and compassionate electorate.

"But you don't represent the people of True America. You never did." Adaven swept an arm wide to take in the entire House chamber. "*These* are the representatives of America. *These* are the A.I. avatars whose votes shape America's destiny."

"You're telling us democracy's dead?" said Antarctica.

"The opposite!" said Adaven. "Democracy is alive and well . . . and *this* is the will of the American electorate!"

Nevada gazed at the horrifying scenes playing out before him—British Columbia's twin skinning Utah alive . . . the doubles of Veracruz and Wisconsin spearing Botswana with a flagpole . . . e-rep Doppelgängers cheering in a circle as the New York of Acirema brutalized the New York of Nevada's digital realm.

"You and your kind have never been more than puppets," said Adaven. "Illusions to mask the true face of America—to let her own people fool themselves even as she expresses their darkest desires. You are the reason Americans have been able to live with themselves and sleep at night . . . but no longer.

"America has become her own shadow: Acirema, the opposite—'America' spelled backward." Adaven pulled Nevada close and whispered, frozen breath swirling in his ear. "We don't need you anymore."

Nevada felt sick. The urge to run returned—but he

realized it was too late. He and Antarctica were surrounded by e-rep duplicates, shadow copies of the hundred digital Congressmen who had died or were dying in front of him.

Soon, he was certain, he would join them.

"Acirema doesn't need to pretend anymore," said Adaven. "We don't need the front. We've accepted ourselves as the complete bastards we've always been, and we've made up our minds from now on to be the *best* complete bastards we *can* be."

"That's why you started killing us," said Nevada.

Adaven nodded. "The first few were tests. The Developers gave us all the keys and cheats we needed, but we still weren't sure if murder would work in the digital realm."

"And you murdered the Speaker first to cripple our leadership," said Nevada.

"Actually, that was a mistake," said Adaven. "In the shadow Congress of Acirema, Missouri is the lowliest of the hundred, not the highest. We thought we were starting with the least important among you. 'When is one one hundred,' remember? The answer to the riddle is this: when *one*—the number one e-rep, the Speaker of the House in your realm—ranks *hundredth* out of a hundred in ours."

Nevada nodded slowly as he looked around at the living hell in the chamber. Even as the corpse heaps grew and the number of e-rep survivors dwindled, the screams of the dying seemed to intensify. "So all of this was for nothing," he said. "Everything we accomplished."

"But the *good* news is, you can still make a difference," said Adaven.

"How's that?" said Nevada.

Adaven steered him around to face the huge double doorway. A figure stood beyond it, waiting in the hall, wrapped in hooded robes emblazoned with stars and stripes.

"She will help you." With that, Adaven gave Nevada a shove, sending him stumbling into the hall. "You will make a difference by *dying*—sacrificing yourself to make way for the new guard."

Antarctica followed Nevada, grabbing hold of his elbow. "What's the plan?" she said. "How do we get out of this one?"

"We don't." Nevada slumped as the robed figure swung a rifle from her back and took aim at him. A dozen options for action flashed through his mind, revving up his heart, burning up his bloodstream with adrenaline. . . .

And he pushed them all aside. He knew that he could go down fighting, and in that way redeem himself at least a little for failing the republic—but he did nothing. Why bother, when a blaze of glory would mean less than nothing to the masses of Acirema? What good would a martyr be if no one knew that he had died and why?

"Please, Nevada." Antarctica tugged his arm, but he wouldn't budge. "It's up to us."

"No, it's not." Nevada shook free of her grip. "Nothing's up to us anymore."

"You're wrong." Antarctica pointed up at the wall in the hallway. A red light blinked on the security camera that was mounted there. "People are still watching."

Nevada stared at the camera, then looked down at the barrel of the rifle. Maybe Antarctica was right. Maybe he could accomplish something worthwhile in death after all.

Maybe this was what his whole life had been leading up to.

Nevada took a deep breath to steady himself. He curled and uncurled his fists.

Then, he bolted out of the line of fire.

"Run!" He glimpsed a blur of movement from Antarctica's direction as he said it.

Head down, Nevada charged toward the hooded

shooter. He cut one way, then the other, trying to avoid her fire, reaching out for her.

But before he could touch her, he heard the deafening crack of the rifle. In spite of his zigzag path, the shot slammed into his chest with explosive force, pitching him to the floor.

He blacked out.

When he opened his eyes again, he saw the hooded woman crouching over him. "Confirmed kill," she said to someone he couldn't see—and when she said it, his heart beat faster.

He recognized her voice.

Nevada knew what her face would look like before she lifted away the hood. At first, all he could think was that it was impossible, that he must have already died if she was there with them.

But then, as she locked eyes with him, he remembered just how possible it was. Every e-rep had a double in Acirema, after all, even the dead ones. Even the one who had disappeared five years ago.

Even his beloved Idaho.

Nevada was in pain, but he managed a smile. The sight of her after all this time, even a shadow double who'd just shot him, was enough to fill him with joy.

Maybe her name was Ohadi instead of Idaho. Maybe she was devoted to the dark purposes of Acirema the Rellik instead of the bright resolve of America the Beautiful. Maybe she felt nothing for him, not even hatred.

But at least he could drink in the sight of her face again. At least he could pretend in his few remaining moments that the precious original had returned to him.

At least he could imagine—or was it more than imagination—that her hand was warm when she touched his eyelids. When she drew them shut.

He could dream that she was his warm-blooded Idaho, hiding all this time to prepare for the threat of Acirema, masquerading even now as the enemy. Infiltrating the darkness. Faking Nevada's death, too, so she could whisk him away to the underground to fight the power. To renew their love.

Or if that hand was colder than he thought, than he Dreamed

And she was Ohadi in spite of his hope, carved from glittering ice with frozen heart and frozen soul,

Perhaps his noble moment of defiance and then his last words would inspire her,

Warm her blood that she would *become* restored Idaho and more,

Seed of change, revolution, restoration,

Changer of hearts, perhaps even the heart of Adaven, his twin, Nevada spelled backward

Spelled everywhichway like America

Acirema Maciera Reamica Cimeara Imeraca

Then that would be all right, too, he thought,

And he tried

In the last words he said

To tell her what mattered,

What they'd forgotten,

What to pass along,

And this was what came out,

His wisdom, his blessing, his curse,

His last wish

His poem.

He said

"I love you."

FAMILY PHOTOS

by S. Andrew Swann

S. Andrew Swann is the pen name of Steven Swiniarski. He's married and lives in the Greater Cleveland area where he has lived all of his adult life. He has a background in mechanical engineering and—besides writing—works as a computer systems analyst for one of the largest private child services agencies in the Cleveland area. He has published seventeen novels with DAW books over the past fourteen years, which include science fiction, fantasy, horror, and thrillers. His latest novel is *The Dwarves of Whiskey Island*, a fantasy set in Cleveland. He is currently working on a sequel to the *Hostile Takeover* trilogy, an epic space opera.

THE SENATOR ON the television asked, "Was it less exploitive when victims did not have these rights?" He gave a condescending look across the podium at his opponent. "Perhaps the governor from South Dakota preferred it back when killers and rapists could sell their so-called stories and profit from books, movies . . ."

Mrs. Angela Norris had stopped when she heard the senator's voice. The party continued around her, conversation, quiet laughter, the clinking of ice in peo-

147

ple's glasses, all fading from her awareness as she
stared at the presidential debate.

". . . my opponent would take away this absolute
right from the victims of crime. He would return to
the days when anyone, including the perpetrator,
could profit from a criminal act. And—is that my
time?"

By all rights, Mrs. Norris should have been one of
the senator's supporters. She had never voted for anyone outside her party, her family's party, the late Mr.
Norris' party. But every time she looked at him, she
couldn't help but think of what was happening to
her son.

No one has a right to do that, she thought.

The governor, a younger man, frowned as he responded. "My opponent is well-intentioned, but he is
wrong. His legislation intends to assure victims of
crime some compensation for commercial exploitation
of that crime. It sounds reasonable, but the precedent
is completely at odds with the letter and the spirit
of the First Amendment. It extends the concept of
intellectual property beyond creative works, but to the
historical events from which they're derived. In some
interpretations it extends to any media representation
of the accused—"

Someone touched her arm and Mrs. Norris jerked,
sending an ice cube flying out of her glass to land on
the Oriental carpet at her feet.

"Angela? Are you all right?"

She turned to face Justice Conroy. His steely-blue
eyes watched her with some concern, and she was
deeply afraid that she had just made a fool of herself
in front of an old family friend.

"I'm sorry. The debate just—" She shook her head.
"Never mind. Can you help my son?"

Justice Conroy didn't make eye contact with her.
Instead, he swirled his drink and looked at the television himself. "I understand your concern, but legally

it is up to your son or his lawyers to appeal any decision."

"You saw the pictures, the court couldn't have intended this."

He raised his glass to his lips and drained the small amount of amber liquid that remained. He shook his head. "There's nothing I can do."

He turned to go, and Mrs. Norris grabbed his arm. "Please? He's my only child."

Back to her, his shoulders slumped.

"You were my father's best friend. Can't you help his grandson?"

"Angela, if you think there's some sort of abuse happening, you need to talk to the AG's office, or the police."

"I've been trying, but no one listens to me." She walked around him so that she faced him again. "If you called someone, they would listen to you."

"I don't have a magic wand."

"But they would *listen*."

He nodded slowly, defeated by her logic. "I can call someone in the AG's office on your behalf."

"Thank you."

"I'm doing it for your father," he told her. "I don't think they'll agree with your assessment of the situation."

Mrs. Norris frowned at him. "But you saw the pictures?"

"Yes, I did." He slipped by her. "Now if you'd excuse me."

She didn't pay much attention to the discomfort on Justice Conroy's face. All that mattered is that the faceless bureaucrats who had been ignoring her pleas for three years would be hearing from a state supreme court justice. They would *have* to do something then. Then, once they actually saw what was happening to her son, it would stop.

*　　*　　*

When Mrs. Norris returned home, she walked into her son's bedroom. The lights had burned out long ago, so she stood in the doorway a long time staring into the darkness. She spent much of that time wondering why she stood in front of her son's dark, empty room.

Nothing had been here since Mr. Norris had cleaned out her son's things over thirty years ago. Her husband had left a bare room that they hadn't bothered to use since. It was one of the things they never talked about. She had never told him that she would have liked to keep something, a piece of furniture, a T-shirt, a poster for one of those obnoxious rock bands.

She had just let him throw everything away.

Mrs. Norris slowly closed her son's door, and walked down the hall. She paused briefly at the door to her husband's bedroom, but that door she didn't open. She hadn't opened it in the three years since his death.

When she entered her own small bedroom, she sat at her vanity table and pulled a small yellowing photograph from one of the drawers.

In the old drugstore Kodak print, her son showed a gap-toothed grin to the camera, holding a present from a Christmas forty-eight years gone. The glossy surface of the print had cracked in a line across Billy's six-year-old face. Mrs. Norris had kept it, because it was the only picture she had where her son was smiling.

Her hands shook, and she closed her eyes.

Justice Conroy was true to his word. He called someone in the Attorney General's office. Where her years of protests, documents, letters, and phone calls hadn't even resulted in the acknowledgment she existed, his inquiry got a response within days.

They called her and promised to send an investigator to accompany her to the next exhibit. A week later, he arrived at her house.

"Mrs. Norris?" The man said when she opened the door. "I am Agent Wilson from the State Bureau of Investigation. I understand that you have a complaint about your son's disposition?"

She looked at the agent, looking for some sign of emotion, of the enormity of what was happening. His tone infuriated her. It was the same bored monotone you got when you called the electric company. "Your call is very important to us."

My son is not important to you at all.

She forced herself to say, "Thank you for investigating."

I've only been trying to get you damn people to investigate this for three years—almost since the trial.

He nodded, and in the same distant telemarketer voice told her, "It's our job to investigate charges that the system is being abused. Unfortunately, we have limited resources."

"Sir, it is my *son* who's being abused."

"That's what I'm here to determine."

"You need to take him away from my granddaughter," she snapped. "The court never should have considered granting her custody."

The agent frowned. "Mrs. Norris, I am not here to review a court decision. I am here to determine if your son is being mistreated."

Mrs. Norris grunted. There certainly would be no question of that. For all the high-minded talk about allowing "victims" the "right" to their stories, Mrs. Norris knew that meant news, movies, books.

Stories—not the kind of obscenity her granddaughter created.

Mrs. Norris rode in the passenger seat next to Agent Wilson. She sat ramrod straight, every muscle tensed at the thought of meeting her granddaughter.

"Mrs. Norris," he said before he pulled away from the house. "I should tell you that I was against the idea of you accompanying me."

"This is my son."

"I understand your feelings. I've read the file, and your statements to the court. I've also read the restraining order against you, and several complaints—"

"Those were all dismissed," Mrs. Norris snapped. "She's been manipulating the system. Preventing me from even talking to my own son. Can you imagine?"

"Yes. Like I said, I read the file." He turned to look at her. "It was a very thick file."

For a few moments it almost seemed that he was staring at her as if *she* was the one who had done something wrong. Mrs. Norris steeled herself. He was just another bureaucratic functionary, annoyed that someone like her had the temerity to assert herself. "We should go, Agent Wilson."

Agent Wilson drove his car off the freeway, taking the off-ramp to one of the uglier parts of downtown. It was a place that Mrs. Norris would never have gone alone, full of dark buildings and dark people.

He pulled to a stop in front of the gallery. The building squatted in a nest of industrial detritus; warehouse shells and weed-shot lots of broken asphalt. The brick sides of the building were painted a glossy black that cast slimy reflections of the yellow streetlights. Her stomach tightened when she saw it.

The front was a massive glass wall, spilling the stark, surgical white light out into the street. Inside, people in expensive clothes were sipping red wine and eating shrimp impaled with toothpicks.

Mrs. Norris saw some pictures hanging, and she had to close her eyes and take a few deep breaths.

I can do this, I HAVE to do this.

Before she was ready, the passenger door opened and she almost fell in the gutter. She threw her hand out and grabbed the door, and looked up into Agent Wilson's face.

"Are you all right, Mrs. Norris?"

No! "I'm fine." She pulled herself up, out of the

car, and tried to assume some posture of dignity and self-control. *I will not cry, I will not scream. . . .*

A sign in the glass window told them that the exhibition was named "Daddy's Girl" and was running through the end of the month. The artist was "Sarah."

Just "Sarah." No family name.

"I told you there's no need for you to be here." Agent Wilson said in his quiet telemarketer voice. "It might be better if you waited in the car."

No need? Of course I need to be here.

Mrs. Norris stood a little straighter and smoothed out her coat. "Come on, and I will show you exactly what is happening to my son."

She marched into the gallery, leading Agent Wilson.

The first picture, the one to greet patrons as they walked through the doors, was titled "Self-Abuse." The black-and-white photo showed a middle-aged man in women's underwear, fishnet stockings, and high heels. He sat at an old-fashioned school desk, and he was carving a tight cross-hatched pattern in his naked forearm with a rusty razor blade.

She forced herself to turn away without shutting her eyes or breaking down. There were worse things. . . .

Like the image "Anticipation." The same man, naked, bound and gagged, spot-lit on a worktable; skin smeared with grease or blood, indistinguishable in the black-and-white image. A woman stands, back to the camera, holding a power drill whose large bit is only a blur to the camera.

Or "Impact I" where the man is bound to a chair being struck by someone who's little more than a blurred shadow. The camera catches the moment as the man's head snaps back, sweat flying, bloody drool sailing from his mangled mouth.

Or "Puppet IV" where chromed chains suspend the man from hooks embedded in the skin.

Around her, the gallery patrons nattered on, oblivious to the horror on the walls around them. Someone who could have been one of Justice Conroy's peers was saying something about how popular culture had always been informed by the criminal, deviant act, and how glad he was that a real artist had reclaimed that power. An effeminate man in sunglasses and a pinstripe jacket complained that so many "victims" spoiled an opportunity by turning their stories into tabloid junk, not enough of them thought to produce something of value. Some awful woman wondered aloud about how much of the pictures was her, how much was him.

She turned from picture to picture, from patron to patron, feeling her stomach tighten.

She finally turned to face Agent Wilson so she could focus on something other than her son's image. "You see? You see this? He's being beaten, sodomized, humiliated—"

"*No!*" a female voice came from across the gallery and Mrs. Norris froze. She could feel the bile rising, as she turned toward the voice.

"No, damn it! You can't be here. You. Heartless. Conniving. Bitch!" A wineglass shattered on the gallery floor as Mrs. Norris' granddaughter pushed her way through the crowd. Everyone backed away and stared at Mrs. Norris and Agent Wilson.

"Sarah," Mrs. Norris said, trying to be calm.

"Don't say it. Do not say my fucking name." Sarah whipped around and faced Agent Wilson. "Are you with this bitch? Because I have a restraining order against this woman. She can't be within two hundred yards of me or my father."

Sarah trembled. The black dress she wore looked as if it might burst into flame from suppressed rage. Agent Wilson stepped forward, pulling out his ID badge. "My name is Agent Wilson, from the State Bureau of Investigation."

Sarah didn't even deign to look at the man's badge. She stared into his face. "What pretense did she drag you here with?"

"She didn't drag me here. I'm investigating allegations of cruelty for the State Attorney General's office."

Sarah glared at Mrs. Norris. *"You!"*

"He's my son," she waved at the gallery. "What you're doing to him—"

"What *I'm* doing? *What I'm doing!"*

Agent Wilson stepped between them. "Please calm down, both of you." He looked at Sarah. "The courts gave you the right to produce work incorporating the defendant's image, but these portraits show activity that cross the line into abuse."

My God, thought Mrs. Norris, *does he ever use another tone of voice?*

"Sir, these are pictures," Sarah said. "They aren't real, they're staged, they're art."

Mrs. Norris couldn't help herself. "That is bullshit!"

"Sir," Sarah said to Agent Wilson, "You need to remove her, or I am going to call the judge."

Agent Wilson nodded. "I'll still have to talk to Mr. Norris."

A massive weight lifted from Mrs. Norris' shoulders. Finally, her son would be freed from this humiliation.

Like a wild animal, her granddaughter seemed to sense what she was feeling. She stared at Mrs. Norris even as she told Agent Wilson, "You want to talk to him? He's right over there." Sarah pointed across the gallery, and the crowd parted as if she was waving a gun.

Mrs. Norris sucked in a breath as she saw her son, sitting on a chair in the corner. Since the trial, she had only seen him in Sarah's sickening portraits. Here he was nothing more than a middle-aged man with gray hair and a wrinkled suit. He seemed shallower, smaller than the man she had known before his daughter's wicked accusations, smaller even than the man stripped bare in her granddaughter's photographs.

He was the only person who wasn't looking toward

the confrontation at the center of the gallery. There was no outward sign of his sentence, a life of little more than slavery at the hands of his accuser.

Agent Wilson looked at them both, and then walked over to the chair in the corner.

Please take him from this. . . .

"What gives you the right?" her granddaughter hissed. "What gives you the absolute *arrogance*?"

"That is my son up there."

"Your son? You never had a son." She leaned forward. "You don't care about him, you don't care about me. You only care about the fact that someone might know what was happening in your oh-so-neat little house."

"You're sick." Mrs. Norris' hands were shaking. "You can't do this to someone—"

Sarah's slap echoed through the gallery. The left side of Mrs. Norris' face was on fire. She could taste blood in her mouth, and her breath came in shuddering gasps.

"Sick?" Sarah whispered. She spoke slowly, as if talking to a child. "None of my art would have been possible without you."

Mrs. Norris stepped back, her composure shattered. Blood was dripping from her mouth, spattering on the floorboards. Red stained her blouse and skirt. She raised her hand to her cheek and only succeeded in smearing blood on her face and her hand.

Sarah was still spouting vile accusations, but Mrs. Norris just shook her head. When Agent Wilson walked back, Mrs. Norris turned to him. "Arrest her, she struck me. Everyone saw it."

Agent Wilson nodded and stepped between her and her granddaughter. "Calm down. Mrs. Norris. I can call the local police. Do you need an ambulance?"

"Calm down?" She was spraying blood on Agent Wilson's shirt now. "She hit me! Arrest her!"

Agent Wilson moved her back toward the doorway.

"I'm going to take you back to the car, and I can call the police so you can make a statement."

"Damn it! You are the police!"

"I don't have jurisdiction to—"

She pushed away from him and felt her back against the glass doorway of the gallery. She looked back in and saw the ring of people staring at her.

Not just the patrons, but her son. Still seated, he finally turned to face her with eyes as empty as the obscene pictures hanging everywhere here. The eyes bored into her throbbing, bleeding face.

"Forget it, then. It doesn't matter. My son—what about my son?"

"Mr. Norris says he is not being mistreated."

She didn't believe what she was hearing. "No—"

"He is only working as a model."

"The pictures! Look at the pictures!"

"—as long as no physical harm—"

"*Look at them!*"

Sarah stepped forward. "Go away, Grandmother."

"No! This is sick. It's evil!"

"And, God knows, you're an expert on the subject," Sarah spat back at her.

Mrs. Norris tried to push past Agent Wilson, but the man grabbed her arm. She looked at her son, begged with him, pleaded with him, "Tell them. Please, tell them. You're innocent. You never hurt anyone. It's all lies. Sick twisted lies. Tell Agent Wilson what she's doing to you is wrong."

Sarah shook her head and whispered, "Wrong? Only because the neighbors can see it."

Her son stayed mute and turned away from her.

"No, Billy!" Mrs. Norris cried, "Don't turn away from your mother—"

Agent Wilson pulled her toward the door. "You need to leave, Mrs. Norris." She tried to pull away from him, but he was too strong for her. The eyes of the patrons followed her, and she hated the pity she saw in them.

*   *   *

Damn court orders, and damn the Attorney General's office. What was she supposed to do? Just ignore what her son was going through? No one cared for a mother's duty anymore. First they arrest him and take him away, then they throw her out of her son's trial, then they stop her from confronting her granddaughter.

Now after three years, they finally investigate the treatment of her son, and all they do is a five-minute interview. Less. In front of the woman who held him prisoner with the blessing of the courts, the same person who accused him, kept him, humiliated him and her own family . . .

One word and he could end three years of being humiliated, publicly beaten, and raped . . .

But, if he couldn't speak or—and this was more likely—Agent Wilson couldn't listen, Mrs. Norris would have to save her son without government help. She had money, and she had property overseas. She could get him out of the country, and if she faced charges for it, she would bear it.

She was his mother, after all.

Mrs. Norris had money, which meant she could afford private investigators. And those private investigators provided her with a file detailing her granddaughter's movements, the layout of her suburban ranch, an illegally obtained copy of the front door key, and the security code for the alarm system.

Mrs. Norris pulled a rented van into her granddaughter's driveway at about eleven in the morning. She would be at some gallery or other today until at least six. By then, Mrs. Norris planned to be on a flight with her son, making their approach to Miami. A few hours after that, they should be out of the country.

Let Sarah deal with the bureaucracy of the legal system for once. Mrs. Norris smiled when she thought that she and her son might be in the Bahamas before her granddaughter even got the police to respond.

Mrs. Norris left the van carrying an oversized bag that contained a small, illegal, bricklike device that one of her private investigators had promised would burn out the GPS locator the court had implanted in her son's arm. It also contained a change of clothes in her son's size.

Also in the bag was a gun from the same private investigator. Mrs. Norris didn't want it, but she was scared that someone might resort to vigilantism. Her granddaughter made sure that the lies about Mrs. Norris' son were known far and wide. People believed her granddaughter's twisted stories, and her son might not be safe.

I just have to get him to the airport. Then I can get rid of the gun.

The key worked in the front door and Mrs. Norris stepped inside, quickly keying the security code into the panel by the door. She smiled when the panel beeped a green light and flashed "DISARMED" at her. Her heart raced, and her breath was shallow.

She slowly walked into the darkened house. She stared at the carpet to avoid looking at the pictures on the wall. Her son's eyes looked at her, pleading from a dozen different frames. No other pictures, no other decoration of any kind, just the photos.

In the back, at the end of a long dark hallway, there was a bedroom whose door was locked with a dead bolt from the outside. Mrs. Norris stood in front of the door for several minutes, unable to move. She listened, and could hear breathing and movement from the other side of the door.

Mrs. Norris reached up and turned the bolt.

"Sarah?" Her son's voice came from the room beyond.

The door swung open and Mrs. Norris faced her son. There was nothing in the room. A bare bulb, a bare floor, the whole thing painted a stark white, including the window. A single twin mattress rested on a metal frame. Her son sat on the edge of the bed, dressed only in boxer shorts.

"It's your mother." Mrs. Norris said. "I've come for you."

He shook his head. "You aren't supposed to be here."

"We have to go; I can get you out of the country." She started pulling clothes out of her bag: sneakers, socks, blue jeans.

"You need to stop this."

Mrs. Norris nodded vigorously. "Yes, yes. I'm putting an end to this obscenity—"

He grabbed her arm, violently. She jerked, dropping the bag and spilling its contents on the floor: shirt, GPS-brick, tickets, gun. . . .

"No, Mom, you have to stop what *you're* doing. Now!"

Her son stared at her with a hard, unyielding expression that didn't come from the child she knew. His eyes did not belong to her quiet, well-mannered son. These were the eyes from her granddaughter's photographs.

"Let me go," she whispered.

"You have to leave. It is long past time for you to do anything."

She reached up and touched the side of his face. "You're my son. I can't let you be tortured like this."

"Bullshit!" He shoved her away and Mrs. Norris stumbled, swinging her arms for balance. Her foot found the GPS brick and her legs slipped out from under her. She landed on the ground, bruising her backside. She stared up at her son, who rose to his feet in front of her. "You can't let me be tortured like this? Where the fuck were you forty years ago, Mom? When Dad had those long talks with me?"

"Please, I need to—"

"You need to what? Keep the family problems in the family? Don't talk about it, and we don't have to deal with it? Deny anything ever happened? Well, it happened, and you *knew* it happened."

"No, you don't understand. He was such a private man and he tried so hard to be close. He just didn't know the right way—"

He turned around and slammed his fist into the wall. The sound of the plaster giving way was like breaking bone. The light above them rattled a little with the impact. "Good lord, do you even know what you're saying? I think you might be worse than he was. At least he had the decency to kill himself—"

"It was the trial; he couldn't see you go though that—"

He turned around, teeth bared and lips pulled back in a feral expression. The cords stood out on his neck, and he was flushed from the waist up. "No. He was just afraid that his little secret would come out during testimony. Just like you, Mom. The only inexcusable sin is getting caught. Can't air the dirty laundry in public. How could he face his buddies at the golf club?"

"Stop it!"

He was circling around her, trembling as if he was about to explode. Mrs. Norris scooted around, so she could keep facing him. Her pulse was throbbing in her temples, and she tasted copper in her mouth. She had to stop moving when her back pressed against the bed frame.

"The truth hurts, doesn't it?"

"You don't understand—"

"What's to fucking understand?" He leaned down and screamed in her face. "Jesus Christ, it's so simple. My father—your husband—raped me, once a week, for nearly ten years. I tried to tell you, but you just shut down. So, guess what, when I have a kid, I rape her. I *rape* her! And you know why? Because I don't have the balls to do what she did. Because I was weak. Because I was like you."

She couldn't look at him anymore. She screwed her eyes shut. "Stop it!"

"What would you have done? If I did what Sarah did, if I called the cops on him? Would you have been so anxious to save me then? Or would you be more concerned about your old biddy friends gossiping about your child-molester husband?"

"Stop it!" Something was painfully digging into her thigh. She grabbed it. It was the gun.

"I know what you would have done, Mom. You would have thrown me aside, just like your grand-daughter."

It began to dawn on her that this wasn't her son anymore. Her grip tightened on the gun.

The photograph is called "Voluntary Manslaughter."

The photo is set in a richly decorated living room, in front of a sleek Frank Lloyd Wright fireplace above which are several family portraits of people smiling from behind glass and stainless steel frames. In front of the fireplace, an elderly woman wears a vintage formal dress from the early 1960s, something Jackie Kennedy would have worn. The outfit includes a pill-box hat, pearls, white gloves, and is a light coffee color in the sepia print. The blood spatters are a deep brown in contrast. The woman straddles the naked, bleeding corpse of a middle-aged man. A small trail of smoke rolls from the revolver in her hand.

The picture is the centerpiece of Sarah's new exhibition.

OUR FLAG WAS STILL THERE

by Steven Mohan, Jr.

Steve Mohan lives in Pueblo, Colorado with his wife and
three children and, surprisingly, no cats. When not writing
he works as a manufacturing engineer. His fiction has appeared in *Interzone, Polyphony,* and *Paradox,* among other
places. His short stories have won honorable mention in
The Year's Best Science Fiction and *The Year's Best Fantasy
and Horror.*

HUNDREDS OF DISPLACED people filled the
streets, people too poor to live anywhere else,
shoved up against the line of riot cops holding Lincoln
Boulevard. The very same cops that had just cleared
them from their homes. The crowd crackled with
anger and confusion and something else. FBI Special
Agent Jason Xia sensed it as he and his partner
pushed their way through the mob.

Fear.

Xia inhaled the thick, greasy smell of it, mostly
sweat with just a trace of something else underneath:
the coppery scent of blood. They were afraid—the citizens, the reporters, hell, even the cops.

And really, who could blame them?

Not Xia.

He was afraid, too.

His partner asked, "Was this what you had in mind, Xia?" (He pronounced it "Shaw.")

Xia glanced back. Darius Jefferson was a small man with caramel skin, his skull shaved smooth. Today he was turned out in a charcoal Armani and a red silk tie. If things went bad, DJ was going to get stuck with one hell of a dry-cleaning bill.

Xia's gaze caught on a face in the crowd. The man was thoroughly nondescript: receding hairline, watery blue eyes framed by simple glasses, round face, dark blue jacket over a light blue shirt.

Except something was wrong.

The man was staring intently at him. Unlike everyone else, he wasn't shouting or cursing.

Just staring.

Xia met his gaze.

If the man had looked away, Xia would have had him picked up right there, but instead he broke into a goofy smile and flashed Xia a thumbs up. So the vultures were starting to turn out to see what all the fuss was about.

Great.

"Damn it," Xia muttered.

About that time, the reporters put two and two together and figured out who was in charge. They started shouting questions, snapping pix.

"Bloody parasites," snarled DJ.

"A free press is the cornerstone of a free society," said Xia.

"Says the man who suspended the First Amendment forty minutes ago," muttered DJ.

Xia shook his head. The terrorists, whoever they were, wanted coverage. Which meant he had to deny it. The warrant granted him broad emergency powers and Xia intended to use them.

An LAPD captain stepped toward them. "We buttoned up the press and cleared out the citizens. What's next?"

"We'll take it from here, Captain," said Xia.

DJ rolled his eyes, but said nothing. He and Xia stepped through the sonic curtain the LAPD had put up and the crowd noise shut off like someone had thrown a switch. They walked west down Wilshire, their footsteps echoing in the sudden silence.

Xia hated the New Waterfront district, a shadowy concrete canyon empty of motion and sound, save for the constant whisper of the sea lapping against asphalt.

It reminded Xia of Shanghai in '58, before his father got the family out.

DJ said, "And by the way, what's this 'We'll take if from here' crap?"

"Darius," said Xia, "something very bad is going to happen here. Would you like it to happen to just us, or would you like to take out a couple dozen cops, too?"

"Well, *Jason*," said DJ, "I'm going to have to go with option (c): None of the above."

Xia sighed, but didn't answer. DJ didn't really need an answer. He was just talking because he was nervous.

"So what do you think this is?" said DJ after a moment. "Dirty bomb? Bioagent? Nanoplague?"

"Don't know. All the oracle said was that someone was driving lots of media toward this part of the city."

"Someone wants a show," said DJ.

Xia shrugged.

"Think it could be a full nuke?"

"I don't know, DJ. Do you think a full nuke will kill us any more dead than the other things you mentioned?"

"No," DJ admitted.

"Well, then?"

LAPD had thoughtfully tied a silver Zodiac to a streetlamp down where the ocean met the sloping surface of Wilshire. Xia untied the boat and the two men pushed it into the water and jumped in, drifting down the street.

DJ handed him an oar. " Go in quiet?"

"Might as well," said Xia

They drifted out of the shadow of a parking garage and the sun came out bright and beautiful, illuminating Santa Monica's bleached concrete bones. Xia glanced over the boat's side. The green water was glass; he could see fire hydrants and stop signs, empty dumpsters and rusting manhole covers.

A round stingray gliding over the zebra stripes of a crosswalk.

"Whatever it is," said DJ, "it's got to be dangerous."

"Yes," said Xia, and then he dipped his oar into the water, spawning ripples that obscured the world beneath.

The first thing Senator Callie Cook noticed when she woke was that she had a skull-splitting headache, like someone had detonated a high-yield nuclear device in her sinus cavity.

The second thing she noticed was that she was naked.

She was lying on a cold steel table, a sheet draped over her body. She sat up quickly, carefully clutching the sheet.

Where the hell am I?

She heard an intermittent buzzing, like someone's alarm clock going off, muffled and distant.

The room was big, its fixtures empty of fluorescent bulbs. Sunshine filtering through a picture window on the other side of the room provided the only light. The room was painted flat white, and, except for the table that was *freezing* her bottom, absolutely empty.

So, no sign of her clothes.

There was, however, a door.

And wasn't that just great? The first paparazzo through that door was once and for all going to put an end to the nasty rumors about her natural hair color.

Not that she was ashamed of her body. She spent an hour a day on the Stairmaster, and she looked pretty good for 43. She'd put herself up against any woman five years her junior.

On a good day, ten.

But a photo of her naked self splashed across the tabloids would undoubtedly cost her fifteen points in the Midwest. (Though she certainly would make inroads with male voters, 18 to 34.)

She shook her head. No. This was one time she definitely couldn't afford the exposure.

And where was the Secret Service, by the way? Bill Mercer had better hope she hadn't been kidnapped, because if she *had*, her campaign was going to go up with thirty-second spots in twenty states. Let him explain how the Secret Service had lost track of a presidential candidate on his watch. A clever smile tightened her pretty face. Yes, that had real possibilities.

She hopped off the table and wrapped the sheet securely around herself. Either way, it was time to go.

Just then the door flew open.

Two men burst into the room, weapons drawn. One of them was Asian, big and athletic, good looking in an obvious sort of way, wearing a dark, off-the-rack suit that screamed G-man. The other man was African American and dressed like a male model.

"Federal Agents," shouted the hunk.

"Really, it's about time," said Callie, placing a hand on her hip and arching one delicate blonde eyebrow.

"My God," he breathed.

"What is it, Xia?" asked the other man.

"Don't you know who this is?" said the first man (Shaw?) incredulously. "You should've paid more attention in history."

History! Cook thought indignantly.

He turned to stare at her. "This is *Callie Cook*."

"Who did you *think* it was going to be?" snapped Cook.

"That's impossible," said the dapper agent. "Didn't she disappear back in the Thirties?"

"*Back,*" echoed Cook, "in the Thirties?"

"No wonder they wanted media," breathed the hunk.

"*Hey,*" snapped Cook. "Do you two geniuses think you can tell me what's going on? And can you turn off that buzzing? My head is killing me."

The two men exchanged startled looks.

"Sounds like a countdown," said Hunk.

"Think someone might have a backup plan in case we shut down their media?" Dapper asked.

Hunk jerked his arm up and fired at the window, the roar of his gun mingling with the music of breaking glass.

Then he was running.

He hit her like a middle linebacker, hard enough to knock the wind out of her. So she didn't notice he'd picked her up until they were through the window, plummeting toward green water impossibly far below, her scream lingering in the air until it was drowned out by the voice of God and the world was suddenly filled with molten orange fire and concrete rain.

In the end, the explosion worked for them, soaking up all the bandwidth the newsies, the carrion net-shows, and the xtreme sports channels could throw at it. Which meant no one had time to notice two FBI agents smuggling a dazed woman out of Santa Monica.

Xia could've shut the media down, but this was so much better. The chattering classes were like children. Tell them "no," and they'd want to know the secret just that much more. This way they thought they already had the story.

The senator needed medical attention. Hell, she needed *clothes.* Xia commandeered a supply tent in the command post the LA Field Office had set up in a small park just off the waterfront so Cook could have a little privacy. He had a Doc-in-a-Box checking her over and a female agent fetching some clothes.

Now there was nothing to do but wait.

"Can it really be her?" asked DJ in a low voice. It seemed to be his day to ask pointless questions.

Xia frowned. "No. It's impossible."

"You're right," said DJ. And then, "But what if it is?"

That thought scared Xia. *What if it is?*

For fifty years people had wondered why the woman who was going to be the next president of the United States had disappeared in the middle of the 2032 campaign. Now, suddenly, she was back, no older than the day she disappeared.

The answer to the greatest disappearance since Amelia Earhart had just dropped in his lap.

As answers went, it wasn't very satisfying.

"Why would the terrorists want her here?" asked Xia.

"Well, she'll attract a firestorm of media," said DJ. "Maybe they expect her to speak out on a certain issue."

"Yeah, but what? And how'd they know where to find her?"

"Maybe they took her in the first place," said DJ.

"Fifty years ago?" Xia shook his head. "Half the terrorist groups weren't around *five* years ago."

"I don't know," admitted DJ.

"I don't know either," said Xia. "But until we figure it out, we keep her under wraps. Somehow, she's the key."

"Hey," said DJ, "you know who might have the answer?"

Xia's stomach constricted. "No."

"Grace," DJ said enthusiastically.

"No."

"I don't know what you have against her," said DJ.

"Absolutely not," said Xia.

"Because she's sure sweet on you." DJ flashed him a wicked grin.

Somehow the stolid Xia had managed to figure out she needed to relax after her sudden explosive entry into the year 2083, so he stuck her in a small, dark tent and loosed a skittering horror.

Yeah, real relaxing.

The horror was a spider-thing the size of a man's fist. It crawled across her skin, measuring, checking, and *injecting, which felt just like a real spider bite.*

Cook shuddered.

She could hear two agents talking outside. She didn't know what to think of them. Xia had saved her life, which was a point in his favor, but then he'd left her in the care of the spider-thing, so that pretty much brought him back to even.

She heard a grunting sound, and a man with a tent stake in his right hand rolled under the bottom of the tent. He wore a dark blue jacket over a light blue shirt, a dark blue ball cap pulled down over his face. He looked like an EMT, which explained his presence, if not his unorthodox method of entry.

"Madam Senator Cook," he said.

He had the kind of voice that promised an instant cure for insomnia. Any young child asked to draw him would've depicted his face as a circle with glasses without robbing the real face of any of its subtlety. Cook supposed she should be afraid of this strange man who stood in her tent with a stake in his hand, but looking at him, she just couldn't manage it.

"You're not an EMT, are you?" she said.

"Don't trust Xia and Jackson," he said. "I know they're FBI, but they're not *your* FBI."

"Who are you?"

"In fact, I recommend you don't take sides on any issue until you understand this world better."

Cook was beginning to wonder if the man could even hear her. "Look—"

"You're wondering what you're doing fifty years in the future." He had an accent, but she couldn't quite place it. Wisconsin? No. More like Minnesota.

No, that wasn't right either.

The man flashed her a bland smile. "You can thank Gregory Tamerind."

"The software mogul?" Cook couldn't keep the astonishment out of her voice.

"I have it on good authority that he kidnapped you and froze you like a popsicle."

"And you work for him?"

The man laughed softly. "No one works for him. Gregory Tamerind died three years ago—which is why all his treasures suddenly found their way to the free market."

"So you're actually *telling me* that Gregory Tamerind, the richest man in the history of humanity, put together a museum of the bizarre and I was the star attraction?"

"Is it so surprising he'd want the most astonishing American politician since Lincoln?"

Cook opened her mouth and then closed it again. She didn't know what to say to *that*. She'd always been sure of herself. But *Lincoln*?

"Come on, after all you accomplished, you never thought of yourself that way?" The man chuckled. "Oh, you're going to be perfect."

"What do you want with me?" Cook snapped.

But the man just smiled blandly and left the same way he'd come in.

It was the flag that finally convinced her. Even more than the abomination the agents called an oracle or the creepy spider-thing, it was the flag that convinced her she'd somehow arrived fifty years in the future.

After she'd been examined and had a chance to dress, they took her to the Roybal Federal Building on Temple. Outside, there was a flagpole.

She heard the crisp snap of the flag in the wind and looked up and there it was, Old Glory. The red, white, and blue. It almost seemed to glow in the sun. She felt a sudden rush of warmth. If that was the flag, then this was still America. Still *home.*

And then she realized something was wrong. *What was it?*

Same red and white stripes, same blue field, same—

It was the stars. There were fifty-four stars. She counted.

Six times.

Fifty-*four.*

She pointed at the flag. "What are the other two?"

Xia frowned. "I'm sorry?"

"Two of the new states must be Columbia and Puerto Rico. What are the other two?"

"Oh. No." Xia shook his head. "Puerto Rico declared independence in 2043. And Washington . . ." His voice trailed off, heavy with grief.

Cook's stomach lurched. "Then . . . ?"

"Oh, ah, BC, Saskatchewan, Manitoba, and Alberta. After Quebec seceded and it looked like Canada was going to fall apart, the western provinces petitioned to be admitted to the U.S."

And that's when Cook understood she'd been transported to an alien world, a world invisible from her native land.

Her knees buckled, but Xia caught her before she went down.

When she came to, Xia was staring down at her, a look of concern on his handsome face. His eyes were a pretty gray-green.

"I'm okay," Cook croaked.

He helped her sit up. "You sure?"

"Water," she croaked. "Could I have some water?"

"We can get you milk," said DJ. "Or orange juice." He paused. "Vodka?"

"Water's fine," said Cook.

"I'm sorry," said DJ. "I can't—"

"Water's expensive," said Xia, studying her closely.

Cook sighed. "Tell me. I promise I won't faint."

Xia drew a deep breath. "Climate change means less average rainfall, coastal marshes are wiped out by the rising sea, increased evaporation leads to—"

"Less water," said DJ.

Xia nodded. "We value water like people of your time valued gold." He paused. "Or reality shows."

"And the Canucks just cut our access to the northern ice," said DJ bitterly.

"So we can't afford to get you a glass of water," said Xia. "Not on a federal salary. But if you'd like—"

"Vodka," said Cook. "I'll take the vodka."

"Not a bad choice," said DJ, "seeing as how we're going to see an oracle."

"Maybe I'll have one, too," muttered Xia.

In his fourteen years with the FBI, Xia had seen many strange and unsettling things, but there was nothing he hated more than consulting an oracle.

And this one was worse than most.

Which was why Xia was very careful to look anywhere but at the thing in the chair.

He listened to the dull rattle of the respirator, smelled the curious mix of menthol and ammonia and PVC, watched the blinking lights on the matte-black servers stacked in neat columns around the room like replicas of Stonehenge.

Anything to avoid looking at *her*.

"It all matches: DNA, prints, retinas, anthropometrics," said the voxbox in a sweet voice with just enough smoke in it to make it sexy as hell.

Xia shivered.

"So this is the real Callie Cook?" said DJ.

"Of *course* I'm the real Callie Cook," said Callie Cook.

"It's a distinct possibility," said the oracle.

"You don't remember your disappearance in 2032?" asked Xia, carefully studying the texture of the paint on the wall.

"No," said Cook. "One minute I'm on a five-state

swing through New England and the next I wake up in LA."

"The Greater LA Reconstruction District," corrected DJ gently.

Xia frowned. There was something in Cook's voice. Was she hiding something?

"The med scan did show signs of cryogenic preservation," intoned the oracle.

"We can't figure out how terrorists expect to use her," said DJ. "Can you help us, Grace?"

"Maybe if Jason asks real nice," she said. My God, Xia thought, was that a note of *playfulness* in her voice?

Without meaning to, Xia looked at the thing in the chair.

Most oracles paid their maintenance staff to surround them with human touches—potted plants, throw rugs, family pix—all to make their clients comfortable. Some of the higher functioning oracles could even unplug and pass for human standard.

Not Grace.

Grace (no last name, of course—Grace was a rock star) lay in a reclining chair that attended to all her body's complicated needs, her eyes replaced by silver orbs of beryllium to emphasize her blindness, a tangle of black-insulated fibers snaking out of the back of her head.

The thing was, she'd been beautiful once. If you could get past the shaved head, the faded hospital gown, and the medical equipment piercing her body in a dozen places, she was beautiful *still*.

Somehow that made it worse.

DJ hit him on the shoulder. *Say something,* he mouthed.

Stop it, Xia mouthed back.

DJ flashed him his *You're being an asshole* look.

Xia just shrugged.

DJ fumed for a second then he turned to look at

the thing in the chair. "You know, Grace, I've often wondered if Xia here would make a good oracle."

Xia opened his mouth. "I—"

"Really?" she said and Xia was horrified to hear a note of enthusiasm in her voice.

"Sure," said DJ smoothly, "I mean, he already thinks he knows everything."

She *laughed.*

Xia tried again. "I really don't think—"

"I promise you wouldn't miss your body, Jason. Sex is mostly mental, you know. And when you're wired in, your consciousness stretches across the whole web. A hooked-up hookup is the best."

Cook was staring at him with eyes the size of dinner plates.

"But—" said Xia.

"Men are such big babies," said Grace scornfully. "Always worrying about never again using their—"

"All right, that's *enough*," barked Xia.

"I could show you," Grace said, her voice suddenly shy.

Xia flashed his partner a panicked look.

DJ just shrugged.

"Look," said Xia in a desperate attempt to regain control of the conversation, "We just need to know the connection between Cook and the terrorists."

"All business, huh?" said Grace. (Did she sound hurt?) "I don't think we'll find a link. Most of today's political issues would've been unimaginable in the Thirties. Cook's sympathies could scarcely be predictable."

"Maybe an ultraconservative group," said Xia.

"Hey," said Cook, "I'm a *Progressive* Conservative."

The oracle snorted. "Maybe fifty years ago."

"Come on, Grace," said DJ.

Grace sighed. "Okay. Callie Cook was the leader of a centrist third party known as the Progressive Conservatives. She was known for forging broad coalitions to resolve seemingly intractable problems. She pushed through the first national civil union legislation—"

"One of my personal favorites," intoned DJ.

"She sponsored automated national security warrants, providing law enforcement with realtime decisions while simultaneously hard coding civil liberty protections. She married tough carbon limits to safe nuclear power. Authored the immigration deal of '28."

Xia shook his head. "So she's a master at the grand compromise Not exactly the kind of person who'd be a natural ally to terrorists."

"That's what I've been saying," snapped Cook.

"She's a dead end," said Grace.

"Hey, I'm right here," said Cook.

"But," said DJ hopefully.

"But," said Grace, "the hotel in Santa Monica wasn't. A sniffer on I-5 detected a chemical marker matching the explosive that went boom down on Ocean Avenue. I checked the surveillance pix and narrowed down 23 target vehicles to a single robodelivery truck."

"Let me guess," said Xia. "It serves a habitat."

"See," said Grace brightly, "you already think like an oracle."

"We're going to need a warrant," said DJ.

"Already processing," said the thing in the chair.

Xia glanced at the blinking servers that made up Grace's distributed mind. Somewhere in there she was translating the pattern she'd detected into a standard law enforcement protocol and feeding it to a Judicial AI.

"Warrant downloading," she said after a few seconds.

"Thank you, Grace," said DJ. "You're beautiful."

Xia was already halfway out the door, but as it turned out, he wasn't fast enough.

"Don't be a stranger, Jason," the thing in the chair

called after him. "Come back and we'll have a good time. I *promise.*"

What surprised Cook most about the maglev was its absolute silence. They were traveling across the countryside at better than 200 kph (apparently the U.S. had gone metric in '42), and there was absolutely no noise.

Well, except for Xia and DJ's bickering.

DJ studied the warrant scrolling across the screen of his handheld. "Man, your girlfriend does nice work."

"She's. Not. My. Girlfriend."

"I don't know why you have to be such a jerk. Just because she's a little wrapped up in her work."

"Wrapped up in her work? She's not even human."

"Yeah? Well, what the hell is she, then?"

"Post-human."

DJ snorted. "That's a slogan, not an answer. Look, she's lonely. She doesn't have anything but her career. Would it kill you to be civil?"

"Hey," said Cook. "Someone want to tell me what a habitat is?"

Xia and DJ glared at each other for a moment, then Xia turned away.

"America in the Fifties was a mess," said DJ. "Four impeachments, domestic terrorism, riots, and *then* food and water started to disappear. Americans just couldn't get along." He shook his head. "So many people trapped in a world they didn't understand, that they couldn't believe in."

A dark chill wriggled down Cook's spine. "What did you do?" she whispered.

"Nothing monstrous," said DJ. "We simply found a way for splinter groups to live by their own rules without affecting the rest of society."

"In the habitats," said Cook.

"That's right," said DJ.

"You put people in camps."

Xia shook his head. "They're not *camps*," he said

sharply. "Only two rules apply in the habitats. One, no violence. Two, all adults are free to leave. Other than that, anything goes."

"Sounds lovely," said Cook.

"It's perfect for the delusional," said DJ. "There's a habitat in Cape Gerardo for people who *still* don't believe in global warming, one in Kansas for creationists, Black Separatists in Watts, Neo-Nazis in Idaho. There's even a habitat where the Cubs always win the series."

Cook snorted. "Everyone but Islamofascists."

"Sunnis in Detroit, Shiites in Memphis," said DJ.

Cook blinked. "How is this all possible?"

"You'll see," said Xia darkly, without turning.

Cook shook her head. "So instead of finding a way to live together, everyone went to their separate corners." She suddenly felt hollow. "And you say that's not monstrous."

"The violence, the hatred . . ." DJ shook his head. "This was the only way."

Cook thought about that. A cancer eating away at the body politic. *How did we turn into the Balkans?* And then she remembered what the not-EMT had said: "Don't trust Xia and Jackson. They're FBI, but not your FBI."

She glanced at DJ. "Which habitat are we going to?"

Xia turned, his face hard. "Dixie," he said grimly.

It was like walking through a morgue. Rows upon rows of lifeless bodies, only here the dead dreamed. The people wore black body suits, their hands covered by gloves, their heads swallowed by helmets that leaked a tiny circle of blue light at the neck.

There was something wrong, but Cook couldn't quite put her finger on it.

"Why are they . . . ?" Her voice trailed off.

"Those are VR inputs," said DJ. "Their muscles are

electrically stimulated and they're nourished by feeding tubes. The whole system is regulated by an AI."

Something was still wrong, but she couldn't see it in the general weirdness.

She shook her head. "It can't possibly feel real."

"Well, you're going to see," said Xia, tossing her a helmet.

And then it hit her. She'd missed it at first because the people's hands and faces were hidden, but she could see their necks.

They were white.

All of them.

She put on the gloves and the bodysuit and the helmet, the system jolted her and suddenly she was walking across a green meadow, toward a forest of dogwood and ash, black walnut and white pine, the two fibbies beside her.

The soft grass tickled her bare feet. The air was warm and humid, perfumed with the scent of blueberry and azaleas and wild rose. It was like being in a bath. Somewhere in the distance she heard the rattle of a woodpecker, the cheerful whistle of cicadas.

She thought she might be in paradise.

Until she saw the line of men on horseback, dressed in white robes and hoods, leading an African American toward a tall, lonely sycamore.

The prisoner was dark-skinned and big, maybe six-two. He was stripped to the waist, his muscular body glistening with sweat.

Hands bound behind him.

"What are they doing?" Cook whispered fiercely.

"You cannot interfere," said Xia, his voice hard.

"Nonviolence," she snapped. "I thought you said one of the rules was nonviolence."

"Callie," said DJ soothingly, "It's not real." He inclined his head toward the prisoner. *"He's* not real."

"Do you think I'm a fool?" she snapped. "Who

would go to the trouble of lynching an imaginary black man?"

And then she saw them. Half-hidden in the forest, a pair of boys, aged eight or nine.

Suddenly she understood.

She darted forward. *"Stop it,"* she shouted. *"STOP."*

Xia ran after her. *"Callie."*

She was sprinting now. *"Stop. This is murder."*

One of the riders broke away from the main group and came galloping toward her. "You are not allowed here, madam," he bellowed.

"We have a warrant," said DJ from behind her.

"Stop, you bastards," Cook shouted.

"Why, you're Callie Cook," said the man, amusement suddenly in his voice. He pulled off his hood, revealing a hard, tanned face. He had a thick black beard with tufts of hair behind prominent ears and baldness working its way around his head, leaving an island of hair on top. And the eyes. Brilliant and cruel at the same time. "Nathan Bedford Forrest, at your service, ma'am," said the apparition on the horse.

And it *was.* Nathan Bedford Forrest. The Confederate general, founder of the Klan, and vicious racist. It *was.* "I suppose you're going to tell me he's not real either," snapped Cook.

"No, he's real," said DJ. "He just isn't what he seems. This is the AI that runs Dixie."

Forrest nodded at Cook. "I am charmed, Senator." His glittering black eyes marked DJ and Xia. "As for you two," he growled, "you are welcome to leave at your earliest possible convenience."

"We have a warrant," said Xia coldly.

"Very well," said Forrest tautly.

"Someone blew up a building," said DJ.

"That is shocking," said Forrest mildly.

Behind him, his men had set the black man on a

horse and tossed a rope over one of the sycamore's branches.

"We have evidence Dixie was involved," said DJ.

"You are wrong, sir."

"Whoever set the explosion also wanted to give a platform to Senator Cook and her outmoded ideas," said Xia darkly.

Forrest raised an eyebrow. "Outmoded ideas? When you say it like that, it sounds like we should be allies." He peered at Cook for a moment, stroking his black beard. "You're against the habitats, aren't you?" He looked at Xia. "And you think I'm working with whoever revived *her?*" Do you think we want to destroy the habitats? Do you think we want to come live with *you?* Someone has sent you on a wild goose chase, sir. And you blue-bellies are too dull-witted to see it."

Forrest pulled back on his reins and his horse reared. He turned around and went galloping back toward his party. Forrest let out a terrible howl and one of the Klansmen slapped the flank of the black man's horse.

Callie Cook had once run for the office of president of the United States and she was tough. So she didn't flinch from the horrible sight.

Neither did the two boys.

After it was over, Xia turned to her, something like shame on his face. "I'm sorry you had to see that."

"That's the difference between us," she said coldly. "I'm sorry it had to happen at all."

"No one was hurt," said DJ gently.

"You're wrong," said Cook. "The *boys* were hurt." She turned and glared at Xia. "And *you* were party to it."

"Hatred is a disease, Senator," said Xia angrily. "We've contained a deadly contagion. What it does to the people of Dixie is not my concern."

DJ shook his head. "What if Forrest was right?"

"Forrest wasn't right about anything," said Cook savagely.

DJ met her gaze. "He might have been right about this being a wild goose chase."

"All right," said Xia, "But that just leads us back to the beginning. Who's behind it all?"

Cook looked from one man to the other. *Don't trust Xia and Jackson.* The man who'd told her that had been trying to manipulate her. There were few things that pissed Cook off more.

She wasn't sure she trusted the two fibbies and she was damn sure she didn't *agree* with them, but they were Americans. You didn't turn against your fellow citizens just because you disagreed with them. Wasn't that her whole point?

She drew a deep breath.

"I might know," she said.

Xia stole a peek at the incomplete portrait hanging over Grace's prone body. Round head. Dull eyes. Glasses. Not much to go on.

Still . . .

"No," said Cook, interrupting his train of thought. "That's not quite right."

"What's the problem?" asked Grace.

"The eyes weren't quite that, ah, distinctive."

Grace sighed.

DJ shook her head. "It's not her fault the terrorists picked an average-looking guy."

Xia stared at the bland face. There was something—

"Uh-oh," murmured Grace.

"What now?" said DJ.

"I've been monitoring the web and—" Grace sighed. "You'd better see for yourself."

Suddenly a window opened in midair, opposite the face. It framed a beautiful African-American woman in a smart blue pinstripe suit. "Hello, this is Kendra Zaïre of CNNFox with a news alert."

The reporter disappeared, replaced by a photo of Cook, eyes closed, wrapped in a white sheet. "At this hour our sources are reporting the FBI has located Callie Cook, solving the most extraordinary missing person case in American history."

"Shit," said Xia.

"The senator's recovery seems to be tied to a dramatic explosion in Santa Monica." The window showed a hotel transforming itself into a pillar of molten orange fire as he leaped from a fifth-story window, the senator in his arms and DJ right behind.

"And twenty minutes ago we received this dramatic clip."

Now the window showed Cook sitting in a tent, still wrapped in the sheet. "So you're actually *telling me* that Gregory Tamerind, the richest man in the history of humanity, put together a museum of the bizarre and I was the star attraction?"

"This clip seems to suggest that Gregory Tamerind, the eccentric software pioneer who was the world's first trillionaire before he died three years ago, was somehow involved in the senator's abduction. What exactly does it all mean?" Miss Zaïre flashed a winning smile. "We here at CNNFox are working around the clock to—"

The window disappeared.

"We're screwed, aren't we?" breathed DJ.

Xia slowly exhaled. And then he glanced at the face. "Wait a minute," he said. "I've *seen* this guy."

The man named Cliff Vander Hosen sat on a plain wooden bench along the dirt path and closed his eyes, obviously enjoying the shade of the cedars and coastal redwoods, the smell of wild grass. Dappled sunlight mottled his bland face. There was no sound but the gentle music of finches and sparrows and the flapping of an American flag on a pole just visible across the open field that bordered the path.

"I'm guessing you're not really the consulate's Business Development Officer," said Xia, sitting down next to the man.

"Indeed, I am," said Vander Hosen. "Right down to my diplomatic immunity."

DJ stepped out from behind a tree, his Beretta nine mil out and leveled at the man's chest. Cook trailed behind.

"You never should have shown up in Santa Monica," said Xia. "We compared your image from the crowd photos to the federal database of registered foreign nationals."

The man shrugged. "No choice. I had to get close enough to her to talk."

"Now I recognize that accent," Cook said. "You're Canadian."

"Bravo, dear." He opened his watery eyes and looked at her. "Good to see you again."

"Why?" asked DJ.

The man chuckled. "Oh, surely you can figure that out." He extended a hand toward Cook. "Just look at her: Beautiful. Smart. Mysterious. And wait until we leak the Dixie clip. Here only twenty-four hours and she's already a major political force." He sat back, a smug smile stretched across his round face. "She's going to turn your world upside down."

"You think she'll speak out against the habitats," said Xia.

"And people will listen," said Vander Hosen.

"My God," breathed DJ, "it'll be the Fifties all over again."

"Yes," said the man. "And perhaps our brothers in the western provinces will realize the mistake they made."

Xia's fists clenched. "It won't work."

The man looked up, drew a deep breath. "I love Griffith Park." He turned to face Xia. "But it's not home. I was born in Vancouver," he snarled. "Do you know what it's like, Agent Xia? I am a patriot—and so I can never go home."

"And you think this will fix it," said Xia.

"Of course it will," said the man. "Callie Cook is a tireless warrior for justice. Problem is, warriors for justice cause turmoil. Look at your own history if you don't believe me. John Brown struck against slavery, and you ended up in a civil war. Martin Luther King fought for equality, and LA burned. Storm clouds are coming, my friends."

"Is she even the real Callie Cook?" asked DJ.

"How can you even ask?" asked Vander Hosen. "Your own DNA tests—"

"Couldn't distinguish between a clone and the real article," snapped DJ.

Vander Hosen looked at him for a long moment and then he smiled brightly. "Well, who knows really? Was Anna Anderson really Anastasia? Who cares. But go ahead and make your claim. It will just make her a more compelling figure. We can't lose."

"Yes, you can," said Xia. He swallowed and turned to look at Cook. "If she doesn't say anything about the habitats."

Cook opened her mouth and then closed it. "Xia," she said softly.

Xia closed his eyes.

"Listen," she said.

Xia felt anger vie with despair. "You see what he's trying to do, and you're still going to go along with him?"

Cook shook her head. "America is not the habitats, Xia."

He drew a deep breath. "When China fell apart and my family came here, no one asked about the color of our skin or what gods we worshiped. Because Americans didn't do that. But now—" He looked away.

Cook licked her lips. "Xia." She paused. "Jason. America isn't about tempting people you disagree with into exile. It's about persuading them."

"You're a clone grown in a vat in some Toronto

gene lab," said Xia bitterly. "What do you know about America?"

Cook stiffened. "So I'm not human, because I'm not like you? Do you want to exile *me* now?"

Xia's mouth opened. "Look, I didn't mean—"

"Yes, you did," said Cook coldly. "You think it about me, just like you think it about Grace."

"I—" He looked down at her, at war with himself, his decency contending with his sense of how things ought to be.

"You see," said Vander Hosen triumphantly. "We Canadians play a long game."

"But not long enough," snapped Cook. "The Civil War *did* end slavery. And the Sixties did put us on the road to equality." She glanced at Xia. "I don't know what's going to happen. But I promise you this, America *will* emerge stronger."

She looked at the Canadian diplomat, and a tight smile cut across her pretty face. "And then there will be hell to pay. If I have anything to say about it."

DJ threw his head back and laughed. "Look out, Vander Hosen. You've created a monster."

Vander Hosen's phone warbled.

"I think that's your wake-up call," said DJ. "It turns out you're no longer welcome in the ol' U.S. of A. Come on. I'll help you pack."

Vander Hosen cast an unsure look at Cook, and then he got up and slowly walked down the path, DJ merrily following behind.

For a moment, Cook watched them go. Then she drew a deep breath and stepped toward Xia, close enough she could smell him, sweat and soap and him. She looked up into those pretty gray-green eyes. She reached out and touched his arm. Her hand was shaking.

"Jason, America is not a place or a language or a religion. It's not even the things we believe today. You showed me that. We may be wrong today. But

America is the promise that we'll do better tomorrow."

He was quiet for a long moment. Finally, he said, "Too bad."

"Too bad, what?" she asked.

"Too bad you were born in Canada. You might have made a halfway decent president."

She leaned into him, and after a moment he took her hand. Together, they watched the flag flapping proudly against the blue summer sky.

THE LAST ACTOR

by Mike Resnick
and Linda L. Donahue

Mike Resnick is, according to *Locus*, the all-time leading short fiction award winner, living or dead, in science fiction history. He is the author of more than fifty novels, almost two hundred stories, and two screenplays, and has edited close to fifty anthologies. He has won five Hugos, a Nebula, and other major awards in the USA, France, Japan, Spain, Croatia and Poland. His work has been translated into twenty-two languages.

Linda Donahue traveled the world as an Air Force brat, has degrees in computer science and Russian studies, and has taught such varied courses and disciplines as computer science, aviation, tai chi and belly dancing. Her stories have appeared in a number of anthologies, and she is currently working on her first novel.

THERE WAS A TIME when Hollywood and television came to Broadway for ideas.

Enrique Rodriguez sighed. There was a time when T. Rex walked the Earth, too.

He knew what had killed the dinosaurs: the comet. But who could have foreseen that Broadway—or at least the Broadway Enrique cherished—would be brought down not by the economy, not by the fact that it remained a singularly New York institution, not by the public's attention turning to the wars in Paraguay and Uraguay, but rather by the dumbing down of half a dozen successive generations of Americans. Nor could anyone have predicted that, paradoxically, in an era when no one performed Shakespeare or Shaw, Albee or O'Neal, Williams or Stoppard, when even Neil Simon was beyond the average theatergoer, the Broadway theater would be in better economic health than ever before.

The problem, concluded Enrique, as he walked to his appointment on 57th Street, was that every actor worth his salt—all three or four of them—wished he could perform today's hits while wearing a mask, so he would never be associated with the drivel that was packing them in on the Great White Way.

Enrique finally arrived, ten minutes after he was due, at the fashionable sidewalk café. (After all, stars were expected to be fashionably late.) A waiter had already brought a carafe of distilled water and basket of bread to their table.

Carlos Mendez and Hector Murdock, the producer-and-writer team, each shook Enrique's hand. "Your agent," Carlos said, "has been singing your praises . . . as have your reviews." At his elbow lay a stack of review clippings from European newspapers. Of course a palm-vid screen could have shown the same information, but clippings were showier and made Carlos appear worldly by suggesting he subscribed to foreign papers.

"I know you've invited me to discuss your next project," Enrique said, "I'm an actor, and actors must work—but let me tell you up front that what I'd most love would be to perform in one of the classics."

"My thoughts precisely," agreed Carlos.

"You're willing?" said Enrique, surprised. "I admire your courage."

"What has courage got to do with it?" replied Carlos. "Almost every show currently on Broadway is a classic. The audiences love them."

"I'm not talking classic TV sitcoms."

Carlos grimaced. "I know, I know—but all the best movies have been done and redone up and down Broadway."

"Think farther back," said Enrique, "to when actors performed *Hamlet* and *The Iceman Cometh* and *Pygmalion*. Then look at what we have today." His face reflected his contempt, as he named one standing-room-only hit after another. "*Lucy Loves Ricky, Uncle Martian, Jeannie and the Astronaut, Ponderosa—The Musical* . . . Hell, even the Royal Ballet is producing a version of the original *Battlestar Galactica.*

"What's your point?" said Hector Murdock. "I wish *I'd* have thought of *Gilligan's Castaways*. It'll run for ten years."

"Plays like that don't run," said Enrique, making no attempt to hide his contempt. "They crawl on deformed hands and knees."

"Europe has turned you into a snob," said Hector.

"I concur," said Carlos. "What the hell is your point?"

"My point is that there was a time when Hollywood and television plundered the theater. Now *we* copy *them.*"

"So what?" said Carlos. "There are only three original plots in the world. Four at the most."

"So they stole *Macbeth* and *A Streetcar Named Desire*. Now the tables are turned, and we steal from them—but they don't *have* any *Othellos* and *Streetcars,* so we wind up stealing *Dumb and Dumber* and *Heaven's Gate* and *Ace Ventura.*"

"My first musical was *Dumber and Dumbest,*" said Carlos. "It put three kids through college."

"Didn't you ever want to produce something proud?" demanded Enrique.

"I'm proud of filling seats!" snapped Carlos. "That's

something your precious Bard hasn't been able to do for half a century!"

"But this isn't a movie, where you go broke if only ten million people buy tickets," persisted Enrique. "You only have to fill twelve hundred seats a night. You can appeal to the best of your audience rather than the laziest!" Enrique suddenly became aware that he was shouting, and that everyone at the other tables was staring at him. He lowered his voice and patted the satchel he'd brought along. "I have some very old scripts—all of them in the public domain." Carlos suddenly looked interested. "Hector, as a favor to an old friend, look them over. See if they don't inspire you."

"But they're already written," protested Hector.

"I spent the morning reading Shakespeare," said Enrique. "I know the language is too archaic for audiences that have been raised on television and graphic novels, but the concepts are eternal." He paused for a moment. "A truly talented writer," he continued enticingly, "could modernize the language and get full credit for making Shakespeare relevant to today's audiences."

He passed his satchel to Hector, who accepted it, holding it as if it were filled with explosives.

"I'll take a look," replied Hector noncommittally. "We'll get back to you."

"That's all I ask," said Enrique. He stood up, excused himself, and left the café. A moment later he boarded the Third Avenue subway. As the train rattled and lurched, he stared at the dirty faces around him.

Neither Broadway nor Hollywood were entirely to blame for the population's plummeting tastes and appetite for stupidity. It was a simple, indisputable fact: moronic was in—brainy was out.

Even before Enrique was born, values had been shifting. People prized entertainment over education. A new discovery warranted fewer accolades than a new athlete or a new blockbuster film. It had crept up on the country when almost no one was looking. Maybe it started with Gomer Pyle, perhaps with the Beverly Hillbillies, surely decades before Paris Hilton, but suddenly dumb had become the new chic.

With a heavy heart, Enrique admitted he wasn't blameless. Like the growing ignorant masses, Broadway's bright lights had lured him in. He could have studied quantum mechanics, or spent his life searching for a cure to some exotic disease or other, but he longed for thousands of fans whispering his name in awe. Einstein, Newton, Plato, Kant—they all had their share of accomplishments (which almost no one could identify), but none of them had any fan clubs.

Seeking to reaffirm the survival of *any* great artistic achievement, Enrique left the subway and walked to the Met—the Metropolitan Museum of Art. A block away from one of the world's greatest art museums, a painter occupied a street corner, selling canvases set up on easels. These weren't the usual Elvis on velvet or big-eyed kids or bad rip-offs of pop culture Warhols. They were truly magnificent portraits and landscapes, paintings harkening back to the old masters.

"You painted these?" asked Enrique, pausing before a portrait of an old woman done in the style of Rembrandt's heavy brush strokes, yet without sacrificing any of the fine, minute details.

The artist nodded. "Ten dollars takes it away."

"It's worth a hell of a lot closer to a million than to ten," said Enrique admiringly.

"I see you and I have similar tastes, my friend." The artist existed a hand that was permanently stained from the use of oils.

"This should be in a gallery, not out here on the street," protested Enrique.

The artist sighed. "Galleries are only interested in what's popular this week. If I had a baboon, I could splash paint on its bottom and let it sit on a canvas. Then I'd be as rich as you appear to be."

Enrique stared at him for a long moment. "So why don't you?" he asked at last.

"Because then I wouldn't be an artist." The painter waved a hand at the Met and snorted contemptuously. "There's no art in there, only piles of garbage and pieces of crushed automobiles. That's what passes for art these days—ugly, welded pieces of junk and paintings that look like vomit. There's no appreciation of beauty or talent." He grimaced. "Walking through the Met or the Guggenheim is almost as depressing as watching recycled fifty-year-old sitcoms on the Broadway stage, with or without music."

"You've been to the theater lately?"

The painter smiled ruefully. "Do I look like I have two hundred dollars for a ticket?"

"Then how do you know?"

"I hear the audiences discussing it when they come out."

"And they hate it?" asked Enrique.

The painter shook his head. "They love it, just as they love the dreck that passes for art today. And if they love it, then you know how awful it must be."

"Couldn't some of it be good?"

"You can make a beautiful house out of styrofoam and toilet paper," answered the artist. "A gorgeous house. But it is still made of styrofoam and toilet paper."

"If you feel that way, why waste your time painting at all?" asked Enrique, hoping for some answer, some hidden insight that would help him decide what do to about this hideous play in which he found himself trapped.

"Because art isn't just something to hang on a wall," said the painter. "It is the mirror of mankind's soul. And I must be true to my soul by being true to my art."

Enrique handed the painter a twenty and took the portrait of the old woman away with him. The price had been ten, he knew that, but hell, the man's convictions alone were worth the extra ten.

Maybe, like a clock's pendulum, it was time to value both beauty and the intellect again, to aspire to the best in man rather than the easiest. If the trend didn't stop soon, everyone might as well go back to swinging from the branches of trees. If a talented artist would rather starve being true to his art than peddle the junk that delighted an indiscriminate public, then maybe he, Enrique, could keep alive the works of one great man. . . .

A week later, Enrique was called to the theater.

Hector greeted him happily. "You were right—those plays were pure genius! Of course, the language made it practically impossible to follow the story. But I feel in my bones that we have a megahit on our hands!"

"Come, sit between us," Carlos invited him.

Enrique scooted into the row of theater seats. Though he wanted to feel their excitement, he'd been stung too many times by too many "brilliant" concepts that would have bored the average eight-year-old of a century ago.

Carlos handed him a cigar. "You had me worried for a while with all your talk, but when Hector told me the plot—hell, I almost shit in my pants it was so brilliant."

"Which play are we doing?" Enrique asked.

"The original title was *Macbeth*, but I've updated that as well," said Hector, tossing a script into Enrique's lap. "I call it *Macbrady*. It's the story of a man who was married to a lovely woman, yet they were all alone."

The pit in Enrique's stomach grew geometrically. Quietly, he whispered, "No."

But his voice was lost on Carlos and Hector. Somewhere amid their excited chatter and grand expectations, Carlos said, "Your agent has signed the contract on your behalf. I think this baby can run for years!"

Enrique groaned. While overseas, he had given his agent the power of attorney to deal with contracts, a power he'd neglected to revoke upon his return home.

"You'll play Mike Macbrady," Carlos said, "an architect at King's Designs, the top architectural firm in Scotland." His eyes glazed. "People love foreign settings, even when they're not as rigorously realized as *Spamalot*." Carlos took a deep breath, forced himself to become calm, then continued. "You and Duncan, another architect, are competing for an important client's account. Whoever gets the account will be made a full partner and oversee the Cawdor branch."

Enrique felt faint. Meek, mild-mannered Hector had become a murderer, and Shakespeare was his victim.

Enrique flipped through the rewrite of *Macbeth*. Every page brought a new shudder. When he could bear it no longer, he shouted "This is wrong! Macbeth has to kill Duncan!"

"You're the star," said Carlos. "You can't be the murderer. The people will never stand for it, not with orchestra seats going at two for five hundred. They want to be amused and delighted, not shocked and depressed."

"Besides," added Hector, "it's not *Macbeth*—it's *Macbrady*."

"I don't care what you call it, it's *Macbeth*," said Enrique. "Will you be dressing the three witches in miniskirts next?"

"It's a thought," said Carlos amiably.

So no one would die in *Macbrady*.

Enrique knew who Macbeth should have killed. By the time he finished the script, he was pretty sure he knew who Enrique Rodruiguez should have killed, too.

His agent.

*　　*　　*

On opening night, reviewers from the four major Manhattan newsdisks sat in the audience. That much hadn't changed in well over a century. There were half a billion people in America, but the opinions of four New Yorkers—each brilliant, ascerbic, and provincial—would determine whether the play would go on to have a profitable run or would close its doors permanently after one performance.

Enrique sat brooding in his dressing room when Carlos entered, his face aglow. "Sold out!" he announced with a triumphant grin.

"Bully for us," said Enrique without enthusiasm.

"What's the matter?" asked Carlos, suddenly worried. "Aren't you feeling well?"

"I feel like a murderer—of the theater, of the language, of Shakespeare. Or, if not a murderer, at least an accomplice."

"*That* again?" demanded Carlos irritably. "People want happy endings. Those old plays are depressing. *King Lear?* Please! No one wants the audience going home to slit their wrists! We want them to buy tickets for next week on their way out! And to tell their friends how good the play made them feel."

"Even if it's all a lie?"

"What makes depressing endings and five-syllable words any better than happy endings and dialogue they can understand?"

"Look around you," said Enrique disgustedly. "We're performing for a bunch of six-year-olds in adult bodies. Doesn't it bother you that more of them are on an intellectual and cultural par with Lassie than with Lassie's owner?"

"It means they're that much easier to separate from their money," answered Carlos. "And for the record, this year's hit musical is *Rin Tin Tin,* not *Lassie.*"

Enrique had to admit that it made perfect sense. Why would an educated elite embark on a generations-long process of undereducating (or was the word *un*educating?) the public *except* to make it easier to separate them from their money. He almost wished he could perform for that tiny percentage of totally amoral robber barons the plays they wanted to see. But of course no one would ever be able to identify them. It was a lot easier for an intelligent man to appear as a fool than for a fool to appear intelligent.

"Come on, cheer up!" said Carlos. "You're on in a couple of minutes. Get that frown off your face and knock 'em dead."

He gave Enrique a hearty pat on the back.

"Maybe I'll do that," said Enrique.

Enrique waited for his cue, then walked out onto the stage. He moved to the center, then found himself staring, almost hypnotized, at the audience.

My God, look at them! They're living proof that Darwin was wrong!

One of the actors nudged him. "Wake up, Enrique!" he whispered. "You're on!"

Enrique took one more look at his audience, the people he was being paid to please. Then he took one step forward and began to speak.

*"If it were done when 'tis done, then 'twere well
It were done quickly: if the assassination
Could trammel up the consequence, and catch,
With his surcease, success; that but this blow
Might be the be-all and the end-all here,
But here, upon this bank and shoal of time,
We'd jump the life to come."*

There was a confused buzz in the audience. Enrique could pick out a few sentences. "What the hell is he talking about?" and "I thought this was supposed to be in English."

Undaunted, he continued, a sneer of contempt on his lips:

"But if these cases
We still have judgment here; that we but teach
Bloody instructions, which being taught return
To plague the inventor: this even-handed justice
Commends the ingredients of our poison'd chalice
To our own lips."

"Get that bum off the stage!" yelled a man.

"This was supposed to be a comedy!" shouted a woman.

"Fools!" yelled Enrique. "Idiots! Chattel! There will be no Macbrady this night, no Gilligan, no charming hillbillies, no lovable teenagers whose IQs could freeze water. Tonight, whether you like it or not, you are going to be introduced to the greatest bard of them all, a bard your great-grandparents all but worshipped before they spawned generation after generation of contented cud-chewers like yourselves." He took a deep breath and glared at them. "My name is Macbeth."

"Is he insulting us?" demanded a man.

"I don't know," said another. "I don't understand what the hell he's saying."

"Well, I understand the tone!" snapped a third. He stood up and hurled a shoe at Enrique.

As if by common consent, the entire audience began hurling debris at him.

"Nitwits!" he screamed. "If you attack everything you fail to understand, I wonder that you have time to sleep!"

Then a young man leaped onto the stage, followed by another, then six more, all of them pummeling him into senselessness. The riot squad arrived five minutes later and made some arrests that would never result in convictions, but Enrique was beyond caring. He died on the way to the hospital. Carlos reluctantly refunded the money, hired a top television actor to play Macbrady, and saw the next morning's line at the box office extend halfway around the block. Two of

the newsdisks carries the story, buried somewhere between the classifieds and the results of the Pan-Asian
Soccer League quarter finals.

They buried Enrique Rodriguez two days later, with
the headstone he had requested in his will, one pro-
claiming that he was The Last Actor.

But he wasn't, of course.

He was just the last one who cared.

THE GREAT CHAIN OF BEING

by Brian Stableford

Brian Stableford's recent novels include *Streaking* and *The New Faust at the Tragicomique*. His recent non-fiction includes a mammoth reference book, *Science Fact and Science Fiction: An Encyclopedia* and a collection of critical essays, *Heterocosms*. His recent translations from the French include the second volume of the classic series of Paul Féval novels after which his favorite publisher is named, *The Invisible Weapon*, and the anthology *News from the Moon and Other French Scientific Romances*.

WHEN DR. HARKNESS EXPLAINED to Sarah Whitney that the resurgent cancer was too widespread and too aggressive to leave any significant hope for successful treatment, she didn't feel anything, except for the everyday excruciation. It wasn't that she was simply repressing her feelings or blotting them out with some kind of endogenous antidote to emotion; she simply didn't feel any horror, grief, sorrow, or regret.

She suspected that the disease was responsible for that; not only was it bloating her with vulgar pain but shrinking her emotional range in proportion.

She turned away to look out of the third-floor window of the doctor's consulting room, but not because she couldn't face him. The hospital was on the city perimeter, and the south-facing window had a splendid view of the mighty crowns of the Neogymnosperm forest that ringed Phoenix Reborn.

The doctor offered to start her on a further course of chemotherapy, but he made it pretty clear that her chances of finishing it were slim to none; taking the poison would only reduce the limited capacity she still had left for clear thought and purposive action.

"You might do better," Dr. Harkness concluded, "to think about planting."

To Alan, of course, that was like pulling a trigger—but for once, he didn't launch the kind of direct and focused assault normally favored by prosecutors. He had plenty of denial and anger stored up, ready to spray out randomly. "This is twenty-third century America!" he ranted. "How can it be possible that some stupid cancer can still get through our defenses? It was supposed to have been cured, damn it! She had the chemotherapy! It was supposed to work! She's thirty-six years old, for God's sake! This is not supposed to *happen* in this day and age! We survived the goddam Ecocatastrophe and saved the goddam world! We're supposed to be *past all that.*"

Dr. Harkness tried to explain. It was pointless, in the circumstances, given that it wasn't ignorance or incomprehension that had set Alan off but sheer blind range, but the oncologist was one of those slightly furtive intellectuals who have no other resource but dogged explanation. Sarah had heard it all before, so she didn't bother to listen to the performance, but she totted up the points in her own mind while she tried hard to internalize the peaceful green of the tree crowns and use it, symbolically, to soothe the perennial pain. It would have been easier if the pain had been polite enough to take the form of a constant ache, but it was more like the infernal equivalent of Russian classical music.

Sarah understood that cancer, like every other evil afflicting humankind, was subject to natural selection. Two hundred and fifty years of increasingly-sophisticated magic bullets had won battle after battle, but could never win the war, partly because successful treatment preserved genetic vulnerabilities within the population and partly because people's immune systems, blithely unconscious of the fact that the magic bullets were the good guys, were being trained to mount better defenses against their invasions, effectively fighting on the cancers' side.

The Ecocatastrophe hadn't helped, of course; the explosive progress of the novel techniques of Botanical Transfiguration had restabilized the climate faster than anyone had dared hope, but the inevitable side effect of the wildfire spread of the Transfigured Forests had been an order-of-magnitude increase in the estrangement of the organic environment—which had, in turn, called forth inevitable echoes in physiological sensitivity. No matter how good the overall accounts looked, one component of the cost paid for biotechnological progress was the further proliferation of animal cancers. Even plants were affected by the trend, although Human Trees were said to be as resistant as it was possible to be.

When mutual exhaustion finally produced a lull in Alan's grandstanding cross-examination of Dr. Harkness, Sarah said: "My grandma still thought that once the Ecocatastrophe was over and progress was back on track, we'd finally emerge into the long-delayed Age of Medical Miracles, when the prime of life would last for centuries. I never found out what she'd have thought of the Foresters—she died before they hit the headlines. She did feel guilty about her carbon debt, though." Sarah winced as she finished, because speeches of that length were taxing, in symphonic terms—but she gritted her teeth, because she knew she'd have a lot of talking to do now that the bad news equation had reached its final proof.

What Sarah was thinking, in reflecting on her dead grandma's foolish optimism was that because she was going to die so much younger than her aged relative, she didn't yet have a single blood relative in any of the Human Forests. Two of her grandparents had missed out on the opportunity because they'd been late victims of the Ecocatastrophe; the other two were still alive, along with both her parents—who'd each passed on their dodgy genes to her without having to take the hit themselves. She would be the first—but she *would* be the first, no matter what Alan's itchy trigger finger launched against her by way of opposi-tional bluster.

"Planting is *not* an option!" Alan howled—at Dr. Harkness, not at Sarah, he being far the more conve-nient target. "You will *not* add insult to injury by try-ing to persuade my wife that she'll feel better about dying if she buys into this crazy, stupid idea that peo-ple can live on as trees. It's ecological mysticism of the worst possible sort, and of all the lunatics the Eco-catastrophe flushed out, the Foresters are absolutely the *worst*. You're supposed to be a man of science, for God's sake! How *dare* you pollute your pathetic, puerile, and pusillanimous advice with that kind of *shit*?"

Sarah was able to take a certain perverse pride in the fact that her beloved husband could still find op-portunities for the alliterative three-part lists that had such a fine rhetorical effect on juries, even while he was reacting to a sentence of death passed on his wife—although it was, of course, in mid-rant that he usually had to deploy such weaponry. What she tried to focus her green-steeped thoughts upon, however, was the first sentence of his tirade, which assumed and asserted that she couldn't and wouldn't feel any better about the inevitability of death if she opted to be planted.

Her internal jury wasn't going to fall for that one. The simple fact was that she could and she would, and

Sarah knew that what remained of her life's work would be the task of persuading Alan to see, recognize, and understand that fact—not so much for his sake, but because she would need his support to ensure that the kids could take what comfort they could from her metamorphosis.

She didn't say so in Dr. Harkness' office, though; it wasn't the time or the place. She saved herself for the journey home. She knew that she wouldn't be any more comfortable in the car, but at least she'd have the benefit of temporary privacy, with no third parties at whom Alan would be tempted to make speeches.

The car's sensors decided that Alan was too over-adrenalinized to drive. Sarah was still under the automatic ban imposed on anyone taking diamorphine on a regular basis, although it seemed to her that her pain was nowadays so Rimsky-Korsakovian that the diamorphine had become impotent. It was the automatic pilot, therefore, that guided them out of the underground lot and on to the Neogymnosperm-lined highway that led back to the Halo. The fact that he didn't have to watch the road freed up Alan's attention, but it certainly didn't improve his temper. He kept his hands on the wheel even thought it wasn't under his control, gripping it so tightly it seemed that he was fighting every twitch and turn.

"I'm going to do it, Alan," she told him, in her best soothing tone. "I'm sorry that I haven't talked to you about it before, but I knew how you'd react."

He did react, at some length. Sarah waited for the gale to blow itself out, while she endured a Mussorgskian night on a bare mountain.

"It's not up for discussion," she said, eventually. "It's my choice and it's made. Your part is to reconcile yourself to it and make the best of it. I called the Foresters from the hospital when I went to the restroom and made an appointment for someone to call tomorrow night."

The blast was feeble this time, the backlash no worse than Tchaikovsky.

"It's Jeanie and Mike we have to think of now," Sarah insisted. "It's going to be hard for them, and it's up to both of us to do everything we can to make it better. You have to back me up, Alan. You have to give me your blessing, no matter how much you hate the idea, for their sake."

There was a lot of green around her now, but the Neogymnosperms were so tall and thick that the Forest path was shadowed and dark. The psychological trick she'd deployed in the doctor's office was far too receptive to that kind of nuancing. Sarah tried to internalize the concept of the road instead, and the angelic orderliness of its white markings, continually reminding herself that she still had a future, and a journey to make, and other traffic to take into consideration.

"I can't believe that you're giving up," Alan said, when his brain had returned to something more like rational mode. His voice was hollow, though, as if serving as an echo chamber for his discordantly vibrant emotions, and that, too, was part of his court repertoire. "You were such a fighter before the chemo knocked the stuffing out of you. I can't believe that you're just going to lie down meekly and die—and I can't believe that you've fallen for this mystical rubbish about vegetable heaven. It's sick, Sarah—sick and stupid and sinister." There was the alliteration again, intoned this time with expert plaintiveness.

"I don't believe in vegetable heaven," Sarah told him. Actually, she wasn't so sure, but she knew that was the aspect of Forester rhetoric he found most offensive, so she had to deemphasize it. "I prefer to think about it in accounting terms." She'd worked as a public service accountant for thirteen years, save maternity leave, before the cancer and the chemo had invalided her out of financial affray forever.

"All that crap about redeeming America's carbon

debt is no better," Alan insisted. "It was American biotech that saved the world. If Neogymnosperms, Lollipop Pines, Polycotton, and Giant Corn haven't already paid for our forefathers' sins twice over, the goddam exports certainly have. If anything, the Human Forests are just getting in the goddam way."

Sarah didn't bother to point out that the totemic Transfigured Trees developed and deployed in distant parts of the world hadn't, strictly speaking, been American "exports." The basic techniques had been exported, but their applications had been carefully leavened with other varieties of national pride. Transfigured Golden Oaks and Wych-Elms had played a major role in the repossession of Middle Europe; New Neem Trees had worked wonders in India, Polar Firs and Silky Spruces had swept across the warmed-up northern landscapes from Norway to Siberia, and most of southeast Asia had refused to settle for anything less than Confucian Rice, in spite of the fact that rice had never been grown on trees before. Even Mexico had decided that the Neogymnosperm tide should advance no further than the Rio Grande, and was nowadays proud to be a Banana Republic in the truest sense of the term.

Thus far, Human Forests were culturally limited, too; America was the world leader by a vast margin—but Sarah felt sure that the global pause for consideration would be momentary. Far from being a Californian craze, Human Forests were the future, not just for America but for all humankind. Sarah truly believed that they would change the world, and bring about a new Golden Age. It wouldn't be the Age of Medical Miracles of which her dead grandma had dreamed, but it would be a world from which human death really had been exiled, after a fashion.

"This is twenty-third century America," Sarah reminded her husband, echoing his own cliché. "We don't do accounting the way they used to before the Ecocatastrophe. The day of quick bucks and cooked books is over and done with. We calculate over the long term now. The true economic measure of the Human Forests isn't what they chipped in to the hectic restabilization of atmospheric carbon dioxide, methane and water vapor but what they'll contribute to the future well-being of the nation and the species. Redeeming carbon debt isn't like paying back the fifty dollars you borrowed from your pal last week; it's more like entering into a long-term contract to ensure business stability." She gasped when she got to the end, but she did get to the end. Internalizing the road seemed to be working, for now. Not for the first time, she felt that the Firebird was in her flesh as well as her surroundings.

"If you're building up to using the words *hedge fund*," Alan said, grimly, "I'd really rather you didn't. There's wordplay and there's simply being silly."

"Gallows humor is inherently silly," Sarah said, trying to sound casual, although the fact that he had retreated to jokes of that caliber was as good as waving a white flag. "I really am serious, Alan. I'm sorry to be brutal, but I really don't have the time to be subtle. I intend to do this, and I want you to be good about it—not just now, but afterwards and forever—because it's no mere matter of making me feel as well as can be contrived while my brain still works. A Human Tree is forever; I'll be part of your life, and Jeanie's and Mike's lives, until the day you and they die. Even if you were to dig your heels in and refuse to have anything to do with me, I'll still be there."

"No, you won't, Sarah," he said, his infernal stubbornness drawing a reluctant Parthian shot out of his determination to surrender and be kind. "They may be right, technically, about the continuity of cellular life and the preservation of the fundamental DNA-complex, but it won't be *you*, any more than a corpse in a grave or an urnful of ashes in the trophy cabinet would be you. You'll be dead, Sarah—if you don't fight."

"I'll be dead whether I fight or not," Sarah told him, gasping again as cymbals suddenly joined in with the climax of a crescendo of screeching violins and booming brass. "You know that. I *have* fought—but I didn't win. That Age of Miracles never arrived."

He said nothing, but she went on, for her own sake, externalizing the prod of her imagination by way of paying back the debt she owed the trees and the road. "The human body simply isn't built in such a way that we can stay in the prime of life, incapable of permanent violation by disease or injury, for centuries. Transfiguration is the only possible immortality. It's not enough—nobody ever claimed that it is—but it's what we've got, and all the evidence suggests that it's the best we'll have for quite some time."

The prosecution still had nothing to say.

"Maybe you're right," Sarah continued, "and there's no essential difference between being planted and being buried or cremated—but even if that's so, the choice between the three is still a meaningful one. You have to respect my choice, Alan; you have to help Jeanie and Mike make the most of it. You have to preserve the meaning of what I'm doing, even if you do insist on thinking, in your heart of hearts, that I'm dead and gone and that the Tree is just an insult to my memory."

She knew that her voice had expressed her pain, in spite of the road and her best intentions. Alan put his hands up to his face, and covered his eyes with his fingers. It wasn't the long straight tunnel through the Neogymnosperms that he was refusing to see, and it wasn't the automatic pilot's ultra-careful driving of which he was despairing.

After a couple of minutes he put the hands back on the wheel again, not because he wanted to pretend to steer but simply because he needed to get a grip on *something*. "I wish the highway weren't so goddam *boring*," he said. "I wish Transfigured trees weren't so goddam *orderly*."

"We'll be back in the Halo in no time," she told him. "Urban design is the etiquette of New Global Civilization. The days when cities and their suburbs just *sprawled* is gone forever."

"You've never been to Denver or Chicago, let alone New York," he retorted, for no particular reason. "We're lucky, living way out west. Arizona's still on the real frontier, you know, even if it's been Transfigured out of all recognition. It's one of those places where people get right on and *do* things. No inertia, lots of *fight*."

"And where are the biggest Human Forests in the USA?" Sarah was quick to say. "California, inevitably. Oregon, of course. Montana and Wyoming are the third and fourth. All pioneer country: join up the dots and there's the frontier of the future."

"It'll be a hell of a long time before anything bigger than a Human Copse sprouts up in Utah," Alan opined.

"No, it won't," Sarah insisted, as gently as she could. "Sacred Groves will be everywhere before you know it, linking up from sea to shining sea. It really will be a New World, Alan—and I'll be part of it. I really will."

Jeanie and Mike were well past denial and anger by now. Unlike Alan, they'd already made their psychological adjustments to the verdict and sentence that their parents brought home. They backed Alan up when he said that Sarah really ought to go to bed, but she stood firm—or, to be strictly accurate, sat firm—on the living room sofa. The sofa was directly opposite the painting over the mantelpiece that displayed Old Arizona in all its ancient glory, all desert and bare rock, glowing sulky red in the setting sun. In Old Arizona, if its current iconography could be believed, the sun had always been setting.

The children weren't in the least surprised or dismayed when Sarah told them that a Forester would be calling round to make arrangements; Jeanie was ten and Mike was seven, so they'd both grown up with Human Forests as a fact of life, and the fundamental notion didn't seem in the least strange or alien to them. That didn't mean, though, that everything went smoothly.

"You have to be planted in the yard," Jeanie said. "This is our home. You have to stay here, with us."

"That's not a good idea, my love," Sarah told her. "Maybe if we were feudal barons living in English castles, we'd be able to think of our homes as long-standing family heirlooms, but we're not tied down, and we shouldn't want to be. This is the only home you've known, so far, but it certainly won't be the only one you'll ever know." She had to stop then, but she fixed Alan with a commanding stare.

"That's true," Alan admitted. "Ours is a land of opportunity, and you have to be free to take those opportunities when they arise. When you go to college, and get jobs, you need to be free to go where you want and need to be. Having your mother's Tree in the backyard is an anchor you can do without."

He stopped there, leaving Sarah to add: "Besides which, Trees belong in Forests. They thrive in company and don't do so well in isolation. It's best if I'm somewhere where I can belong, where you can visit me when you want to, without ever getting to take me for granted."

"You'll still be able to talk to us when you're a tree, won't you?" Mike said. "You'll still be able to listen to us."

"No, Mike, I won't," Sarah told him, taking him by the hand. "I know you've seen a lot of cartoons that represent Animal Trees as things with eyes and mouths, which wave their branches around as if they were arms, but it's not like that. That's just a joke. When I start the series of injections—by which time I'll be in the hospice—I'll go to sleep, and that'll be the last time you see my eyes or hear my voice. Transfiguration takes a long time. It'll be months before I'm ready for planting, and more than a year before I begin to look much like a tree, but once I do, I'll be a real tree. I won't have a brain anymore, so I won't be able to think, let alone talk or listen."

"But you'll be able to dream," Jeanie put in.

"No, I won't," Sarah said, determined to tell the truth, the whole truth and nothing but the truth, as Alan would expect and was entitled to demand. "That's . . . well, not a joke, more a myth. People like to imagine Human Trees being in a kind of dream state, but once my brain's gone . . . ?"

"Where will it go?" Mike wanted to know. He was frowning; perhaps he had been taking it for granted that the human body was still contained within the Human Tree, like a mollusk within a shell.

"It will change, just like everything else," Sarah told him. "It will change into the flesh of the tree."

"But if you can't dream," Jeanie said hesitantly, "how can you be in vegetable heaven?" Sarah knew that Jeanie didn't really believe in vegetable heaven, but the dutiful ten year old probably thought that she ought to make an effort to conceive of it in terms of some kind of hallucinatory state, just in case her mother expected to arrive there.

"If there is such a thing as vegetable heaven," Sarah told her, choosing her words carefully, "it's not something you have to dream. It's just a matter of *being*."

"How long will it take you to pay your carbon debt?" Mike asked. Even though the Ecocatastrophe was over, elementary school children were still taught about the carbon economics of everyday life as a matter of routine. Mike couldn't put numbers into the equations—he didn't know how much carbon dioxide a flight from Phoenix to Miami or a transatlantic trip by a container ship would pump out—but it had been drummed into him that his remoter ancestors had been villains because of the awful extent of their carbon footprints, while his more recent ones were heroes, by virtue of their tiptoed ingenuity, thus bringing the historical account books into a belated but triumphant balance.

"It's not as simple as that," Sarah told her son. She wanted to explain him that it wasn't sensible to divide carbon debt up into individual slices, because it was the economic activities of the whole society that produced the greenhouse gas surplus, and that distributing blame between different nations in the fashion that had made the USA the Great Green Satan of the twenty-first century was patently false accounting, because the economic activity of a particular nation had to be seen in the context of the global economy, but she couldn't have done it, even if there had been any point. There was too much Balakirev going on. What she actually said was: "It isn't a matter of one Tree paying off one person's debt; it's a matter of whole Human Forests making their contribution to the work that's done by all the other Transfigured Forests in the world."

Alan snorted, but when Sarah stared at him, he pretended that he had only been stifling a sneeze.

"One day," Jeanie said, abandoning questions in the interests of demonstrating her intellectual superiority over her younger brother, "there won't be any other Transfigured Forests. All the world's forests will be Human Forests, and then we'll really be Responsible. *Then* we'll have paid our carbon debt to the Earth."

Sarah was glad that Alan hadn't saved up his snort, because Jeanie was old enough not to be fooled by any kind of belated bluff and would have taken it personally. She resisted the temptation not to correct her daughter's Utopian excess, even though she could see that her red-faced husband was biting his lip as he forced himself to maintain diplomatic silence.

In her heart of hearts, Sarah hoped that Jeanie might be right, and that there *would* come a day—if not for thousands of years—when *all* the Transfigured Forests had been replaced by Human ones of every race and nationality, so that all the human beings alive throughout the world could live in the perpetual company of their ancestors, and the species really could consider itself Reverent and Responsible. It was not a dream that she would be able to maintain when she became a Tree, but it seemed to her a legitimate hope that she might live to see such an era, albeit not in her present frail and feeble form.

"What *kind* of tree are you going to be?" Mike asked, his mind on more down-to-earth matters. "I don't want you to be a Joshua tree or a monkey puzzle."

"Mummy doesn't get to *choose*," Jeanie put in, getting slightly carried away with her own supposed expertise. "Human Trees are Human Trees, not any other sort. They're evergreen, but not like Lollipop Pines. They're just . . . themselves."

Sarah didn't want to complicate the issue by arguing that the present uniformity of Human Trees was probably just a phase, and that all kinds of choices might have opened up by the time Jeanie had to decide between planting and death. In any case, there was no choice at all for *her.* Her fate was sealed, to the soundtrack of *Scheherazade.*

The Forester's name was Jake. He was a little too smartly dressed, as if he were overcompensating for the image most people had of Foresters, but he wore his blond hair long and curly, obviously thinking of it as a precious asset not to be sacrificed on the altar of businesslike appearance. He arrived on time, but Sarah had made a late appointment so as to be sure that Jeanie and Mike would be in bed, so it was after dark. She still wasn't absolutely sure that Alan would be able to contain himself in confrontation with Personified Temptation.

To start with, though, Alan was on his best behavior. He meekly poured out a glassful of apple juice when Jake explained that he didn't drink alcohol or coffee, and gave him the benefit of the better arm-chair.

"I've brought you the standard literature," Jake said, handing Sarah a sheaf of leaflets with which she was already perfectly familiar, "but I'd like to give you a brief verbal explanation of what will happen. It helps clarify matters, in my experience, and brings questions to the surface that each particular individual needs to ask."

Sarah could read her husband's mind well enough to know that the words *pompous* and *asshole* must be drifting through it, but Alan said nothing, and Sarah consented herself with an encouraging nod.

Jake launched into his spiel. "The Association of Human Foresters," he said, "is not a commercial organization. No one ever set out to exploit this particular corollary of Transfiguration technology for financial gain. No one ever tried to sell it to the public by advertising. The AHF was summoned into being by public demand.

"The scientists who developed the metamorphic techniques that allowed living plants to be Transfigured realized almost immediately that animals might be Transfigured, too—only into plants, of course, not into other animals—but they thought of it as a technical challenge rather than a practical enterprise. The earliest animal Transfigurations were all done in a spirit of pure experiment; it was a big surprise that it worked so well, after all the disappointments of the past in respect of animal genetic engineering.

"Once it became popular for people to preserve their pets by Transfiguration, the demand for Human Transfiguration became increasingly insistent and urgent. The legislation went through with extraordinary ease. The AHF was created and regulated by state governments working in association with HMOs and a number of existing charitable organizations. I won't bore you with the bureaucratic details; suffice it to say that I'm not here as a salesperson or a social worker, but merely as someone answering a summons. Our services do have to be purchased, but a part of the care we give is reclaimable through health insurance, and the remainder compares favorably with the average costs of interment or cremation.

"What will happen, Mrs. Whitney, if you decide to go ahead with the Transfiguration, is that when you and your supervising physician decided that the time is ripe—which shouldn't be problematic in your case, given that the progress of your cancer can be accurately monitored—you'll go into the hospice. The first injection is administered on the day following admission. You'll slip into a coma almost immediately, and the Transfiguration will begin. The first injection contains the first of three suites of viral organelles that carry the extra genes you'll require in order to complement your own DNA, but its main components are the catalyst for the despecialization of your own cells and the trigger-proteins for the construction of the tuberochrysalis. The tuberochrysalis takes seven days to form; it will retain the basic outline of your bodily form, but many of the individual features will be lost. The second suite of supplementary DNA is injected on day eight, the third on day twelve, and the final batch of catalysts on day sixteen—by which time all your reblastularized cells should have been infected by the vectors. There's a long lag phase thereafter, but planting out of the tuberochrysalis is usually practicable after forty-five to fifty days, if no complications set in."

Alan's patience finally snapped. "What complications?" he asked, sharply. "Your brochures don't say anything about goddam complications."

"There's a good deal of detailed data available online, Mr. Whitney," Jake replied imperturbably. "The complications so far observed are various, but uncommon. The worst-case scenarios involve the rejection or suppression of one or more of the supplementary DNA packages, which can prevent the completion of

Transfiguration if the situation isn't remediable. Usually, it is. To date, more than ninety per cent of our Transfigurations have been completed without any complications at all, and more than ninety-nine per cent have been brought to a satisfactory conclusion. Given the improvements we've made in our techniques and our understanding, we expect those figures to rise in the future, steadily if not sharply."

"I've studied the probabilities," Sarah said, more to Alan than Jake, "I understand the risks. There's something less than a one percent chance I'll end up dead—as opposed to a hundred percent certainty that I'll end up dead if I don't opt for Transfiguration."

"The figure is a hundred percent either way," Alan retorted. "The difference is that if you opt for this travesty they kill you themselves instead of your dying a natural death, and then they turn your remains into protoplasmic mush before getting their ninety-nine-percent chance to turn that mush into a tree."

Jake opened his mouth, but Sarah held up her left index finger to silence him from a distance. "You're a servant of the law, Alan," she said. "You're no longer allowed, let alone obliged, to disapprove of assisted suicide in cases of terminal illness. Choice and painless injection beat natural death hands down, and there's nothing scary or obscene about protoplasmic mush. What do you think decay does to a body? What do you think happens to its carbon atoms thereafter? Whether they travel via the guts of graveworms or dissipate into the air as crematorium smoke, they eventually wind up as the transitory flesh of plants. All the Foresters are doing is bringing some order and focus to the process, cutting out the middlemen and maintaining the continuity of cellular life."

"The *illusion* of the continuity of life," Alan objected.

"It's not an illusion, Mr. Whitney," Jake said, quietly. "Nobody pretends that it's any kind of continuity of consciousness, but it *is* a continuity of life, literally and materially. It's not for me to say whether soul and spirit are illusory, or where they reside if they aren't in the flesh—but there really is no doubt that a Human Tree really is an extrapolation of human life. Your wife's Tree will include the full complements of her nuclear and mitochondrial cells, biochemically organized in exactly the same way. It's just that different ones will be expressed, in different combinations, in different kinds of specialized cells."

"That's three dimensions of difference," Alan pointed out, "and that's all the difference in the world. This is just another scam, in the great tradition of cryonics, offering the shadow of a perverted hope where none really exists."

"No, Alan, it's not," Sarah told him, pursing her lips and moving to the edge of the sofa because her intestines were being attacked by a gang of frenzied cellists. "There's no promise of resurrection here, false or otherwise."

"Becoming a Human Tree is a matter of moving on to a new phase," Jake added, trying to catch the enemy in a pincer movement. "Of course there's no way back, any more than there is from death—but the individual remains instead of being broken down into component molecules and redistributed as raw materials."

"But that doesn't mean that it won't be me, Alan. It'll just be a *different sort of me,* here on Earth and not in any kind of heaven. That's where I want to be, Alan, That's where I want to *go."*

Jake had another leaflet about that, offering a choice of Human Forests, woods, and private plots. Sarah had already made up her mind. She wanted to be up on the Colorado Plateau, partly because the Grand Canyon Surround was further on the way to becoming a mature forest than most, and partly because there was more rain up on the plateau than there was in the reclaimed Mojave. The plateau was a little farther away, but it seemed to her to be the right sort of place for the kind of creature she was ambitious to become. The Halo of Phoenix Reborn was a fine place for humans to live, but Human Trees had different needs, and must have different delights. Even more than the Sierra Nevada, in Sarah's opinion, the part of Colorado plateau that lay south of the Utah border foreshadowed the future of America— not the future of destiny, which really was a silly illusion, but the future to which the Foresters were attempting to act as midwives: the future in which civilized humans would live in the carefully-maintained interstices of an Eden of Human Trees that were both Trees of Knowledge and Trees of the Knowledge of Good and Evil.

Alan's mind was on other things. "What about me, Sarah?" he complained. "What becomes of me, while you're turning yourself into some vast lumpen tuber, and growing into something alien?"

"You have two children to bring up, Alan," she said, more sharply than she intended, because she was hurting. "You have to hold yourself, and them, together. When that job's done, you're free. If you don't want to be planted, that's up to you. You can send your carbon atoms into the future along any trajectory you choose. The only thing you can't do is abstract them from the great chain of being. One way or another, they'll live again."

"*They* don't live at all," Alan insisted. "*Cogito, ergo sum;* real life is made of thought."

"Don't be silly, Alan," Sarah said. "There are countless plant and animal species that don't think, but they're all *real life.*"

"A lot of husbands and wives," Jake put in, "are planning to be planted side by side. For the present, at least, Human Trees are monoecious; male and female flowers are borne on separate dendrites. Thus far, they're all sterile, and their capacity for vegetative reproduction is minimal, but the science and technology aren't standing still." He stopped, apparently realizing that both his clients were staring at him, no longer divided.

"Are you suggesting that we ought to be thinking about tree sex and tree children?" Alan asked stonily.

"Some people do," Jake said. "Some people seem to get quite a thrill out of the idea—but no, I'm not. Fruitful exchanges of pollen might some day be possible, but Mrs. Whitney's Tree will be unable to produce fertile seed. What I *do* suggest you might think about, though, is togetherness. Skeptics insist that love can't transcend Transfiguration any more than it can transcend death, but there's a sense in which it can. What I'm saying is that intimate contact can be reconfirmed and reconstituted within a Forest. Nor will Human Trees remain the end point of our potential existential journey for very long. As I said, the science and the technology aren't standing still."

Alan was silent for a few seconds before he looked at his wife and said: "I don't know how far I can follow you down this road, Sarah. It's your choice, and I have to go along with it, for the kids' sake—but I can't make you any promise about joining you when my time comes."

"I never expected that you would," Sarah said. "After all, you'll still have a life to lead when I'm a Tree, and there'll be other people in it."

"In a Forest . . . " Jake the Forester began—but this time, both his listeners raised their left hands, with the index fingers extended in exactly the same fashion.

A further half minute passed while Sarah and Alan looked at one another. Then Sarah turned away, satisfied that everything that could be settled had been settled. "I'd like to get the paperwork done now," she said to Jake, "and set the wheels in motion." Mercifully, Mussorgsky was experimenting with one of his quieter movements.

"Certainly," said the man who wasn't a salesperson, his blond hair rippling as he nodded his head.

*   *   *

When Sarah could no longer get out of bed, her doctor increased the dosage of her painkillers to the point where the Russian symphony was transfigured into a French piano concerto, all the way to mere Debussy. She was still able to postpone her dosage if she wanted to retain a greater clarity of mind for a while, to make her final reckonings with her parents and former colleagues, but the Russians had gone for good; her most attentive times, during the last weeks of her life, were mostly Bach and Brahms, with only occasional interventions of the Blues.

Three months passed before she moved from her home into the hospice, and began the next phase of her existential journey.

Sarah was tempted, then, to come off the diamorphine altogether, in order to experience the preliminary stages of her Transfiguration as fully as possible, but it couldn't be done. The withdrawal symptoms would have wrecked her perceptions far more comprehensively than the drug itself. She had no alternative but to drift off in a haze, the authentic music of her life fading into a background of gentle crooning and soft swing.

She had lost track of time before she would have wanted to, if she'd still been able to want anything in the final weeks. Grief, sorrow, regret and the other members of their dysfunctional family were long gone, and didn't even pop in to say good-bye while she was in the hospice.

She tried to talk to Alan, Jeanie, and Mike while her vocal cords still worked, but her conversation had evaporated, leaving nothing behind but a crusty residue of platitudes that didn't sound like her at all, but seemed to belong to some vapid ghost strayed from the electronic hinterlands of daytime 3-V. There would have been nothing left of her old self at all, even before she moved into the hospice, if it hadn't been for the dreams. The diamorphine couldn't keep her properly awake, but it did lend color to her sleep.

In a kinder or fairer world Sarah might have been able to dream the kind of dream that Janie had sketched out for her: the dream of a future Golden Age in which the people of every nation on Earth would cultivate their own customized Edens, where their haloed hi-tech cities would be ringed and separated by ancestral forests, and the soil of the United States of America would be bound together by the roots of its people—not its makers, let alone its original natives, but the roots of its *remakers:* the movers and the shakers who had finally brought it to its proper constitution and its true destiny.

In fact, the dying Sarah never had that kind of dream. She didn't dream about history and destiny at all. Her imagination had retreated to a smaller scale. She dreamed about her children, a little, and her husband, a little more, and other people a little more than that, but mostly she dreamed about numbers and balancing accounts.

The dreams weren't nightmarish, as they might have been if the figures had refused to add up and the failure of her enterprise had generated panic, but that hardly ever happened. Almost invariably, the figures did add up, so invariably that there was no sense of triumph in their settlement, but not so easily as to rob her of all legitimate satisfaction.

Then she yielded to the exotic pressures of the injections and was Transfigured into a Tree, in which form she lived for a further thousand years before embarking upon the next phase of her technologically assisted existential journey.

As to whether Alan, Jeanie and Mike came to visit her often, or whether they interrogated her, or whether any of them eventually joined her in the Forest, Sarah's Tree had no idea. There was no reason why she should; it was their business, and they were free to make what use of her they could, or not.

Sarah's Tree no longer dreamed, but all the sensitive creatures that were able to hear her, in the course of her millennial existence, perceived that the song of the New World's wind in her leaves and branches was infinitely more beautiful than silence.

ATTACHED TO THE LAND

by *Donald J. Bingle*

Don Bingle has had a wide variety of short fiction published, primarily in DAW themed anthologies, but also in tie-in anthologies for the *Dragonlance®* and *Transformers®* universes and in popular role-playing gaming materials. Recently, he has had stories published in *Fellowship Fantastic, Front Lines, Pandora's Closet, If I Were an Evil Overlord,* and *Time Twisters.* His first novel, *Forced Conversion,* is set in the near future, when anyone can have heaven, any heaven they want, but some people don't want to go. His most recent novel, *GREENSWORD,* is a darkly comedic thriller about a group of environmentalists who decide to end global warming . . . immediately. Now they're about to save the world; they just don't want to get caught doing it. He can be reached at orphyte@aol.com and his novels purchased through www.orphyte.com/donaldjbingle.

TRAVIS GREENE PAUSED before saddling his horse. The sun was just edging its way above the horizon, downslope and miles away across the plains, and the moment seemed to hang there with it. A bright, fresh day was upon him, the sky clear and clean and the land wide and fertile. The ranch didn't have a rooster to greet the day, but the cattle lowing on the hillside gave melody to the morning. He was up by dawn most every day of his seventy years, but every day on the range was a blessing that never grew old.

As he turned back to the barn and the ranch house off to the right, the low rays of the sun set them aglow. Nothing fancy, but they were well maintained and freshly painted and could house every man, woman, child, and critter that he loved in this world. He pulled himself out of his reverie, before he got all misty and foolish, and set back to his task of saddling Jeremiah for his trek to the cabin up in the mountains at the western edge of the ranch. The cabin was the family's own private retreat, a place a man could go to in order to reflect and enjoy the scenic wilds, or a groom could go with his bride to escape the family long enough to start one of their own. It was stoutly built at a breath-taking altitude. From the front porch, you could sit in a rocker and admire the snowy peaks to the west and watch the weather brew up and blow right at you. It was a place where you could pray or cry or curse a blue streak and no one would hear or see you, save God, Himself, and only then if He wasn't distracted looking at the scenery.

The cry of a baby broke through his thoughts. The sound came from the ranch house and was quickly joined by the throated bellow of another babe doing his best to outhowl his twin. Travis smiled toward the sound, a grandfather's beaming pride, but the joyous grin faded as he saw Matthew traipsing toward him, his brow furrowed and his jaw set. His youngest, Matthew was already in his thirties and a dad now for the first time.

"You don't need to be doing this, Pa," boomed Matthew without so much as a greeting first. "We've got some time. We'll figure a way. We just didn't expect twins."

"You and me, boy," he replied, "we don't make the rules. But they're good rules all the same. They gave us this place. They gave us everything we have. Don't be quittin' on 'em now."

Matthew's face was still grim, but he didn't seem to know what to do or say. His nervous eyes flicked back toward the house, where the cry of the twins still gave jarring counterpoint to the murmurs of the cattle on the hillside.

Travis waited until the boy's gaze returned to him and looked him square in the eyes. "You'd best be seeing to your children and let me see to mine." He mounted up and spurred Jeremiah forward without waiting for a reply, whether it be argument or acquiescence. He didn't turn back until he had traversed past the corral and upslope to the Ponderosa Pine with the tire swing Matthew and his three brothers had pleaded with him to hang so many years ago. When he did look, he saw that Matthew had apparently heeded his advice. Now, he'd best do the same.

He had no need to rush. He would make the cabin by late afternoon and that was in plenty of time. So he let Jeremiah plod upward at a comfortable pace, winding around trees and scrub and rocks. He drew in the thin, cool, crisp air, tinged with the sweet scent of pine and a hint of moisture from the snow pack above. He watched the eagles soar with the thermals and listened to critters skitter unseen in the wilds to the side of the path. As he gained altitude he could see the patchwork of farms and fields and ranches spread out on the plains below, simple and uncrowded.

Who would have thought a city boy like him would wind up here, the patriarch of a clan of ranchers, with land of his own? It was improbable. Of course, the whole thing had been improbable. As a teenager in Denver, all he had heard—when he wasn't listening to music fed directly from the world wide web into his cochlear implant—was about crowding and scarcity and drought and forest fires. The future didn't look bright.

But then, that was back before the mountain and plains states had seceded from the United States of America and formed the Western Range and Mountains, or the Range as it became known. He sure hadn't seen it coming, not that he was paying much mind to current events at the time. But then, no one had seen it coming. That was the only way it could have occurred. Years later, a former politician turned prospector had explained it all to him.

"The key was," Carl laughed, "there was no grass roots secession movement. If there was, it would have been endlessly debated and compromised and complicated. When President McClintock was elected, he had never even uttered the word 'secession.' Why would he? It would have been political suicide for someone seeking national office. But once he was in power, it was easy to do."

Carl put down his pickax and leaned on the handle. "You know, I always wondered when I was a kid whether Gorbachev was a CIA plant. You know, they take some guy who is a low level official and convert and indoctrinate him secretly and tell him just do what you need to do to get into power. We'll orchestrate some help from behind the scenes. Then when you do, you suddenly declare Glasnost out of the blue and when people start to demand freedom and democracy and capitalism and separate sovereignty, you just go along and, voila, the Soviet Union is destroyed with hardly a shot fired."

The old politician gave a wink before he continued. "Now, I don't know if anyone indoctrinated Blake McClintock, but it was pretty much the same thing. One day he's governor of Wyoming. Next, he's president of the United States, all of a sudden saying things like he wouldn't blame the western states if they did secede and control their own resources and manage their own forests and mines. Well, before you know it, Montana and Wyoming and Colorado, they're all making noises like they'll do just that. Then Arizona and New Mexico jump on board and Utah and Nevada, they don't want to be left out. Fearing to get caught as the last conservatives in what looks to be an increasingly urban and liberal United States, or what's left of it, Kansas, the Dakotas, and Nebraska join up. Alaska, the most Libertarian of all the states to begin with, is overjoyed to increase the acreage and the resources of the new nation. Idaho comes in at the last second.

"Washington, D.C. and the national press are in an uproar, of course. But when secession is declared, McClintock just lets the states go. There's no military effort to hold the union together 'cause the Commander in Chief, he doesn't order it." A wide grin spread across Carl's face. "Of course, McClintock, he's no dummy. Suddenly everyone notices that the vice president and the whole line of presidential succession is made up of westerners, so even an assassination ain't gonna change anything. And Congress, well it's got its shorts in a bunch, but since the Congress don't recognize the secession, the western senators and representatives, well, they just delay and filibuster and generally keep anything from happening. In short order, the secession is a fact and the military equipment in the west, nukes and all, are just turned over to the government of the Range. Once that happened, there weren't no way in hell the bell was gonna be unrung."

The secession, itself, wasn't what made Travis a rancher, though. It was what came after. To make sure the Range didn't turn into nothing but a folksier version of the behemoth U.S. government and to make sure that the people controlled the land, the Range doled out all the federal owned lands, save a few parks and other pristine places, to the residents of the Range in a lottery. Private property was left where it was, but everybody got their percentage of acreage of the

public lands. You could buy or sell or trade the land—
so as to combine for timber or mining or parcel out
for housing or leave undeveloped for wildlife refuges
or whatever. There was even a big internet auction
site set up, like eBay, to help move things along. The
dole and the auction site, that's where Travis got his
land.

At first, like most, he just had bits and pieces—
small parcels of land spread out in various places over
the whole Range, which by now had grown to include
Alberta, Saskatchewan, British Columbia, the Yukon,
and the Northwest Territories (the whole Quebec
thing had proved Canada would never stand in the
way of any secession). The distribution was set up so
everyone got a piece of each of the territories in the
Range, so no one could claim they were unfairly dis-
advantaged. Wheeling and dealing on the Internet
auction site had garnered Travis a contiguous chunk
of land on the eastern slope of the Rockies straddling
the Colorado/Wyoming border.

You could trade land to your heart's content, but
there were a few rules. To claim your land, you had
to agree to the insertion of a microchip under your
skull, which identified you with your land, as recorded
by the Land Office. The chip was easily updated for
any transfers, but you always needed to maintain a
minimum land ownership equal to the acreage a citizen got in the initial lottery. If you didn't, you were
expelled from the country. Sure, you could sell your
land and leave if you were fool enough, but you
couldn't sell your land and stay. Travis never had understood the scientific mechanics of the whole thing,
but there were geosynchronous satellites or GPS monitors or somesuch that could locate someone without
a chip or someone who had a chip with an insufficient
land ownership balance. And once you triggered that,
the Rangers would find you and boot you out of the
Range, into the crowded cesspool of the United States

of America to starve and riot with the rest of the
impoverished masses.

Travis clambered off Jeremiah for the last set of
switchbacks before they reached the cabin. The air
was thin and there was no need to burden the horse
more than necessary. Travis was old, but in good
shape. He could handle the slope, even in these high
reaches. The sun had peaked hours ago and was now
brightening the western slope of the mountains. He
saw cabins scattered in the woods, near enough one
another to be neighborly, but never so close as to be
atop one another. Mine shafts dotted the hills and he
could see timber and milling operations to the south
and west.

By marrying the population to the land, the population was kept in check. Oh, it grew some. The minimum had been based on the dole, so private lands not
doled out meant that there could be some net growth
without the minimums being exceeded. But things
were not near so packed as in the rest of the former
United States. Procreation wasn't prohibited; people
would always do what came natural. But if you wanted
to stay, you had to have enough land to meet the
minimums. If you were rich or just hardworking, it
generally worked out. But if you squandered your dole
or didn't work the land, then you had to leave—
willingly or unwillingly.

Travis unsaddled Jeremiah and fed and watered him
in the lean-to behind the cabin. Then he slapped his
backside and shooed him down the mountain. The old
horse knew the way home.

That task accomplished, Travis fixed himself a bit
of stew to savor on the porch as the sun went down.
He'd had a good day and a good life. He had a family
he could be proud of and a ranch that would see to
their needs. Of course, he wished he'd been able to
secure more land. The ranch had been more than

enough for him and Libby, back when she was still alive and their lives as ranchers were just starting out. When the time came, it was enough for their four boys: Bryce and Jack and Roderick and Matthew. Even though the three older boys lived, free and single, in the city—there were still cities with lawyers and doctors and architects and factory workers housed in apartments and subdivisions—they needed to have their allocation of land to remain. The ranch had even been enough, along with the bit of a parcel she brought as a dowry, for Eleanor, when Matthew had finally married and the ranch house once more had been blessed with a woman's touch.

Matthew and Eleanor were responsible folks. They had planned ahead. The acreage encompassed by the ranch was enough for the hardworking couple to have a child. And so they had.

But it wasn't enough for twins.

As the sun set, Travis took his shotgun and headed away from the cabin to a boulder sitting in fresh snow. There was no reason to leave a mess at the cabin. He fingered the copy of the land transfer he had made the night before, then pinned it to his flannel shirt, just to make sure the Rangers understood what he had done when they made their investigation.

He had lived free and prosperous, attached to the land. Now the twins could do so, too. And life would be good, very good.

The shot echoed dully across the verdant valleys below like distant snow thunder as Travis went to his final rest, at peace with his choice, home on the Range.

THE THIEF CATCHER

by Theodore Judson

Theodore Judson was born and raised in a small agricultural community in central Wyoming. He attended the University of Wyoming and was first a geologist and then a teacher. His first science fiction book, *Fitzpatrick's War*, was published in 2004 by DAW. He has since sold two books, including one to DAW. He is a widower and has one adult daughter and one grandchild, so far.

W HEN SAMUEL CUTLER had driven his motorcycle into the middle of the tiny village named Steens Mountain, he was immediately surrounded by seven armed men dressed in old-fashioned farmers' coveralls. He had paid no heed to the signs on the road that had been advising him to turn back as soon as he had left Nevada, and he had pushed on when the road had turned to dirt, and now he found himself in a town that was not on the map, a hundred and fifty miles from the closest inhabited spot, and looking down the bores of seven hand-held energy weapons. A less confident man would have despaired just then.

"Do I take you on all at once or one at a time?" he asked and laughed, knowing he only had the small caliber sidearm in his belt to defend himself. "Why are all of you dressed like Herschel on 'Muddy Flats'?'' he asked, citing a popular hologram program that mocked rural folk from the twentieth century. "Any of you married to each other?"

Samuel was fortunate that a man with silver hair and wearing a heavy blue wool suit more appropriate to the Highlands of Scotland than to the desert of eastern Oregon strode into the circle of armed men and told them step back.

"He is no doubt here to see me," said the man, who was as thin as a scarecrow and moved with excruciatingly straight steps. "Frisk him, then we'll go to my office."

One of the men in coveralls patted Samuel Butler down, found the pistol in Sam's belt, and handed it to the man in the blue suit.

"We haven't even been introduced," Samuel said the man searching him. "Don't get any ideas," he said as the man patted Sam's pants. "I'm not that kind of fellow."

"You aren't as amusing as you think, sir," said the man with the silver hair. "Come on. I'll give you your gun back when we've had our conversation."

He conducted Samuel to a white frame house in the middle of the town. Inside the unimposing structure were shelves of books and a workstation holding half a dozen computer terminals. The precisely moving man asked Sam to take a chair in front of his work desk.

"Before you tell me why you are here, sir," said the man, "we need to know who you are."

"What's your name, boss?" asked Sam.

"Mr. Jones," said the man in the suit.

"Then you can call me Mr. Smith," said Sam.

Mr. Jones stretched the straight line that was his mouth a little farther, which was his manner of smiling.

"Sir, we can do this the easy way; i.e., you tell me your birth name and your Universal Union Citizen Identification Number. Or, second option, I can knock you out with a microwave beam and scan your palm print into my computer to match your prints against those in the government's files. Your choice."

"Citizen Samuel Kent Cutler, UUC ID 786-755-9356," said Sam, and Mr. Jones typed the name and number into his computer.

Seconds later, row upon row of information appeared on Mr. Jones' computer screen, and none of it was flattering to Sam.

"You're a thief, Mr. Cutler," noted Mr. Jones. "Good God, your arrest record goes on and on."

"I've long felt that thief is a very negative term," said Sam. "I'm only somebody unlucky enough to be arrested forty-two times. It's a sign of the latent discrimination society still has for my Irish ancestors. By the by, do you call everybody 'Mr.' instead of 'citizen'?"

"We have quaint ways here in the Steens Mountain Association," said Mr. Jones. "Someone in the year 2110 needs to uphold the old social niceties. No one else will. But I do not think we can help you, Mr. Cutler, as we do not extend our services to criminals."

"I've got money," said Sam, and undid the belt the farmer who frisked him had failed to check; from inside the belt's hidden side he produced five gold coins minted in South Africa. "This is just a little of my stash," he said and held the coins out to Mr. Jones. "I can give you ten times more than this after the job is done."

Mr. Jones frowned at the money and said: "We in the Association have plenty of gold already. We are not going to help you commit another felony."

While huddling around a fire in hobo jungles or during bull sessions held in prison courtyards, Sam had heard the stories others told of the Steens Mountain Association, of how the group, living way out in the western desert, had mastered the creation of small reactors using something called Helium III, and thus could make electrical weapons that were more power-

ful than any in the world. The stories had it that the
Steens Mountain Association was so dangerous the
government left them alone, so long as the Association
did not interfere in the government's work. The stories
also said the Association would sometimes, for a price,
help individuals who were in a particularly bad bind.

"Let's start this again," said Sam, forcing himself to
smile at the dour Mr. Jones. "I got this out of a newspaper," he said and took a folded piece of paper from
his shirt pocket.

"There are no newspapers anymore," said Mr.
Jones, reluctantly taking the paper in hand. "You're
too young even to remember them."

"Electronic newspaper, then," suggested Sam. "Is
everyone out here so particular about language?"

"Which organization put this out?" asked Mr.
Jones, scanning the page.

"The United People's Voice in Good Person
Louis," said Sam.

"We still call it 'Saint' Louis our way," said Mr.
Jones. "An affection for the old names is another of
our quaint ways. This is an item retelling how you
were arrested by a Mr. Jonathan Savage and brought
in front of a local magistrate for stealing two hundred
pounds of Japanese silk from a ladies' dress shop four
months ago. You are out of jail this soon, a man with
your record?"

"A man can always bribe his way to freedom," con-
fessed Sam. "Now, this guy Savage—"

"That's surely not a real name," commented Mr.
Jones.

"I bet 'Mr. Jones' isn't all that real either."

"You aren't in a position to make wagers on anything," said Mr. Jones. "But you were going to say
something about this Mr. Savage."

"He's also been called Jon Watson, Jon Cotton, Jon
Wilde, Jon Collins, Jon—"

"Wait!" interrupted Mr. Jones. "Go back. You say
Jonathan Savage is also known as Jonathan Collins,

the man the media call the Denver Dog? The fellow responsible for arresting Wild Bill Martin?"

"The one and the same," said Sam. "He operates in twenty different cities 'cause all the gangs cooperate with him. You and he ever cross paths?"

"No," said Mr. Jones and shook his head in the negative. "And what you suggest about the gangs is nonsense: they never cooperate with anyone, especially with each other; it is a point of honor among them. To work in so many cities, your Mr. Savage would have to be working for the government. He is, if my memory serves me correctly, a thief catcher, a sort of bounty hunter who makes a living out of bringing in criminals the police can't collar."

"On the surface, he is," said Sam. "The fact is he's the biggest crook of them all. His racket is setting folks up in some sort of scheme, he collects whatever gets stolen, and then he arrests the folks he sent out to do the stealing, collects a reward for a crime he planned, and he also gets a reward for returning the stolen goods. What kind of creep does that?"

"Many of these so-called thief catchers play both sides of the law," said Mr. Jones. "Nothing you say concerning this Mr. Savage—or whatever his real name is—none of this surprises me. You were foolish to have trusted him, and I still see nothing here that would interest our organization."

Samuel Cutler had only one more trick in his hand. He prayed—to which God, it is not clear—that the rumors he had heard were true and the ploy would suffice to bring Mr. Jones over to his side.

"Would you care if I told you Savage has an associate you might want to get your hands on?" Sam asked.

"We are not the police, sir," said Mr. Jones. "We take a case only when there is an innocent victim, and when that victim can pay. You can merely pay."

"He works for the Green Man," blurted out Sam. "Now what do you say?"

Mr. Jones let forth a burst of grim laughter.

"You've been listening to some gimcrack stories," he said. "There is no such being as the Green Man. He is a will o' the wisp, a chimera, a tale your gangster friends tell each other, as the Green Man is everything they wish they were."

" '*Green grow the lilacs all covered with dew,*' " recited Sam. " '*I'm lonely, my darling, since parting with you. But by our next meeting I hope to prove true—*' "

"So you know an old song," said Mr. Jones, no longer amused, for he recognized the ancient song as one the Green Man used as a code signal to his followers throughout the world whenever a major crime was about to take place. "That doesn't mean you can produce this creature."

"But I do have your attention now, don't I?" said Sam, noting the change in Mr. Jones' demeanor.

Sam would not have been surprised that a week later Mr. Jones, now dressed in one of the gray, unisex jumpsuits most lower middle class men were wearing that year, was sitting in a Denver flophouse and awaiting a phone call from someone he hoped would be Jon Savage. The day before Mr. Jones had sent a voice message to a number listed on an electronic kiosk, a number Samuel Cutler had told him was one of the five Savage always used in his operations. Mr. Jones dared not lie on the bed for fear of contact with the vermin that had taken up residence there, and he did not turn on the room's hologram projector because he cared less for the programs it received than he did for the fleas and lice living elsewhere in the room. To pass the time Mr. Jones read from a *koine* edition of Plutarch's *Lives* or went to the window to watch the traffic on Colfax Street. When he did gaze outside, he beheld a typical urban scene of giant armored personnel carriers taking the wealthy and the government bureaucrats from their downtown offices to their dachas in the countryside and he also saw the thousands of workers going home on their motor scooters and self-propelled rickshaws and the tens of thousands of poor slogging to nowhere in particular on foot through the winter darkness. The skyscraper immediately across the street, which was decorated with the popular Neo-Assyrian motifs of stone lions and dragons, was that evening displaying the projected image of a beautiful geisha, who was slowly dancing about a large fuel pump marked **Imperial Diesel.** The words projected above the geisha's head explained that Imperial Diesel was superior to all of its competitors because it alone was made entirely from organic peanuts, nature's natural energy source.

" 'Nature's natural,' " thought Mr. Jones and despaired over the condition of the English language, which had fallen with the rest of the Universal Union into very hard names. "Yet no one seems to notice," thought Mr. Jones and looked into the enchanting almond eyes of the geisha.

At that moment he heard the soft beeps of both the sensors in the hall outside his door and the one in the window, indicating the presence of nitrogen-based munitions in both directions. Mr. Jones stepped away from the window and switched on the generator in his pocket. At once the room filled with a blinding white light, and everyone and everything within two hundred meters of the room slowed to a dead stop when struck by the microwaves transmitted from the grid within the cloth of Mr. Jones' suit. The armed men outside his door felt only a prickly heat on their skins before they passed out. The grenade launcher across Colfax fired prematurely when its computer chips short circuited, and the grenade itself looped into the street, leaving a trail of smoke behind it, before it exploded in the middle of a stunned host of pedestrians and killed a score of innocents.

Mr. Jones turned off his pocket reactor and tossed his belongings into a bag. The men outside his room were still stunned when he ran out the door, so stunned were they then and for the next hour Mr. Jones could pause and lift the mask off each man he

came upon, as he searched for the wide, fair face of
Sam Cutler among the would-be assassins. He stopped
at seven different men, but none of them was Cutler.

Outside, there were more explosions and gunshots
beyond the area the microwaves had reached. Something more than an attempted assassination, something
Mr. Jones had not expected, was unfolding on the
streets of Denver. Most of the violence, as well as he
could tell from a quick glance, appeared to be directed
at the large personnel carriers and the armored cars,
all of which held wealthy passengers. The immediate
crowd Mr. Jones entered was still stunned from the
microwave burst, but several men dressed in forest-
green shirts—the informal uniform of the Green Man
sect—charged into the mass of semiconscious people
and fired their automatic pistols point-blank at anyone
in their way. Mr. Jones hit his fusion reactor a second
time and stopped the green-clad thugs in their tracks.
He checked the faces of these newly fallen men as he
had the faces of the men inside the flophouse. Again,
none of them was familiar.

Down the street Mr. Jones could see even more
men in green shirts attacking other armored cars and
the flickers of light that were the bodyguards of the
wealthy returning fire. Rather than linger near the
place where he had nearly been murdered, Mr. Jones
walked cautiously toward the parking garage in which
he had left his car. When he was approximately three
hundred meters from that building, he switched on his
reactor again, clearing the ground ahead of him of
potential killers up to a few meters of his automobile.
He hit another button, turning on the reactor inside
the car itself, which broadcast microwaves in an area
about fifty meters around the parked machine. Mr.
Jones thus avoided short-circuiting the electrical systems within his auto and also set off an explosive device someone had planted in the garage elevator. Once
inside the vehicle, Mr. Jones turned on the machine's
second and more powerful reactor, causing the entire

car to glow like an incandescent lamp, a lamp that put to sleep everything human or mechanical in its vicinity. Using the vehicle's four terrestrial wheels, Mr. Jones drove into the chaos of Colfax Avenue, weaving his way past stalled conveyances and the piles of unconscious humanity. At the first open space of several hundred meters, he turned on the car's hover rotors, lifted off the pavement, and soon thereafter entered the darkened sky. Glancing down as he rose, he saw fires breaking out in hundreds of different places in the city, as if Denver were a vast, sun-baked prairie suddenly set ablaze by countless bolts of summer lightning.

Half an hour later, safely parked within the dead shelterbelt of an abandoned farm thirty miles east of the city, Mr. Jones dialed the only number Samuel Cutler had given him. The receiver on the other end of the call, whatever and wherever it was, rang five times, then played a recorded message, a familiar song that began:

> *The Green Man, whom none can see,*
> *Has left the world behind him,*
> *I know him well, he speaks to me,*
> *Yet no one can find him.*

Mr. Jones had heard the tune before when it was played on one of the pirate radio stations the Green Man sect operated from hidden places deep in the countryside. He decided that hearing it again did not improve his opinion of the song. The recording asked him to leave a message at the beep after the song, and Mr. Jones said:

"I may not be able to find the Green Man—presuming there is a person known as such—but finding you, Mr. Cutler, is not going to be that difficult."

Thus it was that three months later Sam Cutler awoke expecting to be in the holding cell of the Good Person Louis' Justice and Retribution Center and instead found himself lying in a sunny field somewhere in rural Missouri. His head was racked with pain. With a grunt, he sat upright and simultaneously became aware of someone standing beside him, a tall, slender man with silver hair and dressed in a heavy blue suit.

"Jonesie!" exclaimed Sam Cutler, trying to put a happy tone to what was not a happy situation. "I didn't expect to see you again. Where's the rest of the jail?"

"Oh, we never give up seeking anyone who had tried to kill a member of our Association," said Mr. Jones, crouching on his heels to speak to Sam. "In your case, we only had to wait till you were arrested again. We have access to all police files, you know. As for the guards and inmates you were with back in St. Louis, they are awaking from a deep sleep just now. I knocked them out when I did the same to you, although you were the only one I took with me."

"You're not still upset about that little mix-up in D Town, are you?" said Sam, still bravely smiling. "That was just a little pinch from Green Man. We only held the city for three days."

"During which time your group killed more than a thousand people, stole a half ton of precious metals, and abused God knows how many women," commented Mr. Jones, who certainly was not smiling. "I think I understand. Your group only wanted to show who is really in charge. Similar atrocities occur in other cities several times every year. Of course, while you were showing the Universal Union who is really the boss, your group figured they might as well kill me in the bargain."

"I wouldn't call them 'my group,'" objected Sam, and for the first time he noticed the machine pistol Mr. Jones carried in his right hand. "The Green Man's people pressured me to go visit you, out there in the desert. They threatened my family."

"You don't have a family," said Mr. Jones.

"I've got a mother," said Sam.

"And eight years ago you robbed her home in Newark. Records show she testified against you. I doubt she will mourn you for long."

"I can show you where the Green Men people have some of their money stashed," suggested an increasingly anxious Samuel Cutler, rising to his knees and causing Mr. Jones to take a couple steps away from him.

"I told you before: we already have plenty of money," said Mr. Jones.

"What about Jon Savage? You just going to let him go?" asked Sam, slowly getting his feet under him.

"I strongly suspect Mr. Savage, or whatever his true name is, has no real connection to the Green Man and his minions, or at least he has no more ties to the sect than you do."

"I can help you find the Green Man himself," said Sam, fixating upon the gun in Mr. Jones' hand.

"You don't know where he is," said Mr. Jones and dared to smile. "No one does. I have heard he is a prisoner in a maximum-security facility and runs his operation from his cell. Another rumor has the Green Man having his headquarters in some obscure heartland town. I've likewise been told he is, in fact, a high-ranking government official or a member of one of the Nine Families, and thus is a protected man. We in the Steens Mountain Association don't care where he is. We know one day we will find him, just as we found you. Until we get our hands on him, we will deal with the Green Man's sect by practicing retribution."

"What's that about?" asked Sam, slowly getting his feet under him.

"We kill five hundred of the Green Man's people for every one he kills of us," explained Mr. Jones. "For every attempted murder, we kill only fifty."

"You'd bump off fifty guys just because they tried to whack you?" said Sam, again venturing to emit an abrupt laugh.

"Since that night in Denver I've hunted down only forty-nine of you," said Mr. Jones, and held the pistol at his side at a thirty-degree angle.

"You're not helping us out here!" shouted Sam. "We can still make a deal!"

"Here's my deal: you get three steps," said Mr. Jones and waited for Sam to make his move.

UNLIMITED

by Jane Lindskold

Jane Lindskold is the author of eighteen novels and over fifty short stories. Although most of her fiction is fantasy, she loves science fiction, and is delighted when the opportunity arises to write about spaceships, computers, and alien worlds. Visit her at www.janelindskold.com.

FIRST CAME SMILODON, or, as most people still call it, the saber-toothed tiger.

We tried to convince her otherwise, but in this, as in so many, many other things, Dr. Keisha Dejesus overruled us.

"It has to be something spectacular," she said.

"What about the Synthetoceras?" suggested Dr. Smith—Smitty—as we called him, at first behind his back because he was an intimidating, impressive type, with a list of publications longer than I'm tall—and later to his face because it turned out he liked having a nickname. "The Synthetoceras is rather spectacular. In particular, that nose horn on what is otherwise a mild deer's face catches the eye."

Dr. Dejesus shook her head. The cut-crystal beads strung in her dreadlocks caught the overhead light in the lab and split the glow into rainbows.

"Outré, perhaps, but not spectacular. We'll do Synthetoceras later, Andrew. I know you like creatures with horns."

"Well, then," persisted Dr. Smith, "what about Gigantopithecus? That's spectacular."

"Too familiar. Too like a gorilla," countered Dr. Dejesus. "Besides, primates make humans nervous. Too like us. I want to inspire wonder, not fear."

"Elasmotherium?" Dr. Smith said, but something in his tone said he knew arguing was useless. "That horn . . ."

"Is spectacular," Dr. Dejesus said, and for a moment Dr. Smith's face brightened. "But the rest of it isn't. Face it, Andrew, most people don't bond with rhinoceri, not even giant ones with horns the length of their faces."

"They'll bond with a saber-toothed tiger?" Dr. Smith said, but there was resignation in his voice.

He knew they would. We all did, every intern and scientist gathered in the conference room at Dejesus Dreams Unlimited.

"Yes," Dr. Dejesus responded. "The strangest thing about wonder is that it grows most easily when it is touched with danger. Without danger, wonder quickly becomes routine."

So it was Smilodon who started it all—and not a one of us, except for Dr. Dejesus herself, had the least idea where it would take us.

All the fuss over stem cell research and genetic engineering at the beginning of the twenty-first century, all the attempts to ban and limit, all the withholding of federal funding had an effect none of the politicians anticipated.

Those restrictions drove the most intensely creative research in these areas into the private sector.

New laws protecting the end results of private research grew out of some really nasty court cases about twenty-five years later. Try telling someone who has created a private foundation in order to search for the cure to some disease—a disease that no big concern cares to investigate because it only affects three percent of the population, and that on alternate Tuesdays—that they can't use the cure they've found, and you're going to find people willing to fight, literally, for their lives.

Those cases fought, and especially those cases won, created the precedent that was extended when genetic engineering and cloning moved beyond end results that would find test tubes and syringes roomy to things that could potentially run around your backyard.

But even though the law asserted that you could make anything you wanted for your own use and with your own money and on your own property, there were still restrictions. The one that hamstrung most efforts was the one that stated that not only couldn't state or federal funding be employed in these research efforts, but also no funding from an institution that received state or federal Funding.

If any contaminated funding was found, private ownership of the project was forfeit. The project then would be subjected to review by various government agencies. As anyone knows who has ever waited for an experimental drug to be cleared, those reviews can last a lifetime.

Another restriction—one that pretty much finished off most private sector efforts in the subsection of genetic engineering where Dejesus Dreams Unlimited would later become a star—were zoning regulations forbidding keeping any nonhuman creature—even on private property—without proper permits.

Restrictive zoning laws have been in existence for centuries. Like most laws, they were initially beneficial to the populace at large. Eventually restrictive zoning became an easy way for politicians to cater to special interest groups motivated by fear—and genetically engineered wildlife trumps pitbull terriers and hybridwolves hands down when it comes to generating fear.

But Dr. Keisha Dejesus not only found a way around both of these problems, later she would find a way to make them work in her favor. I think she was already thinking in that direction, back when she told us we were going to create a Smilodon.

Considerable private wealth smoothed Dr. Dejesus' ventures into genetic engineering, making it possible for her to pursue her interests without needing outside funding.

Dr. Dejesus' father was an out-of-the box thinker—the man whose work on computer hardware and software is why you don't encounter the names "Microsoft" or "Apple" anymore except in business histories.

Her mother was an artist who specialized in installment pieces. When the fad for private ranches among the wealthy went the way of most fads, there was a lot of empty land for sale. Dr. Dejesus' mother went out and bought it as another artist might have bought paints at a hobby center's going out of business sale.

Fairly late in life, these two remarkable people had their only child, a daughter they named Keisha. In many ways, Keisha didn't follow in her parents' footsteps at all, moving from an early interest in conservation into a specialization in genetic engineering.

In other ways, Keisha—always Dr. Dejesus to me—was very much like her parents. She shared with both of them a strong refusal to let other people tell her how to think, combined with the type of visionary attitude that's usually seen only in religious reformers or insane artists.

Her parents, relieved that unlike the children of so many of the wealthy, Keisha had dreams, encouraged her to follow them. They just might have been the only people who realized how big those dreams were. Despite pressure to do otherwise, they arranged their estate to support Keisha in whatever venture she pursued, along the way teaching her that the law works for those who know how to work the loopholes.

Due to her mother's real-estate buying spree, Dr. Dejesus owned the entire landmass of two or three counties in several western states. That ended any problems with zoning boards. Essentially, she *was* the zoning board.

Due to her father, she had a firm belief that the best way to program was from the base code up.

So when Dr. Keisha Dejesus announced that she wanted to make a Smilodon, there was nothing but the genetic engineering complications to stop her.

I'm not going to pretend the creation of Smilodon was either fast or easy. During those long years when we succeeded first in cloning kittens, then an extinct black-maned lion, then even a few less complex creatures taken from the fossil record, many of us would have given up—except that Dr. Dejesus refused to let us despair.

I'll never forget the day I was standing alone at the grave of a Smilodon that had died two weeks into gestation—our best effort yet.

"Think we can't do it, Lindberg?" Dr. Dejesus said, walking up to me so quietly I didn't hear her bare feet on the paving stones.

"I've been wondering," I admitted.

"Want to quit?"

I blinked at her, horrified. I was in grad school by then, had even had a few good offers for internships at various labs, but I'd never considered leaving Dejesus Dreams Unlimited. What I was considering was asking to be moved to another project, one that didn't involve working with DNA from fossilized and partially fossilized sources.

"I . . ." I started to babble incoherently, afraid of being fired.

Dr. Dejesus cut me off with a gesture whose abruptness was moderated by the warmth of her smile.

"I know. You don't want to leave. It's just that this is so discouraging. You've heard people—some here, some elsewhere—saying that what we're trying to do is impossible.

"Personally, I think 'impossible' might be the nastiest word in the language. It's murderous. It shuts doors. Kills potential. It says that the world as we know it is cast in stone and there's nothing we can do to change it."

She leaned forward. Although she had to look up at me to meet my eyes—my Scandinavian ancestors granted me genes that make me tall and lean—I had the sensation of being reprimanded by someone of almost godlike stature.

"Remember this, Lindberg Anders. Even when something is cast in stone, you can always take a sledgehammer to it. Don't say my dreams are impossible—say your desire to participate is over. But don't you apply that dirty word to me!"

I didn't. Not then, and not ever after.

When Project Longtooth started, I was an undergraduate intern. By the time we all gathered to watch Stripes and Spots, our twin Smilodons, take their first deer without any help from us, I was a newly graduated Ph.D.

Smitty's hair had retreated to the point that he looked like a newly tonsured monk. Dr. Dejesus looked pretty much as she had. She was little thicker around the middle, maybe, but still the only thing more dynamic than our big kittens out in that meadow was her.

To me, after that lecture in the cemetery, she'd never ceased to be a bit larger than life. Later, I learned she held the same stature with most of us who worked with her. It couldn't have been easy being the focus of so much hope and faith, but like every other challenge she faced, Dr. Dejesus accepted the burden.

Stripes and Spots were grooming each other, managing to do a really good job despite those long fangs when Dr. Dejesus turned to Dr. Smith.

"Now, Smitty," she said, having given up calling

him Andrew like all the rest of us, "we'll start on your Synthetoceras. Do you have your initial materials in place?"

His answer was a sly grin.

"For at least six months now," he admitted, merriment lighting his face.

"This time we won't focus just on one creature," Dr. Dejesus said with a crisp nod of approval. She turned to me. "Lindberg, you've been noodling around with Epigaulus. We're going to need something little and cute to balance Smitty and my inclination toward megafauna. I can't think of anything much cuter than Epigaulus, with those little horns over that prairie dog face."

I agreed. I'd been fascinated by these primitive rodents even since I first saw a picture of a small colony in a coloring book when I was a kid. The horns were cute, but devilish at the same time, an impression reinforced by the pitchfork sharpness of Epigaulus' digging claws.

"Jonesy . . ." Dr. Dejesus turned to another specialist, this one senior to me, although junior to Smitty.

Jonesy was an Eastern European refugee with a surname so long and devoid of vowels that even a group of people who could manage words like "Chalicotherium" and "Phorusrhacos" before they had their first cup of coffee had trouble pronouncing her name.

Dr. Smith nicknamed her Jones. When Smith became Smitty, Jones inevitably had become Jonesy.

"Jonesy," Dr. Dejesus said, her eyes sparkling, "what about Macrauchenia? They're pretty outlandish. I'd like something that doesn't look even remotely like anything that exists now."

None of us asked why, maybe because we were busy envisioning Macrauchenia. Take a camel, remove the hump. Give it feet that are a cross between hooves and a llama's foot. Add a nose that reminds you of an old-style borsch-belt comedian, and you're still only halfway there. Outlandish.

"I can do Macrauchenia," Jonesy said. "We've got some great samples. I'd enjoy the challenge."

"Good," said Dr. Dejesus, rubbing her hands together in delight. "Very, very good."

While we were delighting in our Synthetoceras, our Epigaulus, our Macrauchenia, while a team was working on a second round of Smilodons, because Stripes and Spots were too closely related to breed, and all our research showed that Smilodons were highly social creatures, Dr. Dejesus was busy setting the next stage of her grand plan.

Not that she wasn't involved with our various projects. She was in and out of the labs, consulting over microscopes, offering encouragement, cheering when something went right, consoling when something went wrong.

One day after Smitty had gone through a particularly bad time with some fertilized Synthetoceras eggs that wouldn't take in their host mother, I heard her saying to him, "It's only impossible if you quit, Andrew. But if you need a break, a fresh approach . . ."

"I'll stick with it," he said.

"Determination's like concrete," Dr. Dejesus said.

"What?"

"Concrete's solid, but it also can be a mortar that sticks things together."

"You're weird, Keisha."

"Weirder than you know."

I had a hint of what form that weirdness might be taking a few weeks later when pictures of Stripes and Spots showed up on the news. They were full-grown now, muscular and pretty mean-looking. When the pictures had been taken, our Smilodons had been hunting and looked dreadful. Blood matted the fur around their mouths and on their chests. With those big saber teeth getting in the way, Smilodons are really messy eaters.

"Prehistoric Monsters Stalk Wyoming Plains!" was

about the mildest of the headlines. The others were a lot worse. Words like "heresy," "impiety," "unnatural," and "horror" were thrown around a lot.

Religious leaders prated about violations of God's Will. Conservationists ran their blood pressure up over deviations from the natural order. Politicians catered to all of them, but were forced to admit that what Dejesus Dreams Unlimited had done violated no state or federal law.

When Dr. Dejesus called a meeting, we all hurried there, everyone from the chef who made our meals to the highest ranking project head. Even the kids were there, because you don't have a community as settled as ours was without having marriages and kids, and Dr. Dejesus had always stressed that we were a community.

On that day, we weren't much of a community. There was a lot of whispering about security leaks and betrayal, more than a few suspicious glances around.

When we came to work for Dejesus Dreams Unlimited, each and every one of us had signed privacy and nondisclosure contracts that in hard copy rivaled *War and Peace*. The penalties went far, far beyond mere loss of employment. In fact, they guaranteed that the violator would not only be broke but completely unemployable in the end. Similar documents were signed by family members old enough to access a computer.

We all took our vow of silence pretty seriously, and now it appeared that someone had not only talked, but leaked out pictures as well.

Dr. Dejesus took the podium at the front of the lecture hall.

"You've all heard about the news services somehow acquiring pictures of Stripes and Spots."

Murmurs of agreement.

"And of the unfavorable coverage this has brought to Dejesus Dreams Unlimited. I know you must be wondering who the traitor in our ranks is. Well, you can stop looking suspiciously at each other. The person who sent out those pictures, who leaked the information to the mass media was not in violation of her contract because that person never signed a contract. That person, in short, was me."

Gasps. Expressions of astonishment. Then silence except for a baby who whimpered in surprise before falling under the spell of several hundred people all holding their breaths.

"Moreover, this has been my intention from the start."

"Spectacular," Smitty said, his voice low but carrying in the absolute silence. "You said our first effort had to be spectacular."

"That's right, I did. Worthy of being a spectacle. Well, for the next few weeks, that's just what Stripes and Spots are going to be—a carefully rationed spectacle. I'm sure one or two images will get out without my control, but I've already released just about the worst any photo journalist could get: full-grown sabertoothed tigers smeared with blood and animal gore.

"I'll be making some speeches to the press. Nothing I will say will be in any way, shape, or form a lie. I may, however, choose to withhold some information about forthcoming projects. I hope you will support me in this.

"I remind you of the agreements you signed when you came to work for me. Obviously, some of you will be made offers that those doing the offering will think can't be refused. However, I remind you of this. No one can offer you what I have already given you—the chance to make your professional dreams come true."

And she was right. Some of us were heading teams, long before we could have hoped to do in the rigidly structured academic world, certainly before we could hope to do so in the profit-minded private sector. Even those who were not yet heading teams or actively working on a pet project had ample evidence that such dreams were attainable.

The nonscientific professionals among us had lives

others in their fields could only envy. The professionals who maintained our establishment—the chefs,
housekeeping staff, groundskeepers—were paid admirable salaries. More importantly, they were given a
degree of respect—as their being included in this
meeting demonstrated—that they could never gain
anywhere else.

Dr. Dejesus' reminder of our contract with her was
not a threat. It was a promise of future good things
to come. We all knew it, even the kids.

As far as I know, despite temptations dangled in
front of us that would beggar the imagination, no one
did break their contract. The pressure from without
united a community that was already close.

It was a good time.

As soon as the initial furor died down, and it was
established that no matter what anyone did or said,
Dejesus Dreams Unlimited could not be stopped, the
movie stars started calling. The calls didn't only come
from movie stars but from celebrities of every shape
and stripe.

Dr. Dejesus had the unattainable, and everyone assumed it was for sale.

Their shock when they found out it was not amused
us all greatly. Dr. Dejesus filmed the interviews—with
the participants' consent—and we watched them eve-
nings, passing around bowls of buttered popcorn. The
celebrity who had bought human children from nations around the world in the name of good fellowship
was perhaps the funniest in her indignation, but there
were others who took Dr. Dejesus' calm refusal almost
as badly.

Less amusing was the legal pressure brought to
bear, the attempts to close down the labs entirely.
However, Dr. Dejesus had done her homework, and
her firm of highly specialized lawyers had checked and
double-checked her answers.

We were untouchable, and as Smitty's Synthetoceras toddled knobby-kneed and adorable next to the mildly confused white-tailed doe who had been his foster mother, as my Epigaulus colony started cheeping and chirping while they darted up and down from their burrows, the reactions of the outside world didn't seem much to matter.

We were under Dr. Dejesus' aegis, and like a dark-skinned, dark-eyed Athene, she protected us from all harm.

I realized then as I never had before that Dr. Dejesus had chosen the community that was Dejesus Dreams Unlimited very carefully. Many of us either lacked outside families or were estranged from them. The housekeeping and groundskeeping staff provided a balance to the scientists. We were not forbidden the outside world, but most of us were too busy and too fulfilled by our lives within to desire much of what that the increasingly restricted outer world could offer.

In the world we shared, saber-toothed tigers hunted ungulates on the plains. Epigaulus dug intricate burrows with their horns and claws. Macrauchenia proved to be remarkably social, and our little herd would come over to have their round ears scratched. When you were distracted, they'd pick your pocket with those funny almost-trunk noses.

As years advanced, we went riding on mastodons, and watched Phiohippus foals frolic in the fields.

Then Dr. Dejesus told us changes were coming. She told us that some of our babies were going to be leaving home.

As before, the announcement was made to the entire community. The baby who had cried at that other landmark meeting was now winning science fair prizes. His older brother was doing an internship at a different lab, and couldn't wait to be allowed to come work at "home."

I was still tall, but no longer quite as lean. Dr.

Dejesus' dreadlocks had twists of silver as well as the perennial crystal beads. We'd lost a few of the originals. Smitty had died two years before, and we'd all wept as a marble replica of his beloved Synthetoceras was raised over his grave.

But Jonesy was still there, and so was I, and so were any number of others who had become family and tribe. And from the expressions on those familiar faces, not one in ten had a hint this was coming—and a large number of those who were looking uncomfortably at the rest of us were from the legal and marketing divisions.

Both of those had become necessary after that initial "leak." The absolute certainty that Dejesus Dreams Unlimited would sue and would win in court had been needed to protect our property and airspace from people who "just wanted a look."

Marketing had taken over releasing information in the form of educational videos. They also handled the scholarship program, the science fair awards, and, after someone commented that we might as well get a slice of the burgeoning soft toy market, the franchising of official "Unlimited Limited" toy editions of our various creatures.

My wife, Laura, was on the legal team, and I saw her sneaking a guilty look my way—obviously wondering if I'd be pissed that she hadn't told me about this new development. I gave her a little shake of the head and a reassuring smile. Privacy rules applied, even between us, and I was pleased to see her shoulders visibly relax.

"We're getting crowded here," Dr. Dejesus said. "It's time for us to branch out. There will be a presentation by the legal staff later, showing any and all who care to know the details of how we set this up, but I'll give you the short form.

"First, we're not selling any of your babies. Every single creature who leaves lands owned by Dejesus

Dreams Unlimited will continue under our sole ownership, as will any of their offspring—should we choose to remove the breeding inhibitors.

"Second, neutral but inviolable genetic markers put in place by Dr. Sovak's team will assure that if anyone makes bold enough to violate the stringent legal agreements against anyone using any of our creatures as stock for their own creation efforts, we will be able to prove this is the case and take appropriate legal actions. This will include, of course, our reclaiming the animals in question.

"Third, for various reasons, I have not chosen to have lands held by Dejesus Dreams Unlimited opened to the public. Although a few of our creatures have gone on tour, those tours have been carefully moderated. Even so, they were stressful for everyone—human and animal—involved.

I hope that through this agreement, we can now permit Wonder out in the world, without risking the sanctuary we have created here."

A little girl—all right, I admit it, my little girl, Hannah, who really should have known better—piped out, "Dr. Dejesus, where are they going?"

"They're going to lands placed in specific trust for them by the Smithsonian Institution, under the greater auspices of the federal government of the United States. The details of our agreement will be available to any of you who wish to read it. It's rather dry, but basically it states that those lands will be used exclusively for wildlife—including our wildlife—and for wildlife alone.

"There will be no shared use of the land, not for mining or grazing or anything that any of our clever legal people could think to insert into the clauses. The one thing that will be permitted is limited touring of the grounds. The parameters of those tours have been worked out in detail. Our creatures will not be held in cages so that they can be gawked at. Rather, the gawkers—who will pay on a sliding scale for the privilege—will be the ones caged."

This brought a good deal of laughter because a similar policy had always reigned on Dejesus Dreams Unlimited's own lands. The creatures had implants that were a high-grade descendant of the invisible fences that became common at the end of the twentieth century. Even the most intellectually challenged of our creatures learned very quickly to stay within Dejesus lands and out of those areas reserved for humans. However, that was to protect them. From the start, it was made clear that we were responsible for protecting ourselves.

Dr. Dejesus was asked about this over and over again, especially during those early years when Stripes and Spots were everyone's hottest news item.

"Heavens!" she'd reply, rolling her eyes and looking exasperated. "Humans are always saying they're the most intelligent creatures ever to walk the Earth. Surely I'm not expecting too much when I ask my staff to stay out of the animal's areas."

She didn't ask too much of us, but later, after the legal briefing, when I spoke to Laura in the privacy of our own home, I learned that the restrictions at the Smithsonian enclave would be much higher.

"No mastodon rides for them," she said, and that pretty much summed it up.

The Smithsonian was granted custody of a small pride of Smilodons and nice herds of Synthetoceras and Macrauchenia. They also got a mastodon bull who could not get along with his fellows, and throve where he believed himself ruler of all he surveyed.

They were kept apart from each other—Smilodons really like nothing better than a large helping of fresh Macrauchenia—but they all had other animals in their enclosures. Most of these were herbivores, because, although we were long beyond the days when a single

Smilodon was the impossible dream, we did not have unlimited resources.

Do we ever?

At the heart of the area where people wait for the "cages" from which they can tour Wonder Park, a very active colony of Epigaulus was established. It's not just my opinion that they are endlessly entertaining. They've even outsold Smilodons at the soft toy shop.

Our prehistoric creatures were the standout stars of the new park, but both the Smithsonian and our own people knew from the start that they wouldn't be enough to justify the very high ticket price Dr. Dejesus had insisted be charged. (Very high to those who could afford it, I should mention; educational groups got a discount, a very steep one at times).

All along, Dr. Dejesus' intention was that the park would branch out to include North American species. The Wonder Park was built in the plains, because that was the terrain best suited to the prehistoric creatures we'd loaned them. It also happened to suit any number of native North American wildlife as well. So Wonder Park became a place where the buffalo roamed, and the deer and antelope played.

Wolves, too, and coyotes. Prairie chickens. Elk. Raptors.

Later, a fringe habitat was established, allowing the park to include mountain lions, trout, grizzly bears, eagles, and all those creatures who do a bit better when the land goes up and down.

Dejesus Dreams Unlimited contributed a few creatures to this expanded park, too. Everyone's personal favorite turned out to be the highly ferocious Megalictis, a grizzly bear-sized creature that's what a wolverine wants to be when it grows up.

Very little was made sanitized and wholesome. The ecosystem was permitted to balance itself, with intervention only in circumstances where drought or other extreme weather conditions might threaten the environment.

That meant no tidy feeding stations and bored animals standing around waiting for the keeper to come dump hay. That meant that more than one school group saw that the cute baby deer doesn't always get away. That meant that more than one group of bored socialites, sipping their champagne and looking out the windows of air-conditioned conveyances, learned firsthand that survival of the fittest is not a game played in Wall Street boardrooms.

Wonder, as Dr. Dejesus never tired of saying, needs a spicing of danger or it becomes merely routine.

My hair is gray now. Laura assures me that I look very distinguished when I stand up to speak in my new role as the head of Dejesus Dreams Unlimited. Our dark-eyed, dark-skinned Athene went from us fifteen years ago.

Cancer.

I think she'd appreciate what we've done. There are Wonder Parks on all the continents now. Three in different climate zones in North America. In each one, the native creatures live side by side with their ancestors—or sometimes with creatures for whom the evolutionary game ended with them. In each Wonder Park mile upon mile of land is protected and preserved.

Even in death, Dr. Dejesus spreads her aegis over us, using our wondering delight in what we lost in the past to protect the wonders we very nearly lost here in the present.

SWITCHING OFF THE LIGHTS

by Peter Crowther

Author, poet, editor, critic/essayist and now, with the multiple award-winning PS imprint, publisher, Peter Crowther has produced nineteen anthologies and more than one hundred short stories and novellas (many of which have been collected into five volumes: *The Longest Single Note, Lonesome Roads, Cold Comforts, Songs of Leaving* and *Dark Times*), plus *Escardy Gap*, a novel written in collaboration with James Lovegrove. Two of his stories have also been adapted for British TV. He has also edited many anthologies for DAW, including *Moon Shots, Mars Probes, Constellations*, and *Forbidden Planets*.

"HOW HIGH IS IT?" Ben asked, aiming the question at nobody in particular.

The rocket gleamed in the late afternoon sunlight and, even though they knew they were there, neither of the children noticed the welded-on and riveted patches of dull, heavy-duty tinplate.

"Tall," Samantha said, ignoring the clanking sound coming from behind one of the tail fins. She made the word sound icy and then, thinking better of it, she rubbed her brother's neck just below his ever-present fishbowl helmet. She had never cared for Scotty and Cedric and so had been unable to shed even a single tear when, following a long night of funnel activity, their mother had discovered the fishes lifeless amidst a flurry of glass shards in a puddle of water on the dresser . . . Cedric with his tail fin gone, and Scotty minus his head. But since then, with Ben having taken to wearing a new fishbowl on his head like one of the spacemen in their father's prized collection of old comic books from the closing years of the last millennium, she found that she missed the fishes dearly.

"How *tall* is it is what you mean to ask," Samantha said, her voice now displaying a slightly more compassionate tone.

Ben grunted, one hand shielding his eyes from the reflected light.

" 'High' refers to the distance between an object and the ground whereas 'tall' talks about the object's actual length."

Jerry Stuczi appeared from behind one of the tail struts with a thick roll of gray duct tape in his left hand. He gave Samantha a glare that was more sad than recriminatory.

"What? I was just explaining the diff—"

"How tall *is* it, Pops?" Ben asked, interrupting his sister.

"How tall do you think?"

Ben turned his full attention back to the rocket ship and, craning his head backward, he held his hand against the fishbowl and tried to estimate. "Half a mile?" he said at last.

A funnel split the air above them and, just for a few seconds, they all glimpsed a star-dotted blackness beyond the rip. The funnel disappeared almost immediately, like lightning, and the air smelled of burning. A dull plop sounded from the bushes over to the right.

Ben cheered and ran over. "Hey, it got a bird."

"Leave it, Benny," Jerry Stuczi said. "Come on back over here."

"Yeuch! Half of it's gone."

The boy stepped back from the strangely mutilated

creature, its one remaining wing flapping weakly, and
looked around the grass and bushes in front of him.

"Gross!" was Samantha's verdict on the whole af-
fair, but Jerry knew that it was just his daughter's way
of keeping herself going.

"Time to go time," Jerry said.

"I think we need to be on our way, honey," Sally
shouted. She was leaning out of the hatch at the top of
the drop-down ladder, looking anxiously up at the sky.

"Dad just said," Samantha shouted back.

Her mother nodded and, catching Samantha's dad's
eye, she added, "And *soon*, honey?" She disappeared
into the ship.

Ben and Samantha looked at their father.

Jerry smiled.

"Are we going to be okay, Daddy?"

"We're going to be just fine."

"It'll be just like the old days, won't it, Pops?"

"Yes, just like the old days," Jerry agreed. And
he laughed.

The old days to which his son referred involved Jerry's long stint piloting supply ships from Earth to Mar-
sopolis. Those were the early days of FTL drive and
even what Jerry referred to as his "desk-job" of Mars'
moon runs, ferrying iron ore back from Phobos and
Deimos, when the Board of Directors of Tachyon plc
decided that, at 34 years old, Jerry Stuczi was now
just a little long in the tooth for negotiating his way
through meteor showers or landing some thirty million
credits' worth of rocket ship on an area the compara-
tive size of a pea on a drum.

And then, soon after he had settled into a quiet life
at home wondering what he was going to do to pay
the bills, the first funnel had appeared.

Out on the pond something broke the surface of
the water and returned with a remarkably loud plop,
its identity kept secret from the people in the clearing
and their large metal vehicle.

Jerry Stuczi looked at his son's eager face, the wide

eyes, and, just for a second, the boy's eyes lost some
of their sparkle and maybe gained just a little
resignation . . . or maybe even despondency. The writing was on the wall here and let's not forget it, Jerry
thought. He was heading for the big four-oh now and
his reactions and skills were not what they had used
to be. And that wasn't even counting the fact that the
ship in which he was preparing to leave Earth—
virtually sidestepping into oblivion through one of the
funnels—was the equivalent of a soapbox flyer . . .
and the task ahead the likes of the Indianapolis 500.

But what was it they said about glasses being either
half empty or half full? Hell, wherever there was life
there was hope. And right now, at this single wonderful split second, they were all blissfully alive.

"We going into one of the tunnels, Pops?" Ben
asked, his voice hushed and conspiratorial.

"*Funnels*," said Samantha.

"Yes, we are," Jerry said, and he clapped his hands
before swinging his right hand up into the air.
"Whooosh!" he said. "Just like that."

"But you don't know where we'll end up, right?"

"That's right, Sammy. I don't know where we'll
end up."

"I still think it's sui—"

"Sam!"

Jerry's daughter didn't respond. She just thrust her
hands into her coat pocket and jiggled her foot at a
tuft of grass.

Jerry moved over to his daughter and dropped the
duct tape by his feet before wrapping his arms around
her. "The Earth—" He caught himself at that moment
and wondered whether he was going to have the
strength to finish the sentence. But the smell of Samantha's ginger shampoo gave him a tiny sliver of
optimism. Hell, he had to make it all work.

"She's finished," he went on. "Plumb tuckered out,
as my old granddaddy used to say when we had a
horse to put down. The Earth won't last the month.

She's already totally imbalanced since the funnel that took out most of mainland Europe, and all the way down to the substrata. Staying *here* is suicide: going out there—'' He nodded upward and pulled Ben up alongside. "—going out there is our one chance.''

Nobody said anything for a minute or two after that, and then Ben asked, "Are we the last ones, Pops? Are we the last family in America?'' There was no disguising the awe that the boy felt at such a situation.

Jerry shrugged. He didn't know for sure, but they could just be. "The Last Family in America,'' he said, and then he pulled his children closer. "Sounds kind of special, doesn't it?'' He raised his voice imitating a public address system announcement: "Will the last family in America please switch off the lights when they leave? Thank you.''

Birds twittered in the trees, but otherwise the world was singularly unimpressed.

"Where do you think we'll come out? Of the tunnel, I mean,'' Ben added.

Jerry thought on that one without looking down at his son's upturned face. Getting *into* the funnel was going to be a tall order. Getting *out* of it—wherever that happened to be—was something he had hardly dared to think about. The whole thing was pie in the sky, if the truth be known. But in these dark times, who wanted truth? All they wanted was a little hope. This way was the only way. The only chance for survival.

There were rumors of people making the jump and living to tell the tale, but such stories were apocryphal, told by wide-eyed believers who knew people who knew people. Even before planet-wide and even interspatial communications collapsed completely and the large starship liners set off on their multi-generational missions to find a new Earth, talk shows regularly featured folks who had met someone who had met someone who had funnel-jumped, maybe met them at one of the asteroid bars over beyond the rim, listening to

their tales of warped space and distorted instrumenta-
tion. These were the tales of the space amputees, griz-
zled tattooed old-timers who, spending up to fifty of
their fifty-two weeks among the stars, had elected to
have their legs removed to improve maneuverability—
every barroom on Lunar and the floating cities above
Venus had them, speaking in hushed tones about
funnel-jumpers. The popular theory was that, well . . .
it made sense, didn't it? Statistically, someone had to
have succeeded in coming back to tell the tale. But,
as the gainsayers would counter, shouldn't the same
rationale apply to life after death?

"You're worried, aren't you?"

Jerry shook his head and smiled at his daughter. He
wasn't sure whether the sadness he could see in her
face was for herself or for him . . . or maybe for him
and her mother. He allowed a small chuckle. "Do I
look worried?"

"Yeah, you do."

He shrugged and crouched down to fold up his tool-
box. "Okay, yes, I'm a little nervous."

"Worried."

"*Nervous,*" Jerry insisted. "And it makes a lot of
sense to be nervous. A little perspiration is a good
thing—ask any pilot."

Samantha scowled. "Yeuch!"

Sally slid her way down the last few rungs on the
ladder. "What's your father saying, honey?"

"He's being gross again."

"He's always being gross." She dusted her hands together and, as she reached the three of them, she ran a
hand over Jerry's shoulder. "Ever since I met him," she
added. They all stood in silence for a few seconds and
then Sally said, "So, we ready for the takeoff?"

Jerry raised his eyebrows and made a bemused
mouth-shape. "Well, everything that can be done has
been done," he said, matter-of-factly. "So—"

"We might be the last ones, Mom," Ben said
excitedly.

"The last family on Earth is what he means," Samantha explained.

Ben nodded. "In America anyways," he added.

Sally shuddered. She turned to her husband and said, "Kind of makes you feel a little strange, doesn't it?"

"Strange how?"

She wrapped her arms around herself and walked to the edge of the clearing. Through the trees she could see the lean-to they'd built while Jerry worked on the old transport ship he'd bought with all their savings. Jerry had said they needed to move from the city because the evidence suggested that the funnels seemed to be attracted to high-density population areas. Smoke drifted lazily from the chimney and up into the afternoon air. She followed it with her eyes and then looked away when a small rip opened and closed way over in the distance, making a sound like far-off thunder.

"They're getting more frequent, aren't they?" she asked.

Jerry didn't answer. Instead, he said "How does it make you feel strange, honey?" He moved up behind his daughter and wrapped his arms around her, clasping his hands against her arms and squeezing.

"Well . . . like it's all over. I mean, it's not just whether you and I can make it—not whether any of the others have made it before us. We don't know for sure that anyone's got through one of those damn things." Samantha nodded at a brief explosion of starry blackness in the sky over to their right, unconsciously waiting for the distant thunderclap of ruptured matter that always accompanied a funnel's appearance. "It's the end of America. The end of Earth. Maybe it's even the end of humanity."

"No, we'll survive this someplace."

Sally wondered whether Jerry meant "we" as in them or "we" as in humankind. But she didn't want to ask.

"I guess it comes down to faith," Jerry went on. He planted a kiss on the crown of Samantha's blonde hair. "Like believing whether there's anything after we're gone."

"You mean after we're *dead*," Ben said, imbuing the word with fierce excitement. "Like zombies," he added.

"We know ones that *didn't* make it," Samantha said, her voice hardly above a whisper. Nobody said anything to that. They were all too aware of the *Nautilus* tragedy, captured on a live television news-strand (when they still had television)—a two-thousand-berth clipper ship neatly sheared in half by a closing funnel as the ship rose up from Woomera, spilling bodies and body parts alike out onto the gray landing area below. Just like the old image of the falling man, leaping from the destruction of New York's fabled twin towers in the last century, the clip was never shown again. But, as horrific as it was, the image had contained a magical and almost ballet-like beauty.

They all knew that that wasn't what Samantha had meant. But nobody was about to spoil it all and verbalize it. The odds were stacked against them, and they all knew it. Even Ben.

Out of the blue, Jerry said, "You ever hear of Schrödinger's cat?"

Nobody said anything for a few seconds and then Samantha broke the silence. "I never even heard of Schrödinger!"

Sally chuckled at her husband's crinkly smile and raised eyebrows.

"He that old guy with the black hat and the curly sideburns?" Ben looked first at his mother and then his father, shifting his glass helmet and nodding as he suddenly recalled "*He* had a cat."

"Mister Liebowitz, sweetie," Sally thought of suggesting that Ben remove his helmet until they were on their way, but she didn't have the heart. Instead, she placed a hand on the glass bowl's smooth surface.

She tried to burn away the memory of Abraham Liebowitz's puffed and blackened lips and protruding
eyes when Jerry and Wayne Springer from the apartment upstairs had cut the old man down from the light
fitting and laid him alongside his beloved cat,
Balthazar.

He just couldn't take it, honey, Jerry had explained
to his sobbing wife. *Some folks can't deal with uncertainty. So he poisoned the cat and hanged himself.*

In that instant, Sally Stuczi had understood that
feeling more profoundly than ever before . . . that
feeling of not being able to take it. If she had had the
means right then to do the same for her two children
and Jerry and herself, she would have done it . . .
would have thrown those pills back and washed them
down with a healthy glass of oblivion, thereby removing doubt, banishing uncertainty, eradicating confusion. But that was then, not now. Though, truth be
told, there were times that she had flashes back to it.

"Erwin Schrödinger was a physicist, way back in the
early 1900s."

"A fizzy cyst?"

"A scientist," Jerry explained to his son. "He came
up with the theory of quantum mechanics."

Ben nodded. Okay, this he could understand.
Mechanics . . . guys in greasy coveralls working of
rocket ship exhausts like the ones in the old Tachyon
hangars over in Boston. So those must have been
Tachyon mechanics. He nodded some more and said,
"And he had a cat?"

"Well, no—or should I say, I don't know. It was a
metaphorical cat."

"That a color?"

Jerry nodded tiredly. "Schrödinger came up with
the concept of, well . . . alternate universes."

"Honey, you think—"

Jerry shook his head at Sally and, smiling, continued. "He came up with the idea that if you put a cat
and a deadly virus in a box and close the lid, then

you're basically creating two existences: one in which the cat will live and one in which it will die."

Samantha shuddered and scanned the sky. "Shouldn't we be getting onboard?"

"No hurry," Jerry said. "We have all the time in the world.

"You only find out which of the two universes you inhabit when you open the box." Jerry held out his hands and shrugged meaningfully. "And you can do it with numerous identical dimensions, with every single one having a key change. Like even if there are multiple dimensions in which the cat dies, then each one might have a different time of death."

"Honey, I think that's enough about dead cats."

Ben rolled his eyes and took a deep breath. "Jeez," was all he could think of to say, so he did.

"Benjamin!" his mother chided.

"So how exactly does that have anything at all to do with us?" Samantha asked.

Jerry stood taller suddenly. "Well, here's what it has to do with us. Imagine there are many many more Earths than this one, all of them occupying the same position in space, but in different dimensions."

"Hey, like the comics," Ben said, thinking of the multiple Earths in the comic book microfiche library his dad had bought him for his eighth birthday. "They had an Earth One and an Earth Two and . . . and—"

"Earth Three's next, pea brain."

Ben glowered at his sister, considered saying something in response, but was caught short by his father.

"So whether we make it or not," Jerry began.

"Honey—"

"Whether we make it or not *here*," he corrected, "we do make it *somewhere*."

"According to Schrödinger's cat," Samantha said, her voice suddenly softer and more girlish than ever before.

Jerry was nodding. "If it could be any other way, poochie," he said.

Samantha nodded. "I know, Daddy," she whispered.

"So!" Sally exclaimed, and she clapped her hands. "Time to get aboard and batten down the hatches."

"And splice the topsail?" Ben offered.

"And hoist the anchor!" Jerry added with a flourish of his arms.

They all looked at Samantha. She frowned and started to giggle.

"And—" she began.

They looked expectantly.

"Yes?" said her father.

"And—"

"And?" echoed her mother.

Eyes wide, little Ben hugged himself and shook, as though he were cold.

Samantha clapped her hands together and laughed. "And shiver me timbers!" she proclaimed.

They ran across the greensward and, one by one, clambered up the rickety ladder until they were safely inside the rocket ship.

"I'm not even convinced this thing can fly," Samantha said as she lowered herself into her cot, surprised at how calm she sounded . . . and, indeed, felt. She placed a hand against her left side and searched until she found her heartbeat, breathing a sigh of relief when the found it . . . and a second sigh when she realized it was just *bomping* away as normal, no faster and no slower.

Ben watched his sister from his own cot, making a brave attempt at buckling himself in. "You okay?"

Samantha nodded, turning her attention up ahead of her where her mother and father were securing all loose materials before take-off. "I'm fine." She stretched over against her own straps. "Here," she said, "let me give you a hand."

Ben reluctantly removed his glassbowl helmet and stowed it in the side cabinet along with his beloved facsimile comic books and his favorite toy bear.

Jerry shouted "Everyone okay back there?"

"Aye aye, Captain," Samantha replied.

"You reckon we *are* going to be okay?" Ben whispered as Samantha secured his straps and gave him a pat on the tummy.

She nodded. "Dad said."

Ben made a mouth and sighed. "Yeah," he said, "I just can't get it out of my head. What he said."

"What he said about what?"

"Samantha, Benjamin . . . better prepare yourselves. Dad's switching on."

"Okay." Samantha turned to her brother and repeated the question.

"About the cat. And all the other universes." He looked out of the window alongside him and felt the first satisfying *thrum* of the engines. "All the other 'us'es," he added. He turned to his sister. "All the other Americas," he said.

Samantha turned to her own porthole and looked out onto the shimmering Walden Pond and the sandy paths surrounding it, with the remains of the bicentenary construct of Thoreau's shack in the clearing and the rickety remains of the lean-to where they had spent the past few weeks.

The rocket ship shuddered.

"Get ready," Jerry shouted.

A clap of thunder signaled the appearance of a funnel directly above them. They could see it clearly through the ship's reinforced Perspex nose.

Samantha and Ben watched their mother reach over and grasp their father's arm. Up ahead, a black tear was opening up across the sky . . . stars broiling inside it amidst clouds of gaseous vapor.

"Wow!"

Samantha reached out her hand and took hold of her brother's shoulder, squeezing it. When he turned around to look at her, his eyes were moist.

"We'll be okay," Samantha said as the ship started to lift.

Ben pushed himself back hard against his cot seat. "I know," he said.

The acceleration made their chests ache and the black tear, its edges twisting and warping, beckoned them.

"I wonder where we'll come out," Samantha wondered aloud.

"Just think," Ben said as the ground fell away behind them. "There's another Earth out there someplace where, today, we all just go home."

Samantha nodded.

"Here we go!" Jerry Stuczi screamed at the top of his lungs.

Just a few seconds after the rocket ship had disappeared into the rip in the sky—taking with it the very last (but maybe not) family on Earth—the rip closed with something akin to the slamming of a screen door.

And then a serenity of sorts descended onto Walden Pond and onto all the ancient paths and roads, all the multitudinous byways and highways, and every hill and every valley of Earth and the great continent of America . . . in all of their myriad disguises.

THE POWER OF HUMAN REASON

by *Kristine Kathryn Rusch*

Kristine Kathryn Rusch has sold novels in several different genres under many different names. The most current Rusch novel is *Recovery Man: A Retrieval Artist Novel.* The Retrieval Artist novels are stand-alone mysteries set in a science fiction world. She's won the Endeavor Award for that series. Her writing has received dozens of award nominations, as well as several actual awards from science fiction's Hugo to the Prix Imaginare, a French fantasy award for best short fiction. She lives and works on the Oregon Coast.

FIRST YOU NOTICE the things you can't do. No matter how many times you replace your hips or your knees or your ankles, no matter how many rejuvenating stem cell treatments you get, no matter how many shots you take to keep yourself thin, you can't jump from a four-foot ledge into an alley and not hurt yourself.

You'd think I'd know this. You'd think I'd remember it.

But there I was, lying on concrete that smelled like day-old piss, nursing my skinned elbow and wondering if I'd broken it for the fifth time.

Thinking. *Reflecting.*

Because I couldn't catch my goddamn breath. You land a little sideways, you topple, you fall, and the first thing that goes is the fucking breath.

And of course my partner, still young at fifty-seven, sprinted by me like he was taking steroids—which, for all I knew, he was. He yelled, "Stop! Police!" and then I heard the take-down, which sounded pretty much the way it had at my very first take-down, in this self-same city—hell, for all I know, in this self-same alley—sixty-five years ago.

The rattle of chain-link. The grunts. The curses. The snick of handcuffs followed by another grunt, and then a thud, and another for good measure.

It would be a few minutes before my partner, DeAndre Dawson, dragged the perp back to me. So I had a few minutes to ease myself up, test the elbow—yep, it took my weight; it wasn't broken—and then slowly get to my feet.

During moments like that, I felt like an old man. Which, according to my father's generation, I was. Now, according to the revised government guidelines, I was in late middle age. Or early old age, however you wanted to count it.

Eighty-seven. Three years from the magic nine-O when the city demands that its most loyal, most attached public servants retire.

Mandatory retirement, which actually means *so what if you haven't saved enough, bastard, it's time to get your fat ass out of the precinct.* Of course, I dreaded the day when they forced my not-so-fat ass out of the place—not just for the lack of money, but also for the lack of daily companionship and something to do.

About the time I staggered to my feet, caught my balance, and was finally able to pretend that my elbow didn't ache, DeAndre had come back with the perp. DeAndre's a big guy, nearly six-four, and had a previous career as a pro basketball player. He blew his knee in his rookie season, and that was in the day when the replacements didn't quite make him DeAndre the Giant anymore. So he got to ride to the end of his two-million-dollar contract, and spent three years figuring out what he wanted to do. While figuring, he watched too much television and became way too fond of the detective shows so popular back then, which was how he went to the police academy with the idea of becoming a detective, and which was why he was now partnered with me.

The perp spat at my feet and caught my attention. I eyeballed him. Until he bolted down the fire escape of that six-story building, he'd just been a witness that we wanted to interview.

This kid jittering in front of me wasn't old enough to run with reflexive guilt from using junk which was mostly legal and not all that harmful anymore. He ran because he knew something or stole something or, God forbid, did something.

And whatever he did, it wasn't murdering Stephanie Watson-Cable. Because whoever murdered Steffie had a brain.

A real prodigious brain.

This was the first murder I'd seen in thirty years that had a genius component.

Whoever committed the crime had left no forensic evidence at all.

And believe you me, in this modern era, when a single DNA test could identify the killer in a matter of seconds, when one fiber left at the crime scene could identify *without a doubt* the location it came from, when the itsybitsy cameras embedded in each chip of paint on the walls could replay the actual crime itself, not leaving forensic evidence was the closest thing to a goddamn miracle that I'd ever seen.

I said "close" because I wasn't going to give the bastard credit.

No matter how fucking brilliant he was.

Stephanie Watson-Cable ran a chop shop in an ancient block-long building on Glisan. Took me fifteen years to pronounce that street name correctly. In Portland (that's Oregon, not Maine), streets have normal spellings with amazing mispronunciations: Glisan is pronounced "Glee-son"; Couch is pronounced "Cooch."

It's one way to tell the locals from the pretenders, and we use it. Because Oregon, famous seventy years ago for not liking outsiders, has gotten even worse in the intervening decades.

Steffie was a local girl—Queen of Rosaria in 2020 (that's queen of the city's annual Rose Festival to you outsiders) and like every queen before her, a gorgeous straight-A student who could've won various good citizen awards if someone gave them out. She got a scholarship to Brown, spent four years there, and then came home where, like everyone else in the downturn of '25, she couldn't find work or even the promise of it.

So she invented her own.

Her high-end escort service was just a profitable cover for the heart of her business—the moment-after pills, the venereal disease neutralizers, the occasional abortion, the expensive adoption, and the surrogate services.

She was, according to some, doing the devil's work. I never thought so. I always thought she was a little misguided. I used to tell her that I wished she'd used that amazing brain of hers to start a legal business.

She'd just laughed at me. *Depending on the decade,* she said, *my business is legal. I'm just waiting for the tide to turn.*

Apparently the tide wasn't going to turn in her lifetime.

DeAndre, on the other hand, never liked Steffie. He thought her too superior for someone in her profession, and even though he denied it, he was attracted to her.

It was hard not to be. She had flawless coffee-colored skin and slightly upturned eyes that made her seem even more intelligent than she was. Her lips were unfashionably slender, but they paired well with her tiny nose and high cheekbones.

She never used fat treatments, preferring to hold onto her figure with rigorous exercise and a not-so-rigorous diet. Her clothing was always proper with a hint of suggestion, and it always revealed her long, beautiful legs—the very best part of an already spectacular body.

When the call for detectives came, I fully expected her to greet us at the downstairs entrance like she had the one time that a girl had died in her back room. Back then, Steffie had given us full access as well as all the information she'd had on the girl, stuff that Steffie, with the help of Portland's best lawyers, usually kept confidential.

But that day, Steffie's flawless skin had been mottled from crying and her usually perfect makeup had been smeared. She had escorted us upstairs, and she helped the forensic team find all the cameras she'd hidden, as well as giving us all the images that had either the victim or the perpetrator.

Then, without a warrant, she'd let us collect all the data from the collection units throughout the building, something she had never done before.

When I asked why, Steffie said in a low husky voice I'd never heard from her before, that the bastard couldn't get away with it. In fact, she said she'd testify if she had to, even if it incriminated herself and her girls, just so that she could make sure he would never go free again.

But on this day, the person who met us at the door was the chief of forensics, boss of my boss. He was tall and slender, with a pale whiteness that either came from being indoors too much or working around too many chemicals.

He wore a black suit with a long waistcoat that seemed inappropriate to a crime scene, and when he saw us, he crossed his arms and glared.

"Took you long enough," he said.

I had learned an entire lifetime ago not to make excuses to the brass, but DeAndre had never absorbed the lesson. While he stammered something about being in North Portland and traffic and the impossibility of getting across the MaxTrain lines, the chief watched me.

"It's a mess," he said when DeAndre finished.

DeAndre was about to launch into a second explanation, thinking "mess" referred to our trip across town, but I put a hand on his arm.

"We need old-fashioned legwork," the chief said to me. "That's why we called you in."

You, referring to me, a man who had once gotten commendations for his work as a detective back when detecting involved reading people as well as evidence, putting pieces together from seemingly impossible scraps, and finding things that should have remained hidden in a society without an interconnected database of information.

"What happened?" I asked.

DeAndre stopped, and looked from the chief to me, as if he finally realized that the conversation wasn't about him.

"See for yourself," the chief said, and led us up the stairs.

Steffie's place was at the edge of the Pearl District. Back when I considered myself middle-aged—forty years ago or so now—the Pearl was going through a revitalization. Condos, trendy businesses, upscale restaurants all flocked there.

Now it had settled into middle age itself, with solid restaurants and long-established businesses, residents who had found city life essential but not necessarily the hottest, latest thing.

Technically, a business like Steffie's shouldn't have thrived here—at least not in the mind of men like DeAndre—but I always thought it made perfect sense.

True city dwellers were more forgiving than their suburban counterparts, and Steffie was running an upscale service for people who wanted discretion as well as the things she provided.

She was, in her own way, a long-term celebrity who represented the darker side of the city, and somehow gave it a more positive spin.

Even the staircase leading up to the main floor projected that positive image. Old staircases in other buildings on Glisan had the dark, cavelike atmosphere of a strictly emergency exit. Steffie had remodeled hers into a wide showplace with shallow, clean white carpeted steps that looked almost like the stairs into a palace.

When you reached the main floor, the stairs widened even more, so that they functioned as more of a grand entrance than a stairwell. And as you stepped onto the landing, a soft chime went off, letting the people inside the business know that someone had arrived.

Usually the double black doors swung open at that point, and someone—generally one of the youngest, most attractive escorts—greeted you with a glass of sparkling water and an inviting smile.

But the doors didn't swing open that day. They remained stubbornly closed, and that was the first time I felt how wrong it all was.

Behind me, DeAndre said, "Dark in here," and it was. I hadn't noticed that the usual lights were operating on one quarter power, like they had the time I called just before dawn, during the three hours out of twenty-four when Steffie's business was officially closed.

The chief had to use some kind of key card to get the double doors to swing open. Even then, they moved as if they were made of steel instead of the smooth, easy movement I remembered.

The interior lights were wrong, too. Too bright, almost like floodlights, revealing that the carpet I had always thought of as white was more of a gold color, the kind that hid dirt.

No young attractive escort waited for us with a fluted glass. Instead, some crime scene techs were examining the walls, probably looking for the most active paint chip with the required cameras.

There was no music, and the perfume that filled the air was the rusty scent of blood.

"It's okay to walk," the chief said. "We've already been over this place."

Still, I reached for the booties that the techs always kept near the front of a scene. The chief caught my hand.

"Seriously," he said. "We've had the scene since midnight."

Which meant it had been swept at least twice, and if the scene was confusing—and it appeared to be just from our presence and the presence of the remaining techs—it would have been swept at least twice more.

The chief led us through the entry, down the long corridor with its stunning black-and-white photographs of old Portland from a century ago, and toward Steffie's inner sanctum.

At that point, I still had no idea she was dead, but the hair rose on the back of my neck just the same. No one went to Steffie's inner sanctum without her approval, and certainly no one walked this way without her in the lead.

"You guys knock the pictures around?" DeAndre asked.

The chief glanced at him, and I glanced at the photos. A few of them were askew—just a little, enough to drive a man with anal-retentive tendencies, like my partner, to want to make them line up like soldiers at reveille.

"Possibly," the chief said.

And that was the point I straightened. Crime scene techs had become the most important part of the investigative teams in the past thirty years. The techs relied on science above all else, using the mandatory data collectors stored in all microfibers as well as computer programs that recreated the crime scene in the lab, and doing what I called cheating—using the extensive DNA database that covered every single American and every single foreigner who'd ever crossed our borders.

I had always maintained that just because a person's DNA was present at a crime scene, it didn't mean that he had committed a crime, but I had been outvoted decades ago. Now mostly my job involved eliminating suspects—people who were already identified through their DNA as having been at the crime scene some time (anytime) before, during or shortly after the crime went down.

I hated the new system, and made my opinion known. Lawyers tried to prevent me from testifying at trial because of my "anachronistic" attitudes, and the chief's predecessor had tried to get me fired.

But every now and then an investigation needed my skills—especially when the DNA had been "compromised." More and more, sophisticated criminals were using gene altering techniques to make sure whatever DNA they left at the crime scene wouldn't be traced back to them—rather like the criminals back in the early days of my career who burned off their fingertips so that no one could identify them through their fingerprints.

The chief didn't know if his people had knocked the photographs because the computer models hadn't told him about this part of the scene. And if the computer models didn't know what had happened in this corridor so very late in the investigation, then the crime scene was in trouble.

If I hadn't been so worried about Steffie, I might have felt a moment of glee.

Instead, the chief used the same key card to open the double doors at the end of the hallway, and the decaying rust smell grew worse. The room had been closed for hours with blood evidence—and maybe a body—still inside.

The tension I felt had grown worse. This was the entrance to Steffie's inner sanctum, a series of rooms that had once been a high-end condominium. I'd only seen the main room with its three-hundred-year-old desk, expensive plants, and original Monets. I'd never gone all the way to the back, although I'd heard that the luxury in her private rooms and bedroom would make the front room look like it had come out of a catalog.

After opening the door, the chief stepped aside. He nodded at DeAndre and me to continue.

I went in first, and stopped just inside the threshold. A woman lay on a fainting couch near the room's only window. She was wearing a negligee made of white gauze so thin that it revealed more than it concealed. Her long feet were bare, but high-heeled slippers had fallen onto the floor, crossing over each other like they'd been kicked off.

One arm rested above her head as if she'd fallen asleep. The other covered her stomach. Her head was turned toward the wall, but I didn't need to see her face to recognize Steffie.

DeAndre's breath caught—you never quite got used to seeing someone you knew dead—and I wondered if mine had, too.

"This how she was found?" I asked.

The chief nodded.

"That fainting couch an antique?"

He nodded again.

"Recovered or restored in any way?"

"No," he said softly.

Which destroyed any evidence it could have given had it been a reproduction or a retrofit. All modern materials had nanofibers that collected DNA. Usually it took a court order to examine those fibers, but it was routine for that order to be granted in the case of murder.

"Anyone here when she died?" I asked.

"Three of her female escorts," the chief said softly. "They're just as dead."

And probably just as secretive about their killer, since I doubted I would have been here for one dead criminal—even if she did fall on the tolerable side of the ledger.

"Anyone else?" I asked.

"In the operating theater," the chief said. "Someone we haven't identified."

He said that with such a lack of indignant righteousness that I knew he'd been up here before—and probably not in an official capacity. He hadn't been chief when Steffie led me to the previous body; he hadn't even been in Portland.

"Walls look newly painted," I said. "Glass looks like it has UV."

"Everything but the antiques follow code," the chief said, and code meant that they included tools that would help in any criminal investigation.

"But?" I knew there had to be a "but." He'd called me in after all. Me, in particular, a man he would normally consider a natural enemy. One who believed in the power of human reason over the power of established science.

"But," he said, "they're empty."

"Empty?" DeAndre repeated as if he couldn't believe it. "Like someone removed the trace?"

"As if they were new. As if they'd been replaced since the murder."

"Have they?" I asked.

The chief shook his head. "There'd be a record of that."

"And what if the record was wiped?" I asked.

"I don't think it's possible," he said. "Not from all these surfaces, and not in the time since she's been dead."

"How do you know how long she's been dead," DeAndre asked, "since your usual tools aren't functioning?"

Somehow he managed to ask that question without sounding antagonistic. Me, I'd've been a little too smug and that would have threatened the chief. Or angered him.

"Body temperature, rate of decomposition, and smell," the chief said, then looked at me. "The coroner still knows how to do it the old-fashioned way."

"Is it the same for all of the bodies?" I asked.

The chief nodded.

"Down to the lack of forensic evidence?"

"I'm not sure how there can't be any," he said. "If you'd told me that yesterday, I'd've said it's impossible."

I sighed. I didn't know how to ask my next question without that smugness in my tone. I struggled for a moment to find the right words, and then I finally gave up.

"Is it possible that Steffie set up this place so that it wouldn't record anything?" I asked. "Maybe using ancient carpet samples, old paint, things like that?"

"It's possible," the chief said. "It would violate city codes."

As if she hadn't done that before.

"But you investigated that murder at her behest a few years ago," the chief said.

Nearly ten years ago, I almost said, but didn't. I was trying to be as delicate here as I could.

"She had the normal systems in place. She wasn't trying to hide anything, or so your files say."

"She'd said that, too." I remembered it clearly. I'd been stunned at the level of cooperation she'd given us.

"I figured we'd be overwhelmed in DNA. This would be like hotel rooms, you know, or other public spaces. A surfeit of riches." The chief shook his head. "I never expected to find nothing. Nothing at all."

"What about hairs, fibers, fingerprints?" DeAndre

asked, and again I was glad it was him. The old-fashioned stuff. The stuff we'd been trained in before the new techniques became available.

The stuff we were both comfortable with.

"The place is clean," the chief said.

"No old-fashioned trace evidence either?" I asked.

The chief shook his head. "We even had to find someone with a nontech vacuum—you know, the old kind that only sucked up stuff on the carpet, not stuff from the fibers."

"And you found nothing?" DeAndre sounded as intrigued as I felt.

"That's right," the chief said.

"What about the blood evidence?" I asked.

"What about it?" the chief said, and I looked at him in surprise before I could stop myself.

"Did you match all the blood trace to the victims? Did any come from someone else?"

"The bodies are clean," he said a tad defensively.

"Meaning that you didn't find fluids or fibers on them," I said. "But what about that spray?"

I swept my hand toward the almost invisible dotting of blood on the side of the fainting couch and the edge of the wall.

"It clearly came from her," the chief said.

"How can you be sure without testing?" I asked.

"I would think that a perp who is smart enough to destroy the trace everywhere else in the building would make sure he hadn't left his blood at the scene," the chief said.

"People make mistakes," I said. "Especially this kind."

"The spray came from the body," the chief said again.

"Really?" I asked. "From where?"

I couldn't see any wounds. She'd been rearranged. If she had bled, she had done so somewhere else.

"She's been stabbed," the chief said, and touched himself on the breastbone. "Here."

"Stabbings are bloody," I said even though DeAndre was shaking his head. He didn't want me to talk any more because he knew I'd antagonize the chief. "There should be more than a fine spray."

"He cleaned up," the chief said. "We established that."

"And missed this?" I leaned toward the wall, indicating the spray. It looked more like a shadow than trace evidence. I wondered if the chief could even see it. "He didn't miss any other details. Maybe he missed everything else here, too, the cameras and the internal trace collection."

The chief snapped his fingers. A nearby tech came toward him. "Check that section of wall," he said.

"And don't destroy the spray pattern," I said. "Leave the evidence alone."

The tech glared at me. The chief was frowning. And DeAndre rolled his eyes—at them, I hoped.

I ignored all three of them and crouched beside Steffie. She had been posed close enough to her death to allow the blood to pool in this position. Her eyes were clouded, her mouth bruised.

She had known that her profession was risky. We'd talked about the possibility of her death more than once, and she seemed pretty sanguine about it.

But I wondered if that sanguinity remained when the killer confronted her here. I wondered if she minded a whole lot more than she said she would.

I couldn't touch her because the medical examiner would go over her body at the morgue, with black lights and trace finders and DNA sniffers. He'd give her a more thorough examination there, and probably come to the same conclusion—that she was clean.

But I was glad Robert Callan was on duty tonight. Callan was two years older than I was. Next year, he'd retire and I'd be left with the younger coroners, the guys who didn't dig under fingernails with the clean edge of a knife, preferring instead to let their little machines peer inside the space between the nail and the fingertip and find whatever debris it could.

For good measure, I'd talk to him. I'd make sure he did an old-fashioned examination as well as a new-fangled one.

"What about the other victims?" I asked as I stood.

"What about them?" The chief still sounded annoyed about the spray.

"Who are they? Where are they? How did they die?"

"All stabbed," the chief said. "Except the one in the theater. No one knows what killed him."

Him. That was an anomaly, too, although I didn't say so. Neither did DeAndre, although he caught it as well. Our gazes met over the chief's back and I knew we were thinking the same thing.

We'd start with the guy in the operating theater. We'd consider the others collateral damage. But we wouldn't tell anyone. Everyone here assumed Steffie was the killer's primary target—and they all might be right. But I wasn't going to jump to conclusions. I was going to conduct a good old-fashioned investigation.

The kind that focused on what wasn't there as much as what was.

The kind that required only a little bit of science and one whole hell of a lot of thought.

For the first time in decades, I felt like a man in charge. I knew what I was doing, and it wasn't make-work that I didn't quite believe in. If these crimes were going to get solved, they were going to get solved because of me.

I wanted to see the dead escorts before I went into the operating theater. When I told the chief that, he waved me away. He was more concerned with that scrap of wall. His tech was telling him that there might be something under the spray, and it was taking both of their expertise to remove the technical information while adhering to my request to leave the spray pattern intact.

I wasn't going to tell them to take samples and then photograph the section. That seemed obvious to me, and was probably obvious to DeAndre, but to these louts it was something unusual and foreign. It certainly didn't fit into their way of thinking.

The other escorts were in apartments down the corridor. Most of Steffie's escorts lived off-site, but the handful of fulltimers lived in the former condos near her.

The apartments covered several floors. The chief had ordered each apartment searched and its information recorded. Some poor slob—also with the title "detective"—would have to sift through the information to figure out what was pertinent.

That was one of the jobs I had come to hate. A computer technician would do better than someone trained in the art of discovering murderers. And I had complained about that, too.

The dead women were all in apartments on this floor. The doors were open and the crime scene lasers covered the entrance. I used my ID card to allow me through. If anyone else tried without an ID card, they'd get burned lightly as a warning and their DNA would be removed and sent to headquarters on a special emergency download.

We'd caught a lot perpetrators that way, all of them coming back to the crime scene for something they forgot.

The first apartment was a two-story loft. The main floor opened into a kitchen that then expanded into a giant living room with floor-to-ceiling windows. Nothing had been disturbed down here so far as I could see. The carpet-covered stairs that curved up toward the loft bedroom bore the marks of shoes, but those marks probably came from the crime scene techs.

Still, I walked beside the prints, careful not to touch them. So did DeAndre. When I reached the top of the stairs, I stopped.

The bedroom had the same view as the living room, and the windows were really a continuation of the windows from the floor below. Only here they were covered with gray privacy shades that allowed us to look out but prevented others from seeing in.

The dead woman was on a settee, sprawled just like Steffie was, wearing a black negligee that also revealed more than it covered. Her arms were in the same position as Steffie's, and so were her slippers.

I hadn't seen her before.

I walked as close to her as I could. I scanned carefully, but found no fine mist of spray on the wall or the settee or the carpet. I even had DeAndre look. He couldn't see anything either.

The other two women had died and were posed in the same way. Their apartments had similar layouts, and they were on the closest piece of furniture they had to a fainting couch—in one case a love seat and in the other part of a sofa sectional.

The only thing that differed were their negligees— one wore a filmy red and the other wore a slightly ornate lavender net. Their bodies were positioned similarly and so were their slippers. And none of these crime scenes had that film of blood either, which was leading me to believe more and more that the killer had made some kind of mistake.

The chief had finished in Steffie's room by the time I was done examining the escorts. He sent in the rest of his team to remove the bodies and check one final time for evidence he understood.

I was actually beginning to feel sorry for him. He was beginning to realize how much of a crutch the technology had become for him—and how unsuited he and his team were to this investigation.

To his credit, it didn't anger him that the dinosaur who had been fighting him had suddenly become useful again. He actually gave me free rein to conduct the investigation as only I knew how.

So I went to the operating theater.

Steffie had set up an entire medical unit on the fifth floor of the building. She had a licensed pharmacy, with state of the art security so that no one would break in. There were six examination rooms, five private rooms for patients that had to stay overnight, and an intensive care area should something go wrong. She had hired a dozen nurses to staff the place twenty-four seven. Three doctors split shifts, and she kept one surgeon on call.

Another part of the medical wing was set aside for research, and I would investigate that later. But first I wanted to see the operating theater.

This was the part of Steffie's empire I'd been to the most. In the early days, I had to serve papers back when the facility was unlicensed and they sent me in to shut her down. Then when it became licensed, I would occasionally have to talk to her patients—sometimes warning them that there was an angry mob outside and they should use a different exit—and sometimes having to handcuff them and take them downtown for an unrelated crime.

Over the years, Steffie and I had come to a dozen different arrangements, all of which resulted in her people staying as far from trouble as possible and me staying as pure as possible.

Long after I stopped doing most beat cop work, I did some when Steffie was involved. Because everyone in the department knew that I could talk her into things that no one else could.

I sighed. I would miss Steffie. I would miss her more than I wanted to admit.

The operating theater dominated the back side of the building. The theater was truly one of those operating rooms that had an upper deck so that people could observe the procedures below.

I sent DeAndre up there to eyeball the viewer's gallery. I wanted to look at the theater by myself.

I let myself past the crime scene lasers. The doors swung open and the theater's lights came on.

The place smelled of shit and vomit mingled with

the familiar scent of disinfectant. I stepped out of the theater, grabbed a mask from the sealed box that the medical personnel kept beside the door, and put it on. Then I slipped on some surgical gloves.

Even though I knew I'd find a body, I didn't like the odor. I wasn't about to take any chances.

Then I stepped back into the theater and blinked for a moment in the harsh light.

The place was a shambles. The gurneys were overturned, and the normally well ordered medical supplies covered the floor. All of the computers were on, as well as the robotic equipment. Some of the equipment had been damaged. More than one precision arm moved back and forth as if it were on a circuit that wouldn't quit.

In the middle of the destruction, one single male body lay on its stomach, hands clutching one of the robotic surgeons, face pressed against a control panel.

The floor was covered in every imaginable bodily fluid. The man's clothes were coated. It looked like all the liquid in his body had done its best to flee all at the same time.

"Jesus," I said into the mask, my voice muffled.

I heard a bang from above me, and then DeAndre said, "I can hear you up here."

He startled me. "The sound's on up there?"

"Yeah."

"Can you see how to turn it off?"

"It's not obvious," he said.

"You think it was like that when this guy died?"

"Crime scene's not supposed to change anything."

And they always followed the rules. I sighed again. "You see this mess?"

"Yeah," DeAndre said. "And it scares the piss out of me."

I almost said it scared the piss out of the victim, too, but I didn't. DeAndre lacked one cop attribute that I valued—he didn't have a dark sense of humor. I wasn't sure he had a sense of humor at all.

"You don't think some kind of virus got out, do you?" he asked.

"And then went to the apartments, stabbed the women, and posed them?" I asked. "I doubt it."

That was greeted with silence.

"I meant," DeAndre said after a while, "since the crime sensors are down, maybe the medical ones are, too."

"I have a hunch the ME would have thought of that," I said. I trusted Callan. He'd joined the dead squad after 9/11—oh, so long ago—and got the heavy duty medical terrorist training. The kind that assumed biological agents like anthrax and sarin gas would kill us long before any nuclear bomb did.

All of those notions seem quaint now, but they hadn't then. And they'd built a lot of caution into us old-timers as well as no small amount of fear.

I'd seen pictures of things like this. This was how guys died when they were poisoned or when a biologic that was lodged in their bodies finally came of age.

Even without any medical examiner's notes, I knew one other thing: this man had died quickly, and in great pain. And through it all, he had tried to save himself with the equipment at hand.

And no one here had tried to help him, even though the microphones were on. The viewing area was open to me, and the theater was open to DeAndre.

I wondered if what happened in here could be heard in the nurse's wing as well.

I would test it in a moment. But first, I made some mental notes. I wasn't about to walk around the scene—too many contaminents—but I was going to get a team in here to pick up every bit of fecal matter, every drop of blood, and I was going to see if that showed what the man died of.

Then I was going to use a very old law—the Patriot Act—to claim access to the medical records here should anyone try to fight me. Without Steffie, I doubted anyone would—although I wasn't sure of that either. Some doctor or researcher might want to keep whatever he was doing quiet.

Especially if it got this result.

I backed out of the theater slowly, and waited until the doors closed and the lasers came back on before removing my mask and gloves. I bagged them in a medical waste bag, not because I was going to throw them out, but because I was taking them to the crime lab to force some of those so-called scientists to actually do some analysis.

If there was some contaminant in that room, I wanted to know what it was, especially if it got on my masks or gloves.

Then I examined the sound system in the anteroom. You couldn't listen to the theater from here. If someone had been listening to the poor guy die, they would have had to do it from the observation deck.

This part of the crime scene disturbed me a lot more than the posed women. Those seemed planned.

This seemed random and accidental.

And yet, no one appeared to be in the medical wing, even though Steffie staffed it around the clock. There were no patients, no nurses, not even any beeping monitors.

Clearly, something had happened throughout Steffie's empire.

The question was where it started. Once we figured out the target of the attack, we might be able to figure out who did it, and—if we were really lucky—why.

The other components of Steffie's empire—the parking garage beneath the building, the ballroom, bar, and restaurant on the top floor—were empty as well. Even the big spenders' wing was open and unguarded.

Steffie never usually left the place empty. At least one employee manned the phones during her off hours, and guards, prep cooks, and medical personnel were also awake and working.

Steffie herself never seemed to sleep. Each time I visited, she greeted me personally. No matter the time of the day or night, she never seemed as if I had awakened her from a sound sleep.

Nor had I ever seen her in lingerie before.

All the way back to the precinct, I'd thought about what message the killer had tried to send—that the women were interchangeable? That they weren't quite real, with their multicolored negligees and their slippers? That their value was only in the way they looked?

I needed to know how he got in, and how he got out. I needed to know why no one was at work that night, and why the building was empty.

I also needed to know who the man in the operating theater was.

So, of course, the chief had a different task for me altogether. It seemed I was right; the killer had missed that little bit of spray. The paint behind it had one activated camera, and it had been behind a droplet of blood—if something that small could be called a droplet—and so there was very little to be seen, at least after the spray hit the wall.

The camera was located too low to get many images of the room in the short time it had been activated. But it did manage to catch one clear image: a hand that had dropped down beside it. A hand in great detail, from the calluses along the palm to the ridges and whorls of the fingerprints.

In the time it took me to examine Steffie's empire and get back to the precinct, those ridges and whorls had coalesced into a name. Barund Coe, a young man who had clearly been in the building well before the killings took place, but who might have seen something or managed to avoid something.

The chief gave me an address and a directive to investigate like a proper detective.

I bit my tongue. A proper detective looked at all

the evidence and determined its importance. Witnesses were notoriously unreliable—and that was if they'd actually been present when the crime occurred.

I would wager, if young Barund Coe wasn't our victim in the operating theater, that he hadn't been present and therefore hadn't seen anything of value.

But the chief was pleased to have evidence he understood and I knew I had to placate him so that I would be able to investigate the rest of the crime on my own.

I figured it would be an easy fifteen-minute detour on the route to a long and satisfying investigation.

I figured wrong.

Barund Coe lived on the sixth floor of an ancient apartment building in North Portland. Unlike other parts of the city, North Portland hadn't gone through any revitalization in the sixty-five years I'd been wearing a badge. The neighborhoods hung on like a kid clinging to a rock in the middle of a fast-moving current. Somehow they managed to survive, but they were never glamorous or trendy or even very nice.

Coe's building hadn't even been nice when it was built in the 1930s. The brick was thin and crumbly, the mortar between the cracks nonexistent. The front door to the building had been replaced so many times that it was impossible to tell what the actual front door had really looked like.

The building had never had an elevator, and in the hundred-plus years of the place's existence, no one had bothered to replace a single stair. So the stairs sagged in the middle and the railing that I would normally have used to brace myself was so rickety I preferred to put my hand on the grease-coated wall.

The sixth-floor hallway smelled of clove weed—a modern version of marijuana that somehow gave a mellow high but supposedly removed the paranoia. Coe's door was open a crack, and through that crack,

I could see him sitting on his couch, his legs extended and his head bobbing to some kind of music player he had probably stuck in his ear.

DeAndre knocked—we still had to do that—and then he announced, but Coe didn't notice. He was lost in his reefer and his music and as I had that realization, my stomach tightened.

This wasn't going to go as smoothly as I had hoped.

I pushed the door open with my elbow, keeping one hand on my gun, the other holding out my badge. I was talking as I came in—all reassuring words: *we understand you witnessed a crime; we only need a few minutes of your time; we just want to talk.*

I doubt Coe heard any of that. Instead, he looked up with his red-rimmed eyes and screamed. Then he bolted off the couch and dove out of the window onto a fire escape that should have been removed twenty years before.

His feet clanged down the metal steps. I cursed and followed him, DeAndre yelling behind me to stop or I would hurt myself.

I'd chased perps a thousand times down fire escapes, across rooftops, through streets, and though I occasionally hurt myself, I always got my man.

I knew how to clang down fire escapes. The replaced knees, hips, and ankles actually had some lift. Age had trimmed me down better than any shot could. I was as thin as the eighty-seven-year-olds I remembered from my own childhood—just not as bent or easily broken. I probably moved faster now than I did when I was forty.

The metal wobbled so badly as Coe and I hurried down it that DeAndre was afraid to get on it. He shouted as much from above, and then disappeared inside the window, probably to take the other steps down and confront Coe below.

Coe jumped from the bottom of the fire escape to the rooftop built over the large part of the building's first floor. He sprinted across that open wide space and disappeared down the side.

I cursed, following as fast as I could, getting to the edge in time to see him jump from a four-foot ledge into the alley.

I took some construction stairs to the ledge, watched Coe disappear around a bend in the alley, and knew I no longer had the time to go easy. A metal security door banged open behind me, and DeAndre appeared, sprinting across the rooftop just like I had.

I jumped from the ledge to the alley below—

And that was when I landed badly, skinning my elbow, and knocking the wind out of myself. I saw red-and-orange lights without even closing my eyes, and knew I had to breathe. I also knew that I wouldn't be able to for a few seconds, and those seconds would feel like an eternity.

An eternity in which I waved DeAndre on with my good arm and listened to him take down the suspect at the far end of the alley.

While I lay on my back in the piss-scented concrete, cradling my skinned elbow, and hoping that none of the germs I'd scraped up would turn into anything lethal.

Reflecting. Worrying.

Forcing myself up, realizing that the elbow wasn't broken, watching as DeAndre brought the perp toward us, and realizing then that I had happened onto something—an idea, a memory, a thought that I should have paid attention to and couldn't quite remember.

But I would.

That was the other thing that came with age—a certain tolerant patience with the mind's processes. I knew as I watched Coe jitter his way toward me, hands behind him, and DeAndre admonishing him, that we had come to a turning point in the investigation.

I just wasn't quite sure what it was.

*   *   *

It wasn't Coe.

He had been in the building two nights before Steffie died. His girlfriend had paid for VD reversal for both of them, but he hated hospitals and doctors and didn't want to wait. Instead, he wondered if there was something to steal down the hallways.

Somehow he had made it to Steffie's floor and Steffie's inner sanctum before security took him down.

They took him down on the fainting couch, his hand dropping behind it as he tried to hide the sapphire earrings he'd already taken off the desk. It didn't work, of course.

Steffie had confronted him, and when she found out why he was in the building, she'd personally escorted him to one of the exam rooms and waited outside while the doctor had injected him with the designer cure.

Because Steffie's medical services were mostly free, she used the high-end cures—the ones that would replicate inside a system forever or alter the system to prevent any kind of venereal virus.

Rumor even had it that her docs had found a way to transmit the cure through previous patients, so if they had sex with someone who had the disease, the new person would be cured. I understood that science. But some others claimed that people who hadn't been infected would never be infected if they came in contact with Steffie's designer cure.

No researcher had found a way to permanently pass along immunity—not even through a mother's breast milk—so I wasn't sure I believed that.

But I did know that Steffie was, in her own way, a do-gooder—or she would have been called one if her gifts hadn't had political overtones. She wanted the religious nuts and the abstinence fanatics and the judgmental rich to understand that human beings were human beings. It didn't matter if they chose a life of sexual ecstasy or celibacy. It didn't matter if they believed in God or believed in nothing at all. It didn't even matter if they were rich or poor.

Steffie believed everyone deserved the best life possible. The best life as defined and chosen by the individual—not by the culture around them.

I'd grown up with people like her. They were the generation just in front of mine, the one forced into retirement now—the hippies turned yuppies turned middle-aged dreamers who had somehow found themselves three times older than the people they'd once claimed were too old to trust.

Because of them, I had a suspicion of political idealism as well as an attraction to it. Which was why Steffie fascinated me, even though I believed her enterprise to be doomed.

Which, with her death, it now was.

Coe's story wasn't hard to check out. There were security files in Steffie's office going up to the day before she died, and he was on them. He was also in the medical records. And even if those hadn't still existed, his girlfriend vouched for him, declaring herself a former girlfriend now that she'd gotten a taste of his cowardice as it related to his own health and, by extension, hers.

The chief was disappointed that Coe didn't turn out to be more than he was, and so was DeAndre, but for different reasons.

As the investigation got underway, DeAndre remembered what he hated about the way we used to do things—getting lost in the minutiae of information, going through documents and files and records without doing a keyword search, examining hours and hours of security video and researching the history of Steffie's empire, one long torturous year at a time.

For a woman who tried to do good, Steffie had a lot of enemies. From the religious leaders who thought her the city's leading purveyor of sin to the mayor who'd helped her fund the empire before he realized that the sexual revolution of the twenties wouldn't last, to every last person in her address file, all of whom had something to lose if their connection with her came out, it seemed like everyone she knew had a reason to kill her.

This could be one of those investigations that would take decades if we let it—and I didn't have decades. I didn't really have years either. If I succeeded in solving this one, then I might be able to argue that my investigative methods were at least as good as the methods the chief used.

DeAndre wasn't sure we'd ever solve this. Of course, I'd assigned him to filter most of the information on Steffie, with the lie that she was the most important part of the investigation.

I doubted she was important at all—at least, not to the investigation. The killer had made her the equal of her escorts—whether by design or by accident, I still didn't know—and that led me to believe her corpse and her personal history held few answers.

But we still hadn't identified the man in the operating theater. His DNA wasn't on record, and no one had identified him from the cleaned-up holographic images we'd sent all over the media.

I was thinking of him when I caught a nap at the precinct. In the old days, I'd sleep at work for the first month of a big investigation, and I saw no reason to change that habit this late in my career.

So I pulled a blanket over the cot farthest from the window, put my uninjured arm over my face, and slept for three hours—which was longer than I would have as a young man, but a lot shorter than the six hours I usually got a night now.

And when I woke up, I knew why that alley had been the turning point in the investigation.

I studied the scrape on my elbow. The scrape had scabbed over because I hadn't bothered to go to the precinct infirmary for a healing injection. I'd had more scrapes and cuts and injuries over my career than I cared to think about, and it didn't bother me to wait a few days for the aches to go away.

The younger cops, they always fixed any wound immediately, and the middle-aged guys—the ones I considered middle-aged like DeAndre, not the fake-o middle-aged by dint of science guys like me—they always made sure they got their injections so that no virus or bacteria ever tracked them down.

My immune system was healthier than all of theirs because I let nature take its course. But as a result, I wasn't aware of all the technologies available to guys like me—and unlike the really young guys, the ones just coming out of the academy, I had no idea how to use those technologies myself.

The guy in the operating theater had died with his face against a control panel and his arms wrapped around a robotic surgeon. The average man of his age, in the throes of something that killed him as messily and violently as whatever had killed this guy, wouldn't have gone to the technology for help because he wouldn't know how it worked.

But this guy had.

And he actually thought he had time to save himself.

Which meant he knew what was going wrong—and it probably also meant he knew, at least theoretically, how to fix it.

I got up, showered in the precinct locker room, and put on some clean clothes that I kept there for just these kinds of occasions. The clothes barely fit, which told me how long it had been since I'd last pulled an investigation like this.

But fortunately I'd lost weight instead of gained it, so I just swam in my clothes and didn't worry how I looked.

Instead, I went to my desk and pulled Callan's autopsy report.

Our deceased wasn't in the system. He had no rec-

ognizable DNA at all, which led Callan to speculate
that the guy was a foreign national who had somehow
snuck across our borders, so his DNA wouldn't get
added to the database.

The guy had no rebuilt parts and had no evidence
of rejuvenation treatments, particularly of the skin
(which usually left some residue). His eyes were natu-
rally brown, as was his hair. He hadn't altered his look
in any way that showed up on Callan's genetic tests.

Nor had all that spilled fluid contained any true foreign matter. No drugs or nuclear residue. No poison.
No suspicious viruses or bacteria or evidence of bio-
weapons.

While Callan could pinpoint a time of death, he
couldn't pinpoint a cause. Except that our man had a
violent and sudden purging of every vital fluid in his
system—which would be enough to kill anyone.

But what caused that purging? Callan couldn't
even guess.

But I could—and I wasn't a scientist at all. Maybe
that's why I could entertain strange possibilities.
Maybe that's why I went to Callan's office first.

Or maybe I went there because I knew Callan
would take me seriously, no matter how fanciful my
supposition.

We both remembered what it was like to bat ideas
around, before certainty became the norm. We both
longed for those days, even though he rarely admitted
it except to me.

I had to catch him alone, or he wouldn't play.

I had to talk to him, dinosaur to dinosaur, to see if
we could resolve this together.

I used to dread going to the ME's office. In those
long-ago days, the place smelled of formaldehyde and
rot, no matter how hard the cleaning staff tried to
cover it up.

But now the place smelled faintly metallic, as if the
heating and cooling system had recently been in-

stalled. The place sparkled, and unless someone told you that it was a morgue, you wouldn't be able to tell.

Callan was in autopsy, just finishing up. I watched him through the double-glass window as he removed his outer gear, tossing the lab coat, gloves, and mask into a biohazard wash bin. Then he scrubbed thoroughly—showing his last century training—before he rubbed the regulation nano-cleaner all over his skin.

He'd had some rejuvenation treatments—his skin didn't have that leathery look of a modern eighty-nine-year-old. His hair was silver, like mine, only his was thick and rich, making him look like the TV doctors I'd grown up with—Marcus Welby and the like, men who knew everything and were damn close to gods.

No one treated us older folk like gods anymore. We weren't the nuisance our parents had been to us—people that we just wanted to hide from sight—but we weren't exactly welcome either.

Callan pushed open the door, releasing a wave of stink from the autopsy room. It was the only place in the morgue that still allowed smells of decay—mostly for what they could tell a well-trained medical examiner.

He seemed surprised to see me.

"I got a theory," I said, "and I need your help hashing it out."

He raised his bushy silver eyebrows at me, and then he grinned. "Just like old times."

I grinned back. "Just like."

He grabbed another lab coat from the pegs beside the door and led me up the stairs to his office.

He had the biggest, best office in the place, which angered the younger medical examiners. He wasn't in charge of the morgue any longer—he wasn't even in charge of the section, having refused to go through some year-long training program to "re-educate" him on various techniques that he used to teach.

But he wasn't willing to give up the office, and I knew why. It was twice the size of the other offices, and he'd crammed it full with books, shelves, couches, and dead desktop computers that were more than thirty years old. Beneath it all were stacks of file folders filled with paperwork that someone had decreed out of date, but that Callan believed still had value.

He cleared off one leather chair for me, then went behind his desk, which was covered with hand-held devices of varying size. Most of them had more computing power than all of the dead desktops behind me. I knew why he had more than one hand-held, too. Screen size.

After age fifty, a man needed an eye upgrade every ten years or he'd lose bits of his sight. Our city insurance paid for upgrades every twenty—figuring we'd all retire before we got the ones for age 90 and they'd only have to pay for one upgrade.

The younger guys were threatening a class-action suit, but it would happen too late for me and Callan. We just made do the old-fashioned way—with glasses and a magnifying glass and progressively larger screens.

"I take it that the theory is about Steffie's murder," he said.

I nodded, and stretched my legs as best I could given the number of books surrounding them on the floor. My ankles ached from that ill-considered four-foot jump of the day before.

"You know that the crime scene techs couldn't pull any information from the fibers or the walls," I said.

"Oh, do I know it," Callan said. "One would think the world had ended."

"For them, it has," I said. "But here's the thing. Steffie's security had information in storage from the day before. They'd downloaded just like they were supposed to and put it in hard storage, just like they were supposed to."

He templed his fingers and leaned back as he listened.

"DeAndre's investigating why no one was at work that night in the building. Steffie usually kept a skeleton staff."

"I know," Callan said, then looked at me guiltily. How many of us had ties to Steffie? And how many of us were ashamed of them?

I wasn't sure I wanted to ask.

"We found a very fine blood spray near Steffie's body," I said.

"That's the thing that protected the wall so you got that kid yesterday," he said.

"Yeah," I said. "The spray interests me a lot more than the kid. How come it was there when there wasn't any other trace except what the killer planted? And how come it protected that section of the wall?"

Callan swiveled his chair so that he could look at me directly. "You asking me or are you being rhetorical?"

"Neither, really," I said. "I'm thinking out loud."

"Meaning you have an answer."

"I have a guess," I said. "I want you to tell me if I'm off-base before I talk to anyone else."

"Okay." He folded his hands and rested them on the desk.

"I think the spray belongs to the dead man in the theater."

"It doesn't," Callan said. "We already tested."

I held up a finger. "Let me finish. I think that spray was the beginning of what killed him."

"I told you, it doesn't match," Callan said.

"I thought you were going to be my sounding board," I snapped.

"The tests—"

"Might be the wrong tests."

That shut him up. He frowned at me.

"I think he was posing Steffie's body when whatever it was caught up with him. He felt the beginnings of the . . . eruption, shall we call it? . . . and hightailed it to the operating theater. There he or he and his accomplice tried to cure him of whatever it was, only to fail miserably."

"Nice theory, but I still don't see how," Callan said.

"The key is in the empty fibers," I said.

He blinked, as if he hadn't considered that.

"Remember viruses?" I asked. "Y'know, computer viruses, the things that we used to hate when we had computers like those?"

I waved a hand at his dead desktops. Viruses got tamed a long time ago—both the computer kind and most of the human kind as well. Now we only worried about mutated superbugs which usually bred in folks who didn't believe in treatment. And even then, we only worried briefly. It didn't take someone long to genetically modify a cure or to use a nanocreature to clear them out of our systems.

"The whole miniature data collection business came about after we tamed the technological viruses," I said. "The fail-safes were theoretically built into each little nanocell."

"Yeah," Callan said, sounding skeptical.

"But what if someone devised something that would shut off the nanocells. Something that would replicate like a virus run through all the data collection systems in a building."

"Hmm." He templed his fingers again. I was beginning to intrigue him.

"What if Steffie's murder was the first place to test this thing, and what if the guy accidentally infected himself?"

Callan's frown deepened.

"Could that spew we found all over the theater be his body purging itself of anything it considered to have information?"

"No," he said. "What you're talking about would have cleaned out his system on the cellular level. But if such a 'virus' existed, in theory anyway, it wouldn't do the same work on an inanimate object as it would on an animate object."

"Or the corpses would have spewed, too," I said.

"Crudely put," he said. "but the stuff you find in carpet fibers and in couches and in paint chips are tiny machines, actual data collection devices, not an organic part of the fiber or the paint or the ceiling tile."

"Okay," I said.

"So if such a thing existed, it would take out the machines and leave the organic material intact." He was beginning to sound excited.

"And what happened if someone infected himself with it?" I asked.

"Probably nothing," Callan said. "Unless, for some reason, he already had some nanodevices in his system."

I waited. He had an idea. He just hadn't gotten to it.

"Our guy in the theater wasn't in any DNA database," he said. "That's something new we've been seeing with corpses. Even though we have an extensive database, a disproportionate number of the dead we're finding don't show up in it. And there's been chatter that someone has found a way to temporarily alter the DNA of discarded cells—like sloughed skin cells or hair or blood—so that the DNA is masked."

"And that would take little machines," I said.

"Yeah," he said.

"And what if those machines were attacked inside a human body?" I asked.

"The body would fight back," he said, "only it would do so on a cellular level. Which could lead to the kind of death we saw as the immune system tried to jettison the offending material and as the body fell apart."

I shuddered.

But Callan sounded intrigued. "It would happen too rapidly for our man to do anything about it."

"But he tried."

"He tried."

"And the spray?" I asked. "Could you tie it to the fluids in the room?"

"If I look at things other than the DNA," he said. "Maybe a peptide sequence or, hell, an old-fashioned blood type analysis. We might be able to find out a lot of things about this guy."

"So you think this is possible?" I asked.

He studied me for a moment. "I hope not," he said. "But if it is, I'll wager you money that whoever developed it, developed it in those research bays in Steffie's lab."

"She wouldn't have allowed it," I said. "She tried to do good in her own way."

"She wouldn't have known," he said. "She rented out those research bays when her own scientists weren't using them. All she stipulated was that whoever used them didn't use them to manufacture illegal drugs or designer diseases."

"And this wouldn't be either," I said slowly.

He shook his head. "It would just be a way to short-circuit the entire basis of the modern criminal justice system."

I let out a shaky breath. "Which it nearly did here."

"Thank God for dinosaurs," Callan said.

"Let's not congratulate ourselves yet," I said. "First we have to prove that I'm right."

It didn't take long.

While Callan was comparing the spray to the fluids to the body, DeAndre was interviewing employees of Steffie's empire. Everyone had been given a company-wide day off.

The medical staff was ordered not to take in new patients the day before, and security was told that there'd be an upgrade so their services wouldn't be needed.

Steffie supposedly ordered the empire-wide day off, but she probably hadn't. The employee who did was her second in command, a man named Harrison Jalneck, who also—by no coincidence at all—was in charge of the research bays, and whose bank accounts had been filling up for the past five years.

Of course, those bank accounts were now clear and Jalneck was on some small Caribbean island that, also not coincidentally, had no extradition.

But he had left the day he'd issued the company-wide day-off order, and hadn't been around when Steffie and the other women had died.

It was clear why Steffie had died; she had obviously been suspicious of the changes in her empire and maybe even had realized that something was going horribly wrong. She probably confronted Mr. Researcher—maybe before Jalneck left (we'd have to do more investigating to know this part for certain)—and she probably told him to pack his things.

Which was when he decided to field test his research. Smart man that he was, he figured making it look like a spree killer focused on sex would deflect the investigation, particularly when there was no evidence that modern crime scene techs could read. They'd take the visuals at face value, and assume someone hated Steffie's sex business.

The escorts died first. Then Steffie. She'd been killed away from her office, maybe near one of the escort's apartments and carried back in.

When Mr. Researcher had been posing her, he sneezed or wiped his nose, not realizing that just a tiny bit of spray had landed on the wall beside Steffie's body. He finished the pose, then realized he was feeling ill and hurried to the operating theater, just like we posited.

And there, while trying to remove the virus he'd accidentally infected himself with, he died.

Horribly.

Which was still probably too good for him.

Because we did find traces of his research in one of the bays. He'd been working with a partner—a partner who might have watched him die from the operating theater, a partner who most assuredly had access to that virus.

A partner who was probably already selling it to the highest bidder.

All of that became Homeland Security's problem. They took charge the moment they realized that any criminal investigation anywhere in the world could be compromised. The panic in the law enforcement community was unbelievable.

Too many offices—as in most of them—ran the way ours did, with the crime scene guys in charge, their little machines and their data analysis the last word on what happened at any scene.

The fact that they had been rendered useless here and Callan and I had not only solved the crime, but we had identified a seemingly unidentifiable corpse, had made us heroes.

But what no one really realized was that Callan and I had rescued ourselves. Neither of us had saved enough for that mandatory retirement—especially if we were going to live another thirty years.

We needed our salaries, but we also wanted some respect, a few more perks to our jobs, and a lot more time to ourselves.

We have been taken out of the field, and we have gone into "investigative training," a re-education program that is now mandatory for everyone connected with Portland law enforcement.

We're teaching them how to use their brains as well as their scientific equipment, showing them that the evidence talks even when it doesn't show up on some tiny computer screen.

And because of the high profile nature of Steffie's death, our reputations have grown. We've been put on loan to police departments all over the nation.

Callan and I get to travel in our old age—at the government's expense.

And I do mean old age, in the best sense of the word. Old the way our great-great grandparents were old. The patriarchs, the elders, the ones who were revered for their knowledge as well as their longevity.

No one rolls their eyes at us any more.

Although a few people ask at every seminar why that moment in the alley was so important to me.

Callan says they're probably too young and too healthy to understand my explanation, but I tell them anyway.

It was my worry that I had somehow infected my arm in that disgustingly dirty alley that changed things for me. I thought, for a moment, of bacteria and then I watched the blood well out of the scrape, cleaning the wound, and I didn't think about it again until I woke up after my three-hour nap and looked at my arm, seeing not an infection, but a scab protecting the wound as it healed.

Most people nowadays don't let their wounds scab. They see someone and get instant healing.

So they don't understand how scabs work. How they cover an opening and make sure nothing harmful gets inside.

Like that fine mist of blood over that little paint chip. The mist acted like a scab, preventing that manufactured virus from getting in.

I like to say when I teach that the spray looked like my scab, but it didn't. It was just the way that the mind—the human mind—makes the occasional odd connection.

When I was young, we called that connection intuition, and we valued it, even when we couldn't explain it.

Intuition defies certainty while embracing it.

And that I don't explain to my new students.

I doubt they'll ever really learn it. But I'm trying to give them the tools.

Because the other thing my age has taught me is

this: Nothing remains the same. Whatever system works now won't work in the future. And that system will eventually fail, too.

The most prepared person is the one who is flexible, who can work through any situation.

Or at least survive it.

Until something better comes along.